Far From
Maddy

C. C. Saint-Clair

978-0-9803344-2-5

Saint-Clair, C.C.
Far From Maddy
2nd. ed.
ISBN 9780980334425

1. Lesbians - Fiction. 1. Title
A823.4

Book design by www.bookmakersink.com

Lazy Moon Productions
Moorooka, Queensland, Australia
lazymoonproductions@netspace.net.au

QUEENSLAND, AUSTRALIA – Lesbian romance has a new voice, that of C.C. Saint-Clair. She belongs to a rare breed of contemporary lesbian writers who achieve a lot more than mere titillation in their fiction. Her writing is solid, sensuous and evocative. It deserves the tag already attributed to it - that of 'the thinking woman's lesbian romance'.

Born of French parents in Casablanca, Saint-Clair is a native French speaker though she completed her formal education in the United States, at The University of Texas, majoring in English Literature.

Since her return from a challenging trek inside the jungles of Sarawak, Saint-Clair has written the screenplay adaptation of *Far From Maddy*, which came at 2nd at the *Rhodes island Film Festival* [GLBT Barren Branches] screenplay competition in 2005, and made it to the quarter finals of the international but stritcly mainstream Scriptapaloosa comp in 2006.

She has also written the screenplay to the stand-alone sequel, *Morgan in the Mirror*, her seventh novel.

She now lives and works in Australia with her long-term partner, pursuing several interests which include writing, cinematography, computer imagery, and collecting rustic antiques.

Also by C.C. Saint-Clair

North and Left From Here (Take II)

Benchmarks

Silent Goodbyes

Risking-me

Jagged Dreams

Morgan in the Mirror

SYNOPSIS

In **Far from Maddy**, C.C. Saint-Clair displays her keen ability to recall how it feels to be a child, a young woman, a young lesbian. She conveys her recollections and imaginings through her skilful use of language and imagery, which vividly evoke feelings and memories from childhood. Many of us relate to the feeling of powerlessness that we experienced as children, and which still can be triggered by current interactions, particularly those with intimate others.

As a child, Jo tried to survive, the best way she could, her mother's illness, alcoholism and suicide; her father's emotional absence; and the loss of her much older sister when that sibling left home. As a young woman, Jo's interactions with Maddy, despite their loving relationship, trigger the fear of being emotionally dependent on her lover and of being vulnerable to the potential loss inherent in an intimate relationship. It is that fear that, subsequently, leads to her 'disappearance'.

C.C. Saint-Clair's usual poetic language contrasts starkly with the parental violence it describes; deepening the threat of that anger, making the child's pain and bewilderment unbearable.

> *The light from the garden is trapped inside the glass.*
> *Jo watches the refracted light as it spins, as the spray*
> *of transparent liquid curves outwards and back. She's*
> *already traced its path. She won't have to duck for this*
> *one ... The thing is Jo doesn't know, not fully, why her*
> *mother has hurled the glass at her. And it is the not*
> *knowing that makes her a bad daughter. A bad daughter who precipitates her mother's bad moods. Bad girl.*
> *I'm a bad girl, she reprimands herself silently.*

Once again woven throughout this gritty tale is the leitmotif of this 'thinking woman's lesbian romance' writer: her erotic, subtle and sensuous language of desire, lust and love between women.

F.T. Johnson

Acknowledgements

I wish to thank Myahr for her caring involvement with all aspects of my writing, Joy and Sue for their careful reading of the final draft and K.C. for her insider's knowledge in regards to some aspects of Queensland police procedures.

From C.C. Saint-Clair ... more strong, substantial and sensual writing in the tradition of *'the thinking woman's lesbian romance'*

With her debut novel, **North And Left From Here**, C.C. Saint-Clair launched her series of trademark romantic and sensual plots centred around strong lesbian characters.

Though thirty-five year old Alex lives in Australia, poignant flashbacks return her to earlier moments, be they in Spain, in the States or in Algeria, when love and desire, the exhilaration of self-discovery and the fear of vulnerability gave her life a vibrancy that is painfully lacking in her present day reality.

Benchmarks, set in the Montmartre district of Paris, the French snow-fields, and the Riviera, is a lyrical meditation on female desire focused on an ultimately unattainable release.

Silent Goodbyes, set on board a yacht sailing the Whitsunday Islands in The Great Barrier Reef, and in the river city of Brisbane, Australia, introduces forty-five year old Emilie Anderson as the central character. A particular set of emotional triggers forces Emilie to grapple with her insecurities and, in her own way, to say hello to life.

The bleak backdrop of **Risking–me** is woman to woman violence but, as in all Saint-Clair's novels, her main focus is the delicate and sensual web that she weaves around her central female characters, whose main desire is to get on with life through love.

Jagged Dreams, her fifth novel, another BookMakers' Ink publication, begins when Emilie finds her lover, Tamara, unconscious near her Jeep. It soon becomes apparent that a violent blow to the head is the cause. Beyond the fear of possible complications not yet ruled out by Tamara's doctor, Emilie and the police need more clues than they have regarding the attacker's identity and motive.
This novel is about the disturbing reality that becomes Tamara's during the time she spends in the ward, inside her bed, inside her head, while her thoughts go on, sliding and slithering away from her.

Sexual violence. Emotional violence. For most of the thirty-odd hours since Tamara collapsed on the ground of the parking lot, her thoughts have been a shaken and stirred cocktail of patches, stretched and distorted by the warped, time-controlled reality of nightmares. Father to daughter, uncle to nephew, woman to woman, the violence she has intellectualised only makes her restless in her sleep. Other moments that her psyche has yet not processed successfully, no matter how dated, are brought back, distorted by thoughts that slip away from her.

Visit **C.C. Saint-Clair**'s website for downloadable extracts and choice author cuts:
www.ccsaint-clair.com

PROLOGUE

When Maddy returned with a bottle of brandy and two plastic tumblers and found the wooden picnic table empty, she simply assumed that Jo must have decided to have a look around to stretch her legs. So she bridged the few steps to where, come high tide, the sea would just about meet the grass of the esplanade.

In a loose and watery horseshoe formation the waves, though strong enough to knock her over, came only close enough to lick the sand and retreat hastily, like meek dogs. She looked to the left towards the restaurant where, earlier that evening, at a little table set on the edge of the sand, they had enjoyed a candlelit dinner. Then she looked to the right where the night was darker. Only a few lights inside apartments rented, probably like theirs for a few days of beachfront frolic, broke through the darkness. There was no one in sight, not even a solitary dog-walker. The cul-de-sac was quiet. The moon was high and Burleigh Heads had hunkered down for the night.

Unperturbed, Maddy reconsidered her lover's absence figuring that Jo must have, after all, gone for a pee. She walked back to the picnic table and resumed her earlier position facing the sea. Fancy taking her bag and leaving mine just there, she groaned at the sight of her backpack, only partially tucked into the darkness of the picnic table. Wallet and all.

The breeze was gentle on her face, gentle over her bare arms. What a great idea, she thought, pulling the cork out of the bottle of brandy, a moonlight nightcap right here by the surf. It had been Jo's idea to finish off the night, their last on the South Coast, facing the waves, sipping a little brandy. To get right into that breeze and, hey, grab a hold of that pounding, you know, the surf, and take it home with us, is what Jo had said.

Hey, didn't even know you liked it so much here. Just goes to show. We'll just have to retire by the sea, Maddy had replied simply. Should be easy considering Australia's got like … zillions of miles of coastline. It's not like we'd be after prime real estate or anything, had been Maddy's afterthought.

Jo had been silent for a moment as if considering her reply. No, she said, we won't be into prime real estate at all. A little cabin, or chamferboard, tucked away in some obscure cove, is all we'd be after. Her grey eyes had grinned at Maddy through uneven tufts of dark hair. That'd do just fine, she had added emphatically.

And for *now*, Maddy had asked, reaching for Jo's hand across the wooden top of the picnic table. Her round blue eyes under arched eyebrows seemed more round. You're still OK for next weekend? She hadn't meant to sound worried about a possible change of mind.

Jo had produced the special smile that etched two tiny creases at the corners of her lips. Sure, I'm OK. Her long fingers had closed over her lover's hand. Won't take long to shift this backpack right here, she had added, tapping her rainbow-coloured bag. It, and the two other boxes, plus the few bits and pieces I've got back at Fairfield. It's not like you'll even notice I've moved in. Jo had grinned like a schoolgirl about to do something naughty, and Maddy had ginned back at her, back at the grey eyes that were grinning from behind the odd longer strand of dark hair that flopped over her lover's forehead.

Oh, I'll notice all right, Maddy had answered vigorously. Like I'll notice you in my bed just fine, thank you. Beaming at Jo, she had added, Last thing at night. First thing in the morning. *And* whenever I get up for a pee. She had tightened her fingers on the back of Jo's hand. *Yes!*

Jo had leaned across the tabletop to kiss Maddy on the lips and it was then she had come up with the idea that a nip of brandy would go down well, right there, facing the outgoing surf on the little knoll across the street from their block of flats.

Finding Jo gone as she had come back down, Maddy had automatically looked in the direction of the toilet block they had passed on their way back from the restaurant. She could not see it from where she was seated but she knew it to be less than two hundred metres away. With a shrug, she had poured herself two fingers of brandy and, absent-mindedly, swirled it around the glass before bringing it to her nose. She had inhaled but the plastic tumbler with its wide mouth had not trapped much of the aroma. She sipped it anyway and grinned as the liquid clung to her insides, warming her up in that particular way. She smiled contentedly because she remembered their early morning lovemaking.

Jo had woken up randy, wanting to make love, but that was not so unusual in itself. Better than that – Maddy *and* Jo had been able to bring Jo to orgasm. And when Jo had opened her eyes, detaching herself from Maddy, she was still flushed and breathless and *that* was the fairly unusual bit. Jo had taken Maddy's hand and had placed it curled around her sex. Yes. Just … there, she had said, once again closing her eyes. It's still all … tingly. And feeling cockily, happily connected to her lover, Maddy had grinned. And still, seated at the picnic table facing the surf, she smiled to herself.

The wind shifted and the pounding of the surf brought her back to where she was. She looked at her watch again and frowned the first frown of the night. She felt the first flutter of apprehension. She stood up and brushed the seat of her jeans. Across the bay, the glittery lights of Surfers' Paradise made her wince. Too bright, too shiny. Too fucking *festive*.

Again, between sips of gut-warming brandy, Maddy considered various possible scenarios for her lover's prolonged absence but she finally figured out what had been keeping Jo. Jo would not be coming back to the picnic area because she knew that Maddy, not finding her there, would just *guess* that the venue for the nightcap had changed. She would just know that the nightcap would be even more romantic closer to the outgoing surf. She could've waited a couple of minutes and spared me the crap angst. Maddy pushed the cork back into the brandy bottle. She was not annoyed and she was not worried anymore.

She simply stood up and hitched the low-slung jeans a little higher on her hips. She gulped what was left of the brandy at the bottom of the plastic tumbler and retraced her steps back to the beach, past the toilet block, past the restaurant, already visualising Jo seated off to the left on the dark rocks exposed at low tide, close to where they had had dinner, looking up the path, waiting for her, Maddy, to figure it all out.

*****

ONE

Tuesday morning, the Tuesday on the other side of the Australia Day long weekend, Maddy left a message on the answering machine at Terry's Tyres where she worked, knowing that the boss's wife would be the one to hear it.

"Viv, it's me. Look, it's 7.35 already. I'm still at Burleigh. Something's ... uh ... Listen, something's come up," she said, knuckles white and tight around the phone. "Ah ... I'll be there as soon as I can, but can't say when. I'm ... Uh, Viv, tell Terry I'm really sorry about not showing. Can't be helped." She hung up and hooked the mobile back on her belt.

The morning sun, already hammering heat into the sand and into the bitumen below, had ignited the tips of Maddy's rust-red hair into a fiery translucence. She ran a hand through it and, from her vantage point on the balcony, stood squinting into the ocean. The sea was once again full, sparkling and totally blue except for where the surf broke and rolled onto the sand.

In the distance, the apartment towers of Surfers' Paradise, like uneven femurs planted for a ritual in crooked rows, were already hazy and sunbleached in the strong morning sun. Maddy's eyes returned for the umpteenth time to the little picnic table six storeys below, the last place where she had seen Jo. Maddy swallowed hard.

"And all because of a bottle of bloody brandy?" she moaned, freckled knuckles clenching the balcony railing of the unit she and her lover had rented for a three-night holiday. *If it hadn't been for that fucking bottle,* her thoughts crunched, *I would've been right there with her. I would've stopped it. It just wouldn't have happened.* Like a woman overboard desperate for a buoy, Maddy turned away from the ocean to face the bed visible through open sliding doors. *She'd be right here with me. Still asleep.*

The previous night, at around 2 a.m., she had watched from the grassy mound below as a rubber duck yellow Zodiac from the Surf Lifesaving squad, had combed the rolling surf. She could tell it was following diverging currents, troughs and rips nearer the shore and further back where the sea breathed and swelled before breaking. Backwards and forwards it rode the waves, cyclopian spotlights sweeping over each cresting swell as it presented itself ahead of the inflatable boats.

Once her brain had let in the reality that her lover was no longer anywhere logical or visible, Maddy had run over to the Surf Lifesaving Club. She ran back to where she and Jo had had a late afternoon drink before going back to the apartment for a nap and prepare for their evening. She had pounded on the only door that she could see thinking that someone *had* to be in there, on duty. Even if the beach was totally deserted. And she pounded on that door until a young man, half-naked and more than half-asleep, reluctantly cracked the door open.

"Hey, lady," he said, rubbing the flat of his hand across his manly chest, "where's the fire?"

Seriously wrong answer from a dude on duty, Maddy almost snarled, not realising that, though the man was a Lifesaver, he was not on duty because there was no night duty for him to be on. For every squad on the coast, duty ended at 5.30 p.m.

Maddy blurted out that a friend, *her* friend, might have been dragged away by the outgoing tide. Or a fast receding, churning rip. Or an undertow. "Or taken by a shark, for all I know," she had added, fingers raking through her hair in utter frustration.

"Take a breath, lady," the young man answered over a yawn.

Don't you tell me when to fuckin' breathe, she had wanted to snap back, but instead, she made herself breathe and replayed her account, more in control, for the Lifesaver who, in spite of a visible urge to roll back onto his cot was doing his level best to be the kind of guy that made the squads renowned – a team of blokes who care. And so, he rubbed his scalp through tousled ginger hair and ran splayed fingers over his washboard abs to the low waist of his boxer shorts, but he also asked her a series of baseline questions. *No,* she hadn't witnessed the event. *No,* her friend had not indicated to her that she was going for a swim. *No,* a swim had not been on the agenda. *No,* she hadn't witnessed anything at all. *No,* her friend did not have a bathing suit with her.

"But the beach is there, *isn't it?*" she had enunciated clearly, her voice bouncing against his eardrums. "And people *do* get dragged away. And since she's nowhere to be found and – *No,* she's not on drugs, and uh – *No,* she's not inebriated," she had answered, once more bristling. "*No,* not drunk either – Yes. *Yes* we have *imbibed some alcohol* but, *no* I'm not drunk and neither is Jo … my … friend."

The young man had persisted. "And why you think that your friend has gone into the water at all, or even near it?"

"We're on holidays. We're going back to Brisbane tomorrow," she had answered staccato, pressure building up inside her chest. "Why *shouldn't* she decide to go for a dip, huh? That's not such an odd thing to do, is it?" she had asked, pitch rising.

The Zodiac disappeared on the other side of a wave and Maddy sat on the grassy mound, lost in thought, sandwiched between the black surf and the black sky till her mobile buzzed. A male voice said that, luckily, the crew hadn't found anyone requiring intervention and that the *person* was probably safe and sound elsewhere and that the best thing for her to do was to get herself home and to bed. "In the morning," the voice had concluded resonantly, "things will probably have worked themselves out."

Maddy had half a bottle of wine and two nips of brandy sloshing around in her belly by the time she began searching for the Burleigh Heads police station but, quite a while ago already, her brain had figured out that a quick rethink was needed. This was not, after all, to be one of those nights when it was OK to mellow out on alcoholic vapours and lie around languidly tucked alongside Jo's long body.

So, having followed the little street information signs strategically placed at all main intersections, mostly for the benefit of tourists, she had found the blue and white checkerboard neon-lit shingle she was after.

To the policeman at the duty desk, she repeated her story almost verbatim because he was asking the same baseline questions as the young man back at the Surf Club but this time, Maddy was careful not to exhale alcoholic fumes in the officer's direction. She regretted not having thought to stop at the all-night petrol station she had passed along the way to buy a little box of mints.

Again, though Maddy had wanted to launch immediately into the details of how she had already scoured the area for Jo, she had been brought to a quick halt.

"Before anything else, young lady," said the officer behind the duty desk, "we need to confirm who *you* are, right? And *so,* we need to take down a few details," he explained with a too-sweet smile. "So, I'll need to have a look at a driver's licence. Do you have one on your person?" Maddy blinked at him, wondering how her details could be in any way relevant to Jo's disappearance but, nonetheless, from her back pocket she had produced her driving licence.

"Good, good," the officer had clucked, checking Maddy's bright, freckle-splattered face and wide shoulders against the tiny, impassive Maddy-face on the driving licence. "Maddy Collins," the policeman read. "Twenty-five years of age. Residing in Cronin Street, Annerley." He looked up. "Is this still current?" Maddy nodded. "And where *exactly* is Annerley?" he asked with a smile meant to be engaging but before she could answer, he redirected himself. "Ah ha! A 4103 postcode would place it somewhere near Brisbane, right?" He had slid the laminated licence off to his right, next to a PC's keyboard, away from Maddy's direct reach.

"Right. But who cares where I– "

"How close to Brisbane *exactly*," the policeman persisted.

"Fourteen minutes from the CBD *exactly,* but look, what's that got to do with– "

"Hold your horses, young lady," the officer cut in with a firm but patronising pleasantness, and his manner began rubbing Maddy the wrong way. She moved her eyes away from his waxy round face and onto his nametag. *Constable John Comino.*

"First thing's first," Constable Comino said, palms of hands in front of his chest as if slowing down invisible traffic. "Before considering any action in regards to your current query, young lady, we need to know who *you* are. So ... when you're ready, we need your home phone number and workplace details," he insisted smoothly. Maddy had obliged frostily. Resentment at the officer's irrelevant line of questioning was just about getting the better of her when finally, though he hadn't entered any of Maddy's details anywhere, he had finally asked about this friend of hers who *she thought* had gone missing.

"And this person's name is?"

"Jo Brenner. Joanna Brenner," Maddy answered. Her lover's formal name resonated in her head, full of dread and foreboding.

"If one of the measures that needs to be undertaken involves distributing pictures of..." the officer glanced at the name he had jotted down, "this Joanna Brenner, the first thing you need to provide is a good, clear picture of the missing person. One that will blow up nice and– "

"A picture like, right here in my back pocket?" Maddy snapped. "No, no picture." The officer rolled his eyes.

"I can tell you what she looks like," Maddy said tightly. "Five-eleven, short black hair, grey eyes. Thin. Tall and thin."

"Nice," he grinned appreciatively. "How old?"

"Twenty-three."

"Mmm. Any distinctive features? Or–" he was asking when a tall policewoman appeared behind the duty desk, an armload of files under one arm. She looked twice at the young redhead who was visibly scowling at the officer on duty.

Maddy shook her head before answering the Constable's question. "No distinctive features. Only that she's tall and thin and– "

"What? No scar? No tattoo– "

"No scars, no. No tattoos. No piercings." Maddy frowned again before adding through tight lips, "But, hey, her favourite band's Soundgarden, if *that helps*."

"Now, now," Constable Comino tut-tutted, "you might not know this woman well … uh, well enough, I mean, not *intimately* enough to know about any of these personal details. Perhaps you need to have a chat with her boyfriend and see if *he* wants to report her missin... "

Maddy had drawn in her bottom lip, pulling in, at the same time, the silver lip loop that split it right in the middle. Forehead tight, blue eyes tense, she cocked her head at the tall policewoman who had deposited the pile of files she had been carrying on a corner of the duty desk. Desperately seeking some kind of confirmation that, surely, her distress deserved better than what Constable John Comino was giving her, she squinted at the strapping woman in the white uniform shirt, somewhat reassured by the chevrons on her epaulettes.

It was not just the short red hair standing on end that had caught DS Jensen's attention. It had been what she had seen, beyond the glower, in the young woman's eyes that had intrigued her, a tired nervousness, the fear of the little child lost for too long in a shopping mall. So, instead of going back to her desk to make a dent in the back-log of paperwork, she had stood by the duty desk, listening in on the exchange, listening to the young redhead explaining that though her friend had not been found in the sea and was nowhere else to be found, not in the public loos, not on the beach, not in the water, and not back at the flat, then some kind of accident must have happened to her.

"Look, the thing is that *maybe* she's been mugged, right? *Maybe* more than two hours ago already," Maddy had finally cut in pointedly. "Anything could've happened." Nibbling at the inside of her bottom lip, a habit from childhood, and sounding close to defeat, she had added, "She's missing, that's all I know."

Just as the policewoman had moved in closer to the night-duty officer, her junior in rank if not in age, to signal to him her interest in the young woman's predicament, he replied somewhat sardonically that this *missing* friend was probably already "tucked in with the boyfriend".

The glare of irritation in the policewoman's eyes had buoyed Maddy's sinking spirit.

"Oh, I don't think so, Officer," Maddy replied coolly. "She's ... uh ... I mean ... I'm her lover. *Me*. There isn't any boyfriend."

"Like I said," the Constable persisted undeterred, "that's what women do when they're upset." He had grinned like an oversized schoolboy at a toilet humour joke. "First thing they do is run back to the boyfriend– "

"Ah, knock it off, John," the policewoman broke in sharply, "you're not funny." And to the redhead she said, "Come." DS Jensen had rounded the desk, leading Maddy off to the side, towards a quiet corner.

"Is he always such a dickhea– uh ... a troglodyte?" Maddy asked shakily, looking over her shoulder at the policeman who was still grinning behind the duty desk, but apologetically this time.

"Never mind *him*. Boys' humour," DS Jensen replied, lightly but clearly distancing herself from the male officer's remarks. "Can be a bit of a prick when the mood takes– "

"Well, I reckon the mood must've gripped him good and strong," Maddy replied icily, looking straight ahead, jaw muscles bunched.

The tall policewoman hid a grin before bending her head to meet Maddy's eyes more squarely. "I'm DS Jensen. Christen. Chris." The woman had smiled easily. "Look," she added, "I only tuned in at the post-introductory phase back there, so I missed out on ... Never mind that. You are...?"

"Maddy Collins."

"Right. Maddy. Nice. Short for what? Madeleine? No? Maddison?" The young redhead had shaken her head again. "*No?* Not Maddison? So, what does that leave? Uh ... Mad– "

"It's not short for anything, it's my name. That's it. Maddy."

"Oh right. OK. So ... how old are you, Maddy Collins?" DS Jensen asked gently, visibly intrigued by the young woman who, she didn't doubt, would be quite vibrant if it weren't for her obvious distress.

"Twenty-five." Round blue eyes looked up, focusing on DS Jensen for the first time. The policewoman's eyebrows arched in disbelief. "Why?" Maddy asked defensively.

"Oh … nothing." The tall woman smiled, spreading her hands in self-defence. "Just that I didn't make you to be one day over twenty, that's all. Twenty-*one* at the most. In any case," she snorted good-naturedly, "it's good to know you're, uh … old enough to drink alcohol."

Maddy blushed but tapped her cheekbone, where constellations of freckles were permanently clustered. "Yeah, well, it's the freckles that do it, the young-thing bit," she explained flatly, as one used to a recurring comment made by strangers. Her tone was the same as the one that often accompanied the staple rejoinder she gave people who enquired about her lip ring. Just about everyone she came across on the floor of Terry's All Treads and Tyres wanted to know if the silver loop ever got caught around her food.

"My lip loop?" she would ask, cheekily poking with her tongue the loop that split her bottom lip in even halves. "Nah! Never. Not even when I kiss. Not even on a big-time pash." Because her round blue eyes smiled even when she didn't, people often missed the mild sarcasm of her retort and they nodded back with a newly-found understanding of the piercing thing.

DS Jensen grinned. "Could be right about the freckles." One hand on the buckle of her utility belt, she added with the kind of enthusiasm a nurse saves for a flailing patient, "Something tells me *you* need a cup of something hot. Tea? Coffee? Milo?" Maddy blinked at her. "Don't tell me I'm wrong *again*. Twice in a row? So you think a hot brew would do you good?" the woman asked, dipping her knees a little, like Jo sometimes did, to find Maddy's averted eyes. The policewoman's theatrics helped divert Maddy's attention, if only for a brief moment, and she smiled in spite of herself. "Something hot would be nice, thank you," she replied softly. "Coffee, black."

"Good girl. Uh…" The policewoman sat down again. "I'm not sure what the last shift's left us in terms of the better coffee, as in *not* the Caterer's Blend. Hang on a minute." DS Jensen stood up. "Hey, John," she called out. Officer Comino looked up. "Anything left in the Lavazza tin?" she asked, brushing back what blond hair had loosened itself from the otherwise neat eight-strand plait that rested against her neck.

Officer Comino grinned back. "I'd say there might just be enough for two good ones. Let me." He walked from behind the duty desk to disappear inside a hallway. "Won't be a tick," he called back.

Eyebrows arched humorously, DS Jensen grinned at Maddy. "As I said, he's not all bad. Not *all* the time."

A moment later, both hands around a chipped mug, Maddy listened to what DS Jensen told her about people. About the unknown number of persons who *disappear* in the night, on any given night, everywhere in the world.

"Most of them…" she corrected herself, "Just about all of them, pretty much *all* of them, show up in the morning or the next day with one hell of a good story to tell. Of course, if we're talking about alien abductions, the *return* process has been known to take a bit longer." Not feeling in the mood for any kind of humour, Maddy glared ahead.

"Right. Bad joke," DS Jensen said easily. And then, sitting down across from Maddy on a contoured grey plastic chair, she posed the question while rearranging the two-way radio that, at first glance, appeared simply stuck on the cloth of the uniform shirt stretched over her powerful shoulder. "Maddy, is Jo *married?"*

Blue eyes flashed a not-you-too warning because Maddy was not intimidated by the policewoman's physicality. She stood up. Hot coffee spilling over her fingers, Maddy winced.

"No, look, Maddy," DS Jensen said, staying seated. Maddy flicked liquid off her fingers, too late aware of the proximity of the officer's pale blue, starched shirtfront. DS Jensen remained focused. "This is the *one* very basic question *you* need to handle." From her position on the grey plastic chair, the police officer had to look up to maintain eye contact with Maddy, now that she had stood up. "Whether Jo's in real trouble or not, wherever you're going to seek help, or a solution, or simply some professional to chat to, now or later…", Maddy sat down again, "…you'll be asked that same question every time. So, Maddy, is Jo married?" The officer had paused, keeping her eyes on the young redhead's face, reading her conflicting thoughts as easily as the pages of a book. She waited for Maddy to settle.

The night was quiet out there in the streets of Burleigh Heads. Things would be different up in Surfers' Paradise, the teenage and tourist Mecca where students and visitors flocked to let their hair down. But until something major happened up there or until the bank's alarm went off at the Burleigh Heads cop shop, all seemed as it should, except for this young dyke who had lost her girlfriend. And DS Jensen figured that more important than her stack of unprocessed paperwork was the time she could spend to soothe young Maddy Collins away from her loop of fear, doubt and confusion.

"Truth is," DS Jensen began again, easing the heavy utility belt against the unyielding plastic of the chair, "husbands *and* boyfriends are truly, too often, a woman's worst enemy. It can also be the brother or the uncle, even grandpas, but that's another story again." She paused, waiting for Maddy to lift her eyes off the beige carpet and look at her. She sighed and shook her head imperceptibly at the slumped shoulders, bare, freckly and sunburnt, made more vulnerable by the skimpy T-shaped muscle shirt. "For many, it comes down to just that, *Sleeping With The Enemy*. You know like the title of that film with…. Anyway, Maddy, you know what I'm talking about, don't you?"

Maddy shrugged, shoulders uncharacteristically rounded.

"So … Jo, is she married? Or did she have *any* relations with a male, any male, that you know of, that you've heard of or met, say during the past year?"

Eyes planted on the beige carpet somewhere between her runners, Maddy shook her head.

"No, you *don't know* or no, she *isn't* or *hasn't?*"

"I don't know that much about her … like about her past." Maddy did not look up. "We've only been together nine months. She's not married, though. That, I know for sure. Never has been. I mean, she's a–" Instinctively, she altered the end of her thought. "She only twenty-three!"

"Fair enough, but can you say *for sure* that no male might be involved, directly or indirectly if, as you say, Jo's not where she should be?" DS Jensen watched as Maddy finally registered the true meaning of the question. She watched Maddy swallow hard. She noticed, too, the bunching muscles just above her jawline, the glint of the lip ring and more importantly, the straightening of the shoulders that indicated the young woman was regaining some control over her thoughts.

The police officer had already considered the width of the young woman's shoulders and estimated it at a good two and a half hand-spans. While she had ushered Maddy along to the sitting area, her eyes had roamed the graceful sweep of taut muscles that spread gently from the middle of her back to pad her shoulders and how it ended in a smooth wedge that tapered off, level with the clavicles. The rounded oblong deltoids and the elongated smooth mass of the young woman's biceps at ease, far from making her look bullish or boyish, lent definite grace to her movements. Nothing knotted, nothing bunched, nothing bulging; only smooth, feline, gentle and understated strength. "You work out a lot, Maddy?" DS Jensen asked to engage the young woman differently.

Maddy looked up, eyes misty, Adam's apple dipping. "Don't need to," she replied grimly. "Got a couple of hours to spare? Have a go at nipple trimming. It'll do it for you too."

DS Jensen opened her mouth to speak but closed it again. Finally she said, "Say again?"

Maddy blushed even under her sunburn because she realised that she was being rude to the woman who was only trying to help. "Sorry," she said with the best smile she could muster. "I'm a mechanic, a tyre fitter, too. It's quite physical … for a chick."

"I bet." DS Jensen was impressed. "Demanding, even for a bloke. I'm pretty sure our friend John out there," she pointed a thumb back towards the duty desk, "I'm sure he wouldn't last long on *that* floor. But what's the … hmm … the nipple trimming thing about?"

"Oh that." Maddy grinned. "That's when the tiny little thin teats have to be trimmed off tyres. They all still have them from the moulds back at the factory. We don't sell them with the teats on, looks untidy."

"So?"

"So what?"

"Hey, I'm curious. How do you trim those *nipples* off the tyres, surely not one by one."

" Ah … no. Not one by one. It's like there'd be a hundred or more on one single tyre."

"So, what's the shortcut?"

Maddy glanced at the policewoman. *What's with the questions? It's not like it's riveting stuff or anything.* "The tyre gets fitted on a rotating machine and there's a fork, something that looks like a fork, that's hand-held, and as the tyre rotates past, quite fast really, the teats get snipped off. The thing is that it gets done in that tiny room, no air coming in and the temperature's often well over forty and it's just … Well, it's hell. The only good thing is that it makes me sweat buckets. Really litres, so it's even better than a sauna. Keeps me cut."

"Right. I see what you mean about your job keeping you fit. "

"That and swinging and stacking and lifting and fitting the tyres, again and again. Good fun," Maddy added, looking like she meant it. And because she fell silent, again returning to contemplating the space on the floor between her shoes, the policewoman kept going. "I was just asking ... you know ... about your workout because I spend many hours in the gym, myself. Comes with the job, right? But all I get is the bulk. Strength and bulk. Like here." She pointed to her shoulders, full and round, under the navy blue shoulder-boards of her uniform. "I've varied the weights and the reps and the pace and just about everything I can think of but I still end up shoulder-heavy. Impressive ... sometimes, but not sexy." Then she beamed at Maddy. "I'd die to have half the muscle definition you have."

That made Maddy snort on a grin. "Oh, hey ... yeah, well that's the tyre thing that does it and, also I get a bit of that from my parents." And on an afterthought, she added, "That and the red hair, and the freckles. Even my mother is ... put together like, wiry and all *she* does is the housework."

"Right. It's in the genes then." DS Jensen chuckled before her face grew solemn again. "Look, Maddy, there's something I need to make sure you understand." She paused and Maddy looked up again. "The way you came in, I mean here, to the station, the same way you can leave, right? I mean, you can leave any time, right? You do understand that nothing much is going to happen here, tonight? All I can do is enter the MP data in the computer and send someone for a sweep of the area once we can define a realistic radius to cover the ten minute span when you were up in the flat. You understand what I'm saying, Maddy?"

"I understand," she snorted again, but this time derisively.

"Reality is that there's nothing we can do about Jo besides taking down a statement to the fact that she's not where she should be and someone, namely you, is worried about it. Date, address, signature, that wraps it up. OK?" Maddy shrugged to suggest that she understood but that the system stunk anyway. "But here's the deal." DS Jensen tugged at her tie. "If you don't have anything better to do, like it's ... " She glanced at the wall clock in front of her. "3.04 a.m. On the one hand it's late but again it's far too early for ... for many things. So ... if you think you're not ready for sleep and you want to hang around a little, maybe we can go on *chatting* a while longer. Maybe I can help you think more clearly about your options. Or maybe I can help you anticipate what *might* happen in the days ahead. That's *if* you feel you want to talk about Jo ... with me." She stopped and scrutinised Maddy's profile. "What d'you say?" she asked gently. "Got some time to hang here a bit?"

Maddy stood up. She rotated her shoulder blades, one at a time, to loosen the tension that had settled. She looked at the policewoman who, again, had remained seated. "D'you guys have a loo I can use?" she asked hoarsely.

"Sure." The policewoman turned to Constable Comino still at the desk behind them and called out. "Hey John!" She waited till the policeman looked up from whatever he was reading. "Something useful for you to do, mate. Can you just *point* her towards the johns?"

"You got it," was all the officer replied.

Maddy's blue eyes settled briefly on the woman's face. She seemed about to speak but, wheeling on the balls of her feet, she walked away without having answered the woman's question.

DS Jensen unclipped the wide leather utility-belt from her waist and eased her back more comfortably against the chair. The Glock, in its holster, clanked dully against the metallic chair. She stretched her legs and sighed.

One day, some nine months ago, minutes before closing time, a tall woman about her own age had come into the bay, at Terry's All Treads, pushing a bicycle. Maddy glanced up from what she had been doing. One look at the customer, at the well-worn combat boots, dark-green acid-washed pants and black rib-hugging T-shirt under a flannelette shirt told her the young woman was into grunge. Another look at the bike was all she needed to know that they didn't sell what she'd be needing. At All Treads, they neither patched up tyres, nor did they carry anything that could be fitted on a bike.

"A truck's no problem, but a push-bike? C'mon, lady! Give us a break," she heard Drew tell the young customer. So Maddy got up from the tyre where she had been sitting, chucked the piece of chalk she had been using to mark a stack before shelving them, and walked over to have a look at the bicycle. Holding up the handlebar with one hand, she spun the front tyre around and it became immediately apparent that no amount of goodwill would mend the long tear that snaked up along the tread. Not even temporarily.

"Too far gone. It's like—" It was then that Maddy noticed the general aspect of the bike. "I was going to say it's like it died from old age but looks to me like the whole bike's about to cark it." She noticed the woman's grey eyes looking at her intently. *Young chick,* Maddy thought and yet she did not smile.

"Fifty bucks. That's what I got it for," the young person offered in lieu of explanation. Her grey eyes were very grey. Very grey and very serious. Up close, her hair was not only short and almost black, Maddy noticed it was cut in some sort of unaffected, untidy style. The 'grunge chick', as Maddy had quickly labelled her, was as thin as she was tall. Stringbean, Maddy thought, though she had returned her eyes to the bicycle frame. Willowy would have better suited. "Thought it was a pretty good deal," the dark-haired girl continued. "Actually, been riding it around for a month already. Still reckon it's good value what with the fifteen speeds and all."

Maddy glanced at her and back at the bike and chuckled. She ran her hand over the rusty frame, looked at the fine rust that had clung to her fingertips and gave the derailleur a quick once-over. "Might be right. Solid joints. Only surface rust. Chrome's totally shot, paint's as dead as it gets but that don't kill a bike. Just makes it look old." She looked squarely at the bicycle owner.

The tall girl frowned. "And so ... what's wrong with old?"

Maddy was about to answer that old was fine provided it could still do whatever it had been designed to do when Drew broke into the conversation abruptly, as he always did when only women were involved. "Well, lady, old or new makes no difference to us but we're closing shop here so, if you don't mind ... " Rudely, he pointed to the street beyond the great hangar doors. To make amends for his curtness, Maddy ushered the woman and her crippled bike towards the sunlight and, to be more helpful than her colleague, she asked her how far she had to go. The young customer explained she was on her way home, somewhere off Fairfield Road. Only a fifteen-minute bike ride from Terry's All Treads but probably walking was more than twice the cycling time in the late afternoon heat. As it happened, Fairfield Road was quite close to Annerley, the next suburb, where Maddy lived. And though she had planned on going in the other direction, straight to the university pool for an hour of muscle-relaxing laps, she offered to give the young person a lift. The lame bicycle got tossed in the boot of her equally old but much fitter Holden Commodore.

Maddy and the passenger, who had simply given her name as Jo, didn't talk much that day except about the bike and how Jo had found it in an op shop, 'preloved and all,' she had said.

"Just standing there in front of the store, between two crates of books, a skateboard and an ancient looking lawnmower. Fifty bucks, nice and even. Good buy." She nodded to herself. "There's still some life left in it, you know."

"The tyre'll cost almost as much as the bike."

"Them's the breaks," Jo said matter-of-factly.

Why not get a proper second-hand one like from the Trading Post? Maddy had almost asked but instead, one hand loose on the steering wheel, the other loose on the gearshift, she simply replied, "I reckon." That's all she said but, as she shifted back into second gear, she became aware that the passenger seat's usual position didn't allow the stranger to stretch her legs comfortably. She became aware, too, of the very long and thin fingers, bare of jewellery, that tap-danced on the dashboard to some silent tune. *That's one thin chick,* Maddy thought, bringing the engine back into third. *Nervy, too.* She turned on the radio to give the long fingers something real to tap-dance to. The beat on the B105 station was definitely not Seattle grunge, but Jo wouldn't have expected it to be.

When Jo said, "You can pull up right behind that truck over there," Maddy had looked around to guess which was Jo's dig.

"So ... which one's yours?' she asked, unable to hazard a guess as all the houses in the street kind of looked the same, in urgent need of a good scrape and a fresh coat of paint.

Jo pointed at a very wide and squat chamferboard Queenslander. "That one."

The entire ground level, even the wrap-around verandah, encased in concrete and louvred windows, might have been painted in some shade of yellow ochre, once, a long time ago, but it had faded to an uninviting shade of dingy yellow. The large Queenslander, once con-verted, had obviously been left to fend for itself. *Fairfield House* the sign said in washed-out lettering.

"What, you live in a boarding house?" Maddy was surprised.

"That's where I hang up my hat, my bag, and tie up my bike. So, yep, that makes it home."

"Right."

"Right, what?"

"Uh ... nothing, really." Maddy shook her head, keen to dispel any negative inference. "It's just that I've never met anyone who lived in a boarding house," she admitted quickly.

"You're strictly houses or flats?" Jo asked, eyebrows knotted in an expression that Maddy interpreted as incomprehension. "Which one?"

"House. Not far from here. Just a shoe box but– "

"*But* it's a house."

"Right, it's a house. Room to move," Maddy shrugged, not about to apologise for what Grunge Chick, still on the passenger side, might perceive as aspiring capitalism. "Many things needing fixing but yeah … You been living here long?"

"Nah. I'm new in town."

"How new is new?"

"Four months."

Maddy glanced at Jo to check that she was serious. She had almost said *Right!* again. Four months took it well beyond *her* understanding of new-in-town. New-in-town in terms of housing, for her, meant a couple of weeks, before she'd settle on one of the many rental possibilities that abounded in Brisbane.

Every day in the *Courier-Mail,* or even in the free local rags, there was also a fair range of shared accommodation, for those who privileged saving some rent money over privacy. Or for the convivial types, Maddy figured, though Jo didn't impress her much as the convivial type. Maddy, on the other hand, could be as convivial as the best of them but when she came home wrecked from having bounced tyres around all day, when she wasn't head-under-bonnet or slid under one chassis or another, she longed for privacy and her own space above all else. And, partly thanks to the money dear Aunty Ida had left her, the walls around her, no matter how basic, were more hers than the bank's.

"I wish I could do more for you, little one," Aunty Ida had said the day she disclosed a clause of her will. "But if you have a roof over your head, Maddy, and you *own* that roof *and* most of the walls *and* most of the pipes around it, you'll be safe. You're still very young but I want you to know that when you're ready for the responsibility of home ownership, you'll have enough to walk into any bank manager's office and proudly say, 'I want to buy.' I reckon there's enough money here for a deposit." Aunt Ida had reached for Maddy's hand and held it between her own bony fingers. "But you'll still have to put some of your own money into it, Maddy. So you *will* have to make your own sacrifices and put in your own determination, but you'll be fine.' And when the time came, late last year, Maddy had honoured her dear aunt's final wish.

She had researched various lending authorities, she had done her homework in terms of repayments and taxes and variable or fixed interest rates and, confident of her eligibility for the First Homebuyer's Rebate, one day she walked proudly into the Annerley branch of the

Commonwealth Bank of Australia and told the lending manager with whom she had secured an appointment, "I want to buy."

So, the way Maddy figured, four *months* should have afforded the new-kid-in-town enough time to commit to something, anything, beside a room in a fleabag of a boarding house and communal space to share with–

"How many rooms are in there?" she asked, as neutrally as she could.

"Around twenty."

"Right. Well … anyway," Maddy threw in, eyeing her passenger's long legs as she slid out of the car, "if you want to stretch out a little, I mean, one little room can't possibly feel like *real* space … I mean, if you'd like to walk over to my place, sometime, and I could throw us a couple of chops on the barbie and…"

And that's pretty much how Maddy remembers both of them getting together, except that Jo hadn't walked over. She had ridden the rusty bike that sported a handsome new front tyre to Maddy's place. Maddy knew the tall girl would eventually turn up. It's just that she hadn't been game to bet how soon that might be.

Maddy had dropped the bike and Grunge Chick Jo, her private nickname for the young woman, in front of *Fairfield House* and by the time she had walked through her own back door, and into her kitchen, she had lost the momentum to drive to the St Lucia pool. Instead, she plugged in the kettle, thirsty for a cup of tea. But in what seemed to be the same fluid movement, as she passed by the fridge, she took down one freezer bag of chops and another of sausages … just in case.

The butcher had been categorical. "Real Spanish flavour, these sausages," he had promised, "They'll be a sure hit the moment they start crisping up."

If Jo comes soon, as in this *evening,* Maddy had rationalised, *I'll zap them to defrost. If she comes later, as in a couple of days later, well … they'll just thaw out slowly.* Though she didn't want to gamble on how soon Jo would drop by, Maddy still knew she'd drop in before the end of the week. She didn't know *how* she knew, she just knew she would.

By the time Jo had pushed through the back gate, the sausages were half-thawed on the bottom shelf of Maddy's fridge. The beer was as cold as beer gets in the middle of an unseasonably hot Saturday in April. Cold enough to stick to unsuspecting fingertips. Cool for the time it takes to gulp four swigs. Definitely warm by the time of the last ones. *Hey, what the hell, the Poms have theirs warm all the time,* Maddy thought, though she didn't really know that for a fact. She had never been outside of Australia, but you know how it is. You hear things, you repeat things and if you don't think too hard about them, if they're pretty much irrelevant anyway, you don't really need to know if they're true or not.

"So, yeah, if it's good enough for the Poms ... at least we don't drink warm beer by choice, now do we?" she had asked, head lingering inside the freezer where, earlier, she had placed four beers against hard pillows of stone-frozen meat. She was grateful for the immediate cooling effect of the freezer-cold air against her cheeks.

So, as Jo had pushed through the back gate, chinking the little bell affixed to it as a perimeter-penetrated warning device, the rusty squeak of the gate always let Maddy know someone, anyone, friend or foe, had come through.

From behind the kitchen window, Maddy had watched Grunge-Chick Jo carefully close the gate behind her, and push the old bicycle in front of her, leading it over the concrete driveway with one hand on the saddle. Bottom lip drawn in, Maddy had watched her lean it against one of the supporting patio beams. *So, she's made it here after all,* she had finally grinned. *Only took her three days.*

The back door was open.

"Anyone home?" Jo had called out, peering into the chiaroscuro of the hallway, unaware of Maddy's face framed, off to the left, by the chamferboards of the kitchen window. So Maddy rapped the glass pane. Three sweaty knuckles left their imprint on the glass. Jo's grey eyes, following the sound, had found Maddy's face. Grey eyes smiled from under uneven strands of short black hair.

"Hey. I've come to stretch my legs," Jo called out. "It's like you said, not much space inside a small room." Her lips curled up and two little grooves had appeared at their corners. *Cute,* thought Maddy. *Nice smile that.* Jo hadn't smiled the day Maddy had given her a ride to *Fairfield House.*

Jo slid a funky rainbow-coloured bag off her shoulders. "Brought a couple of beers along."

"Didn't have to but ... Right, why don't you come in and we stick them in the fridge? I'll crack open a couple that're already nice and cold, huh? You OK with Cascade?"

"I'm OK with whatever."

And Jo had come in, grey eyes serious in spite of the little smile that could also have passed for a little smirk. All legs and arms. The legs, Maddy got to learn much later, were the steady part of Jo. The smile could falter. It could come and go. It could go and be very long in coming back. She always understood what made Jo's smile come on but she seldom understood what made it go away. And she never understood what made it stay away for such long stretches of time.

In terms of personality though, with Maddy, what you saw was what you got: flaming dark-red hair, a smattering of freckles more dense across the ridge of her nose and cheekbones than anywhere else except across her shoulders. What you saw was what you got *except* for the lip ring that split her bottom lip evenly. And the *attitude* the lip loop gave her face was quickly belied by round blue eyes that smiled even when she didn't.

Jo had stepped into Maddy's kitchen for the first time, long legs clad in a pair of worn-through jeans low on her waist. A rib-hugging T-shirt sporting the face of Chris Cornell, Soundgarden's charismatic front man, was only long enough to reach past her belly button. Over it, an equally well-worn green and black flannelette shirt that dangled to mid-thigh. Jo looked like a long stem, lithe and striking in a most understated way. No bangles, no chains, no dog collar, no makeup, no nailpolish, no gel in the hair, short for the most part, that fell over her forehead in uneven strands.

Jo had cast her eyes about the kitchen and made an immediate beeline to peer at the many pictures and haphazard arrangement of bills, mementoes, and notes held to the fridge door by a horde of differently coloured tree-frog magnets. She returned her attention to Maddy, cute in her jungle-coloured muscle shirt.

"You're into frogs?" she asked Maddy, who stood in the middle of the kitchen trying to think of what she needed to do next.

The sleeveless T reached just below her buttocks. In spite of the blue togs, the swimsuit bottoms she wore underneath, Maddy felt suddenly naked. *Right! Well, it's not as if I was expecting company, like right this very moment, now was I?* she argued with herself, turning away from her guest as a slow blush crept to her cheeks.

"Not into *frogs*. It's more like I am totally into *tree*-frogs," she said from inside the pantry. "It's not the same thing. The ones that live in rainforest and what not." Maddy came out of the pantry empty-handed. She reached for the beer bottles she had retrieved from the freezer and twisted the top off the first one. Jo's eyes had first flicked, then lingered, over the bare well-defined shape of Maddy's upper arm. "Know anything about them?" Maddy asked over her shoulder.

Jo shrugged. "Can't say that I do. Except that, like all frogs, I suppose they blow themselves up to horrible proportions. And what, they're prettier and smaller than the usual garden ones? Right so far?"

"Not necessarily smaller."

"But they're just as slimy."

Maddy smiled quickly. "Right on the *slimy*."

"So, what's this one here?" Jo had asked, pointing at a handsome wood-carved frog magnet that was lime green on top and orange below. Even its eyes were golden with orange outer rings.

On her way back to the pantry Maddy glanced at the miniature carving. "That one's a Northern Red-Eyed Tree Frog. Its real name's something like Litoria Xantho ... something or other."

"So like, where do these little guys live, I mean, with a name like that? Up a tree somewhere in Northern Australia?"

"Close. They live in rainforests but in Northern Queensland. And they're easier to spot after the rain when they come out to call. But these little guys ... they grow up to some six and a half centimetres, so that's not so small at all. And the Giant Tree Frogs ... they get between ... ten and fourteen centimetres long." Maddy was still rummaging inside the pantry. "But the Red-Eyed, what they like to do ... is call from low branches and ... once they start they easily keep going for hours, like nine hours non-stop."

"Sweet! I think I'd really like to fall asleep to the sound of that, all tucked in deep inside a rainforest, like inside one of these great big buttress roots," Jo had said as if she had simply said, I'd like to listen to them from inside a log cabin. "So what's the name of the glam frog of Frogland, you know? That little tiny one we always see on postcards," she had asked, eyes fast on the wide sweep of Maddy's back.

Maddy finally made up her mind and pulled down a couple of packs of assorted nuts. "Oh, there's a few really that are, uh, more photogenic than others but my favourite would have to be ... that one." She pointed at another magnet, that of a green frog that had rather large pads. "It's a Dwarf Tree Frog and it only grows some three centimetres long. Thing is, it has a real high-pitched call and that one wouldn't be *that* pleasant if you're trying to go to sleep. Not even inside tree roots, like you said before."

"Hey, I'm impressed." Jo grinned but Maddy had already turned her attention to something else. So Jo tapped the fridge door. "No pets on the fridge."

"No pets in the house."

"Good."

Maddy sliced the top of the first party-mix foil. "Awh … Pets are nice to have around."

"Right! Cute and nice. You get attached, they die."

"Well…" Maddy began, surprised by Jo's clipped tone. "We all kind of … die, sooner or later." She turned to look at the gangling young woman who was still standing in the middle of her little kitchen.

"Ah yes, we die but it seems that most humans in this world of ours manage to live past the age of ten."

Maddy grinned an appreciative sort of a smile. "Right. So what? You lost a pet when you were– "

"A pet, two grandmothers, two grandfathers and my mother." Before Maddy was able to proffer an awkward 'I'm sorry', Jo had added wryly. "All but my dog managed to live beyond ten, though."

Eyes rounded, mind blank as to an appropriate rejoinder, Maddy nibbled the inside of her bottom lip and stayed still against the kitchen counter. Jo came to her rescue with a casual, "Hey. Don't sweat it. I've got it all under control. That was six years ago that mum died. I guess I've had my time to grieve."

Front teeth nipping at her lip ring, Maddy hesitated. "Right. Still…" The words she would've liked to say didn't come to her. Instead, she blushed again before remembering the beers that, coat of frost already puddling at their base, were about to reach room temperature in a record time.

She twisted the top off. "Here," she said, handing it to Jo before taking a gulp of her bottle.

The waist-deep side opening on Maddy's top bared the length of her ribs padded by intercostal muscles. "Cashew-peanut mix. Unsalted. OK with you? And chips?"

"Sure, whatever. Just as long as you don't give me anything that's got celery in it."

Eyebrows cocked in a comical expression, Maddy answered, "Not much celery in any of the party packs *I* buy."

Jo grinned in the way that created double tiny creases near both corners of her lips and Maddy stood there looking up at her, feeling too short. *Too short for what?* crossed her mind and remained unanswered because the visitor was again talking to her.

"Need help with those?" Jo was pointing at the packets once again in Maddy's hands.

"Uh … no. But yeah, why don't you grab me those two bowls over there."

Hips slightly forward, Jo bridged the couple of metres to the draining board. "Three bowls here," she said, hefting the three bowls, feeling their contour with long fingers. "Which two? Terracotta white? Terracotta blue? Terracotta *au naturel?*"

Aware of Grunge-Chick's playful tone and unnerved by her own increased heartbeat, Maddy concentrated on the blurb printed on the back of the cashew-peanut mix. "Your pick." Then, preferring to cut rather than slice the air-packed packet of chips, she rummaged in the top drawer, then in the next one down, and when, kitchen scissors in hand, she straightened up, Jo's hands were cool against her shoulders, flat against her skin. Something lurched inside Maddy's stomach as Jo turned her around to look into her round blue eyes.

Maddy raised her chin. Jo bent her head and dipped her knees, just a little, and slid her hands over the smooth freckle-splattered skin of Maddy's shoulders, over the oblong curve of her deltoids and down the soft swelling of her biceps. Maddy frowned because her breath had caught somewhere below her solar plexus but she didn't move. Even her collarbone didn't rise because she had stopped breathing. And when Jo slid her hands under the thin T and ran them slowly over Maddy's warm marble-pale ribs, Maddy closed her eyes. When she heard herself moan, her eyes snapped open and she inhaled forcibly to bring air down into her lungs. And just as Jo's grey eyes were about to become fuzzy, because Jo's face had moved too close to her own, close enough to feel the brush of her lips, Maddy, pupils already dilated by the sudden ache of desire, took one step back.

"Whoa! Hold your horses," she said huskily.

Jo's lips said, "Why?"

"Well, it's like…" she attempted forcing a little more air into her lungs. "Right. It goes like that, we've only just met and–"

"Ah. You're the kind of chick that needs a couple of dates, a film or two, let's throw in a couple of romantic dinner conversations and *then* you'll feel you know me well enough for us to kiss and hop into bed." It was not a question and Jo's tone, in spite of the words, had remained neutral.

If anyone had asked Maddy whether *that* was indeed what she usually expected before a first session horizontal with anyone, she'd have said, *Hello! Wake up! Like who doesn't, right? Who, in their right mind's gonna go and screw around with a perfect stranger, huh?*

Jo suggested that the beers could, perhaps, go back into the freezer. And that's just the way things went because by then, more than a couple of dinner dates, what Maddy absolutely craved was to feel Jo's mouth hard against her own. She absolutely ached to feel the coolness of that Grunge-Chick's hands back under her T-shirt and *over* her breasts. She wanted to know the feel of Jo's thumbs nudging her nipples.

Hands still gripping the balcony railing, still staring out to the open sea, the morning sun already biting her skin, Maddy sighed. Was this the same thing, the same kind of dropping out of sight, as what Jo had done that time when she didn't show for three days? She nibbled the inside of her bottom lip and blinked away the hot tears brought on from having stared so long, too long, eyes unseeing, at the mirror-shiny sea across the esplanade.

Briefly, she tongued the lip loop, resting her front teeth gently against its curve before releasing it. She shrugged and ran a hand through sand-and-salt-stiffened hair, stiffened, too, from the many times she had raked her fingers through it since the previous night, shortly after midnight.

Earlier, she had called the Burleigh Heads police station, hoping to find DS Jensen, hoping the policewoman would tell her something about what had been done past dawn, in terms of searching the immediate vicinity for clues. But the officer who answered the call had told her that DS Jensen was not on the day's duty roster. That either meant, he had kindly explained, she was on her day off or attending to some of her other responsibilities outside the station, as was often the case. Did she want to leave a message, she had asked. Maddy had declined.

Before placing her call to the local police station, Maddy had punched in Jo's work number just to be sure. And when Peta James, the morning crew supervisor, said icily that Jo Brenner hadn't yet reported to work, Maddy was neither surprised nor disappointed. The one thing she had known for certain was that Jo wouldn't be over there, in the Mater Hospital cafeteria, making mung bean and ham sandwiches.

The night before, Maddy had confided in DS Jensen how she and Jo had got together. She had had to do that because the police-woman had asked if Jo had already been unreliable in terms of either her whereabouts or commitments. And the cop's question had triggered the memory of an episode, only one, which Maddy felt would probably count as *weird* and *unreliable* behaviour.

One particular evening, Jo didn't show up for dinner at Maddy's. Later that same evening, after she had paced up and down the garden, worried that Jo had come to grief on her rusty bicycle, Maddy had placed a call to *Fairfield House* where Jo rented a room on a weekly basis.

The young male who had answered the phone said that, yes, he knew Jo.

"A tall chick, right? Kind of skinny with black hair and she goes around like on that old bike that looks like she found it on a rubbish hea–"

"Yeah, that one. So ... could you knock on her door and tell her Maddy's on the phone?"

"No sweat. Can do."

A moment later the young voice spoke again through the ear-piece. He said that no one had opened the door. Yes, there was light in the room. No, he couldn't say for sure that there was anyone in the room. Yes, her bike was there by the toilet block where she always ties it up. Yes, he did have a bit of a look around in the dining area. And for sure she wasn't in the TV room because he would've noticed her there because that's just where he was himself, that is until he'd gotten up to answer the phone.

Maddy was surprised and considerably more worried than when she had first placed the call because *then*, she had expected Jo to be somewhere around the boarding house. Which is why, following that call, she had driven the few minutes down the road to *Fairfield House* to check things for herself and have a look around the grounds. She spotted Jo's bike chained to a post near the toilet block, just like the young male on the phone had said. She'd been about to rap her knuckles on the door with a tarnished number 8 hanging skew-whiff on one nail. Maddy briefly considered trying to set it back in its original position but opted not to. She hesitated by the door but left without hav-ing knocked. She told herself that she should respect Jo's privacy. Just because they happened to live close to each other didn't give her the right to force an encounter, not if for reasons best known to her, Jo did-n't want one.

Ultimately, what had unsettled Maddy the most wasn't the thought that Jo had had a change of mind and had chosen to stay away on that particular night. *That* Maddy could easily handle. She did understand the need for private space and plans that should be kept fluid. So what *had* bugged her was that her lover hadn't bothered to say she wouldn't be coming around, let alone explain why, however briefly. They hadn't had any arguments. Not recently. And the last argument they did have hadn't been a proper argument anyway.

That non-argument had happened after dinner, as they were doing the washing up. Actually, Maddy had already popped the kettle on for the coffee they were going to have out on the patio. There'd be more of a breeze there. Maddy had asked something about Jo's day at work, at the hospital cafeteria, something rather innocuous about the women on her shift or about Peta James, her supervisor, or something equally harmless, she thought, like how early did they start setting up the carvery and salad bars or the dessert counter.

Jo had flown off the handle. And after it had all blown away, the one thing that Maddy had retained from that incident was that Jo didn't like to talk about work because, Jo had explained, things like work and the weather and the rising cost of whatever were not topics interesting enough to waste valuable spit on. When Maddy had asked what, then, were better things to talk about, Jo had simply shrugged a 'Whatever' reply and had made coffee for both of them, ears plugged to the Seattle sound of Euphoria Morning. Later that night though, she had made love to Maddy. Later again that night Maddy had made love to Jo but, unlike Maddy, Jo didn't orgasm.

As it turned out, it was five days later that Jo had totally blown her dinner date at Maddy's. Two days later she still hadn't phoned. Nor had she opened the door to her room at the boarding house. And by then, Maddy was as worried as she was upset. She had refrained from making more calls to the boarding house as it was always a stranger who picked up the phone, some poor sod who'd just happened to be walking past as it rang or someone who had been watching the tube in the communal lounge room. Either way, Maddy wasn't one to impose. Besides, she was too private a person herself to make public her business with Jo. And so it seemed to her that visits to Jo's door weren't any more appropriate than Jo's unannounced disappearance. However, the status quo could not go on forever and Maddy had decided that, if by the following day she hadn't heard from Jo, then she'd punch in the number for the Mater Hospital cafeteria. She'd ask to speak to the morning crew supervisor and ask whether Jo Brenner had made it to work. Knowing whether she had or not would give her a starting point.

But in that one instance, Jo had eventually appeared in Maddy's backyard on the morning of the third day. She had come around so early that Maddy was still under the shower. Jo could hear the water gurgle down the pipe so she had waited for the water to stop running inside the pipes before knocking again.

She apologised for not having called earlier but, as she hurriedly explained, she had had to hop on a train bound for Towoomba. Jarrah, her sister, had phoned late that afternoon of the missed dinner to say that she was unwell and could she, Jo, come over and help her with the baby while Gerry, Jarrah's latest de facto, was away for work somewhere or other. So that's what Jo had done for the previous two and a half days – the sisterly thing with Jarrah – an hour and a half west of Brisbane.

Maddy hadn't known anything about a sister living reasonably nearby, in Towoomba. Well, she did know Jo *had* a sister, but last she had heard the thirty-six year old lived close to their ailing sexagenarian father somewhere in Western Australia. That distance away from her family, Jo had explained early in their relationship, placed father and sister on the other side of a cross-continent line, as far away from south eastern Brisbane as one could wish. Maddy had concluded that Jo wasn't keen on unplanned family incursions into her private world and that she wasn't very close to either her ancient father or her much older sister.

So, not having heard the news that Jarrah had moved to the Towoomba range, a mere two hundred kilometres away from Brisbane, and that she had had a baby, *that* was OK by Maddy. No grief there because she, herself a single child, didn't have much of an understanding of the relevance siblings usually have for each other.

True, Maddy herself wasn't very big on family unity, her father having disappeared from her life before she had begun to walk and her mother having, to all intents and purposes, disowned her over the matter of Maddy's sexuality. Only she had had her Aunty Ida in whom to confide and in return, Aunt Ida had done what she could for her favourite little niece whom she loved to bits in spite of her 'invertedness', her aunt's euphemism for lesbianism. At least Aunty Ida had made the effort to read the 1938 lesbian classic, *Torchlight to Valhalla*, in an attempt to better understand her niece's attraction to women. Aunty Ida had also found herself a copy of *Surpassing the Love of Men* because somewhere on the dustjacket it was written that it focused on 'Romantic friendships and love between women from the Renaissance to the present,' though the present in question had ended in 1981. That year, Maddy had celebrated her fourth birthday. Of course, if Maddy had known of her aunt's efforts to understand the appeal of lesbianism, she would've guided her towards a different sort of text that would've yielded more social relevance in regards to her lifestyle.

After Jo's return from Toowoomba, Maddy did a lot of rationalising on Jo's behalf: she didn't have an answering machine so maybe Jo had found it unnecessary to call STD from her sister's knowing that she'd only be gone two days and that surely Maddy'd understand. And Maddy had understood. At the time.

However, back at the Burleigh Heads police station, when she told *that* story to DS Jensen, the policewoman had frowned. She had simply frowned. She hadn't said anything much but she had looked at Maddy, eyebrows furrowed, mouth twitching as if resisting the urge to say something but she knew that by then Maddy was visibly far too wrung out to explore *her* insight.

Before she let Maddy go back into the night, DS Jensen had initiated a few local phone calls, including one to the hospital that serviced the district. She had grinned to Maddy that Joanna Brenner was not on anyone's book. The night had been quiet everywhere, she had explained. Nowhere was there an unidentified Caucasian female, alive or dead, waiting to be claimed.

"Thank god for that, right?" the policewoman had said, trying to make Maddy smile. And Maddy had closed her eyes with a sigh of relief. She had nibbled the inside of her lip while releasing the breath she had been holding in for much too long. And she had smiled back.

Around 4.00 a.m., just before Maddy left the station, DS Jensen handed her her card. "Keep in touch, Maddy. Let me know how things pan out, won't you?"

Maddy had nodded. She thanked the officer for having taken the time to listen and help and she proffered her hand. DS Jensen took her hand firmly into her own and shook it. With a bright smile, and strapping the heavy utility belt back around her waist, she waved Maddy goodbye and goodluck from the police station steps.

Dawn was breaking by then. The streets were no longer dark and the glow of the street lights was about to become redundant.

Maddy, walking back towards the esplanade and the flat she and Jo had planned to vacate around 7 a.m., looked at her watch.

"4.34. Fuck, fuck, *fuck!*" she had muttered, knuckles clenched. 'What a *fucking* night.' She quickened her steps.

Monday having become Tuesday, the Tuesday on the other side of the Australia Day long weekend, she and Jo needed to be back at work by 6.30 and 7.30 a.m., respectively. Maddy's heart lurched again as she came within sight of their apartment tower. They had been given only one key to the flat and that one key was still inside Maddy's bag. She had hoped against hope that she might find Jo waiting for her on the entrance steps. She further lengthened her stride, imagining Jo sitting there, waiting, then looking up at her as she always did whenever Maddy stood in front of her, the only time Jo didn't have to lower her head and dip her knees to make eye contact with her lover. Heart thumping at the thought, Maddy engaged herself in a silent rehearsal. Would she do the 'Bloody hell, where have you been?' bit or the 'Darling, you had me worried big time! You all right?' bit.

As the front entrance came into view, Maddy looked once more towards the picnic table and bench because, heart sinking below anything she had thought imaginable, she already knew that Jo would not be waiting on the front steps. Maddy bit hard on her bottom lip, repressing the urge to shout, *Where in the fuck are you? Jo!* Her front teeth chinked against the silver loop.

*****

TWO

"What the hell!"

Back inside the rented apartment, Maddy was sitting cross-legged on the double bed which was still tousled from the last time she and Jo had made love. That had been approximately 9.15 a.m. the day before. She knew the hour because hours, ever since Jo vanished, had become important to her. They had become important ever since that hour when she had last brushed Jo's lips at the picnic table with the promise of a quick return and the makings of their brandy nightcap.

The morning was aready too bright. Too blue. Too still. Another perfect day in paradise, she thought grimly. She had just finished a second cup of very strong coffee concocted from three little Nescafe sachets emptied into the one cup. She was about to drop her wallet back inside her bag when the thought occurred to her that she should shake the bag free of sand before returning to the city. And so, seated in a loose Lotus position, she had begun pulling out the few items that were already in it.

Out came her favourite cap with the little rainbow patch on its side, the one she had ordered online. Out came the protection 15+ sunscreen and the lesbian pulp she had bought weeks earlier from The Women's Bookshop. And she had a brief thought about what a pity it'd be for many women that this particular Brisbane landmark seemed to no longer be operating. The last time she had stopped by, the familiar lavender sandwich board was not on the footpath, the door to the shop was locked and all she could see through the glass window was wall-to-wall shelving, empty of books. Cardboard boxes, in various stages of filling, were piled in the middle of the deserted shop.

Suddenly her hand pulled out of the bag an object that was very familiar to her but totally misplaced within the confines of *her* bag. So odd it was finding it there that, though she was familiar with its shape without having ever touched it properly, her mind had refused to recognise it for what it was: Jo's black leather wallet.

Totally startled by her find, heart thudding against her ribs, she cried, "What the fuck is it doing in *my* bag?" Her first reaction was to frown at the worn square of black leather because *that* wallet inside *her* bag was as incongruous a find as if it had been a dark-shelled crab that had crept in there by mistake. Jo's wallet was always either in Jo's bag or in one of Jo's pockets.

Picking up the wallet from the palm of one hand with the thumb and forefinger of the other, Maddy placed it on the white sheet, in front of her knees, and she rubbed her fingertips hard against her eyes. When she released the pressure, her vision was blurry but the dark shape of a man-style wallet was still distinctly visible on the rumpled sheet. She stared at it, unwilling to open it.

Maddy had always considered a wallet one's very private personal possession. Not because of the money angle but because she assumed others, like her, tucked all sorts of little things inside its folds. And all these receipts, mementoes, vouchers and pictures would be, in someone else's hands, as many clues about *her* life. Different clues, perhaps, from those found in a diary, or in a nightstand – less of an overtly intimate nature – but very personal all the same. Unable to bring herself to open her lover's wallet, she ran her fingers through her salt-and-sand-stiffened red hair.

Tears welling, she flopped backwards on the bed, legs still crossed at the ankles. She closed her eyes. The tears ran sideways across her cheeks and onto the pillow. She opened her eyes and sat up again. She hefted the black wallet, opened it like a book and, forehead pressed against it, she let her tears run freely.

By the time she retrieved, also from her bag, the inch-wide woven leather wristband she had given Jo on the night of their six-month anniversary, Maddy was all cried out. All she did was look at it dumbly, the ball of her thumb running against the ridged braiding.

"It's not to make you feel like, feel all tied up or anything," she had explained tentatively, relieved when Jo had slid the band over her hand, presenting her thin wrist to her so she could tie the securing thong. "It's only to remind you that … you know, that someone, *me*, right … It's to remind you that I love you. A lot."

Jo had watched as Maddy tied a careful set of knots. As she lifted her face from the finished task, Jo's serious grey eyes and her lips were there, waiting for hers. Their lips had nibbled and licked the edges of each other's face, the tip of a nose, the whorl of an ear, the brush of an eyelash, the tips of their hair. They kissed with warm tongues and they made love on a lounge chair, just there, off to the side of Maddy's garden. They were careful not to giggle too much because of the neighbours and, for the first time since they'd been together, Jo's body had allowed her an orgasm while tucked inside Maddy's secure embrace.

The very first afternoon she had come through Maddy's back gate, Jo had tried to tip her off. She wanted Maddy to know, right there and then, as soon as their hands had skimmed, caressed and discovered the immediate surface appeal of each other's body, that *her* body didn't do orgasms. Not all that comfortably. Not all that frequently.

Split seconds split further, rearranging the moment around them that afternoon in Maddy's kitchen. Maddy had shifted inside Jo's embrace to better face her, pupils dilated by the burning ache to slide her hand against the tall girl's stomach and let it find its own way to Jo's pubic hair and beyond.

The raw energy of the touch ignited by the tentative tip of Jo's tongue, by the electrified heat of *her* fingertips, by the deep pools of *her* eyes, all that intensity, Maddy thought, can only ever happen once, the very first time two lovers connect. Jo was so close, close enough to pick up *her* scent, too close to breathe but *not too* close to feel her, not too close to discover and combust – all that, Maddy had thought back then as she had reached again, hungrily, for Jo's mouth.

Jo, one arm wrapped around Maddy's shoulders, the other wrapped around her hips, had led her away from the kitchen. Maddy, nostrils flared for air, had pressed Jo's lanky body against her own, eyes squeezed tight against the hot surge of desire that ripped out from deep inside her sex. Both were slowly but inexorably making their way towards the nearest horizontal surface that offered more padding than the kitchen linoleum.

It was then that Jo, in a brief moment of reason, had whispered something like, "I really, *really* want to make love to you. Maddy? You hear me?" One hand against the back pocket of Jo's jeans, firm against the flat shape of her buttocks, Maddy had moaned against Jo's lips. "But look…" Jo lifted Maddy's face inside both her hands. Grey eyes serious. "I need to tell you something…" Maddy strained against Jo's hands because her kiss-swollen lips were hungry for more of that passion, for more of that irrational delirium.

A flutter of incomprehension had reshaped Maddy's round eyes so Jo persevered calmly but, in retrospect, Maddy decided Jo had spoken almost distantly when she said, "I don't come. Hardly ever." Jo had paused, perhaps expecting a response from Maddy, any response, but none came. "Maddy?"

Maddy nodded, eyes tightened by the intensity of her arousal. "Mm," she moaned, breathing in through her mouth, "Jo … kiss me. Now. I … need to kiss you *more*. Some more. A lot more. A lot better."

But because Jo's face still hovered a fraction out of reach, Maddy said, "Yeah, I hear you. But … don't sweat it." One hand on the back of Jo's head, Maddy slowly brought her new lover's mouth back to hers.

It had been all right, deliciously all right for both of them. Even taking into account that, once the high point had been reached and overshot, Jo, not having come, had asked Maddy to stop trying. Instead, she asked her to lie on top her and hold her tightly. *And that had been so good,* Maddy thought, as she peered at the black wallet inside her palm.

And on the occasion of their six-month anniversary, moments after Maddy had tied the love knot that secured the wide leather braid to her lover's wrist, later, after they had lain together, whispering softly one to the other, Maddy's hand protectively light over Jo's sex, Jo had produced something from under the lounge chair – a wind twirly thing, not a chime, not one of those wooden or cloth things that spiralled in the breeze but an object Maddy had never seen before.

Jo had stood up and held the mysteriously attractive spiral at arm's length, allowing it to catch the night's lights on its curved acrylic surface. She blew on it to make it twirl as it would when caught in a light breeze. "I think it's meant to be a bit *Feng-shui* but that's not why I bought it."

The lights trapped on the clear surface curled upwards, giving the strong optical illusion of a spiral, of shiny, elongated bubbles materialising out of the air below to rise languorously in slow succession, only to die and disappear back into the nothingness at the other end of the long spiral. Again and again, as Jo blew on it, it travelled upward and downward, sparkling bubbles of shiny water cascading the length of the spiral.

"I'd like you to hang it right there," Jo said, pointing at the hanging branches of the poinciana tree a few feet away, directly in front of Maddy's only lounge chair. "Just so that … like, you know, when you're out here gazing into space, this thing, the way it catches the light, twirling it around and all, well … I'd like to think that it'll bring your thoughts back to me. On the nights we're not together."

On the rumpled bed, six storeys above the Burleigh Heads esplanade, the spilled contents of Maddy's bag lay touching her bare feet. In her hand, she still held the bracelet found there amongst her belongings. Maddy straightened her shoulders to allow more air to fill her lungs. The leather knot that she had tied on the underside of Jo's wrist that night, some three months earlier, was still intact, tight and secure, but one of its ends was severed from the braid. Maddy brought the band to her lips.

The sweaty saltiness of it against her nose, the tiny patch of salty leather under the tip of her tongue hit her like a door in the middle of a sleepwalker's path. Jo's face, bigger than life, exploded behind her eyes. Jo, with her grunge hair cut that still spilled, shiny and black over her pale forehead, over her grey eyes. Jo's aquiline nose. Jo's smile that creased the corners of her mouth instead of turning them upwards. Every detail was there, too large, too alive, far too unreal for Maddy to accommodate inside her heart.

*****

Dazed but with the automated motions of the undead, Maddy had eventually driven back towards Brisbane. 9.35 a.m. said the dashboard clock. The morning traffic having peaked a while ago, she had been able to keep the speedometer on a steady 110 on most of the freeway, all the way to the Juliette Street exit.

Instinctively, Maddy knew that there was no need for her to stay home by the phone. So, just as instinctively, she headed for her other home: the workmates and the four walls of Terry's All Treads. During the drive back, Maddy had reached two conclusions. Jo had left of her own accord. Her disappearance was only an absence. Jo wouldn't call. Not for help and not to signify her return. She would simply show up, in person, one day, or never. *Just like the woman cop said last night,* Maddy thought bitterly, *things are clearer the next day.*

Why did Jo's wallet end up in her bag along with the bracelet visibly ripped off from her wrist? For *that* she still had no conclusion. None that made sense. But again, she couldn't figure why Jo had done a runner in the first place.

Why that way? That's one sick thing to do. Eyes itchy and aware of a swelling sensation inside the tip of her nose, she wiped the heel of a hand across her eyes, sniffed and straightened herself behind the wheel, shoulders tense, knuckles clenched.

Lip loop trapped under her front teeth, Maddy played back their last lovemaking, the last moment of love they shared the previous morning. *Fuck it. That was like …* she glanced at the dashboard clock, *like* now. *Only yesterday morning.*

They had woken up around 9 a.m. and had made love. Throat tight, eyes riveted on a distant spot ahead of the Commodore's bonnet, she had let that moment play back behind her eyes.

They made love, tenderly, so magically that Jo had come, her face cradled against Maddy's shoulder, one long leg wrapped tightly over Maddy's hip and thigh to better keep her lover against her. When Jo finally opened her eyes and detached herself from Maddy, she was still flushed and breathless. Her eyes were shiny. She took Maddy's hand and placed it back, flat against her sex.

'Yes. Just … there,' she said, once again closing her eyes.

And Maddy grinned, feeling cockily happy with herself. And they had kissed again, the little kisses of the sensually fulfilled.

And why the fuck take off from Burleigh? Why the bloody hurry? Maddy was not grinning anymore. Front teeth biting on the lip loop, she squinted against the rush of blood that pulsed at her temples, threatening to obscure her road vision.

Jo had split, *that,* Maddy understood. *That's why she's torn off the fucking bracelet. But why?* she screamed silently. *Why??*

Intuitively, Maddy knew that Jo had left the woven braid in *her* bag clearly as a symbolic gesture that they were through, but the wallet thing, *that,* Maddy couldn't wrap her head around. *Crazy!* Maddy hit the steering-wheel hard with the side of her fist. Pain shot through to her elbow. *Fucking mad!* She bit her lip and, jaw muscles tight, she drove on towards Brisbane.

She parked the Commodore right in front of the entrance to *Fairfield House* and walked inside the musty corridor. Though she knew there wouldn't be an answer, she rapped her knuckles on Jo's door. Once, twice. She listened for sounds she knew she would not hear and walked to the outdoor toilet block. The rusty bicycle was there, at its usual place, under the chain Jo always wrapped around it, though the chances of anyone stealing the bicycle had always seemed slim to Maddy.

Then she drove towards her place and up the lane that led to her back gate. She popped the car into neutral, hiked up the hand-brake, took the two steps to the fence line. On tiptoes, she scanned the inside of her garden and the recessed patio and once back in the car, she slammed the door shut. One quick glance in the rear-view mirror and she turned the car back towards Ipswich Road.

A few kilometres later, she signalled left and drove under a long and wide plastic banner that proudly announced, in large letters, *Terry's*

All Treads Discount. The message was repeated above the great rolled-up hangar door and accompanied by the alphabetical list of names of leading tyre manufacturers from Cooper to Yokohama.

Somewhere during that drive back, Maddy linked the last time Jo had disappeared for three days with the previous night's desertion from Burleigh. *OK, so she's one seriously screwed up chick,* she concluded, chest heavy, forearms taut against the steering-wheel. *OK, so she doesn't communicate the normal way. She can't. Cool, now I know … for sure. Already knew that … but now that's for sure.* Behind her the highway was empty but Maddy made herself glance at the rear-view mirror all the same. *It's always gonna be like that with her. Here now, gone later, even if she comes back. That's just the way she is.* "Fucking sweet for her," Maddy shouted in frustration, "but where the fuck does that leave me?"

She parked the old Commodore with the usual care, in its usual spot, a couple of metres beyond the banner and on the left-hand side of the hangar. She left her bag where it had landed in the back seat and her weekend gear, along with Jo's, in the boot. She patted the car on its bonnet as she always did. She didn't lock it because she never did and she made her way inside the tyre bay.

The air was heavy with the sweet acrid smell of rubber and greasy oil that Maddy no longer noticed. She aimed her steps towards the office window to let Vivian, the boss's wife, know that she was on the floor, that she had finally shown up for work. Vivian looked up, saw Maddy, smiled, and waved. She mouthed, *You OK?* Maddy shaped her lips into a small smile and nodded. Viv made to return to her paperwork but looked up again. Maddy's face and torso were still framed by the glass pane, immobile. Viv hesitated. She opened her mouth to say something but she shut it again.

Maddy slowly turned away from the window, unaware that Viv was still looking at her. There were only three customer cars in the bay. Maddy registered that her offsider, Drew, was busy fitting a tyre under a Ford ute. Her eyes scanned the other three tyres stacked by the vehicle. Desert Duellers of the common variety. The young man noticed movement from the corner of his eye, looked up from the tyre he was about to heft on to the lugs, and waved.

"Problems with your alarm clock, Tom?" he hollered.

"You can say that again," she replied without stopping. Drew craned his neck, eyes on her, visibly surprised by her flat tone.

Tom was Drew's affectionate nickname for Maddy. Tom as in *Tom Thumb,* the tiny fairytale character who lived in a world of giants.

"Suits you to a T," he had explained the first time he had called out that name.

Although she had only been working at *Terry's All Treads* for a couple of weeks, she already knew that she would enjoy hanging there for a while. She liked the family feel that the boss's wife imparted to the place and it made for an easier boss-employee relationship to know that Terry wouldn't be one to try and get into her overalls. She just knew he wouldn't, even if his missus was not working on the premises. And as a bonus, there weren't any girlie posters anywhere. The calendar, compliments of Firestone tyres, featured various mud, water and sand-splattered four-wheel drives sporting purpose-suited tyres, doing grunt work over a variety of terrains. *Makes a lot more sense than a girl in a bikini,* Maddy had thought at the time.

So when she first heard Drew call her Tom, she automatically assumed that he was on his way to being homophobically stupid. So Maddy had frowned.

"Say again?" Her tone had better suited an order than a question as, eyes narrowed and moving closer to him, she carried on wiping her blackened fingers on the rag she had just picked up.

Maddy needed to spend many hours every day, every week, working, if not necessarily alongside Drew, certainly in his immediate vicinity, sharing jobs, sharing clients, sharing tools, sharing the token locker in a room the boss's wife had glamorously christened the 'locker room'. And she had grown quite fond of him, Big Drew, as the boss called him because of his barrel chest, not his height. *A man,* she thought a few days after she had been hired, *but a good bloke.* Just a decent guy who'd gotten himself a girlfriend, Jen, pale as dawn, who wore long and very blue fingernails cut straight across, tight-fitting little midriffs that seemed far too little to safely contain her generous breasts, and spray-on, hip-hugging jeans over skinny buttocks.

Drew had looked up from the nut bolt he was about to tighten. "Look at you!" he grinned easily, "You're only what, five-five max, right?" He sat back on his heels. "How much you reckon you weigh, huh?' Maddy shrugged, nipping at the inside of her bottom lip, waiting to hear where he would aim the conversation. "I bet little over the low end of fifty Ks, a bit more than Jen because you got muscles she ain't got." Drew initiated the tightening of the fourth nut with two fingers. "When the boss said he'd hired a chick I thought, Fuck, mate, I'm gonna have to do her job and mine and take home a double back strain but only one pay cheque." He wiped his hands on a grimy rag and rubbed it on the inner side of his forefinger and thumb where the road grime had become more ingrained inside the roughened folds of skin. "That's what any bloke would've thought, for sure. And here you go stacking those bloody heavy mongrels like nobody's business," he continued, pointing a still-grimy finger at the rows of tyres high on wall shelves. "You can quote any specs *and,*" he smiled broadly, "you're real lethal with a tyre iron, so now I reckon … Yeah, I was telling Jen the other night, you're just like this little *Tom Thumb* fellow, gutsy and all. 'Cept of course that you're a girl." Healthy white teeth flashed at Maddy. "That's something there ain't cause to doubt. Though a bit on the flat side … " he added jokingly, large hands cupping the air under his nipples. "They're the only muscles Jen's got bigger than you." He was still grinning like a schoolboy busy decorating a toilet wall with a big pair of busty breasts. "But you're a girl aw'right." He rubbed his chin bristles with the side of his thumb. "One thing for sure though, I'm bloody glad all them chicks don't have that strength or else guys like me would be out of business." He pushed himself off the concrete floor and, pitching his soiled rag into the rubbish drum, he stood up full height, five foot ten, and stretched his back.

Maddy had listened to Drew's harmless tirade rocking on the balls of her feet and by the end of it she, too, had grinned, relieved. She lobbed her rag in such a way that it had landed right on top of the young man's head and flopped down over his eyes, down over his ears. Blind but not yet out of the game, he flicked her the finger but she had already wheeled on the balls of her feet, her own brand of caustic humour trailing behind her, "Nah. I don't see it. You blokes'll never go out of fashion," she retorted cockily. "Not till they find a way to get *good* sperm out of mice. And *even* then," she added, "there'll always be *some* women, in fact most chicks I suspect, mind you, none that *I'd* care to know, who'll go on moaning, What would we do without them, huh? No dirty socks inside the bed? Toilet seat's always down. What, no fart jokes? No ball scratching at breakfast? No belching? No grotty mates sprawled on the sofa making beer-can castles? Bo-ring."

"Hey," Drew answered back, "A bloke's gotta do what a bloke's gotta do."

"Absolutely," Maddy answered, unsnapping the top of her overalls. Coffee break meant time for a little chat with Viv, in the office, and a cup of tea.

Vivian stood up from her desk. Through the glass pane, she looked in the direction of the locker room where Maddy would be changing out of her civvies to slip into her grease- stained overalls. She sat down again, picked up her pen, tapped a few keys on her calculator, brought out a big Yokohama catalogue from the shelf near her desk, flipped a few pages and stood up again. Maddy had not come out of the locker room. The boss's wife looked perplexed. One hand on the doorknob, she hesitated. She scanned the bay for her husband. She finally spotted him coming out of the storeroom, carrying a couple of spare parts boxes. She stepped out of the office, caught his eye and gestured towards the locker room. He nodded and kept on walking.

Viv found Maddy clad in a white sport bra, seated on the bench, overalls only pulled up as far as her hips. Elbows resting on her thighs, hands dangling between her knees, shoulders slumped, the young redhead was staring at the floor, somewhere beyond her boots, somewhere in front of the metallic locker. Viv watched her, lost for words.

Every ounce of strength seemed to have abandoned the girl. The graceful angle of her neck, the full curve of her bare shoulder, the soft rise of her biceps and triceps, both slightly contracted to accommodate her elbow's position on her thigh, the tiny folds of skin on the firm plane of her stomach visible in the vee of undone snaps, all that was *uniquely Maddy*. And yet Maddy's form slumped on the bench made Viv think of a stage suit discarded by its owner. It was there, but it only contained the memory of the one who owned it.

"Sweetie?" Viv whispered. "You all right?" She sat on the bench near Maddy and noticed the girl's laboured breathing. Tentatively, she lay a hand on her shoulder relieved by its warmth and firmness under her palm. She left her hand there in an unconscious attempt to ground Maddy through her touch. And then slowly, she moved her hand across the sweep of Maddy's back as she would have done across a small child's. She soothed Maddy as she used to soothe her own daughters before they were grown.

When 'the little redhead' had rapped her knuckles on the office window, two years earlier, Viv had looked up startled. People usually took pains to knock on the office *door* to get her attention. And when the young woman with short-cropped rust-red hair said she'd like to talk to the boss 'in case there's a job going,' Viv's mouth dropped open.

It was not that Viv was unused to female mechanics, for they had had a couple themselves at *Terry's All Treads* and others had worked on the strip on the *Magic Mile*, the local name for that stretch of car yards, car repair, motorcycle and tyre shops that line a particular area of Ipswich Road. One knew pretty accurately who worked and for whom. So Viv knew about female mechanics and, on the whole, she was not overly fond of them. She was a traditional woman with old world values, and about women mechanics she would say, "It's not because they work with lads that they've got to ape them. Why do these women carry on like the boys, crude and all?" And she would add, "And get all tattooed up? It's not as if most lads are necessarily good examples of anything, even if they're good at what they do, now are they?" And Terry would look at his wife above his reading glasses and nod in agreement before returning his attention to his crossword puzzle magazine.

So what had struck Viv about the new girl was the way she carried herself. Like a ballerina, she had first thought, as Maddy paced up and down the bay, getting close enough to the vehicles and machinery to have a look but not close enough to touch anything while she waited for the boss to appear. The ballerina thing didn't stick long because Viv knew that ballerinas were all tall and thin as broom handles. This girl was not *tall*. And though she was trim of hip and thigh in her black jeans, saying that the girl moved like an *athlete* was more accurate, but it was only when the word *gymnast* popped inside Viv's head that she had nodded to herself. But again, she argued, while scanning the Personal and Employment History details that Maddy Collins had filled in, not a gymnast like these little twelve-year old girls who dance on parallel bars. No, *that* girl visibly had muscles that perhaps would have better fitted a *young* male gymnast, minus the long arms and big hands that boys have. Long frames waiting to be filled. That young woman, Viv thought, she's already grown into her body. She shook her head again and paged her husband. Viv knew they needed a fitter and though Terry would baulk at the idea of hiring a female for the fitter's position, that and the fact that, according to the information on the sheet, the girl was a qualified mechanic not a fitter. *If* she needed the job, though it paid less, *that girl,* Viv knew, would cotton on very quickly.

"On the job training, that's how it can be done," she told Terry, her husband.

In the locker room, Maddy was still looking at the space in front of her boots but Viv could tell that, though the girl was worrying her lip ring with her front teeth and had not acknowledged her presence, her *back* was responding to the slow stroking.

Viv had three daughters, all married and all away. So far away they hardly ever visited and when they did, with husbands and children, Viv always felt, by the time they left, that she still hadn't seen her daughters. Or more to the point that she had only *seen* them. They never sought to connect at the other level that Viv had been missing, particularly since the last one, her youngest, had moved out.

Viv felt the tension ease up in Maddy's neck and *inside* the smooth muscles that padded her shoulder blades. A brief moment later, though, she took her hand away.

"Sweetie, I'd like you to look at me now," she said to Maddy's profile. "You don't have to tell me anything but I need you to look up from that spot over there. I need you to look at me."

The freckles on Maddy's cheekbone always gave a healthy, ruddy glow to her skin but even in the poor light of the locker room, Viv could tell that *underneath* all those freckles, Maddy was pale. And she waited until Maddy half-turned towards her.

"That's a good girl," said Viv, who needed to look into Maddy's eyes to better gauge the depth of the girl's upset. Maddy's eyes told her what she needed to know. And, calmly, she said, "Luvvie, what've you done to that lip of yours, huh? You've made a mess of it, haven't you?"

The back of Maddy's hand brushed against her mouth. She winced and looked at the back of her hand where a smear of blood had left a red streak.

"It's OK, Sweetie. You've just been worrying that lip thing of yours a bit too much. I'll tend to that."

Maddy drew in her bottom lip and tasted blood. Like those of a wide-eyed little girl, her eyes flicked from the back of her hand to the woman's face and briefly settled there. In the round blue eyes made tight by the strain of containment, Viv saw pain and incomprehension. From the pinkish shadows that had spread under Maddy's eyes, she understood her night had been sleepless, but differently sleepless from the other sleepless nights Maddy used to inflict on herself, carousing around the Brisbane night scene. *Back then*, Viv remembered, more than blue eyes dulled and bloodshot, more than the mid-afternoon yawns, the daylong cocky air about her, the extra bounce in her stride were always dead give-aways that Maddy's nights had been full of many things much more relevant than sleep. All that seemed to stop around the time Terry had given his wife the account of how their 'little dyke' had tossed a strange woman's rusty nail of a bike in the boot of her car and had given her a ride home.

Viv had only replied one thing. "If she's good for the little one, then I suppose it's OK, don't you think? She does need company of the sort she needs, you know. We all do."

Terry had shrugged awkwardly. "Just as long as she doesn't slack off," he said grumpily, far from being as cosmically understanding of homosexuality as his wife was. As far as he was concerned, it was all a rather kinky business, no matter who was involved, no matter how fond he was of 'the little dyke'. When, on occasions, he thought of what Maddy's after-hours life might be like, he was ever so glad all *his* daughters were normal. Viv knew what *normal* meant for her husband. It meant 'married with husbands to provide.'

Maddy glanced around the locker room as far as she could see behind her boss's wife. She swallowed hard. She squinted at Viv and wanted to smile at her but like a child, helpless at suppressing a sorrow too big to be contained, Maddy threw her arms around the woman's neck and sobbed, forehead pressed against her shoulder. Viv closed her arms behind Maddy's back and rocked slowly.

"Thatta girl. God ... he gave us tears for a reason, you know. No good at all keeping them in. Tears are good," the woman sing-sung near Maddy's ear. "You just go on and cry. You just cry it all out."

*****

Maddy looked at Mitchell Grimes, manager of *Fairfield House*. She looked at the thick black beard that ate away three-quarters of his face. She looked at the lank unwashed hair that brushed the shoulder seam of his unironed T. She winced at the tufts of hair that protruded from under the neckline, and the man's pasty, doughy arms that matched his neck made her very glad there was not more of him to see. *If it weren't for his eyes, who could possibly love this guy?* Maddy thought. *Besides his mother?*

Earlier that afternoon, Viv had convinced Maddy that there was nothing else she could do but wait and see what the Burleigh police would do with what information Maddy had given them. In Queensland, that was all there was to the procedure of declaring a person missing. No forty-eight hours wait needed. No specific form to fill in. Not even a signature. Only a statement.

When Maddy explained what she wanted to know, Mitchell Grimes scrunched up the bushy eyebrows underneath which Maddy had already noticed the two large pools of blue from which she inferred that the man had a certain goodness and hoped that, ultimately, *that* goodness would prompt him to give her the information she so desperately wanted.

"Here you are, asking me questions like the police would ask but you're not the police now, are you? Hey? You, young people," he started again, talking about young people as an old man would, though Maddy had him figured only in his late thirties. *Not that old.* He patted the counter with the flat of his surprisingly small hand. "You just roll up here and ask things, but truth is you don't even understand things like legal implications, and wrongdoings, and the fact that someone might sue me about a breach of privacy or something like that. It's a harsh world out there, young lady. Believe you me, I know."

He pulled his eyebrows together and before Maddy had a chance to redirect, he unpacked his thoughts further. "For all I know, you could be getting facts for some ... maybe on her father's behalf. *Yes* you might," he insisted in response to Maddy's shake of the head. "Or for a psycho brother even. Why not, huh? I can tell you it's been done before... "

Maddy frowned but the manager was visibly intent on taking his train of thought right through to the bitter end. "Could be a twisted boyfriend out for revenge, right? And he's the one wanting that info you supposedly want from me."

Oh, there we go again with the boyfriend bit.

The man stopped abruptly, mouth left open in his beard. Maddy's estimation was that he had finally run out of puff but her estimation was premature. "I mean, how would I feel, *me,* Mitchell, huh?" The tip of his index finger disappeared into his squishy chest. "What say I tune in to the news and I hear some lady's been found at the bottom of a ditch, right? And her last known place of residence is here, right? Room 8 under this very roof. And I'd *know* that it was me what gave out the very info that may have contributed to that lady ending up raped and mutilated and tossed there, to be found by a dog, by children playing in the scrub." Blue eyes glinted under the bushy brow. "You tell me how I'd feel then, huh?"

Mouth open, ready to break in, but impressed by the man's imagination, Maddy looked at him wide-eyed. *Relax,* she wanted to tell him. *Take a breath. A chill pill.* Instead, she told him, "Relax, Max. Maybe you watch too much TV. Does your missus–?"

"There's no missus." Mitchell scrunched up his eyebrows. "Hasn't been for years."

"Right, uh … Look, I'm really sorry to hear that," Maddy said, quickly redirecting the conversation. "But look, I've only asked you the *one* thing, right? And, really I think it's pretty obvious I'm not likely to be her *father*, right?" Maddy chose to sidestep the fact that she might conceivably be ferreting info on someone else's behalf and because honesty was on her side, she found the impetus to plough on undeterred. "Then, I'd say it's also pretty obvious I'm not likely to be anyone's *brother* either, right? So what, you think I might be her *boyfriend* or something?" She bit her tongue. She really didn't want a replay of the high point of her conversation with the cop. "Really! You, grown man and all…" She gave him one of her easy smiles. "Surely you got to recognise a chick when you see– "

"Yeah, yeah, yeah. Bloody right I recognise a chick when I see one, just like you say but I don't know what … what … ultra …ulterior motive that chick *might* have, now do I? And who might be pulling her strings, huh?"

"Can't know for sure but hey, that's what instinct's for. And intuition. And–"

"Awright. Enough with you," the man said plainly giving up. "OK! You're a real pain in the arse." He pulled a ledger from under the counter top. "Look, lady. It's like I told you. I haven't seen *her* since last Tuesday."

"Right, but my question is how far in advance is she paid up to?" Maddy held the man's eyes briefly and followed through with a quiet little smile and a nod towards the red ledger to encourage him to open it.

The manager squinted. "Does she owe you any moollah?"

"Mulla?"

"Dough, bucks, dollars?"

"Oh … no," Maddy replied, startled by the simplicity of his assumption. *If only that was it,* she thought. She shook her head. "She doesn't owe me anything. It's just that … It's more like…" She shrugged, "She's my buddy."

"And your buddy, as you say, she's gone and done a Casper on you, hasn't she?"

"Casper?" Maddy hesitated looking perplexed.

"Yeah. One minute she's there and the next she's gone. Like the cartoon. The little ghost?"

"Oh. Right. " Maddy couldn't remember what the little ghost got up to in the cartoon but she couldn't readily deny the overall accuracy of the man's assumption.

"So you're trying to figure out whether she's been planning it all along."

Maddy shrugged, avoiding his eyes.

"Tell you what I can do for you. I can tell you how much she's paid up in advance. That what you want to know?"

Exactly! she almost shouted. Instead, she nodded, front teeth nibbling at her bottom lip.

He opened the ledger and flipped pages. He ran his tongue along his thumb and flipped many more pages. Maddy glanced at him and glanced at the book. *We're only in January. Shouldn't his info be somewhere at the beginning of this bloody book?*

"There." The man tapped the middle of the page he'd been looking for. "That's her." Maddy's heart lurched. *That's her.* Two little words. So simple. *Her.* So innocuous. Jo. *Where is she?* A hot tingle under her eyelids made her straighten and push more air inside her lungs. She swallowed again. "Says here that your friend, she's two weeks ahead of herself. Well, not quite anymore. It's more a case of she *was* two weeks ahead of herself." *A week ago, she still thought she'd be hanging around.* The man snapped the ledger closed and rested a small hand over the red cover. "Could've told you without looking," he grinned. Maddy was getting a gutful of grinning men. *But at least, this one's been helpful.* She grinned back.

As it turned out, the manager clearly remembered Jo waiting for him last Tuesday night. He remembered because it had been right after *The Bill,* so that made it nine-thirty. He had popped out of his private quarters to make sure 'no one was doing nothing they shouldn't have been doing and there she was. Waiting for me, all quiet like. Could've rang the bell.'

Jo had apparently done what she had always done ever since she came to *Fairfield House.* She paid two weeks in advance. Mitchell said that he had *again* reminded her that she only needed to pay one week in advance but that one day at a time would be fine, too. "But she insisted," he said. "Said it was simpler for her that way so she paid cash as she always did."

"Two weeks in advance and that brings her all paid up till the 5th of February."

He scratched inside his beard with a pale finger and nodded. "So ... that's it, right?" he asked almost expectantly. "That's all I can tell you."

Maddy shrugged. Round blue eyes didn't crinkle but she turned up her lips at the corners. "Right. Fair enough. Yes ... thanks a lot," she said, about to turn towards the front door. "I'm really glad she's all paid up and legit with you." She stopped in mid-stride. "Oh, by the way..." Thumb hooked under the wide leather belt that kept her low-slung jeans from slipping completely off her hips, she pivoted to face the man one last time. "Uh ... Saw her bike on the way up here. It's padlocked like, you know, where she always leaves it–"

"And so?" He peered at her more closely. "Not that I know why she ties it up. It's not like anyone coming in from the street's likely to want it. Not *even* anyone from here. It's only a rusty frame with two wheels. And there's only one good tyre to the bike anyway."

Maddy stuck her bottom lip out. "One good tyre's better than none," she added defensively. "Anyway, Mitch, just one more questi–"

"Ah, no! I said *no more* questions. I run a proper business here. There's rules that got to be followed."

"No, look, Mitch, it's cool." Her hands flew upwards in a calming gesture. "I was only going to ask what happens when someone's rent ... runs out?"

"You mean their rent's up and they ain't got more cash to keep it goin'?"

"Or like if they're not even around– "

"They lose it. Kiss it goodbye. Room's up for grabs. First in, best dressed and all that jazz."

"Right, yeah. Fair enough." Maddy glanced at the flyblown calendar behind Mitch before half-turning towards the street only a few steps behind her. "And what about their belongings then?" She tried to sound almost disinterested by whatever the answer might be.

"They get stored for two days, just out of courtesy like, I'm not goin' to dump them on the street or anythi– "

She was facing him again. "And then what?"

"If they don't show after forty-eight hours, I stuff the whole lot in them big plastic bags and dump them at the Salvos."

"Right. Like what, the whole lot? Everything? Clothes, books– "

"Everything. Kit and caboodle. Says so in the Agreement that I can do that. *That* and not cooking in the room and not drying laundry outside the room and them not bringing members of the opposite sex inside the room."

"Good idea that." She repressed a grin at the thought of the serious lesbian love-making that had gone on behind the door of Room 8. "So, that's what you'll do with her stuff if she's not back by ... by the–"

"By the 5th."

"So, that's what you'll do? I mean dump it at the Salvation Army?"

"That's what it says in the Agreement," Mitchell repeated, as he inched out from behind the reception desk. "They've all signed on the dotted line so I reckon that's what I'll do unless someone else claims it on her behalf."

"Someone else like– "

"Like anyone who's got a note from her saying so."

Maddy moved closer to the man. "What about me, then?" She tried not to sound too eager. "I mean, I don't have a note or anything." Shrug. "But you'd let me keep her stuff *for her* ... You would, wouldn't you? For whenever she gets back. Like, if she's not back by the ... the 5th? That's in ... "

"Today's the 31st."

"Right. Well ... then ... if she doesn't make it back..." Maddy's heart was beating too fast. It interfered with her thoughts like static on the line. "Like, if she's not back on time ... to keep the room. Say in ... five days' time. I know ... *I just know* she'd like to have her bike back when she returns. And her stuff, too. Like whatever she's got in her room."

Mitch's eyes fluttered on the lower part of Maddy's cut-off T. She felt them brush and hover on the hemline that delineated cloth from skin. Instinctively she tightened her stomach muscles.

"You work out a lot, don't you?"

Taken aback by this digression but not totally taken off-guard, she gave him a reply intended to blow him off quickly and painlessly. She had an ulterior motive for not wanting to ruffle him. She needed him to come good on the 5th.

"Damn right I workout. At my father's gym. Should see how big *he* is," she added, palms of her hands apart to show an impressive shoulder width, hoping that it would help Mitch shift his private thoughts away from her.

His eyes narrowed in a freaky sort of way. They settled on her hips. The tip of a too red tongue poked out from his bushy dark beard.

Ah shit! Here we go, Maddy thought. She was used to men eyeing her the way Mitchell was doing but they usually got that stupid boiled-mullet look much earlier in the game.

A slow riser. Maddy took a couple of steps off to the side and became quite absorbed with the label stuck on the red fire extinguisher affixed to the wall, briskly resuming her train of thought. "So, Mitch ... about Jo's things. You were saying I could have them– "

"Yeah, yeah. I reckon I could let you have them. I've seen you around with her. It's not like you've walked straight off the street, is it now?"

"Damn right it's not. Jo's my ... she's my buddy."

"Look, lady, don't sweat it." Mitch patted the red ledger one more time before picking it up. He puffed out his chest. "So, I say check back here on the 5th. If she's not back, you pop in and collect them."

"Cool. I'll even come early enough to pack them myself. That'll save you the hassle," Maddy said, happier than she could afford to let on. "She's a bit fussy with her things, old Jo is."

*****

All's well that ends well. Jo's all moved in now. As planned.

One jumbo plastic bag in each hand, Maddy groaned as Jo's last words, back at Burleigh, seared a strip in the back of her eyes. *She was fucking right too. Didn't take long at all.* She placed the bags in a corner of her bedroom and, throat tight, turned her back on them. She drew in her lip, front teeth resting on her lip loop and sat on the edge of the bed facing the wall.

'Won't take long to shift this backpack right here.' That's what she said. I remember. She even patted her backpack, 'And the two other boxes and few bits and pieces I have back at Fairfield. You won't even notice I've moved in.'

Maddy flopped on her bed. Inside her head, Jo was grinning like a schoolgirl on a naughty thought. Maddy shut her eyes tight against the memory. She threw her forearm over her eyes. "Jo…" she moaned, "Why the fuck did you have to do it? Why *that* way?" *Why couldn't we just talk about it? Everything was going so well between us.* Under the crook of her elbow, her eyes snapped open. *Fuck no! It was obviously seriously not there for her. If things were so hunky-dory between us, she'd be here. Not just her bags.*

The tightness under Maddy's chest was spreading and pushing against her ribs. She breathed slowly through her nose. She wanted to make it stop spreading. But it didn't. It kept on pushing and pushing until she could no longer breathe.

Breath suspended, she had to get up. Feet apart, arms apart, to lift her shoulders, to widen her rib cage, she forced little gulps of air down into her lungs. As Jo does with a bicycle pump when her old tyre's flat. The disturbing feeling that a balloon had inflated where her lungs used to be persisted as, on the edge of the bed, head down she thought, *And now what? What else can I do?*

Black in the palm of her hand, Jo's wallet. Maddy still had not opened it back on that other bed in Burleigh Heads. Unable to rifle through it, as if pulling out its content, like a snapped silver cord would mean the certain death of her lover, she had carefully replaced it back at the bottom of her bag. But now that all of her lover's belongings had been moved into her bedroom, Maddy was getting anxious about possible clues missed.

Flat, black and slim: Jo's address book. She had found it in Room 8, on the nightstand, but she hadn't packed it in the big plastic bags along with the rest of Jo's belongings. Instead, she had slipped it inside her jeans' pocket. She could feel it, stiff against her buttocks.

Maybe I should just look inside that first. There'll be her sister's number. What's her name again? Maddy squinted to make that name pop inside her head, the only name in the world she knew to have a connection to Jo. *Gina? No, not Gina. A G name, though.* No, not G name. It started with a J too. I remember Jo had joked about it. *Jill? Joan?* None of these names sounded right. Too short. Jo had only mentioned her sister once or twice and the last time had been after she had returned from a three-day absence. *The last time she had disappeared.*

Maddy held the address book flat and unyielding between thumb and forefinger. Glossy except for fingerprints smudges. *Her fingerprints.* Maddy sighed. *I need to open the damn thing and look for that name. I just have to. Maybe the sister knows something.*

Maddy flipped the little book open. Her heart sank at the sight of her lover's handwriting. So neat and regular. *So neat like Jo. Neat and tidy.* The thin, gold-edged pages opened at the letter D. Only three entries: *David, Dentist, Deidre* each followed by an address but only the dentist had a phone number written next to it. A phone number and a Toowoomba address. She shuddered. *If anything bad's happened to her, they'll want to talk to him.* They always did on TV. Maddy nibbled the inside of her bottom lip and slid her fingernail under the thin **J** tab. *Jeremy. Joey. Jarrah.* "Jarrah!" she exclaimed, "Right! That's *got* to be it." She looked again. One address in Toowoomba and a phone number. *Yes!*

Suddenly energised, Maddy pushed off the bed, address book open under her thumb. And then she stopped dead, dismayed. "And now what?" she whispered. "What do I do with this number?" *What, I call up the sister and say that Jo's gone – Uh, the cops would've told her so – What if they haven't contacted her? And she'll want to know who I am. So I say I'm a friend. A good friend. Her best friend?* Maddy's heartbeat picked up. *Did the cops even look inside Jo's room? Wouldn't they have kept the address book? Mitch would've mentioned –* "Shit!"

Heart thudding, Maddy dialled the number neatly printed alongside the name of Jarrah. The phone rang against her ear and with each ring Maddy grew queasier.

Ring, ring. *What if she knows what's happened anyway?* Ring, ring. *Because the news is bad?* Ring, ring. *What if she tells me …* ring, ring … *point-blank that Jo doesn't ever want …* ring, ring … *to hear from me ever again?* Ring, ring. *What if the news is beyond bad …* ring, ring … *like something terrible's happen –*

"Hullo."

" ... " Maddy was mentally unprepared for a first ever conversation with her lover's sister.

"Hullo," a woman's voice insisted.

Eyes shut tight, nose wrinkled in the effort it took, Maddy stammered, "Right ... Yes. Hello. Uh ... you don't know me. I'm Maddy. Uh ... and ... I was– "

The voice parroted, "Maddy?"

"Uh ... yes." Like an athlete, a hair's breadth away from the starter-gun blast, Maddy blew out a tight stream of air through rounded lips. "Maddy Collins. I'm a friend of– "

"Maddy? As in *Jo's* Maddy?" the voice asked excitedly.

" ... " Maddy punched the air with a closed fist.

"Hello? You there?"

"Uh ... yes," Maddy grinned. "I'm here."

"So, are you?"

"Am I ... what? Uh ... Jo's Maddy?"

"Well, yes."

Maddy's heart lurched but she would've hugged the woman if she had been any closer than two hundred kilometres away. "Ah, yes. Absolutely. That's me, Jo's Maddy." She swallowed hard to disperse the incipient welling of tears. "Uh, I'm calling because she hasn't– "

"Maddy?" the woman's tone was now urgent. "How long has she been gone?"

*****

The hard drops pelted down on her scalp. Together, they formed thick rivulets of soft water that parted her hair, painting a shade so dark that it looked almost brown. The water parted her hair in the most absurd of ways. From the top of her head, two almost identical seams led directly to the top of each ear. From the top of her head, another pale seam of skin travelled almost perfectly aligned with the tip of her nose. The water came down hard. It came down hard and it was very hot.

The top of Maddy's ears were all red. Wet and red. Her shoulders were red, too, because the spray from the showerhead was also jetting onto her shoulders. The rest of her body didn't seem much affected by the spray apart from the fact that it was wet. Not much could get to the rest of her body. Not from above in the position she was in, seated on the white tiles, knees bent, toes touching the opposite wall of the shower recess. Her eyes were wide open. If she had been using her eyes to see, she would've seen her kneecaps made glossy by the spray. But her eyes were not seeing. Not her kneecaps, not anything. She had disconnected her eyes because she didn't need them to play back the conversation she had had with Jo's sister earlier that night.

When Maddy had opened her back door, back from her round-trip to Toowoomba, the moon was high in the sky, almost too small even. All the houses in her street were tucked away inside the night. The TV stations had stopped emitting, too bad for the insomniacs.

She had gone straight to the bathroom to turn on the shower, wishing she had a bathtub. But Maddy didn't have a bathtub, only a shower. So she had disconnected her eyes to better return to her conversation on Jarrah's sofa, to connect again with the helpless anger that had kicked her in the stomach. *If* she had had a bathtub, she would have filled it to the top. She would've submerged herself, entirely, just as entirely as the houses were submerged, smothered by the night. She would've let herself be submerged by water until it filled ears, nose, mouth, and eyes. And she would've let the water decide the rest for her.

*****

THREE

Maddy stirred on the hard tiles. Numb bum. She lifted her face to the hard spray and let it splatter over her face. The hard drops tapped against her eyelids, but like flat tears they ran away sideways. She pushed herself up against the back wall, brushed her sodden hair back with one hand and pushed herself up with the other.

That much closer to the showerhead, the spray was denser and harder. She let it hammer against her forehead until some of it found its way to the back of her throat, scratching it raw. She spluttered, swallowed hard and winced before finally opening her eyes. Her fingertips were all shrivelled. She rubbed them together but they remained shrivelled. She slapped the palm of her hand hard against the wet tiles. The relentless spray had not yet melted the blend of hurt, apprehension and resentment that had steadily built up inside her during the course of the evening.

When things were bad, Jarrah had explained earlier that night in the living room of her Toowoomba flat, all that Jo did was go to her room. She would turn on the ceiling fan, open the window, lit a pre-rolled joint plucked from the middle of the pen-mug atop her desk, slip on her headphones and settle down with her homework.

In her senior year, Jarrah said that her sister hadn't made it as St Joan's School Captain. She no longer had straight As in everything, the prerequisite for nomination by the teaching staff, but she performed well as a Vice-Captain. At sixteen, one year younger than most in the Year 12 cohort, Jo was still balancing her studies and her sport commitments along with her mother's mood swings, though by then, she'd only ever pick at her food. By then, Jo had become a one-joint-a-day kid.

When Isabel OD'ed on the morphine that she had stashed away, unbeknown to all but Jo and the Head Nurse back in the oncology ward, Jarrah explained that her sister dropped all plans of ever becoming an architect. She had dropped all plans to go to uni.

"Actually," Jarrah had added somewhat cryptically, "it looked to me like Jo had, right there and then, opted out of her life altogether. I mean, out of the life she had meant to have … to take up one that didn't seem to be hers at all."

Maddy understood that when her mother died, Jo's last chance of ever having Isabel's love and approval, uninterrupted like the tinkle of chimes in the breeze, also died. She had lost her drive to be the best she could be because being the best she could be had not been good enough.

"Jo's basic spin was, why else would Mum have preferred to die rather than hang around and be a mother to her. From very young," Jarrah explained, "she had convinced herself that bursting a gut to achieve was a fair exchange for Mum's love. She wanted to be loved unconditionally so over-achieving, she thought, was a one-way ticket to that love." Eyes unfocused, Jarrah added, "She was wrong there. Totally wrong." She hesitated. "You see ... Years before that, Jo had convinced herself in a twisted sort of way, that if she were a *better* daughter, she'd be able to stabilise Mum. Not so much in terms of her cancer ... That had been a major scare but only for two years or so. It was more in terms of the anger and depression that were making Isabel so ... so ... unpredictable." Brown eyes shiny, Jarrah looked away. "As it turned out after Mum died, my little sister dropped out of everything altogether and became an introverted couch potato stoner. That new state became the shrunk focus of her existence."

"Stoner as in ... into drugs?"

"You didn't know?" Totally surprised by the news, Maddy shook her head. "Would it've made a difference to you if she had told you?" Jarrah asked.

Maddy took her time before answering. She shrugged. "I don't do drugs myself but I wouldn't have minded. A joint or two, I mean I'm not ..."

"Not one or two a day, Maddy. I'm talking about a serious habit. Would you have minded if she had told you about it? As a past thing?"

"I ... Uh, before I fell in love with her ... I guess, if she'd told me *that*, like on day one. Yeah..." The slow blush creeping up her cheeks made Maddy falter. "It might've made a difference."

"Why then and not later?"

"Because later, like I just said, I got to know her. I got to love her." Maddy's face felt hot. "So if she'd told me about this past ... *thing,* even like a couple months ago, that wouldn't have been a big deal story or anything. But at first I would've thought like, Is she OK to trust and–"

"Maybe she sensed that. I mean, maybe she thought you wouldn't have given her a look in. That you'd close up on her, if she told you." Jarrah suckled the whiskey from the rim of a Klein-blue glass tumbler. "You'll have to ask her, huh?"

"Right. I will," Maddy agreed tightly. "When she shows up."

"Anyway, for the next year or so," Jarrah continued, "she attached herself to the bloody bong like a mare to a feeding bag. *Time to boot up the bong,'* that's what she'd say and she'd get totally mashed up. Stoned out of her gourd."

"But..." Perplexed, Maddy drew in her bottom lip, "I don't get it. She hasn't smoked a single joint since I've known her. I'm sure she hasn–"

"I know she hasn't. She completely gave up that shit about a year ago. In stages. Her hot-boxing days were a knee-jerk reaction to Mum's suicide but ... you're not into the pot-thing at all, are you, Maddy?"

Maddy shook her head slowly, wondering whether she should have indulged more frequently. "No, not beyond the odd toke. Like, I have a couple friends who light up and when I'm ... there they want to share it three ways." She shrugged. "Never even thought about buying my own." And then, she added. "It's the inhaling thing I can't do."

"So, you don't smoke tobacco either?" Again Maddy shook her head. "Right." Jarrah looked away again. "I guess I'm the one who got her started on her first joint. Hmmm." She cleared her throat and shifted self-consciously in the armchair. "She knew I smoked. Back in those days, while I was hanging with David, a boyfriend. That was a long time ago ... Anyway, back then I was on two a day. After a while though," Jarrah smirked, "what with the munchies and all, I started bulging out so I gave it up. It wasn't a big deal for me. But ... before that, one afternoon I stopped by the house to connect a bit with Mum and the little sister and Jo, she just came right out and asked. Like as soon as we were out of earshot, in the garden, actually. I remember," Jarrah grinned, "it was near that old pond where none of us ever went anymore. Well, she had just about dragged me there to ask if I carried any weed. I was floored. I mean, I had never talked about anything much with her anyway. She was just my kid sister, so I didn't talk much about ..." Jarrah flopped back against the armchair and sighed. "At the time, I really hadn't figured out what was going on with Mum, I mean about her depression so ... Yeah, I thought, Hey, little sister's growing up and testing the system. So ... I left her the one reefer I had on me at the time and ... well ... the rest is history," Jarrah concluded too quickly. She fiddled with one of the plastic coasters on the coffee table but, once her thoughts collected, she looked up and met Maddy's inquisitive gaze. "I ... uh, I mean ... knowing Jo, even if I had done the *reasonable* big sister bit with her, I'm sure she would've found a way to score on her own but, yeah ... OK, I got her the starter kit." Brown eyes slid away from Maddy. "But she was sixteen then. Already as tall as Mum. Vice-Captain of that bloody school. Skinny as a ... as a *weed*. Forever stuck in her books. Books and music. Ah, yes. High adrenaline stuff. Heavy Metal. Old Led Zeppelin stuff." She sighed. "Too many bloody medals she had earned for this and for that. She didn't even display them anywhere. You see, Maddy, they weren't really for her, were they? I guess, Jo's a real Gen X kid. Focused on what she does, whatever it is, but feeling alienated from it all."

"So your parents didn't know about– "

"My father wasn't there *to* know anything about either Jo or Mum. He just drifted in late at night and left early in the morning. I'm sure he wanted to divorce Mum after her remission from bone cancer but he was too much of a coward. It wouldn't have looked good, right? Imagine all the people in his practice knowing ... Maddy, for a while the doctors thought they'd have to ... they might need to ... amputate Mum's right leg.

"We were all devastated, of course, but for Jo ... it went beyond that. Oh, look..." Jarrah threw her hands about. "The thing is Jo's grown up all on her own. And she looked OK. As I said, she was still doing well at school and all that crap. But in retrospect, she wasn't coping all that well, not on her own with Mum but it's after Mum's..." Jarrah finally articulated, "It's after Mum killed herself that Jo blew a gasket and got totally mashed up on a daily basis. And..." she attempted a little smile, "that's when I managed to have her stay with me ... Just so that I could ... Well, I guess I felt like I was being given a second go at doing the big sister thing ... Properly this time." Her eyebrows went up at angles. "Better late than never, right?" She swirled what remained of the whiskey inside the blue tumbler and took a long sip. She exhaled the vapours through her teeth.

Both young women remained silent until Maddy looked up from the collection of muticoloured marbles that filled the glass bowl on the coffee table. "What's hot-boxing?"

Jarrah sucked air between her teeth as she flicked the dark hair out of her eyes. "Quite nasty really. Look, I don't mind telling you but..." She reached across for Maddy's hand, but her fingers only got as far as touching her wrist. "You sure you want to– "

"Jarrah, I *want* to know. I want to know all there is to know about *all* these moments in Jo's life. Later, I'll want to know why I ... Why I didn't know about any of them. Like why she never told *me* about any of that pain that she's been carrying around for ... for so long. But for now ... Yeah, I need to know ... everything."

Like an athlete on the starting blocks, Jarrah breathed in, focussing on the round swirls painted on the coaster she was holding. "Right." She breathed in again. "In Jo's case, she'd sit in her car. Used to be Mum's, right? Windows all rolled up tight." Jarrah glanced at her sister's lover and hesitated again. Maddy blinked a nod for her to continue. "She'd ... she'd light up. She'd spark that bong and do it to death until the damn thing was totally cashed, totally spent. Until you couldn't see the windows, the car windows through the smoke." She stopped. Maddy sensed that *that* particular aspect of the conversation had become difficult for Jarrah too, but she remained silent. She was flat out trying to connect the dots between what she knew: the Jo she loved and thought she knew, and the bong-sucking zombie that Jarrah had summoned inside her Toowoomba livingroom. "A steamroom of floating THC. In a car, that's hot-boxing." Jarrah continued, "*That* and what she'd inhale directly ... Well, there wasn't much wastage at all." She breathed in and shook her head sadly. "You know why she was doing all that, don't you?" Again Jarrah lifted the tumbler to her lips. "Damn! That thing's strong," she said, teeth bared on the exhaled vapours.

Thrown as much by the question as by the revelations, Maddy was too dazed to contribute a worded answer. She simply nodded, then shook her head wondering how she and Jo could have been so close-in-love and *she* knowing so little about her lover.

There was so much she wanted to know about her, about her pain that Maddy didn't know how to begin asking. She just looked at Jarrah, at her standard good looks and found it difficult to truly reconcile her as her lover's big sister except that they had the same shade of dark, almost black hair. Maddy gazed at Jarrah and she envied her the places where *she* had been in Jo's life.

Jarrah reached for another cigarette. She inhaled deeply before blowing out a long plume of acrid smoke that made Maddy's nose twitch.

"I wasn't really there for her when she was living at home. And we *still* haven't talked much about her relationship with Mum." Jarrah shook her head and continued slowly as if talking to herself. "But I don't think she *ever* got resentful of Mum. I'm sure she's never hated her. In fact, I do know it was quite the opposite. She loved Mum too much and the more she loved her, the more painful each of Mum's unpleasant turns became."

"Did you know how it was for Jo ... back then?"

"I didn't, not for a long time ... but again I kind of did." Jarrah considered the tip of her incandescent cigarette. "I'd already left home when Mum became ill. She wasn't sick or depressed when *I* was growing up. There's that eleven-year difference between us, Jo and me. A lot of things get slotted inside an eleven-year gap." Maddy watched Jarrah puff on her cigarette, holding on to the smoke a fraction too long. *Almost like she's smoking a joint,* Maddy thought. *Can't be good for her.* "So anyway, Mum and Dad still shared a life in those days and there were times when we, the four of us, were a *very* happy family." Jarrah dragged on her cigarette and as she did, Maddy saw her lover dragging on a joint. "Mum always knew how to turn on the charm and, before I left home, the three of us often went about playing and walking holding hands. Jo was still very young ... Damn!" Brown eyes, pinpoint-sharp, glared at some unfocused point, off to the side of Maddy's shoulder, while smoke curled lazily away from Jarrah's half-opened lips as if she had forgotten to blow it out. She leaned back against the armchair and tilted her head to the ceiling. Maddy noticed the hard dips of her Eve's apple. *Maybe I could go to her,* she thought. *She needs a hug. Hell, she'll probably freak out if I move now. Probably think I'm making a pass at her or something.* And so Maddy made herself lean back into the armchair too.

After a while, Jarrah brought the cigarette butt to her lips. Its tip, still incandescent, burned like a tiny cone of hard lava. "It's true to say that for a long time, I didn't know what Mum was doing. And again because of the age difference between us, I was already out and working, had a boyfriend, one of many," she smirked. "Had an abortion, too." Off on a tangeant, she added, "I don't think Mum had planned on having a second child." She sighed and made tiny shaking movements with her head before looking squarely at Maddy. "And ironically, Jo, as soon as she came out of her baby-fat phase, was just like Mum's little clone. The same grey eyes, oyster-shell eyes, I used to call them. By fourteen or fifteen, she was already as tall as Mum. After that, I don't ever remember her *not* thin. Not gawky." She twirled a strand of her hair around her finger and brought it forward to show Maddy. "That colour, that's Mum's colour and Jo's. Now, my father," she snorted, "here's one good example of a totally useless male. Man enough to *stay* away from everything, he was. Anyway, later when their marriage ended up on the rocks, like beyond repair, instead of taking on a lover Mum took up a relationship with Mr Smirnoff, from Vodkaland. I resented her for it … well, maybe not *her* so much as her weakness. Jo was convinced Mum had become an alcoholic. I think she just became alcohol-dependent."

"What's the difference?" Maddy asked softly, already thinking there was no difference.

Jarrah breathed in slowly. "Look, Maddy, Mum managed without the booze for most of the day. She didn't have a bottle stashed under her pillow. She drank only from late afternoon onwards. And Jo felt responsible for Mum's drinking and she felt responsible for all of Mum's other pains too. But the real problem, I mean, what became *Jo's* problem with her is that Mum, beyond her severe mood swings, became erratic when she drank. A very bad drunk." Jarrah glanced at Maddy who gave her a little smile.

Maddy couldn't muster more than a little smile because her dawning understanding of her lover's childhood held her, talon-tight, around the throat. She imagined Jo as a little girl with long baby-giraffe legs. She imagined her as a dark-haired little girl who peered tentatively at her mother, hoping for a smile and a hug she may not get.

Jarrah stubbed her cigarette. "Oh, listen to me!" Her voice rang sharp. "A bad drunk, right! That's what I've just said." Again, she glanced at Maddy, still precariously perched on the edge of her armchair. "She's been gone almost seven years, Mum has, and I'm still finding it difficult to … to admit out loud that her relationship with Jo was … Damn it, it was *abusive!*" She took another swig of the whiskey that hugged the bottom of the tumbler. Maddy was still holding hers, cradled inside her two hands. "Nothing truly violent but yes, definitely nasty, *emotionally* nasty." Again, Jarrah sighed and threw up her hands in the air. What remained at the bottom of the tumbler splashed over. "Shit, I'm clumsy," she said tightly. The tumbler changed hands and Jarrah wiped her fingers on her jeans.

Maddy was too tense to grin. "You really think Jo felt *responsible* for your mother's– "

"Look, Maddy," Jarrah replied sharply, "I don't think it, I *know* it. And it's not felt but feels, if you know what I mean. Present tense and ongoing. She couldn't stand seeing Mum weak and she was *totally* unable to have her take responsibility for anything. Jo never even complained but later, I started putting two and two together and came up with something like a *composite* picture of the last few years of Mum's life. As witnessed by Jo." Jarrah stood up and went to the sliding door that, Maddy could see, led on to a balcony barely wide enough for a small table and two chairs. "It had to be one of those Sunday lunches." Jo's sister spoke into the night. "Mum lost the plot with me for the first time. It was … well … it was absolutely awful and once the … the *mess* was over, I asked Jo if, you know … if anything like that had ever happened *to her*, right? I meant, Mum turning *violent*. Yes, … violent and…" Jarrah leaned her forehead against the sliding pane. "She didn't answer me. She went up to her room. I followed her there and, after a lot of prompting, for the first time ever we had a sister-to-sister talk. A couple of joints helped us along." Jarrah looked at Maddy and held her gaze for a brief moment then she looked away and sighed some more. "The truth is that besides trying to convince Jo that none of that, *none of anything* was, or had ever been, her fault … I didn't do *anything* for her." Tension returned to Jarrah's brow and for a flutter of time, there was something in that expression that Maddy recognised. She had seen it on her lover's face when she was trying to convince Maddy that her own inability to climax had nothing to do with Maddy's performance as a lover. "I guess I can also say that I didn't do anything for Mum either, but that's different. When it came to her, I didn't even try to understand. I just wanted her to help herself. To be strong. To seek professional help. To undergo some sort of therapy, voluntarily. Instead, she piked out. She got tired of living. And she … she just gave up. And Jo figured Mum got tired of Jo. That Jo was not worth it as a daughter, not worth it enough for her mother to want to stay alive … That kind of thing."

Maddy turned the shower off and grabbed one of the large bath towels that hung behind the door. Hers was the blue one. The other one, the green one, was Jo's from the last time she had showered at Maddy's, the afternoon they had driven down to Burleigh Heads. She initially had left the green towel there for Jo on the way back. Now, she left it there as others hang yellow ribbons on trees. Jo exists. Jo is her lover. Jo will come home.

Maddy dried her hair, towelling it within an inch of its life but the conversation with Jarrah that had finished only a couple of hours earlier still spun inside her head. She understood better Jo's need for very little. She understood her fussy neatness. And she understood why smiles didn't linger long on her lips and why, when they disappeared, they sometimes took a long time before reappearing.

Earlier that night, on the long drive back to Brisbane, Maddy had realised how their nine-month long relationship had spread itself across two vastly different lives. It seemed as if their love had tried too hard to make itself at home over what now seemed to her very mismatched emotional baggage.

Although Maddy's mother had caused *her* a great deal of pain, Maddy had been able to take that pain in her stride. She had considered herself all grown up by the time her mother cast her off. She had just turned eighteen. Besides, she had never felt very close to her mother. In fact, she had often wished Aunty Ida were her mother. *But if Jo and me are so mismatched, how did we fucking manage to grow such beautiful flowers, wildflowers, together?* she asked herself.

All clean and dry, her body covered by a long T-shirt, Maddy flopped on a beanbag and closed her eyes. *Fucking long day.* She breathed in slowly and then forced all the air out of her lungs. She breathed ou stale air that sat low like smog. *Answers, many answers but not to the questions I had. Not one fucking answer to my question, Where the fuck is she?*

She pushed herself off the beanbag to pour herself a brandy. She had only tasted the slug of whiskey Jarrah had poured in her tumbler because she had been too tense to drink. Too intent on Jarrah's words to drink. And when it was all over, back in the Toowoomba flat, after Jarrah had offered her the spare bedroom to save her from a long drive into the night, she still only finished that one drink. *But now,* she thought, *I more than fucking deserve a drink. Not just a drink,* she smirked, *a double-header ... just to get started. Tonight's the night I'm getting rat-arsed! Starting now.*

She looked at her watch. 2.23 a.m. Lips pressed together in a grim line, she snorted. *Where are you, Jo? You're not with me. You're not with her. Why don't you fucking call us?*

Earlier that night, in her Toowoomba flat, Jarrah had explained more of Jo's pain.

"Jo left home one year after mum died, almost to the day. Dad sold the house on Neilson Street and relocated his business to Perth. He's still there. Can't go any further from here and yet remain in Australia." Jarrah's words echoed Jo's when, early in their relationship, she had quickly dismissed her father. "As far away from south eastern Brisbane as one could wish," she had said matter-of-factly to Maddy. "Western Australia. That's where he went to retire."

Maddy smiled tensely. "That's one of the two family things I knew about Jo. That her father lived in Perth and that she had a sister. Mind you, I only found out about you some three months *after* we got together and only because she had vanish– "

"Look, Maddy, you've got to understand that over the years she's taken the habit of coming here whenever things get too complicated for her. This flat, me, we're like a release valve for her. And she's always wanted to keep that arrangement private, like just between the two of us. So, you know, when she appeared on my door step some what, six months ago– "

"Appeared?" Maddy is surprised by the word. "You would've been expecting her, I mean, when you told her you weren't well and what with the baby and– "

Round eyes, Jarrah chuckled. "Maddy, I think you got me mixed up with someone else's sister."

"Whadda you mean?"

"Well … do you see any babythings around here? If you do," Jarrah grinned, flashing her hands as disclaimers, "they'll have to have been planted by visiting pixies."

"What? You don't have a baby?"

"Tell you what." Jarrah scoots up to the edge of the armchair. "After that abortion I told you about earlier, I've made sure, bloody sure, I never left the house without double protection. You know, one for me and one for him, whoever *he* might have been."

Maddy's blue eyes reflected her confusion. "So … who's Gerry, then? Jo said she had to come all the way out here to help you with … well– "

Jarrah asked amused, "With a baby and what else?"

"Because you were sick and your partner or something like that, some dude called Gerry, was out of town and– "

"My, my. Looks like, this time, my little sister got carried away with the melodrama. I don't think she normally bothers, you know. OK, the baby's fiction but…" She beamed at Maddy. "She *almost* had it right about Gerry. He's my boyfriend. He lives in Brisbane so … yeah you could say he's mostly *away* from here. Right?"

Maddy frowned. *Something's not right.* "OK," she said, unconvinced. "What am I missing here? Why did she lie about that? I mean, what's it to me whether you're married with a baby or single without one?"

"Maddy, hey, don't get upset.' Jarrah lay her hands flat on the coffee table in front of her and looked straight into Maddy's eyes. "She didn't lie to you just to wind you up."

"Oh, like you're sure of that, are you?"

"Yes, I am." Jarrah nodded vigorously. "Jo didn't come to spend three days with me, that time, because there was some chick back in Briz she wanted to play."

"Right. So, why *did* she come here and not tell me?"

Jarrah hesitated. "Because there was a chick in Briz that she thought she might be in love with."

Maddy blinked. "So what's the big deal?" she asked, determined to ignore the flip-flopping feeling in her guts. *Right, Jo loves me and Jo disappears ... twice. What the fuck!* She found it less painful to focus on Jo's half-truths than to understand what Jarrah was telling her about Jo's confusion. "Why'd she come all the way here and like, stay away, and not even call, and then spin me that yarn about you and a ba– "

"Because Jo doesn't deal with *love* very well."

The love word kicked again inside Maddy like a foetus in its mother's womb and still she chose to ignore it. "Oh, *please!* Don't tell me she's really a newbie on the scene and she's confused about her sexuali– "

"That, Maddy, is the one thing I'm not likely to tell you about our Jo." Jarrah grinned to ease Maddy out of her little slough of despond. She had noticed the way the young redhead had begun worrying her lip loop with her front teeth. "I know for a fact that *my* little sister's been on the prowl, on the gay side of the tracks, for quite a few years already, and quite actively at that."

Maddy stuck her chin out. "So?"

"So, Jo is well practised at having sex with women in spite of a difficul– " Jarrah stopped abruptly and shook her head. "No, never mind that. I'm sure you know what I was going to say anyway." She waited for Maddy to look at her before continuing. "Anyway, she's had lovers but what she hasn't done much of, and I'd be the one to know if she had, is ... fall in love. She fucks around, Maddy. That's what she does. It suits her purpose." Whatever had kicked earlier inside Maddy lay cold. Heavy, cold and motionless on the other side of her belly button. *What's she saying?* she asked herself. Jarrah's words were reaching her from a great depth. "She's not trying to prove a point of anything. It's just that she doesn't handle love." Jarrah stopped talking.

A deep frown settled across Maddy's brow and Jo's sister felt moved by the blend of incomprehension and anxiety clearly visible in the round blue eyes, so she got up to squat close to Maddy's armchair. She lay her hands over the young woman's freckly knuckles and very gently, straight into her eyes, she added, "Jo has never tried to deal with *any* feelings of love, if she's ever had any. Not until *you* came along." Maddy's chin quivered, the round blue eyes welled and two fat tears quickly rolled down her cheeks. Jarrah smiled a little smile. She retrieved a folded tissue from a back pocket of her jeans and handed it to Maddy.

Later Maddy heard how Jo had appeared one evening, totally unexpected, on her sister's doorstep. Through Jo's broken words, Jarrah understood that Jo should have been at Maddy's, at her lover's. Jo had tried to explain why she was unable to do just that, roll up to Maddy's for dinner and sleep curled up against her.

Jo had decided that she'd never be able to let go enough to be any good for Maddy. That Maddy would soon realise that *she* wasn't worth loving all that much. Maddy, she knew, would just end up doing a Jekyll and Hyde on her, like her mother. Jo knew that whenever that would happen, the childhood wounds she had covered up, if only with thin tear-away scabs, would reopen. She knew that she'd hurt all over again. She knew that a rejection from Maddy would confirm what she'd already learnt from her mother, that Jo Brenner didn't deserve love. Not her mother's. Not Maddy's. Not the love of anyone who mattered like Maddy now mattered.

"I'll tell you another thing, Maddy. You tell me Jo's been missing ten days? I tell you she's never been missing that long. In fact she's never been missing at all, has she?" Jarrah gave Maddy time to process what she had just said. "She's always been here, right? Every time she got frazzled about things. That's not *missing*, is it? Maddy?"

Maddy looked up and shook her head silently.

"So what I'm trying to tell you, Maddy, is that..." Jarrah counted on her finger, "One: I'm worried. If she's not with me and she's not wherever she's supposed to be and the police haven't even tried to look into the matter, otherwise they would've gotten to me before you ... There's cause to worry." She breathed in through her nose and waited before resuming her line of thought. Her brow was tight. "Two: why would she *intentionally* drop her wallet inside your bag, huh? I mean, wherever she went she'd need money and her papers, right?"

Maddy swallowed and nodded slowly.

"Third: because this disappearance is her first ever, I think you could take *that* as the measure of her confusion about her feelings for you. There's no doubt in my mind, Maddy, that whatever she's doing is all about you." Jarrah held Maddy's blue eyes. "Question: can you handle *that,* Maddy? Can you handle being ... the focal point of what's made her freak out? How strong are you really, Maddy?"

Maddy put the empty tumbler on the floor by the beanbag. The long T that's now all bunched up has exposed the russet freckles scattered over the warm alabaster of her thighs. *Can I handle that?* Absentmindedly, she ran her finger around and around the rim until, dizzily, the tumbler fell on its side. *How the fuck can I handle anything if she's not even here? If she's gonna piss off every time she gets confused, huh?* She watched the tumbler roll away from her. Her fingers raked through the still damp spikes of her hair. With a sigh and leading from the head, she pushed herself off the beanbag. *Anyway, what does she mean by* 'handle'? *What's there to handle, huh?*

*****

In the family of Bridgestone Potenza RE730 I have the 225/60ZR16 and the 225/50R16. Could fit those under a ... under a ... Well, hell! Under a Beamer Z3. In the Bridgestone family of Dueller M/T with Uni-T, we got the LT235/85R16, load range E tread. 6"9 width, 32"2 overall diameter. That could go under ... ah ... under the next Wrangler that comes in. Them or the Firestone Firehawk RMT, if it's for both off and on-road driving.

"Large lugs notched," Maddy recited to herself, "and tapered for max traction. Interlocking centre tread blocks for stability and ... a quiet ride. Yes!" *And why is that?* she asked silently as she went about marking the new arrivals with white-chalk hieroglyphs. *The quiet bit ... that's because ... Well, I reckon it's because the lug and tread-block sizes have been varied.* She cast a quick glance at the spec sheet jammed between the two tyres immediately on her left. *Yep, that's what it says right there.* She jumped off the ladder, grabbed a Timberline A/S off one of the stacks nearest her, hefted it in her left hand and went back up the ladder. Toes curled inside her work-boots, she balanced herself on the top rung and swung the tyre behind her back to grab it with the right hand and, in one fluid movement, she landed it on the shelf, twisting her wrist just so, and set it on its rim. *Could go under one of them Super Duty utes.* She patted the tyre in place and jumped off the ladder four rungs up from the concrete floor.

As she turned away from her work, her throat closed up on her. Only a few metres away, her back to the sunlight, a woman was wheeling in a bicycle with a very flat tyre. Willowy in faded trousers and flanelette shirt. Willowy in spite of the combat boots on her feet. The longer strands of her short hair spilled casually over her forehead.

Maddy blinked to free herself from the vision of Jo as she had appeared to her that very first time. The time when Drew, keen to pull down the huge Roller-door and go home, hadn't been attentive to a customer's need. The time when, because the person with the problem had been a woman, Maddy had thought she could at least see for herself if there was a way to patch up her tyre, if only temporarily. There were, after all, many different sorts of rubber on the premises from which a patch might be improvised.

"Can't patch up a fucking long tear," she muttered, as she wiped her face with a dark green bandanna and turned her back to the streaming sunlight. Viv, the boss's wife, was tapping against the glass pane of her little office. Holding up the phone towards the pane, she gestured for Maddy to come inside.

Maddy listened, earpiece tight against her ear. "Yes, I remember," she enunciated slowly. She listened some more and she blanched. It was almost like all the freckles on her cheeks had been bleached. "She, what? You've got to be kiddin'!" she exclaimed. Her eyes were wide. Like big blue butterflies casting about for somewhere safe to land, they flitted over the blackened crescents under the fingernails of her free hand. She curled her fingers against the palm of her hand. Her eyes flitted through the glass pane and she squinted against the light. Then, her eyes searched the small office for Viv's face, but Viv had left the office to afford Maddy the privacy she knew she would be needing once the nice policewoman broke whatever news she had 'about a friend young Maddy was worried about.'

Viv had immediately understood that the police had found Jo. Maddy closed her eyes altogether and clenched the phone even more tightly. She sucked in her lip loop. Her shoulders rose because she needed to breathe and her lungs weren't doing it for her. And then, "What d'you mean?" she asked harshly. "Why the fuck not?"

"Because, Maddy, if you go to her as a *lover*, two things are likely to happen," DS Jensen answered gently from inside the earpiece. "One: you'll be putting her at risk." The policewoman remembered well the young redhead from that night at the station and she paused to give her time to process what information she'd just given her. "Most important for now, Maddy, you *do* have to understand that Jo's out there, totally on her own. Day and *night*. You do get the *night* part, don't you?" DS Jensen insisted. "Nothing at all around her to protect her. And believe me, whatever male fantasies are out there, including the lesbian porn fantasy … Uh, look, Maddy, I do know that these males' impulses are terribly exacerbated in an uncontrolled environment such as a– " Because of the muffled sound heard at the other end of the line, Ds Jensen asked, "Maddy? You're still there?"

"Yeah … I'm here. I almost dropped the … I'm listening. It's just that I … What *can* I do, then?"

"To be totally honest with you, Maddy, I'm not sure. I'd say you could go to the park and let her see you from a distance. Don't surprise her. Let her *see* you coming. Move slowly. Take your time. Don't corner her. Let it sink in that it's you out there and … Well, after that, I guess it'll be up to her. The thing is, Maddy," DS Jensen added almost urgently, "it's *her* dance. She has to lead it. *I* don't know why she's there but you … maybe you've been able to figure out what might've pushed her to run. Whatever it is," DS Jensen added firmly, "if she's *chosen* to put herself through that, it's got to be because she can't think of anything else to do. Even two weeks later, right? As far as she's concerned, there's still no other way out of whatever has made her snap in the first place. So, that's how it goes, Maddy: if you want to help her, just go there and tread carefully. Forget your own needs. They're not a part of the equation, not this time."

"And?"

The voice hesitated. "And what, Maddy?"

"You said there were two things– "

"Ah, yes. The other thing to consider is that you might well freak her out." Again DS Jensen paused. "By that I mean that you might unconsciously overwhelm her. Your … your … your lover *persona*, not you necessarily. It could make her feel emotionally or intellectually inadequate, you know, for the way she's run away without even talking about it. And she might feel guilty, too, for what she's putting you through. As I said, this particular situation does not fall within my field of expertise. That's more a social worker's thing what young Jo is doing to herself." Maddy sensed a hesitation in the policewoman's voice as she continued, "I did have that Missing Person thing flagged ... so I'd be told the moment she showed up on our system." The voice travelled softly through the earpiece. "What I mean is ... Because of our long talk that night you reported her missing, I felt I'd like to be informed the moment there was news and now that what she's done has become clear, I think this business of yours has turned into a rather complex psychological situation. Maddy, this is not your everyday garden-variety lovers' tug of war for top-dog positioning. This is totally not about the usual mind games people play to score points off each other."

*****

FOUR

"Near the toilet block on the east side of the park," DS Jensen had said. Maddy looked around to get her bearings.

East? Where the fuck is east? She looked up at the sky. Twenty-metre tall Moreton Bay Fig trees, though not trees of the fig-bearing variety, swayed against the grey sky. "East is where the sun rises. A lot of help that is," she grumbled. She glanced at her watch. *5.05. Muggy as hell and cloudy.*

Behind a line of trees she spotted a toilet block. Is that the right one? Her heart, already fluttering under her ribs, switched to a mad tat-too. *What if she doesn't want to know me?* Maddy was slowly freaking out. *What if there's other people around ... people like her? What's she gonna do when she sees me?* Like a bird beating against a glass pane, Maddy's heart would not be restrained. She felt the shimmery release of adrenaline. Cold sweat cooled the palms of her hands. She stopped walking. *Get a grip, girl,* she admonished herself, bottom lip drawn in. She lifted her face to the sky. The grey sky was breaking into sliding patches of blinding white.

A soft breeze that came from the river swayed the long arching branches of a large poinciana. Its gnarled trunk and exposed thick root system suggested its great age. Some of the trees in New Farm Park are centenarians. That's just about as old as anything in Brisbane, itself 'discovered' in 1832 and settled a few years later as a penal colony. Though, of course, the Aboriginal population had been thriving there and everywhere in the vast continent for at least the past 40,000 years, feeling safe in their understanding of the cosmos and their belief in Mother Nature. Safe in their DreamTime. "Right. And even now, they're still strangers in their own land," Maddy said to the breeze. *Can't believe this.* Eyes tight, she nibbled the inside of her lip. *Can't believe she's just like, here ... Somewhere,* Maddy thought, struggling to remain in control of her emotions. *And she's been here all along. Her choice all along.* Maddy bit on the lip loop. Eyes squinting in concen-tration, she scanned the area. *What's done's done. It's the next few minutes I've got to handle right.* The river breeze found her face and ruffled her hair. *Breathe, Mad. Go find the eastern side of the park.*

New Farm Park, with its famed rose garden, had relevance to Maddy, as it did for the great majority of Brisbanites, but only as a lovely inner city park that stretched alongside the river. The park was a place where, over the years, she and friends had gathered for the occasional BBQ or picnic on the lawns, a game of Bocce, or a toss of the Frisbee with someone's borrowed dog. A nice spot to chill with friends out for a lazy Sunday gathering. Never in a million years did she ever foresee the day when this park, or any park, would become the backdrop for a strategic moment in her life.

Maddy approached the toilet block cautiously. DS Jensen had been categorical. 'Let her see you first,' she had said. 'Walk slowly. Don't make her feel cornered.' And Maddy also remembered the policewoman's reminder that *her* needs, Maddy's, were not only subordinate to Jo's, they had to be totally non-existent. So, Maddy made herself breathe again. She became aware of her moist palms and she wiped them on her jeans. *Fuck this,* she thought, annoyed with herself. *I don't do sweat. My hands never sweat.* She rounded her back like a cat, held the position a few seconds, straightened her spine and pushed her shoulders back. *OK. Let's spin this now before I lose it totally.*

Ahead of her, on the other side of a picnic table, a waist-high hedge in a wide horseshoe configuration delineated the brown grass from the adjacent Sydney Street. Heart in her mouth, Maddy sat at a table and scrutinised the area ahead. Followed by a woman whom Maddy immediately assumed was her mother, a little blond girl atop a wobbly pink bicycle pedalled over the patchy grass surface.

"Slow down, Lisa," the woman called out. "Don't you come crying to Mummy if you fly arse over kettle, you hear?"

Maddy watched them as they came more directly into her line of vision. The little girl slowed down and stopped pedalling altogether.

Something to her left, close to the bushes and hedge, held her attention but from where she was seated further away at the wooden table, Maddy was too far to see what it was. The little girl, interest visibly pricked, veered left and began pedalling towards the hedge.

Her mother picked up her own pace and strode after her, calling her back. "Lisa, you come back here now. Right now!" Maddy watched the mother as she accelerated her pace. She watched her toss the magazine she had been holding into a large rubbish bin. "I mean it, Lisa. Won't tell you again!" she threatened.

The mother's words, or had it been her tone, seemed to mean something to the little girl. By the way the back wheel of the bicycle kicked out, Maddy guessed that the little girl had applied sudden pressure to the brakes. By the time the woman turned around and resumed walking in the same direction as before, she was holding Lisa's hand firmly in her own and the pink bicycle frame, off the ground, in the other.

As they retraced their steps, Maddy heard the mother's scolding. "You must *never* go near people like that, Lisa. I've already told you about them, haven't I?" She shook the little girl's hand.

"But, Mummy, I just wanted to see– "

"No *buts*, Lisa, you hear me? There's nothing out there for you to see, they're abos."

"But they weren't doing anythin– "

"They're *Aborigines* Lisa. They're a nuisance." The woman looked over her shoulder. "They don't work. They don't wash. They live off the dole and they spend good taxpayers' money on metho."

The little girl lifted her head. " Mummy, what's *meto?"*

"Metho, Lisa. Methylated spirits. That's what Daddy uses to clean things in his workshop."

The little girl's eyes widdened in alarm, her mother tugged at her hand harder but neither said another word.

"Stupid bitch," Maddy muttered. *I guess they've got their own reasons for living like that. Shit, that woman's way off base, feeding her daughter all that crap.*

With a shrug, Maddy got up from the bench to have a closer look at the Aborigines the little girl had spotted. Just then a tall figure detached itself from the background of bushes and moved in her direction. Maddy plopped back on the bench. Actually, her legs gave in and her tailbone hit the bench heavily. Jo was coming towards her. Breath dried up inside Maddy's throat but her heart, like a piston, thudded hard inside her chest. No thoughts formed inside her head. No words formed inside her mouth. For all intents and purposes, Maddy was transfixed by the apparition.

Jo's long, loose-kneed stride propelled her to the rubbish bin that stood almost half way to the picnic table. She reached inside and retrieved the magazine Lisa's mother had thrown in only a moment earlier. Jo shook it. Something detached itself from the cover. Jo kicked whatever it was along the ground with the rubber toe of the well-worn, lace-up Converse that Maddy knew so well, but kept her attention fixed on the cover of the magazine. Slowly, head bent and reading, she made her way back from where she had come and Maddy stayed slumped on the bench, hands shaking, a thin spray of cold sweat between her skin and her T-shirt. She exhaled forcefully to chase the light-headedness that was threatening to settle inside her head. *So it's true. She lives in the park. Just like the cop said.*

Head on her forearms, Maddy closed her eyes. The slow ebbing of the adrenaline left her faint and shaky but it also allowed in its place a wave of relief that flooded to the tiniest particle of her being. *She's all right. Not hurt. Not dead.* Her first thought, badly phrased as thoughts often are, had been an automatic thought association of relief that went along the line of *Unhurt. Undead.* Couldn't let that hang around though. It made Jo like a Zombie.

"Wow," Maddy exhaled forcefully. "*Yes!* God, thank you," she added, face raised to the sky, fists clenched tight against her thighs. It's only then that she realised how far she had managed to push back the fear that Jo might've come to serious grief, even if, at the time, way back at the Burleigh Heads police station, DS Jensen had reassured her that no woman was laying unclaimed, either in hospital or in the morgue.

After the rush of adrenaline and the wave of relief came the spike of elation. Hot on its heel: the consternation of finding herself not *allowed* to run after Jo. Not *allowed* to turn her around. Not allowed to hug her tight and say, 'Where the *fuck* have you been?'

OK, Maddy made herself reason logically. *One thing at a time. She's alive. She's here. I can see her and she's looking all right.*

She pushed herself off from the picnic table and moved towards the area where the little girl and her mother had seen the Aborigines. Cautiously, because she assumed Jo might be hanging with them, she hugged the line of bushes instead of cutting directly across. And sure enough, some ten steps further in she could clearly see one Aboriginal woman and two men sitting on a patch of dry grass. *Murris,* thought Maddy, who had heard somewhere that Aborigines who came to the Brisbane area from their respective 'nation' clans scattered across the continent

Besides, New Farm Park had already been taken over by too many whites: the trendies, the families, the tourists wanting to check out its famous rose gardens featured on the brochures, the lovers, the druggies, the bleeding hearts, the ferry trippers and basically everyone else who could score something out of the cheery, green openness of a park by the river. Musgrave park, the Aborigines say, that's one

Brisbane place that still holds strong spirit memories of the Dreaming. Not so New Farm Park, no, but Maddy figured that, if a break away from 'home' is as good as a holiday, as the saying goes, then, maybe it worked that way, too, for park dwellers. She snorted at the sad irony of that thought.

A faded calico dress fanned away from the woman's hips to cover all but her thick brown ankles and her bare feet in shades of dark chocolate and dirty cream-coloured soles. What she could see of the men's attire suggested grimy jeans and old shirts buttoned from 'Monday to Wednesday,' as Aunt Ida would say to indicate to her young Maddy that she had buttoned her shirt the wrong way. In the dust at their feet, Maddy recognised a cardboard-clad cask of red wine. Still mindful to approach Jo only in an open area, heart thudding again, she carefully scanned the area for her lover. Her heart sank.

The three Aborigines were alone in the middle of their meagre, dusty possessions, a few clothes inside plastic bags set close to them, the line of shrubs, the only one-sided partition between them and the rest of the street-side of the world that quietly kept watch on them. The younger of the men looked up from the dirt and caught Maddy looking at them. He curled up his lips showing teeth made whiter, even at that distance, by the dark left by missing ones. Keeping his head lowered, he beckoned Maddy.

"Here, sista," he said, as he dipped one hand low towards the ground at his side. "Here … Come," he said, eyes averted as Murris often do when talking because everyone knows that maintaining eye contact is a rude thing to do.

Maddy smiled a little smile but shook her head. She had no intention of settling with the group because, like most city folks, like the little girl's mother, she only knew that Aborigines who squatted park-lands, like derelicts anywhere in the world, were likely to be under the influence of one substance or another. As such, they were known to behave erratically. But unlike the little girl's mother, Maddy didn't find Aborigines to be despicable and objectionable. She did truly think that, as a people, they had many reasons for living it rough though some would, of course, argue that street Aborigines didn't choose to live that way at all.

Scrounging a living from discards, begging for a few coins, sleeping in a park, be it New Farm or Musgrave, or in a train station, surely that couldn't be a lifestyle anyone would choose for themselves. If Maddy had asked the Aboriginal park squatters why they were there, getting drunk on cheap grog at all hours of the day, scaring mothers of little blond girls on pink bicylces, she figured that they'd be more likely to say that their way of living - cut off from their land and traditions - had been thrust upon them the moment the white men robbed their ancestors of their tribal customs. White men, she'd heard them say many times on TV, keep on robbing them, some two hundred and forty years later, of their pride and of their rights as a people.

The older man leered at Maddy. All he saw was one lone white female, there to taunt as he wished simply because he could. Simply because he knew fully-grown white females, more than little girls, were afraid of black men who drank in parks.

And why shouldn't he be drinking? Maddy thought. *What's he got to bloody well look forward to?* But another thought, no longer attached to the Aborigines as such, was nudging her. If Jo did return to this area of the park, it wouldn't do to connect with her from inside this situation, with everyone watching.

Maddy wanted to ask the group if they knew the tall chick who had walked past only a minute earlier but again, she thought that if they *did* know her and they told her someone was asking after her, Jo might freak out and move on. So, head buzzing with what-ifs and why-nots, Maddy flashed to the group a quick wave of acknowledgement, but maxed-out and totally at a loss as to what to do next, she turned her back to them and walked away. She passed the rubbish bin, the toilet block and the picnic table - each a landmark superseding its equivalent back in the Burleigh Heads picnic area.

"Maddy." The voice was barely louder than a whisper but it made Maddy spin around on the heel of her work boots. As she did, instinctively, she knew to lift her eyes a little higher to meet Jo's face. And there she had them; Jo's grey eyes peering down to meet hers, grey and shiny from under unevenly cut strands of black hair. Park sounds and street noises stopped.

From inside Jo's hug, face buried against her shoulder, Maddy only heard the thumping of her own heart and the rush of blood in her ears. *Don't go to her as a lover.* Maddy's eyes snapped open and, gently, she disengaged herself from Jo's long arms and stepped back.

Grey eyes sad. "Maddy," Jo began. "I'm sorry."

Maddy felt the hot prickle of tears rise. She forced down what air already happened to be inside her lungs. She forced it down as far as it would go. Light pink shadows underlined each eye. A dusty smear coated her right cheekbone. Maddy reached to wipe it off with her thumb. Jo nodded with another sad knowing smile.

"Maddy ... I don't know what to say," she began.

Questions and accusations knotted tightly together as a knot of worms. Maddy wanted to shout her relief at having found her lover safe, sound, still able to hug, but she also wanted to hiss out in anger, incomprehension and frustration.

The pressure that had accumulated inside her chest during the past weeks needed to roil and blow. *If you want to help her,* DS Jensen's voice repeated inside Maddy's head, *tread carefully. Forget your own needs.* So, struggling to keep her tone neutral, Maddy simply asked, "Why did you leave?" and held on to her breath, rooted to the spot by the sudden fear of having already blown it. She'd been too blunt, had moved in too quickly, the very thing the policewoman had said *not* to do. *Don't spook her,* she had said. *Don't make her feel inadequate.*

Chest heaving, almost wincing, Jo looked away readying to bolt. She hesitated. "Maddy ... I've ... been like, *so* dreading ... " Her thin sloulders slumped. "Ever since ... " Her Eve's apple bobbed along her thin neck. "I've been dreading this. There's not a *fucking* thing I can say. Not to *you,* not to ... not even to Jarrah, you know ... my sister."

"I *do* know Jarrah," Maddy replied evenly. "We've met. I called her to say they'd found you. She was seriously relieved to hear you're OK."

"The police called you?" Jo's eyes narrowed. "Didn't give them your name, you know. Not even mine." She grinned. "Don't even have an ID to flash at them *even* if I wanted to, which I don't. I'm like the Asylum Seekers on the Teev. First thing they do is lose their papers." Pleased with her reference to current news headlines, Jo grinned.

Maddy opened her mouth to say something but changed her mind. She hesitated. "Right. Well ... they must've figured out you might be the one ... on the Missing Person ... Jo, I reported you missing." She swallowed hard. "I only got the call this afternoon. That's why I'm here. Would never've guessed on my own, would I, now?" she added, unable to totally bite off the bitterness of her words. "So anyway, here you are." She wanted to touch her lover again. She wanted to hug her again, to feel her body, to make sure that her skin was warm as it should be, that her heart was beating as it should. Instead, she only added, "You're OK. That's the main thing."

The park and the strollers were closing in on Maddy. She didn't want to stay there, to stand there. She didn't want *them,* the two of them, to remain exposed. She wanted to take her lover by the hand. She wanted to take her somewhere dark, somewhere soft. Somewhere where Jo would feel safe. Safe to talk. Safe to be. Somewhere where Maddy would feel safe too. Safe to hold her while she listened. Maddy desperately wanted all of that but she knew better than suggest going back to her place.

"Look, Jo … I don't want to … hang here. I need a coffee. Can we just go … just there? Across the street? I need to sit down."

Jo's eyebrows fluttered before settling in a knot. She glanced at the dark crescent of dirt trapped under her fingernails. "I've lost my nailbrush." She met Maddy's eyes and blushed. "That's driving me crazy all that dirt and– "

"Hey, Jo … never mind. We can get you another one." Maddy's fingers brushed over her lover's. "Come. My shout."

*****

Back inside her car, head whirring, painfully aware of the empty passenger seat, Maddy slumped and closed her eyes. Cotton wool filled the cavity inside her skull. Her body overcome by an unexpected sort of lethargy, all thoughts had bubbled away. Her nerves lost all tension. Her muscles lost their natural tautness. She drifted into a restless vacant space.

The late afternoon had turned into evening. Hers was the only car still parked in the area. The children and the mothers had all gone home. Only a lone jogger here and there. Like the electric discharge of a cattle prod, all thoughts of Jo crackled and zapped their way back to Maddy, setting her heart on yet another rib-thudding pace. She looked at the dark patch of the park. *Jo's out there. Alone. All alone in the night. What will she have for dinner? Where does she sleep? How safe can she possibly be? How comfortable can she fucking be?*

"Oh, fuck *you*, Jo!" Maddy shouted inside the stuffy cabin of her car. "What the *fuck* makes you think you can do that, huh?" she shouted again, fist coming down too hard on the steering wheel. She winced and bit on her bottom lip because she couldn't bite off the pain that radiated up to her elbow. So, she brought her front teeth too hard on the lip loop and winced again at that new pain but kept her lip trapped in.

Jo had talked. She had filled in some blanks for Maddy. Maddy had listened. Other blanks still needed answers. Besides, some blanks that had been filled didn't quite have the right feel, they just didn't *seem* right to Maddy and she resented these badly patched up blanks as much as the ones that didn't even have an edge on them, an edge to separate them from the others. Jo had given Maddy an account of why she had fled so suddenly from the picnic table back at Burleigh Heads.

Head heavy against the headrest of her old Commodore, eyes closed to better see Jo, Maddy played back her lover's story.

Jo, her back to the receding surf, is seated at the picnic table facing the esplanade. She watches her lover saunter off across the empty cul-de-sac. She follows her with her eyes for as long as she can, until she disappears into the brightly-lit lobby. She's on her way to their rented apartment. She will bring back a bottle of brandy and two glasses. A moment later Jo sees a light come on at the far left-hand side of the sixth storey.

That's Maddy up there. Jo smiles at the thought of her lover. She plays back a moment of their morning's lovemaking and she grins. She can almost still feel Maddy's fingers inside her, gently stroking her, while the ball of her thumb rubs lightly over her clitoris. And Jo wonders what had been different that morning, different about Maddy's tongue play on her clit. She wonders how she had been so fired up by the time Maddy had slid back against her, back to her mouth. But then again, what with Maddy's tongue copy-catting the slow rhythmic play of her fingers still inside her … That, plus the feel of her lover's clit rubbing lightly against her thigh and Maddy's smooth butt tight under her hand … Jo doesn't quite know what had made it happen but, that morning, she had had one of her elusive orgasms. It had been full of exploding yellow sparkles. The sparkles had surged and peaked twice, leaving her fuzzy-eyed and short of breath.

Jo looks up. The light is still on at the far end of the sixth floor. She imagines Maddy foraging inside her bags, looking for those plastic tumblers she always packs away. Maddy will probably have a pee while up there. Jo wonders what time it is, but without a watch she can't tell for sure. She can only guess that it's got to be some time after midnight.

The little smile of contentment still on her lips, Jo breathes in the night air. By the time she breathes out, the smile has detached itself from her lips and instead of the warm glow that had filled her only a second earlier, in the pit of her stomach is an unyielding lump of dread. She frowns. Her breathing is shallow.

She straightens her back and lifts her chin. She wants to fill her lungs with fresh air from the sea. She needs to dislodge the amorphous murky presence from her insides, but like a pregnant pod, it explodes, releasing thin and nasty little tentacles of panic that all but shut her down as the light at the end of the sixth floor goes off.

Thoughts collide inside Jo's head. An irrepressible fear rises and rises and peaks. She short-circuits. Her mother's right there, purple vein raised on her forehead, spittle flying out on the edge of the words she hisses. Isabel Brenner has materialised in front of her daughter.

"Look at you standing there like a fucking whippet in a blizzard. You make me wanna puke."

And Jo understands that one day Maddy, too, will talk to her that way. "I know she will," Jo says out loud, tone oddly pitched. "She will."

The storm, short and violent like a flash flood, subsides inside Jo's head but its imprint remains. Her mind's made up. No risks, no returns. What's inside her head can't go on spinning the same fucking way again and again. Her right hand tears at the leather band that circles her other wrist. She pulls so hard that the tying thong breaks off. She doesn't know why she's done this, not any more than she can explain what makes her reach inside her bag. Claw-like, her fingers close on the largest object it contains. Finger-quick magician, she slips it and the bracelet inside Maddy's bag, pushes the bag under the table while grabbing her own and, springing to her feet, she bolts. She runs towards the surf. She runs into the darkness.

She spends the rest of that night further on, much further up on the beach, trying to press the meaning of her life out of the fullness of the moon but the moon remains full, untouched, while Jo remains empty and wrung-out by what she's just done. Wrung-out by the realisation of how much more of herself she'd stand to lose through an unsevered emotional connection to Maddy. Though unprocessed, that realisation bonds with Jo like tumour to bone.

As Jo had sat at that picnic table waiting for her lover to return, she had been so full of love for Maddy that she reckons something had to give. Jo's thoughts had been focused on having Maddy already back at her side, the brandy bottle in front of them, the two plastic tumblers still stacked one into the other.

In Jo's mind, as she had waited for Maddy to return, she had reached for her lover's hand. Then she had reached for her lips. Grinning with hungry pleasure, she parted her lips softly, firmly with the ball of her thumb, with her tongue. In her mind, Jo had felt the warmth of her lover's mouth cool under the breeze, the third partner of their kissing game.

Jo had been so full of Maddy that in that crack in time when the moment, *any* moment, slips into its flip-side, its irrational flip-side, Jo had seen herself gaunt and starved and mad. Gaunt and starved and mad because, in the moment that had flared out of the darkness, she was no longer in Maddy's arms. Gaunt and starved and mad, she had seen herself as she would be the day Maddy, her Maddy, would cancel her out with one of her mother's stony stares, with her mother's venom tongue.

"Only a matter of time!" Jo's death-cold thought had shouted. And it had been a frightful glimpse of herself, at the fear shattering under the inevitable moment of Maddy's withdrawal, that had galvanised Jo into flight mode. Not unlike Dorian Grey, she realised that she had brokered a hellish deal but, unlike him, only with herself. The glimpse Jo had had of herself, in that crack in time when the moment, *any* moment, slips into its irrational flip-side, had been just as repulsive to her.

Once on the beach, once the adrenaline rush had receded, her thoughts had travelled back to Maddy only once. Only the first time she had glanced at her wrist. The inch-wide mark of skin shone palely under the white moon and the way her heart kicked at her confirmed she had done the right thing by excising herself from the grip Maddy had on her simply by being her lover.

Not unlike having a tooth pulled, Jo had thought back on that beach, prostrated against the cool softness of the night sand. *Go to the dentist and she'll do what's needed. Or you can do it yourself. Tie a twine around the tooth. Tie the other end to a doorknob. Any fucking doorknob will do. Take a few steps back and slam the door shut. Done!* And that's exactly what Jo figured she had just done. She had slammed shut a door that needed to be slammed shut by her, and now. Not by Maddy, later.

While they had sat momentarily reunited on a terrace, in Brunswick Street, Jo had gone to some length to explain to Maddy why, back at Burleigh Heads, she had disappeared into the night.

"That's sick," was all Maddy had been able to blurt out from across their sidewalk table at Rosati's.

Lips pinched, Jo had simply looked away. They had stayed silent for a long time after that until Jo had tried again. "Look," she said, "it's like … OK! Imagine a silk screen, right? A big one." Jo unfolded the white paper napkin that had come on a saucer under her cup of coffee. With her long fingers and the palm of her hand, she flattened the napkin and smoothed it over the tabletop near her empty cup.

Maddy watched the thick vein that curled up from Jo's middle finger to branch into the delicate pale purple network that always stood out on the back of her hands. She ached to reach across the little table and gently caress it with her fingertips.

"Right," Jo said, intent on her purpose. "Imagine there's something projected on that screen. And what's on that screen, that's what we call reality, right? Now … " Jo tried an engaging smile, "imagine a long tear on that screen. Look." With a dirty fingernail, she scratched the white paper napkin in a way that made the varnished tabletop appear framed *inside* the tear. "There!" she said, satisfied. "See? Behind what *I think* is reality, there's this other thing. There is, isn't there? Another reality. I mean, look. It's there." She tapped her fingernail on the varnished surface that peered at her from inside the torn napkin. "Wouldn't see it, would you, if there wasn't a tear in the napkin but it'd still be there, wouldn't it? Under. Not visible, but there all the same. Can't deny that, Mad." Maddy's mouth was already opened on a rebuttal when Jo added sharply, "No, no! Don't you go telling me what's valid and what's not. Not on this." Jo settled back into her chair. More gently, she resumed, "Top screen reality or behind screen reality? They're both real, Mad. Which one's more valid? Rhetorical question, don't bother answering that." Jo frowned but Maddy saw more than a frown, she saw a glare of determination in the squint of her lover's grey eyes. "So the way it is … The way it was," Jo corrected herself, "my *top screen* reality was one of total trust and dependence on you. I mean, you know, dependent on you for cuddles, for feeling good. For love! So, totally vulnerable, like a fucking pawn. Like a … like a snivelling little whippet type of thing! Huddled *and* fucking scared." Maddy's blue eyes reflected a deepening incomprehension. *What the hell is she raving on about? What's with the snivelling … dog thing? Scared of what, for chrissake?* "The *behind-screen* reality is the one place where I can *never* be hurt because– "

"Because you're fucking putting yourself there. All on your own. It's called … uh … Jo! It's fucking not dealing, that's what it is! All you're doing is spoiling the best– "

"What? Fucking up the best thing that's ever happened to me?"

Maddy bit on her lip loop. "I was going to say the best thing that's happened *to us,* as in to you, to me, separately. And yeah," she tried to grin, "as in to us *together,* too."

"The best thing, absolutely. But I didn't fuck it up, Mad. I've only altered it, that's all. I've only … altered it," Jo repeated tightly. "There's something you've got to understand here." She paused and turned inward for a brief moment.

Maddy slid her eyes away from Jo's. *Oyster-shell eyes,* she had almost said out loud, remembering Jarrah's words about Jo and their mother's eyes. Instead, she looked at her lover's hair. *What the hell has she done to it?*

"The thing is, Mad, I'd much rather have *me* spoil it, I mean the moment, whatever that was," Jo's voice brought Maddy back to her lover's eyes. "I mean by doing what I did … rather than have *you* spoil it for me the moment you'd realise I'm not the one you thought I was. Or had hoped I'd become." Slender neck corded under the effort, Jo was speaking quickly, too fast almost. "Not as lovable as you thought I should be, could be, or needed to be. And that would've been the moment you *too,* you'd realise I didn't have the … the whatever I'd *need* to have to be what you expected me to be." Jo's hands whip up the air above the tabletop. "Sooner or later, Mad. Don't look at me like that! Don't you fucking see what I'm on about? You, too, you would've realised that I could never have been the … the never-messes-up-never-disappoints lover that … " Jo sagged on her chair. "I just don't want to be there when that kicks in, Mad. That's all."

Maddy had kept her silence while trying to keep up with Jo as she unravelled her thoughts. "The moment *me too...* what?" She finally asked. "You said just now. You said that me, too, I'd realise something about you. Me and who else?"

Jo sniffed. She sratched the corner of an eyebrow. "My *mother*,' she eventually replied.

Maddy squinted. "Jo, your mother's been dead for some six or seven years and one of the first things you said, that first time at my place, was that you had done all your grieving. So, I'm like, what's *she* got to do with anything?"

"Oh, I'm over her *death*, all right. That took a while but, yeah, that had to happen. It's the fucking ... things she used to shout at me. That's what I'm not over." Jo returned her attention to the grey sidewalk. "And, Mad, what *I* remember of that first conversation in your kitchen is me saying something about impermanence. That's a word I remember from my days at St Joan's."

When you could've become anything you wanted to become. Maddy remembered what Jarrah had said about her sister's potential back then, the year before their mother suicided.

"Everything dies. Everything passes. And for now, I want you to leave me alone. Right here. In the streets. No attachment. Not even to a fucking boarding house. I just wanna be like, totally free. I want to ... float like a bubble."

"Right. You don't want to deal. You don't want to settle. You want to float. OK," Maddy replied tightly, struggling to keep all *her* pain and frustration out of her voice. "So ... what's wrong with living for the moment, then? Floating could be about that, huh? You and me. Like living one day at a time. Like always in the present." Jo kept her eyes averted and silence settled again over their table. "OK. I won't push it, but Jo ... " Maddy sounded resigned, "why did you leave your wallet behind?"

"Didn't leave it *behind,* Mad." Jo tried on a grin. "I left it with you." She looked at her fingernails and self-consciously frowned again.

"Jo ... Serious now. Why did you leave it in my bag?"

Jo hesitated. She sucked the last dregs of coffee from her cup. "Not sure really," she answered pensively. "Guess it was all part of the lucid insanity of the moment." A wry smile, grey eyes hard on blue: indications of Jo's deep-set frustration at her inability to set up a telepathic channel between her mind and Maddy's. And Maddy ached for her lover. *Right hard it'd be,* she thought, *squeezing what she feels into words. Into practical little words that'll make sense. Not for her benefit,* Maddy sighed wearily, *but for mine.*

Jo shifted on her seat. "That first morning when I woke up on my own, as soon as I reached for that wallet, you know, like automatically, to buy myself some breakfast, I worked it out. Having like, shed my wallet ... that was an unconscious gesture, but it turned out to be symbolic. I had to move on. I had to free myself of who I was right there and then," she explained, brow knotted tightly. "The wallet was a symbol of giving up *everything*. Not just you. Not just a room. Keep nothing. Shed everything, Mad! Wow, like a ... a ... like a snake," Jo explained, infused with her conviction. "Everything that's ... uh ... above *skin* level. To break away, totally, from the way I'd been carrying on ... for so long." She had stopped abruptly, somewhat breathless, head cocked to consider Maddy, and Maddy saw more thoughts rolling out behind Jo's eyes. Grey eyes, shiny eyes. Eyes smudged by sleepless nights and smudged by other things, too, that Maddy didn't know about. "Now that I think of it, it's a bit like a nun. They shed every earthly possession to better make contact. Oh!" she snorted. "Don't you go looking at me like that, Mad. It's not like I'm having a fucking religious meltdown, or anything. It's more like I did ... *I do* need to shed ... *habits*. Uh ... no pun intended." Grey eyes smiled tightly and something kicked again inside Maddy's chest. "Look, Mad. It's really a no brainer. I know that I've been repeating the clingy crap cycle over and over again since I was ten. Or eleven. Or twelve ... doesn't matter. I'm twenty-three, Maddy!" Grey eyes sparked. Black brows made forbidding wings. "The moment is a state, Maddy, only a *state*. Like when one's in an *altered* state. Deliriously happy. Or in trance. Or high. Or fucked. The moment is only a moment."

Maddy hesitated. "Jo, life's made up of moments," she finally retorted. "A succession of moments ... That's what makes a lifetime. What's your fucking problem with that, huh?" Intentionally, Maddy bit too hard on her lip loop.

"I don't know *what* fucking problem I have with that. I don't even know *why* I have a *fucking* problem at all. Mad," Jo stammered, patience depleted, 'let's just agree that I have ... a *fucking* problem. That's it. That's all there's to know."

Her long index finger picked at the paper napkin that still lay by the cup and saucer. More of Jo's brown-varnish-tabletop reality appeared from under the paper napkin. By the time she stopped, the napkin was just about shredded and what remained of it contrasted even more with the exposed tabletop. She looked up and blinked against Maddy's round blue gaze. "There!" she said, in lieu of further rationalisation. She patted the white shreds flat.

They had walked back down Brunswick Street, passing by the New Farm bowls club where players bowled holding bottles in their free hands. They were conspicuously young for the game, usually regarded as the last bastion for the hip-replacement-geriatric brigade.

Lawn bowls rejuvenation's got to be what's happening there, Maddy thought as she glimpsed the turf, bright green under the bright lights, and the too-young players plainly *not* wearing the traditionally compulsory white uniform. *Maybe the old sport's becoming trendy. Born again like Jo wants to be.*

Jo tugged at the hem of Maddy's cut off T-shirt.

"See there? Behind the hedge? Under those big Moreton Bay figs?"

Maddy nodded, but all she could see were very large trunks and the leafy darkness of dense foliage rustling against the pale, early evening sky. The spot Jo was pointing at was almost cave-dark under the thick and low overhanging branches. "That's where I hang some-times, like after midnight. But I don't sleep here often. The cops, they casually stroll in," she indicated the park, "like at dawn, right? just to make us move on." She paused just long enough to cross the street. "And the guys from Chubb Security, they do their rounds, too, while they lock up the toilet blocks." Jo and Maddy had reached the brightly-lit ferry landing. They walked towards the railing. "The signs in the loos say they're to be locked at 7.00 p.m. All of them," Jo went on explain-ing, "but the guards, they don't roll up before 8.30. So, that's like one extra pee in relative comfort," she added, with a grin intended for Maddy but Maddy was tensely looking straight ahead, nibbling the inside of her lip.

It was then that something familiar had shifted inside Jo. She immediately recognised the sensation, the same as the one she had felt, the first night she found herself *alone* on the Burleigh Heads beach, the first time her thoughts had returned to Maddy. That lurch in her stomach was the same as when she had first noticed the inch-wide band of pale skin etched on her wrist. The meaning of that sensation, Jo had worked out, had to do with her attachment to Maddy, her dependence on her for love *and* acceptance. It had to do with the emo-tional dependence that had to be broken.

The flip-flop sensation she felt again, as they stood side by side, simply meant that the task ahead would be arduous. *All the more the reason to persist. Better that pain now,* Jo thought, shuffling a little away from Maddy, *than that other one.* The other one, the other pain was the ineluctable pain that would leave her raw and exposed. The pain that would skittle in with the confirmation that she was irrevocably defective as a human being. Absolutely unworthy of being loved by anyone, be it mother or lover.

Maddy, elbows resting over the railing, had kept staring ahead. Reflected in the water, the lights of Hawthorne across the river had remained her focus while she listened to her own internal monologue.

She had been good. She had listened to Jo and she had, only occasionally, tried to counter some of her arguments. She hadn't lost her cool and she had to give herself credit for that. She hadn't made Jo feel cornered. She had avoided, as best she could, making her feel guilty of anything.

Not a single fucking phone call, she would've liked to shout. *Not a fucking note under the door. Nothing! What the fuck is wrong with you, huh?*

Shouting inside her head did not provide Maddy with any relief and she knew the most important thing she had to do was to *accept* whatever it was Jo had superimposed over *their* reality.

She understood that struggling to *understand* Jo might actually prove to be counterproductive. *Must be like a painting for her,* she reasoned, eyes still on the river's rippled skin. *What we had would be the fresh layer. Lovely, bright. Happy. But she thinks it's been put over an old layer that's dirty, cracking even. Old paintings go like that. They peel, they crack and bits fall off. So, she doesn't believe that our paint's gonna grip.*

Vision blurred on the lights that bobbed over the river's back, Maddy had tried to process the tip of her emotions. *She's flipped.* Maddy swallowed hard. *Let her vaporise into a fucking bubble, if that's what she wants to do with herself.* The wide City Cat ferry cut across her line of vision. *No. Can't cut her loose. Not now. Not like that.*

"You know, the ferry shelter out there?" At her side, Jo was pointing at the white open-sided structure from which the gangplank protruded, "It's actually a great place to spend the night. I mean, the new landing. The old one's fine during the day, great view of the river, quiet and all but at night it can be seriously spooky." Maddy's throat was too constricted to answer. She knew the moment of separation was looming. "A couple of nights ago," Jo rambled on, "the night of that massive storm, remember? Well, you know how everyone just rushes off soon as the sky turns that weird tinge of yellow and green? Like full of electricity?" She could only see Maddy's profile but she saw her nod. "Anyway, I came here, just after the rain started pelting down. And besides the sound 'n' light show, you know, sheets of lightning that'd crack the sky right open," she pointed north, "and awesome thunder claps that were like, *so close,* and the trees bending and the branches twisting … Totally mad." Jo's hand movements indicated the fury unleashed from the sky. "Couldn't even see the houses anymore, I mean the lights on the other bank because the rain was like a thick curtain. White. Freaky. No, not freaky," she corrected herself quickly. "More like wild-scary and beautiful at the same time. So I was all alone, right, rain bucketing down, and the river was whipped up by the wind and whipped up some more by the downpour and so I just stood at the railing over there, and watched it all until it … just vaporised. Awesome!" She looked at Maddy again but again Maddy only allowed her her profile, not her eyes. So Jo looked at the dense rust-red tufts of hair that stood up on ends in an erratic sort of way on her lover's head.

Jo winced. Before Burleigh, she would've reached over. She would've patted down each little tuft. She would've let each spring back against her fingers and she would've pulled Maddy to her and Maddy would've grinned and she would've lifted her face to Jo's. Jo's tongue would've licked her lips. She would've teased Maddy's lips with the ball of her thumb and Maddy would've let her in. She would've carressed the tip of Maddy's tongue. Maddy would've nibbled at her, the tip of her tongue deceptively strong and insistent against the fleshy part of her lover's thumb. Finger Cunting Maddy is what Maddy called Jo's finger foreplay to kissing. 'You know, as in finger counting but … yummy,' she had grinned, round blue eyes rounded some more. 'Could be Finger Lickin' too, but that's too much like KFC.' And if Burleigh Heads had never happened Jo knows that Maddy would've mumbled, *Jo, gimme your tongue.* She would've said that, warm tongue snug against the arousing tips of her lover's fingers. And Maddy would've taken Jo inside her mouth and the familiar ache of desire would've spiralled upward from Jo's cunt. And they would've kissed passionately hard. Soft hard, as they so often did, even in public, totally unconcerned by possible passers-by.

Like a restless filly, Jo stubbed the rubber tip of her Converse against the concrete slab of the ferry landing again and again. Her fingers gripped the railing and she let herself fall backwards. Long arms outstretched, slender hips thrust forward, head back, she closed her eyes briefly, just long enough to feel her hand roam the broad sweep of her lover's back. Just long enough to feel the soft muscles that padded Maddy's ribs, to feel them smooth under her fingertips. Just long enough to cup her lover's butt firmly inside both hands and bring her close, closer against her.

If Burleigh had contained only the memory of a lovely weekend away, that's what Jo and Maddy would've done, right there, at the ferry landing of New Farm park. But because something shattering had happened back there, back at Burleigh, Jo opened her eyes and did not return them to Maddy for quite a long time. She swallowed hard to dislodge the moist constriction that was making her eyes tingle. Like one at the bottom of a pit, she latched on to the thread of the conversation dropped only a moment earlier, as she would to a rope. "And ... yeah ... Like I was saying, I just curled up on one of those nice wooden benches over there and I ... slept there, on the bench." She was hoping that talking about something non-essential would ease away the tightness in her heart. "That would've been around midnight, that the rain really hit. It's only the call of all the birds around here, like the kookaburras and the light from over there ... " She pointed to the eastern reach of the river, "It's what woke me up." Maddy nodded again, jaw muscles bunching. The ferry was already midway across the river.

Watching Maddy stare straight ahead, watching her nibble on her bottom lip, had stirred up Jo so much that she was unable to snap back to the neutral dead zone where she had been safe for the past two weeks. Safe until Maddy had found her. Until Maddy had reappeared in front of her. Totally dismayed, she realised how extremely easy, still, even after two weeks in the park, it would be to put an end to her ache and kiss away the unfamiliar tightness, the unfamiliar sadness that she had noticed in Maddy the moment they had faced each other by the rubbish bin, earlier that afternoon.

It's not too late, she thought. She could still lift Maddy's chin with her hand and gently make her look at her. The thought, that thought had returned. The longing for what had been had returned. Jo looked at Maddy and she knew how safe she would feel tucked in, tight against her strong body. She sniffed. Safe because all would go away. All would disappear. *Safe, melting and oozing from the inside out,* she reminded herself. *Get a grip!*

Jo pulled herself away from the railing. She forced a breath deep inside her lungs. She shook her head. It had happened too fast, so fast she hadn't prepared for it and she hadn't prepared against it. She hadn't prepared herself against the effect that seeing Maddy would have on her and she tightened her cunt against the electric pain that was still biting into her. She tightened her cunt to stem the heat, to hold back the wetness that was already making her sex silky warm. Warm and ready for Maddy. Jo pulled herself away from the ferry landing. A part of her knew damn well how good letting go would feel. That part of her wanted to feel that good, right now. Another part of her, the damaged part of her, knew that this feeling could only be temporary. *If I light up every time I fucking feel like it, how the fuck do I wipe out the craving, huh? If I feed it everytime?* Jo grunted, then she remembered that she hadn't had a shower in two weeks.

"Fuck this shit!" she snarled.

Maddy looked up from the river. She came over to where Jo was standing, looking angry, arms at her side. *No, not angry. More like disoriented.*

"How you set for music?" she asked non-committally. The time was nearing when she'd have to let Jo go back to whatever had become her after-dark routine in the streets of New Farm. She knew not to overstay her welcome. She had already suggested dinner, locally, but Jo had refused. *Don't corner her,* is what the policewoman had said. Maddy had not insisted.

"Discman's still working and I got Badmotorfinger. Had them with me in my bag, you know, back … at the beach. So, yeah, that's holding. Knew the lyrics by heart before and now … well makes no diff." Jo grinned. "Still good."

"Want me to bring you … uh … Ten or Downward Spiral or– "

Grey eyes hard on blue. "No, Mad." Jo's tone was abrupt as she squinted at Maddy who sucked in her lip loop. "If you're nice," Jo flashed a little smile to soothe the bite she knew her tone had inflicted, "I'll show you one of *my* real hideaways … Another day."

Jo was about to disappear into the night of the park with only the contents of her bag as worldly possessions and whatever spare change she might still have in her pocket. Earlier on that afternoon, while they were still at their sidewalk table, Jo had told Maddy that with the fifty-dollar bill that she had pulled out of her back pocket, she had bought herself a tube of toothpaste, a tooth brush, a cake of soap, a comb, a roll-on deodorant and a little bottle of shampoo.

"And a nailbrush and fingernail clippers. That's got to be the hardest thing to keep clean, fingernails … being outdoors all the time," she had added, circumspect. "And whatta you know, that's the first thing I fucking lose." Before Maddy had a chance to ask about the lost nailbrush, Jo had already moved on. "No towel, though. Too bulky to fit in. I'm not quite ready to settle into the bag lady thing. No crap plastic bags all around me. No shopping cart," she had added lightly to ease the tightness out of Maddy's eyes. "So the deal is, what doesn't fit in *this* here bag ... " She had lifted her rainbow-clothed backpack. "If it don't fit in here, it ... don't fit *full stop*." Maddy remembered the thin, small and ever so absorbent chamois towels she had seen in a camping store somewhere but, front teeth hard on the lip loop, she hesitated too long and the moment passed without her mentioning them to Jo.

Jo had not returned to *Fairfield House* for she instinctively knew that once back in her things, meagre as they were, so close to Maddy's place, so close to Maddy, her will to see this *thing* out would've failed her. At the very least, she would've hopped on the train Toowoomba-bound, back to Jarrah's again, as always when in crisis, though none of her crises had ever been as urgent, as compelling, as immediate as the one that had struck her back at the Burleigh Heads picnic table. None had been so powerful as the one brought on by that light bulb being turned off in the apartment she had rented with Maddy on the sixth floor facing the esplanade.

Maddy opened her own backpack. She pulled out a pair of Jo's acid-washed jeans that she had rolled tightly, a sarong, two pairs of undies – *In the sun, they'll dry in a couple of hours,* she had thought - one of Jo's favourite T-shirts and a thin Indian cotton calico skirt, the only skirt Maddy had ever seen her wear.

"Here," she said, handing the neat pile over to Jo. "Thought you might enjoy a bit of a change." Jo looked at the bright colours and looked away. "Jo, take them. Won't change anything about what ... about what you're on about. Please, take them. They'll *fit* in your bag. You do need a change of clothes, for heaven's sake."

Jo reached out for the clothes and nuzzled the clean linen. She smiled the smile that creased the corners of her lips. "A blast from the past," she said, inhaling the clean fragrance. "Yeah, thanks."

Without giving Maddy the chance to say or add more, Jo wheeled around on her rubber soles. Long-legged, loose-kneed, she strode over the grassy slope. Too quickly her black T-shirt and army-greens blended her into the night.

Maddy ran after her. "Jo! Hold on." Jo turned around and waited for Maddy to catch up. "Here," Maddy said, "keep this with you. Just for a while, huh?" She lay her tiny mobile phone on top of the rolled pile of clothes that Jo hadn't yet stuffed in her bag. "It'll fit in your pocket." Jo shook her head. "It'll fit in one of those big pockets," she insisted, pointing at the deep army-style pocket sewn on the outside of Jo's trousers. "Won't even know it's there. Just in case you need ... anything. Jo? Just for a while? Huh? Please?"

"No, Mad. *That* I can't do."

"What you mean, *Can't do?* It's just in case you need someth– "

"Whatever I need, I'll have to deal with it from here, on my own. Maddy, please. You go on now. It's not something you have to understand. It's just ... "

Jo turned her back again on Maddy and strode deeper into the night.

That night Maddy drove to St Lucia, to the University of Queensland pool, the only public pool she knew would be open at that time of night. She had to cleanse herself, of herself, of Jo. She needed to immerse herself, submerge, and get as close to drowning as she could. She needed to drown Jo's voice, Jo's words and the hard-edged determination behind her words. And the steely glint in her grey eyes. *It's not something you have to understand* by way of cutting Maddy loose.

Maddy needed to push herself, her muscles, till they screamed like all of her was already screaming inside her head. Maybe, she hoped, all these screams after a hundred-lap workout, would dim her other pain, that new pain, that of having found Jo, that of not knowing how to deal with her resolve to stay on the street.

Being aware that she was missing the point didn't stop Maddy from asking out loud, "Why won't she fucking sleep in *my* garden, huh, if she wants to rough it? At least she'd be safe there."

Somewhere in the sixth set of ten laps, Maddy stopped counting her tumble-turns. Her last conscious thought, expelled as she pushed off the tiled wall, went along the lines that it would just be a matter of time before Jo got aggressed, raped or killed in that fucking park. Everybody knew that New Farm park was like every park in any major city, a dero hang-out, an area punks prowled for easy preys to roll. *Then, what? What will I do then, for her?*

Maddy forced all the bubbles out of her lungs. She saw them rise in front of her nose and when her head broke again through the surface, when her mouth gulped more of the damp air, she split her focus. One powerful stroke after the other, each drove all thoughts out of her mind. Her body took over. Her brain segmented itself off. Neocortex bypassing the tearing of her muscles, a different part of her brain took over the same muscles and her breathing to keep her going on deeper into her flight towards physical oblivion.

*****

FIVE

"Sweetie ... " Viv waited till Maddy looked up. "You look like death warmed up, but barely."

"Right."

"That's it? Just, *Right?* That's all I get from you?"

"*Right* means, *I know.*" Maddy's tone was gentle but, to Viv, it suggested a huge weariness. "And I say, *I know,* because I *feel* like shit. And that's not even warmed up shit. I'm maxed-out, Viv. Squashed, turd-flat."

"Right," replied Viv.

Maddy's lips curled up a little. "What, *Right,* is all *I* get?" she mimicked.

Viv smiled. The two women sat in silence, both of them nursing a cup of steamy hot tea. *Terry's All Treads,* in gold letters, was wrapped around the circumference of the identical black ceramic mugs.

"Flash, huh?"

"What?" Maddy questioned, blue eyes in a pale shade of blue, not the usual porcelain doll-blue that was theirs.

The older woman raised her mug. "I knew you hadn't even noticed." Maddy looked at her dumbly. "You really *didn't* notice. How can you *not* notice? The mugs!" Viv raised hers and looked at it appreciatively. "For our best repeat customers. A little marketing idea of mine."

Maddy moved to lift her own cup and winced. "I really think I overdid it last night." She peered at the black and gold mug. "Flash, all right. They for Christmas or something?" She rearranged her face so as to replace the grimace of pain that was still lingering on her lips with something more appropriate. "Bit late or ... What, only ten months early. Which?"

"Neither. We'll send them to our special customers on their *birthday.* Get it? That'd be more of a treat for them than at Christmas when everyone's busting a gut to shower everyone with pens, calendars, and fridge magnets and what-nots."

"Absolutely. Birthdays are in. Christmas and cheap commercial ploys are out."

Viv peered at the young redhead seated across the desk from her. "You having me on? You must be feeling better then." Maddy pretended not to see the *What am I going to do with you* look of concern in Viv's eyes.

Maddy used to bounce inside the tyre bay like a big puppy on two legs. Just about did cartwheels every morning. "Always quick with a joke and a smile, our Maddy," she'd often tell her husband. And as she watched Maddy slump, she worried that with all that business, she'd end up making herself sick. And she fretted because she knew there was no one to look after Maddy once Maddy dragged herself out of Terry's All Treads. Maddy looked up just as the older woman looked away. "You don't go worryin' about me, huh, Viv? I'll be right. It's all that swimming that did it last night. You'd think with all the physical stuff I do 'round here– "

"Different muscles, must be."

"You're not wrong. Different muscles that I obviously don't have much of."

"What you need is a good soak in a bathtub and lots of Epsom salts. That'll fix you."

"Viv, the only muscles I can soak are my butt muscles. That's if I sit in the shower recess and– "

"Awh … aren't you the funny one!"

"I don't have a bathtub."

"Well, we do. And I have the salts, too. Why don't you come home when we close shop and I'll fix you a nice bath while Terry– "

"You feeling clucky again?" Maddy interjected too quickly. "You missing your daughters or somethin'?"

Viv looked at the young redhead and shook her head slowly. "I miss them … sometimes, yes, but," she tried holding on to Maddy's eyes a moment longer. "But not right now. It's you I'm concerned about and I– "

"Look, Viv … " Round eyes in a pale shade of blue snap back to Viv's. "I appreciate your … the invite but, truth is, I'm too wiped-out to even think of chewing … anything. The bath thing … sure, that sounds real nice and all but then … I'll hate the drive back. It's not everybody's choice, you know … acreage at Munbullen. I'd fall asleep at the wheel."

"Well, then you could stay the night. It's not as if we're short of bedroo– "

Maddy reached for Viv's hands wishing she, too, had been one of that woman's daughters. It would've been different then. If Viv had been *her* mother, instead of Maddy being the daughter of a mother who wanted nothing to do with her, she would have taken up the offer. She would've spent the evening curled up and snug against this warm and generous woman and, come morning, she would've been all patched up and fighting fit. But she wasn't this woman's daughter and she really hated the thought of driving all the way *there* and *back*. She already had had a long drive into the night that week, coming back from Toowoomba.

"Look," she began, keen to make it up to Viv, "if you've got a minute, I can tell you about Jo. Saw her last night."

"I thought you might've. How is she?"

"Oh, physically she looks ... all right ... except for shadows under her eyes like she's not sleeping much." The image of Jo, shiny-eyed, but paler than usual, superimposed itself in front of her eyes. "She's very thin, right, but I don't think she's any thinner. Never ate much at the best of times," Maddy explained, talking to her hands held, wrists loose, on the edge of Viv's desk. "Always leaving half of everything on her plate, she is. But it's the hair." Maddy looked up. "I guess, that's a bit of a give-away now. That and her fingernails. I know that'd drive her nut– "

"What's with her hair?"

"Well, it's like, more *hacked* than cut." Head cocked, Viv waited for more. "See, she has short hair, right, nice and black. She cuts it herself in an uneven sort of way, intentionally, right?" Viv nodded. "Like *short* short bits and *longer* short bits and yeah, well ... it hangs well on her." Maddy blinked. The tip of her nose began to swell because her throat had become constricted. She drew in her bottom lip and Viv, recognising the tension in the young woman, reached across to rub her shoulders.

Maddy looked up, big blue eyes magnified by welling tears. Chin wobbly, she sniffed and blinked. Large tears rolled down her cheeks and fell flat on her grime-stained overalls. She rubbed the heel of her hands against her eye-sockets and blinked again. Viv held a tissue for her while running a comforting hand over Maddy's hair, from her temple where some hairs were almost baby-fine to the back of her head, smoothing it down as she would a little child's. "You see ... " Maddy explained, voice breaking, "she doesn't ... she doesn't have scissors ... and she doesn't have a mirror ... so she took to her hair with ... with fingernail clippers." Her head dipped and she had to blow her nose which she did noisily. "And she did it in one ... of the toilet blocks and you know how ... public loos, they don't have proper mirrors, right? Like it's only metal or something." Viv nodded. "Right. So … the way her hair's cut now looks … it looks … weird." Maddy sniffed again and ran the dirty cuff of her sleeve across her eyes. "She says she … she only washes it once a week, under a tap in the park. She wants to … to make the bottle last. That's what she says."

"What, the shampoo bottle?" Maddy nodded. "Don't they give them basic necessities in those Salvation Army refuges?"

"Hasn't stayed put long enough to really check that out. Not past the first meal. They didn't have a bed for her. There's only like enough beds for something like twenty homeless women in all of Brisbane. That's what she reckons someone there told her."

Viv shook her head. "Can't be right, surely, when you hear of all these poor women who've got to leave their own homes because of their husbands bashing them. There's got to me more than twen– "

"It's different, I think. If you're a victim of this … domestic violence thing, you call a number and I think you get a bed in a women's refuge or something like that. For homeless women, there's hardly anything at all."

"Why not?"

"Don't know why not. Maybe there aren't that many … women … out there."

Some time later, Maddy replayed for Viv some of the conversation she had had with Jo over three cups of coffee at Rosati's, because Jo hadn't wanted her to pay for a dinner that she thought, as a bona fide street person, she shouldn't be having.

Jo had tried to have her first dinner as a homeless at the Salvation Army soup kitchen. She had looked up the address in the phonebook because, though it was listed in her own little address book under *Salvarm,* the address book was not with her. It was in her room at *Fairfield House.* She didn't fully know at the time, a few months earlier, why she had looked it up, why she had written it down in her address book. She just had.

Once there, she was spooked by all the men there, unkempt, in various states of disarray. Many were filthy, even the younger ones. Many wore Band-Aids or dirty bandages either on their face or around the hands area. Many were missing teeth. Many had suspicious rashes across their face, crawling out of their stubble and beards. Many seemed under the influence of something or other, or completely dejected. *Unnaturally quiet,* she had thought at the time. The old, scary looking ones leered at her in a lewd sort of way. To her, they seemed desperate for a blowjob.

There were hardly any women there at all and the ones she spotted were not only entrenched in a sea of smelly males but also looked equally off-putting. Maddy didn't dare ask Jo what she had expected to find in a soup kitchen. But as it turned out, Jo hadn't stayed there long enough to explore further options.

The dining room was hot. It was full of greasy food odours. Full of the oddest collection of people she had seen but only in movies. Faces, she said, that reminded her of the ones cast in medieval plots like 'In the Name of the Rose'. She hadn't quite freaked out but only hung around long enough to grab a bun and a little square of butter wrapped in foil. She sat on a bench to get into that bun but she was accosted twice in a very short space of time. So she kept on walking.

Once in Ann Street, she bought some grass from a dealer who beckoned her from the shadows. As he handed her a stick of Red, she handed him twenty dollars from the change she still had in her pocket because he had asked for twenty-five. He rubbed his chin, giving her a long once-over. Ultimately he handed her a foil, taking it upon himself to suggest where she could spend the night.

His crib was only around the corner and he'd be giving up the shift within the hour. All his regulars had already visited and passing trade was slow, that particular night being a Tuesday. Tuesday night in The Valley. She glared at him, wondering why he'd even said that to her. And she blushed, realising that she must already have a bit of that stray-cat look about her, not that she had ever been one to be confused with the twin-set, pretty-in-pink-brigade. Urban grunge at the best of times. Clean but wrinkled, second-hand grunge, was her preferred style of clothes.

From a nearby tobacco shop she bought some rolling skins. She turned into Brunswick Street because the thought occurred to her that it would lead her to the river. She had not realised what a long stretch of a street Brunswick was, never having had to walk the length of it.

Once Jo reached the park, she had been totally puffed and desperate for her first blow in months. *Thirteen months clean. My fucking personal best.* She had given up blasting roaches on the way to Brisbane. After her father had sold the house on Neilson Street where Isabel had suicided. After she had turned her back to the Toowoomba range where Jarrah had chosen to remain, ready to roll, Jo had shaken the last little bits of brittle buds on to a skin, but it was obvious that there wasn't enough to make a joint, not even a skinny. So she simply crunched up paper and bits of grass together and turfed the lot out of the train window. *Welcome to Briz,* she muttered. *Stone-sober clean.* She snorted at the memory of how Jarrah had been so proud of her for that. That night, though, the second since she had run away on Maddy back at Burleigh, if Jo hadn't bumped into a dealer, she would've set out looking for a place to connect.

So it was that, on her first night on the streets, as Jo had neared the end of Brunswick Street, a short walk away from where she had scored, Jo discovered the night calm of New Farm Park, the calm of most parks at a time when most people are tucked at home in front of the tube. She sat on one of the little benches that face the river and she sparked the joint she had just finished skinning, the first in thirteen months. She inhaled deeply before suspending her breathing. She inhaled again, deeply.

Jo sighed and let her muscles relax the length of her lanky frame. Each time she exhaled more of the tension, more of the confusion she had so swiftly trapped and bottled up inside her, more of the fear that had harnessed *her,* she almost became one with the night breeze. And the breeze felt good against her skin. Soft river sounds floated back to her through the silence of the park. She closed her eyes and gave in to the emptying feeling.

Maddy, as she had last seen her, on her way to the flat from where she was going to quickly bring back a bottle of brandy and two plastic tumblers, Maddy passed through the interstice cleared by the smoke inside Jo's brain. Through the eye of a needle, Maddy travelled to Jo, rust-red hair standing on ends, the glint of the silver lip loop splitting her cheeky grin. And eyes closed, Jo smiled at her.

She smiled at the face she loved so much and touched the constellation of freckles on her lover's cheekbones. She kissed the corners of Maddy's eyes, both of them, to make her smile because there was a sadness in those eyes and there was hurt in those eyes where there only ever was blue - a happy blue, deep shades of porcelain blue.

In front of Jo, though, with the river as backdrop, the blue in Maddy's eyes did not sparkle. So Jo kissed Maddy's eyelids because she couldn't kiss her eyes, not really.

"How did you get so sad, Mad?" Jo asked the night air. The breeze had nothing to answer. Close to her fingernails, the roach was burning hot. Eyes still closed, she sucked in the last lungful of THC before slouching more comfortably on the park bench.

Face lifted to the sky, she studied the canopy of leaves, how it swayed ever so slowly, so silently above her head. Dark patches of leaves high up there. Pale patches of night sky sliding softly to connect. The susurrus of tall sea-weeds, swirling. Slithering back to touch the–

"Hey, pretty face. Wanna do a B?"

Eyes wider than a moth's wings, pupils dark, Jo had sat bolt upright on the bench, heart thumping. "What the fuck! What you want?" she asked sharply, senses spun around too quickly.

"Hey, man!" the man said, hands splayed in front of him, "Cool chick asleep on bench. The river, the moon. Hey ... what's a dude like me likely to want, huh?"

"No idea." Jo peered at the man standing in front of her. Youngish. White. Clean-shaven. Big baggy gear. Metal jewelry. Rapper poseur. She swung her legs off the bench but unsure as to what she should do next, she stayed seated. "Man, you've just crashed through my cloud ... in a major way."

He moved closer to her and took in the light-coloured eyes, the punk-dark hair. His eyes roamed lower over her breasts, small under the clingy dark T-shirt. They travelled lower over the small creases of her stomach left bare by the low-waisted khaki greens. His eyes glided the length of her thighs. Finally, he shifted his weight on the other foot and grinned appreciatively at her rangy body.

"What say I make it up to you, huh? S'no good frightening a little babe what's all alone in a park. Look," he said, dropping his weight right next to her on the bench. "Forget about peeling me some dough for a B." His knee touched hers. "I say we blow it together, huh? My shout." He slid his hips forward on the bench and from the front pocket of his baggy jeans, he retrieved a matchbox, the smallest dose of dope that can be bought from a dealer. "First the box, then the skins, then the– "

"Whoa there, buddy! Too quick for me." Jo gathered her bag and stood up.

"Hey, girl, don't you be goin' anywhere on me now. Just got started. S'not like you gotta go nowhere in a hurry, right?"

Matchbox half-opened in one hand, the man grabbed at Jo with the other. She half-fell on his lap. His cock was already stiffened. She jerked her hand away and jumped to her feet, flicking her hand as if to dislodge something nasty that had gotten stuck to it. The man saw her expression. His easy smile turned. He dropped the matchbox back in his pocket.

The fuzzy feeling was receding. "Fuck *off!*" she said sharply.

Senses finally on alert, Jo moved away from the bench. The lamp posts gave off enough light to allow her a scan of the patch of park directly ahead. She spun around. As far as she could see, though the little boats bobbed sleepily on the river, though the little park benches were watching over them, there was no one around. *Where's the fucking pleb when you need them?*

She had set off over the grassy embankment to reach the wider, more public area of the park, the man close behind her. Five long strides and she reached the flat ground, broken here and there by flowerbeds and to the right by some sort of gazebo. Most trees, all the tall ones, seemed to have receded to the periphery of the park. *Not a fucking* anyone *in sight.*

The man's breath was on her neck. Her skin broke in goosebumps.

"C'mon, babe," he whispered in her ear. "Don't be so hard on me." He came around to face her. His hand was in his pocket. "What the fuck, Momma, making a dude like me run in the state I'm in." Breathing fast he closed in on her, lips hard against hers. He forced her hand against his cock.

Jo felt the wave of nausea. She felt it shape itself deep inside her stomach. She felt it rise and uncoil like an inquisitive snake. "Look, mate, you're ... You're on to the wrong chick here." She pushed his chin away hard with the heel of her other hand. "Nothing personal, buddy." His neck was exposed. "Just that I don't do *boys.* So why don't yo– "

Before she could finish her sentence, a spurt of vomit exploded from deep within her. The man sprang backward, horrified disgust distorting his features. "Sick cunt! You fuckin' bitch," he yelled.

Eyes wide, Jo wiped her mouth with the back of her hand. Her head had cleared instantly. She tucked her bag under an arm and, low like a rugby man to the goal posts, she ran and ran, while the man stood, too overcome by a primeval repulsion to do more than tentatively touch under his chin and flick away what remained of the bun Jo's stomach had not quite finished digesting.

Back at Rosati's, two weeks later, and over several cups of coffee, Jo had filled in some blanks for Maddy, but she had also edited out a few frames which meant that Maddy went away not knowing that Jo had picked up the old habit again. Not knowing that it was more through celestial intervention than clever management that Jo hadn't been badly hurt on her first night alone in the park. Almost hurt, almost raped, almost killed –Maddy would have said - in the very area she was now calling home. Jo edited her story right after the frame that showed her walking away from the Savation Army soup kitchen and before the one that showed her looking around for a safe place for the night.

She had run out of the park, and was almost out of breath by the time she turned into a side street, then another, lungs screaming for air. She let herself fall behind a parked car and sat momentarily safe in its shadow.

Some time later, she realised that the chamferboard house across the street was dark and all buttoned up, though most of the others showed some light. Most also had cathode tubes flickering through open back porches and wide-open windows. It was another hot and steamy night and the good people in Welsby Street were liquefying slowly under their ceiling fans that could do no better than rearrange great swirls of humid heat above their heads.

Jo pushed herself off the ground, crossed the quiet street and casually peered into the ramshackle backyard she could glimpse from the side of the front gate. Carport, empty. Trees, shrubs, bushes. High besser-block wall, concrete protection at the back. Diminishing in height, one block fewer on each layer until the lower section, street-side, only reached hip-high. *Not much protection there,* she thought. *Weird way to go about fencing.*

Casually, she cruised by the front gate and the low end of the separating wall. No one was watching. Quickly she tossed her rainbow bag over the low part of the concrete wall and straddled it, one long leg easily touching the ground on the other side. Hugging the shadows, she moved quickly to the nearest shrub and stood still, heart in mouth. Nothing stirred. *No dog,* she thought belatedly. In a crouch, she resumed her progress towards the trees at the far corner of the garden. She squatted. She listened. Something slithered near her foot. She prayed there were no blue-tongue lizards around. Her heart beat faster again.

Blue-tongue lizards repulsed her in a way no other native creatures did, not even goannas. Thick, shiny scale-less head. Black, still and slanted eyes. Chunky, truncated snakes. She didn't like the rustling sound they made dragging their body on the ground, in spite of their legs. Maybe they repulsed her, too, because once in Maddy's garden she had come across one of these big blue-tongue lizards riding on the back of another, mounting it while erratically biting the other creature's head, drawing blood with each new bite.

Nothing else stirred. Jo let go of her breath as she let herself drop to a sitting position. From a house down the street, a dog barked. Another answered close by, but the garden and the house sat stone-silent and dark. She drew in her legs and squatted, rocking in the darkness of the garden, arms linked around her knees. She tasted the rancid taste inside her mouth and on her hand from when she had tried to wipe it off her lips.

Suddenly, she realised she desperately wanted three things, to shower - inside and out, to brush her teeth and to make herself a cup of strong coffee. And it was at that moment that the meaning of what it meant to live in the streets began to dawn on her.

Beyond the various dangers that lurked at night, anywhere, in wait for the unsuspecting woman, Jo could no longer satisfy any of her most basic needs. That first night on her own, Jo had neither toothpaste nor toothbrush. She certainly was in no more of a position to brew herself a cup of coffee than to relax under the warm jets of a showerhead. She contemplated the thought of a coffee at one of the terraces she had passed along the way. She did, after all, have enough change left to shout herself one. She could almost taste the strong Arabica, hot on her tongue, but she didn't move.

Having just found herself a piece of turf that she believed safe for the night, Jo didn't dare leave it in case re-access became problematic. Because she had finally stepped out of the frame, she contained the urge to jump back over the wall. She was no longer 'one of them', cool grunge chick at a sidewalk cafe. Already she felt different from the trendies she had passed there, at the edge of the park. Already she was as an outsider. She patted the loose cloth of the army greens over her thighs. Under her hand, the first telling wear-and-tear stains stood out, even under the distant light from the street. And Jo understood, perhaps for the first time in her adult life, the real meaning of the word grunge. Grunge according to the Webster. She looked at her greens, nodding in acknowledgement. She chuckled in the darkness because she had realised the deeper ramification of going about with stained clothes.

She realised she had finally made it outside of the square. She realised that it was too late to go back, that even if she wanted to pretend it wasn't so, her clothes would betray her. So she curled up on the ground, under overhanging branches and, for the first time since she had left Maddy, closed her eyes without seeing her.

Jo is fifteen: Jo holds the navy blue uniform skirt tightly against the back of her legs and plops on the rug. She crosses her legs and watches Isabel, her mother.

Her eyes are closed. The book she had been reading lies open against *her* chest. Her hands are folded over the spine. From where she is sitting, Jo can see that the book her mother had been reading has a hard cover, a dark blue cloth cover with gold letters, but she can't make out the title from where she is sitting. She would have been able to make out the title printed on the spine under her mother's hands if she had sat at the other end of the sofa, next to her mother's feet, but she hadn't wanted to do that. Jo looks at her mother's thin frame wrapped in a black silk kimono, stretched on the velvet green sofa. She's only asleep, Jo thinks, knowing that if she wasn't really asleep, if she was dead, she'd most likely look the same.

Jo spends a lot of time thinking about death. Hers and her mother's. On the one hand, she knows she's not likely to die any time soon, herself. On the other, she knows her mother *could* die any time. One of the differences that exists between Jo and her mother is that, though there have been times Jo would have liked to die, her mind was blank as to how that might best be achieved. Oh, she knows she can slash her wrists in the bathtub and she knows she can climb on the roof and pretend to fly to the ground but such scenarios just don't feel right for her. She's been thinking that maybe *she* doesn't have the suicide gene in her DNA.

For her mother, it's different. Her mother, Isabel, has a death-scenario all ready to be activated. Not a spectacular death that will leave her body dangling in a convenient place. Nothing messy for others to scrape off the walls or off the floor, as would be the case if she were to blow her brains out with her husband's handgun. Much easier on everyone, she will simply inject herself with all the morphine vials she has secreted for that purpose.

The vials aren't a secret to Jo. She has seen them, side by side, in a cigar box, on the floor of Isabel's wardrobe. Nobody else knows about the four vials tucked away in that box behind the fixed panel of the wardrobe, behind the one that holds the big mirror. Not even Jarrah. Only Jo and Jemma Wiggings, the Head Nurse at the oncology ward, know of the vials.

Jo knows because she's the only one who ever goes inside her mother's bedroom. Not her father, whose room is down the hall and who doesn't come home anymore until he thinks Jo and her mother are likely to be asleep. Not Jarrah, who doesn't live at home anymore. Not Jane, the cleaning woman, who only comes once a week. Jo has found the vials because she had been looking for them or, if not precisely for them, she had been looking for a lethal thing that her mother may have stashed away for the purpose of killing herself.

The last time Isabel had been admitted to the hospital, she had a private word with Jemma, the Head Nurse, with whom she went back a long way, way back to the school days at St Joan's when they were both prefects. Later, they connected again during their university days and Jemma had turned up again, two or three decades later, as a regular at the bridge evenings Jo's mother hosted on the third Tuesday of every month.

In the name of their many years of friendship, that woman, whom Jo knew, but not personally, had helped her mother spirit away what vials she chose not to have on the days she felt strong enough to confront her pain unaided, preferring to save these vials for later. For the *greater* need she'd have of them … later. No one knew except for Jo because, as is often the case with bright children, Jo hadn't needed to be told to know.

Cross-legged on the rug, Jo looks on as her mother rests, fairly sure she'll look the same after she'll have emptied all the vials in the syringe that lies, away from the vials, in its unopened wrapper tucked inside the shadows of a top drawer. *Four vials today,* Jo thinks, *but there might be more vials in the cigar box when the time comes unless, of course, the time comes tonight.*

Jo's black hair has fallen into her eyes. She pushes it back away from her cheeks. Another thought crosses her mind. *There might be enough of the stuff left inside that syringe. There might just be enough for me, too.* She looks at her own thin wrists and how they stick out of the pale blue sleeve of her St Joan's uniform. She pinches her thin calf muscle and rubs her fingertips over a protruding anklebone hidden by a ribbed, white uniform sock. *I don't suppose I'd need much to go under.* Jo unfolds her coltish legs and stands up, loosening her skirt on the way up. *This room needs light. Can't be good for her to spend so much time in the dark.*

One hand already poised on the plantation-styled shutter, Jo suspends the motion. "Will she or won't she," she whispers, eyes back to the supine form of her mother. *Will she be upset with me for letting light inside the room or will she smile and say what a wonderful idea I've had?* She shifts her weight on the other foot and considers the most likely outcome.

Jo takes in a big breath and pulls both shutters towards her, folding them back, one at the time, on their hinges. Eyes shut tight against the sudden burst of clear sunlight, she holds on to her breath. Even from behind her eyes shut tight, Jo knows her mother is stirring. She hears the rustle of her silk kimono.

"And what might Little Jo be doing with her eyes scrunched up so tightly?"

Jo lets go of her breath and beams a smile. Her mother is not upset with her. She opens her eyes and lopes to her mother's side. When Isabel Brenner calls her daughter by the pet name of Little Jo, this is the clue that she's feeling well. When Isabel Brenner feels well, she is good to her younger daughter.

More than her father who is seldom around, more than her older sister who only visits over lunch when she does, Jo has had to learn to gauge what reaction any of her actions are likely to trigger. She has learnt to anticipate a whirlwind of vituperations that may or *may not* eventuate at any given moment.

Isabel smiles. She sits up and pats the space on the sofa near her hip. "Come and sit here. Let me have a good look at you," she says with motherly tenderness.

Jo flops on the sofa next to her mother. Isabel makes a mental note to make an appointment for her daughter at the hairdresser's. "We need to do something drastic with that hair of yours, my little darling. I hadn't realised we had let it go so long. Never mind. James will know how to shape it again into that lovely bobbed cut. Have you been here long?"

"Oh, no," Jo lies energetically. "Actually, I just got here and I was deciding whether or not you were ready to be woken up."

"Well, if my little girl's already home from school it signifies that the best part of the day's already come and gone." Isabel reaches for her daughter's dark head and pats the top of it, gently, slowly. "So I'd say it's high time for me to have a look at what's left of it, huh? Before it all … fades away. Don't you think?"

"Absolutely." Jo grins a smile that etches two parallel little grooves on either side of her lips. "The light's still bright but the sun's all soft so, if you wanted to, we could walk through the garden."

"Splendid idea," replies Isabel, lovely grey eyes still tender on her daughter's face. She notices Jo's pale cheeks. *That girl needs to go to bed a lot earlier than she does. Too much late-night studying.* "But first, tell me how was your day?"

"Just fine," Jo says. Absent-mindedly, with a fingertip she traces the shimmers of the silk gown stretched over her mother's legs. "Would've come home earlier but Miss Shay asked me to stay back. She thought I should help one of the other girls becau– "

"And what could be so terribly wrong with this other girl that she can't help herself?"

"Oh, it's OK, Mama. I didn't mind," Jo replied a little too quickly. "Anyway, there's really nothing wrong with Chrissie, the girl, except that she's new and she's always hated Maths and she's finding the catching up a bit too much. What with the other– "

"Oh, well, if you don't mind, then … I don't mind," Isabel smiles into bright, eager grey eyes, eyes that look painfully like her own. Like hers did *before*. Before her life cracked around her like old varnish. Something kicked inside her stomach. "In any case, it's nice to do something for other people, isn't it? Besides, going over what *you* know and being clear enough about it to explain it to someone else is as good a way as any to review and internalise the … stuff."

"That's exactly what Miss Shay said."

"Well, there you go then." Isabel smiles. "And how is the wonderful Miss Shay these days, anyway? It's been a long time since you've … "

Isabel doesn't know Miss Shay, Jo's mathematics teacher, not any more than she's known any of her daughter's other teachers. Though her heartfelt resolution at the beginning of every school year, ever since Jo began the long haul from primary school, was to attend the once-a-year parent/teacher evenings, Isabel had yet to attend the first one. She still manages to gloss over her lacking in front of other mothers by reminding everyone that St Joan's, being one of the best girls' schools in Queensland, maybe even better than those ritzy ones in Victoria and New South Wales, had efficiently shepherded her daughter through all those wonderful teachers who certainly wouldn't *want* her, Isabel Brenner, to tell them how to do their job. 'That's the thing, isn't it?' she'd often tell her bridge-playing friends, 'When the family *can* afford it, there is no better education than a private school education.'

An ex-St Joan girl herself, Isabel had pushed and prodded until Gerald, her husband, had capitulated, agreeing that Jarrah and much later, Joanna, would be enrolled at St Joan's as early as Year One.

'It didn't do wonders for her older sister, but Little Jo has really come into her own.' Isabel was very proud of the fact that her second daughter was one year younger than the majority of students in her year group, that she had been elected the Year Eleven Rep and that, generally, she thrived on achievements, be they in the classroom or on the sports field. Why, she might even be next year's School Captain in her Senior year.

"So, what d'you say, Mama? A walk in the garden and then I can tell you about our netball non-event and you won't believ– "

Something kicks again inside Isabel but whatever it is, this time it stems from a murkiness that is different from the weariness she felt only a moment ago, about her faded beauty and hers that had become a hollow existence. This time, the irritation is more immediate. Its source is her daughter's excited chirps about some teenage irrelevance that is about to make the moment slip away from her.

"So?" Jo stands up, holding out a gallant hand to her mother. "Shall we do the garden rounds, my Lady?"

Isabel ignores her daughter's hand. "We will, dear. Not just now. In fact, I am feeling a little weary after all this chattering."

Sensing too late that she must have become careless at some point in the conversation, Jo looks at her mother more carefully. She can tell her mother is already closing up on her.

"Mama," Jo asks softly. "Would you like me to get you anything? Earl Grey? Rum and raisin ice cream? I stopped for some on the way home." Grey eyes bright.

Isabel is feeling the familiar heat rise up along the length of her body. The heat is familiar, the anticipated outcome, too, is familiar. The middle part is also familiar, and though that middle part is the part she knows she *wants* to alter the most, she cannot harness the energy that it would require for her to do so.

"No, dear. Maybe you should just leave me alone … for now. We'll talk later." Beads of sweat break on Isabel's forehead.

Jo rises again. "OK, then. I'll go– "

Isabel snaps back. "And where would you be off to so quickly then?" The frown that tightens her grey eyes isn't lost on her daughter.

"Oh, nowhere really," Jo answers quickly, keeping her tone soft and easy. "I mean, I thought I'd go up to my room and make a dent in my homework, but I can do that later." Jo plops back on the sofa near her mother's shins.

"Well, my girl, don't let me stop you from your obligations to the world out there. It certainly needs you more than me." The voice is cutting and cold and bitchy. Jo knows not to look at her mother, not to look *into* her mother's eyes, not now. Not anymore tonight. The gentleness that had been there, in the lovely grey eyes, only a moment ago, she knows is gone. The skin around those eyes, she knows, is tight and parched because Isabel's jaw is clenched, because her face is closed. "After all … " the voice rises and the tone becomes too highly pitched, " … that fucking world will be *around you* a lot longer than I will."

Jo flinches. The cigar box and its four vials tucked away in a corner of her mother's wardrobe flash behind her eyes. She blinks. Her heart thuds inside her chest. She knows her mother has just thrown a cheap shot but even a cheap shot, if it is prophetic, cannot be discarded with a simple shrug. Besides, the F word always hits Jo in the guts when it's spat out carrying her mother's voice. It almost physically winds her. It sounds so different *then,* very different from when her school friends say fuck or fucking.

When Isabel spits these words out, they are hard, vicious, truly foul, so Jo absorbs herself with the patterns of the richly coloured rug that spreads across the living room floor, aware, too aware, of her mother's shins against her thigh. "So, by all means, go! Run to it. Do whatever it is you have to do. Go perform for the fucking world. Go embrace it." And with a sudden movement, Isabel's shins connect with her daughter's side, with the soft part between rib and hipbone.

Jo has anticipated the kick. One knee is already hovering close to the carpet. It doesn't hurt. Her mother never hurts her. It's just that sometimes, she moves brusquely, without thinking. It's because she has been very sick. It's because she's still afraid to die. It's because it's all been going on for too long and her father is never home. Jo knows all that, just like she knows it'd be useless to hang around to placate her mother. Once the mood has turned, she knows the best she can do is stay out of sight and out of reach. Out of reach of the harsh, painful words, out of reach of any object that can suddenly become airborne, like the hard-cover book still open on the smooth silk of her mother's kimono.

Such a book hit Jo once and its corner caught her, tearing the skin just above the right eyebrow. It didn't hurt, but Jo had fretted all night, trying to invent a plausible reason to give everyone at school the next day. Even her teachers would be asking her about that cut and bruise. She couldn't have said that she got it playing hockey as all her friends were on the hockey team and they hadn't played a game, not even a practice game that day. In any case, if she had been hit with a hockey stick there, right near the temple, she reasoned, it would've done much more than *graze* the skin. And, well, when it came to net-ball, she really couldn't think of anything happening on the court that could've left such a mark either, not just there above her eyebrow.

Jo moves away slowly. Over her shoulder, she asks, "So, Mama, is there anything you would like me to bring you?"

"*Yes, there is,*" Isabel hisses, "and don't you pretend you don't know what it is." Her voice rings clear. "If Jane's still around, get her to make me a vodka and tonic. If she's not, do it yourself. Didn't think I'd ask for a *glass of milk and bikkies,* did you?" The tone is icy with sar-casm. "And straighten up that posture, will you? Can't stand it when you skulk around all slumped like a beaten dog."

Jane is the woman who comes in to clean the house and do the weekly shopping. She had come in at the time when Isabel's bone cancer had caused her excruciating pain. The cancer had spread from cartilage to bone, but once blasted by an aggressive treatment of chemotherapy and radiation, the tumours that held on to her bones, leech-like, pretty much shrivelled up and died. Once the critical period passed and Isabel no longer truly depended on either the laxative treat-ment or the vials of morphine to dull the strident pain of tumour push-ing against bone and nerve and cartilage, she substituted them for alcohol in the form of vodka and tonics. She "self-medicated" not only the fear of the cancer returning but also the emptiness cultivated by her husband's abandonment, though they still shared the same roof. Jane had remained even as Isabel had moved into remission.

Jo knows that too-precious-to-let-go-Jane has already left because her car was not in the driveway when Jo had come home. Her father wouldn't be home until late and Jarrah, her sister, wouldn't come around until Sunday lunch. So Jo goes into the kitchen where all alco-hol is kept so as not to be "so bloody tempting."

In a tall glass, Jo pours three of the little silver measures and tops them with Indian Tonic. Because her mother prefers crushed ice to ice cubes, she retrieves two handfuls of crushed ice from the freezer compartment and watches the cold crystals slide slowly into the liquid. She sets the glass on a silver tray there for that purpose and, though her mother hasn't asked, Jo adds a little bowl of cashews. Her mother likes cashews and Jo knows that it is best if one eats when one drinks, though she wonders if the eating part still has any relevance when it comes to alcoholics.

*****

The cool flame decals on the eggyolk yellow body of the car attracted her eye at the same time as she realised that the vehicle was parked too close to the driveway to allow her enough of a turning angle. She'd have to drive further and turn around to do a left-hand entry through the back gate. *Cute,* she thought of the Ford Focus coupé. *New to the neighbourhood,* she thought. *Too bad about the tyres*. They were in good condition but even from the seat of her right-hand drive, she recognised them for the factory standards that they were. *Monza wheels, that's what that cute little body needs. Or Yokos A 520. Good sharp response.*

Her own Commodore idling in neutral, Maddy reached over the gate to slide the seven-inch bolt. Movement caught her eyes. *What the hell!*

A woman came towards her. From inside *her* garden. Weary as she was and totally not in the mood for visitors, even less for strangers in her backyard, Maddy asked curtly, "You looking for someone?"

The woman smiled. "Hey, Maddy."

"Have we met?"

"Of course. OK," the woman said with an easy smile, "forget the beach gear. It's my day off." She tugged at her board shorts. "Drove straight from the beach to ... " By the expression on Maddy's face, she realised that the young redhead didn't have the foggiest. "Try this," she said cheerfully. "Try and picture me in a pale-blue shirt, navy blue trousers, a walkie-talkie stuck to the shoulder, a big wide leather bel– "

"DS Jensen?" Maddy asked briefly, wide-eyed.

"Christen Jensen, that's me."

"Uh ... well ... " Aware she wasn't coming up with the right rejoinder Maddy shifted her weight from foot to foot. "Uh, look, I'm sorry.

It's just that I'm like, strung out. Tired. Uh … " Figuring the woman must have had a reason for being in her garden in shorts, T-shirt and sand crawlers, Maddy asked formally, "What can I do for you, DS Jensen?"

"Not much at all," the policewoman grinned in answer to the redhead's scowl. "Actually, I was just in the neighbourhood. My mother lives nearby, in Tamar Street and well– "

The idea that she had a cop in her garden finally registered. "How'd you know where I live?" she asked suspiciously.

"It's on the info I entered on the computer that night … the night you dropped in at the station," the policewoman answered easily. "Actually, home addresses, phone numbers and places of work were about the only facts you were able to give us for you and your missing friend, remember? A picture of her would've been nice. Friends' or siblings' phone numbers would've gone down nicely too but– "

An almost forgotten resentment bubbled up inside Maddy. "The cops could have found out *all that* if they had only *bothered* looking inside her room. Cops are meant to go looking for things, aren't they?" she asked defiantly.

"Yes, things and people." DS Jensen peered at Maddy. "Why do you ask?"

"Looks to me like no one's *bothered* to have a look at her belongings." Maddy glared. "When *I* got her stuff from the manager like, a *week* later, right, no one had even spoken to him. Even her sister didn't know Jo was missing. Her address book was right there all along … for numbers you said might be '*nice* to have at the time'. And I'd say nobody went looking because no one gives a fuck about a missing dyke. Not worth the action … I bet." Maddy turned away and kicked the toe of her leather work-boot. Once her resentment had been aired, she looked undecided.

"That's a very serious thing to say, Maddy, and you don't know that for sure," the policewoman replied gently. "And neither do I. I assume the boys here did the usual checks– "

"Oh sure," Maddy said sarcastically. "Stick up for the boys." And then, with a dismissive wave of the hand, she added frostily, "*Whatever!* I still say the boys in Briz took a few shortcuts. And that's what *I assume*, OK?" Chin up, round eyes narrowed, Maddy was defiant. "I mean, there might have been something in her gear, right, a hint or … clues … that could've been vital if … something *else,* like something dramatic had happened to her."

"Well, all's well that ends well, Maddy," DS Jensen said in a conciliatory tone. "They found her and because I had flagged the report requesting to be advised of any development, they did just that and ... here we are." The policewoman tugged at her T-shirt. "Uh, look, I tried to get you at work but the woman said ... the boss's wife – "

"Viv?"

"That's the name, she said you'd just left and that you would be driving straight home. So ... looks like I got here before you. Didn't know what car you drove so ... " the police officer looked through the half-open gate. "Hey ... an old Commodore VK. Still kickin'?"

Maddy answered curtly, "A good mule." She hitched her bag on her shoulder. "And I suppose the flash coupé that's just about blocking access is yours?"

"Ah ... yes." The woman glanced towards the street and noticed how the bonnet of her car, though not a long one, parked as it was, did indeed interfere with access to the driveway if approach was intended from the right. "I'm sorry. Didn't realise," she said seriously, but quickly added, "Hey, wanna write me up a ticket?"

Maddy retorted grumpily, "Lame cop humour." Without waiting for an answer, she turned away. Something stopped her in mid-stride. "Uh, look, I'm sorry," she began more softly. "I really should've phoned to thank you for making that call, uh, yesterday. Jo, she was right where you said. In the park. Somewhere near the Junior Soccer League shed ... and the, uh, the toilets." Maddy hesitated, gnawing on the inside of her lip. "We had a chat."

"Where is she now?"

"Still there." Maddy shrugged. "I think."

The woman stated the obvious. "She didn't come home."

"Didn't ask her to," Maddy answered brusquely. "Didn't want her to feel– "

"Good girl. You've done the right thing. She knows where to find you. And now that she knows that you know, and that you still care, it's very important for her to feel she's free to– "

"Look, I'd normally ask you in ... " Maddy felt uncomfortable discussing Jo with the officer, even if the officer was wearing shorts and had sun-bleached hair down to her shoulders. Besides, Maddy, quite intending to bypass dinner altogether, was hanging out for a cup of tea, a shower and an early sleep. *Too bloody long a day as it is.* "But ... truth is I'm really not up to– "

"Viv did say you were wrecked but ... "

"Good woman."

"But she also said she thought you could use some company– "

Maddy snorted. "Well, for once, she thought wrong. Now, if you don't mind, I really need– "

"Look, I can see you've had it, Maddy." The woman once again tried to have Maddy look directly at her. "But maybe just a few minutes, huh? Maybe I could start the kettle while you hop under the shower and … well, look," she smiled sheepishly, "the truth is that I have a bit of an interest in the case – "

"What kind of an interest?" Maddy asked suspiciously.

The police officer replied, unfazed, "Just because of that night, you know, back at the station." She shrugged. "You looked so lost and … and we talked, remember?" She lowered her head to better peer at Maddy's face, a gesture that reminded Maddy of Jo. "I don't usually talk to everyone and anyone who like, rolls in with their problems, right? Customer Relations and social work, well … that's just not part of *my* job description." She paused. "But, hey … It's not like you owe me. I *wanted* to be there for you and so ... well ... The point is that I'd really like to know how it's all coming along and how you're coping and I thought we might just talk about it a bit more. Just short. Just over a cup of coffee. *I'd like that,"* the woman concluded in all simplicity.

Maddy sighed. She couldn't see any real reason why she should refuse the woman a cup of coffee and a quick chat. She had, after all, been very good to talk to that awful night when there had been no one else. Helpful too, like she cared.

"Awright then … come on down," Maddy said, gesturing hand over shoulder towards the patio on the other side of the lawn. "I'll show you where the stuff is in the kitchen. And it'll be *tea* for me, not coffee."

Maddy left the woman on her own in the kitchen, tossed her bag on the sofa and made a beeline for the bathroom. Her deltoids and triceps screamed when she crossed her arms to pull the T-shirt above her head. *Bad move,* she groaned inwardly. She thought about it but there was no other way to remove her sport bra than to repeat the arm over head motion and again she flinched. She slid a finger under each of the rivets and let her jeans flop around her ankles, and grumbled. Unable to simply step out of them because of her work boots, she had to sit on the loo and slowly, carefully, ignoring the pain in her calves, lift thigh over knee to ease off one boot at a time, and roll back one sock at a time.

Hair plastered over her skull, eyes closed to better feel the hot jets hard on her shoulders, she shook her head in resignation. On the other side of the wall – a cop watching a kettle boil. *Her* kettle. She reached for the nailbrush and began the daily fingernail scouring ritual. Her heart pinched. Jo's puzzled frown, Jo's dark rimmed fingernails danced, disembodied, over the white tiles.

Maddy had washed most of the grime away with Zep, as she always did after each job, before starting on another and before leaving work, but she still needed bristles to dislodge the last particles that the abrasive liquid soap had not reached. And that had become a part of her daily home-after-work-ritual, *after* a cup of tea.

When she came out onto the patio, hair neatly wet-combed on either side of a straight part, clad in a white T-shirt long enough to cover most of her black shorts, she bore more than a passing resemblance to an altar boy.

The policewoman smiled apologetically as she pushed a mug of steaming tea towards Maddy. "I hope you like it plain. No milk in the fridge. Look," she added quickly, "most people feel funny about having a cop at their table … even honest folk." She shrugged. "It's like a reaction. Can't be helped. But Maddy, I'd really like you to call me by my name, not by my job. Christen, *not* cop." Her eyes brushed over Maddy's and settled briefly. "*And* I'd really like it if you could just treat me as someone you've just met and that you're finding *a bit* nice." She hesitated. "You do, don't you, find me *a bit* nice?" she asked, eyes wide open in exaggerated concern.

Maddy looked at her gravely. "I like you. I do find you … *a bit* nice." She smiled the first smile of the day.

"OK, then. To all these *other* people," Christen said cheerfully, chinking her mug of coffee against Maddy's mug of tea. "To the ones who are *totally* nice." Maddy just grinned and took a first sip through tightly rounded lips.

Christen asked Maddy about her house and Maddy answered simply that the main buying factor had been the back yard.

"When I saw all those big trees and bushes and so like, private, I couldn't even see the fence line, I thought *this* baby's gonna be mine. And … uh, well, as it turned out," Maddy grinned, "the backyard came attached to a house and it's like the house wasn't bad either. Simple, needing a new kitchen, but plumbing was sound and I liked it right away. Could really see myself living here, you know like inside and out.

So, yeah, as they say," Maddy concluded, lip loop flashing, "the rest is history."

Christen also asked about Maddy's old VK. She thought it might be a bit of a petrol guzzler. Maddy asked Christen about her Ford ZX3 and she explained that it was a nice change to her 'copmobile', being so much lighter to manoeuvre but still plenty zippy because of the Zetec 130 horsepower engine. At some point in the conversation, Maddy caught herself looking at Christen Jensen, truly looking at her for the first time since they had met back at the Burleigh Heads cop shop. *And what have we got here?* she thought privately.

Christen had the tall, rawbone look of her Swedish great-grandparents. A look that had stopped being *standard* Australian back in the '70s, the period during which the continent had begun opening itself to multiculturalism.

She was thirty-five, which meant that her face no longer had the mango-skin-tight- smoothness that indicates a life on which one hasn't quite yet embarked. Hair-fine lines ran down the middle of each cheek because that was where her smile creased them. The corners of her eyes crinkled, too, when she smiled her big smile. And when she didn't, little crows' feet stayed lightly etched on the delicate skin around her eyes, a side- effect from too many years spent squinting against harsh sunlight. There was something about sunglasses that had always made her uneasy, something about how they altered the colour of life on the other side of the lenses. She only wore them behind the wheel.

"Great road presence. Fun too," Christen was saying. "And I do quite enjoy that weird dashboard." She explained that its original shape reminded her of Dali's melted watch faces and that she'd show Maddy what she meant later. Maddy, she said, could even drive the thing around the block if she wanted to.

Maddy's diagnosis of Christen's sexuality was accurate, although she would have been at pains to explain why she had reached that particular verdict. The woman didn't wear any make-up. Her fingernails were short and unvarnished. She didn't wear any earrings, be they matching, dangling, or otherwise, and the beach gear she had on, though still bearing the mark of an iron, was unisex and nothing more than cheerful. Cheerful yellow for the board shorts, cheerful electric blue for the T-shirt. If anything, her hair looked more wind-blown than blow-dried, and years of weight training had shaped her somewhat shoulder-heavy. As she had said to Maddy, that night back at the station, her shoulders worked wonders on young punks. They were more impressed by them than by the gun at her hip. Probably because they assumed she'd be more likely to use her strength, if pushed, than her Glock. *Straight chick.* Maddy smiled inwardly. *OK, so the babe's flawed.*

"There's a bit of a torque-steer at full throttle on slippery roads but it's not too difficult to manage at 100 kph. Wouldn't want to kick into a full chase alert in it, though. But look," Christen said, setting her empty cup back on the table, "Maddy … how is Jo?"

So Maddy gave her a summary of her encounter with Jo.

"And … how long do you think she'll hold out on the streets?" Christen asked.

"Not sure, really. She seems quite determined." Maddy looked at the empty mug.

"Well, good news is that apparently sixty-seven percent of the folks who take to the streets remain there one month or less."

"It's already been three weeks."

"A lot can happen in a week out there."

Maddy remained silent.

"Has she told you why she'd taken that particular way out of … the loop?"

Maddy raked her fingers through her red hair, upsetting it along the no-longer-straight part. "Oh, yes," Maddy replied a little too quickly before hesitating, unsure as to what areas her loyalty to Jo needed to cover. "To protect herself from me … From me ditching her."

"Say again?"

"The way she sees it," Maddy began resignedly, "sooner or later I'd have woken up one morning just in time to decide that I didn't love her anymore. And *that* would confirm *to her,* right, that there's nothing lovable about her." Her eyes met the older woman's. "She's convinced herself that she's *long-term* unlovable."

"Mm. So … what, she's pre-empting, being pro-active in a way? By doing a runner on you?" Maddy remained still, hands cupped around the empty mug. Christen asked again, "But why take to the streets? Why not just … break up?"

"Too easy, I guess." Maddy loosened her shoulder muscles and flinched against more of the stiffness. *Like I'm all corroded,* she thought. "Because she says she's been living from hand to mouth in terms of … scratching around for love, her mother's, for too long. *Forever,* she says. But really, yeah, same thing, since she was about eleven years old." She stretched her legs under the table. "Creature comforts don't mean much to her at all, that's why she could live in a boarding house for so long when she didn't have to. I mean, she was working, right, and she does have money, even now. In the bank."

"And?"

"And she's determined not to use any of it, ever. Said I can have it all. Then she said she could take it out and, me and her sister we share it. She says it's time for her to change the way she's tried not to deal with her ... her ... fear of not – Oh ... look, I'm not sure." Maddy's hand flew through her hair. "I don't get it, not really."

"Look, maybe you won't want to answer this but ... Do you know anything about a mental health history she might have?" Maddy looked at her blankly. "I'm asking because it seems that at least *half* of the homeless population is out there because of some sort of mental illness, others because of some kind of violence done to them, either sexual or physical or emotional, and others because of substance abuse. But again ... I say maybe for some it's got to be in the genes, just like any other predisposition. Like suicide. Not everybody has it in them to even *think* about it." Something shifted inside Maddy's eyes. Something in what Christen said hit a chord.

Abruptly, she got up. Christen watched her spin on herself like a weathercock in search of wind before loping up the back stairs on her way to the kitchen, determined not to let the pain stiffen its hold over any more parts of her body.

Christen continued as, through the open window, she could see Maddy reach inside the fridge. "Maybe there's a distinctive type of person who simply rejects our day-to-day routine. You know that crap aspect of our lives that's based for the most part around paying bills and keeping up with other people's expectations of what we need to do, and how we should go about doing it. And maybe what we find horrifying – that utter lack of everything – for them is nothing less than liberati – "

"I think she's been abused, emotionally, by her mother."

Christen sat up on the wooden bench as Maddy curled off the beer caps. "Maddy ... share some of that with me, please."

Maddy felt the tear. Torn by the urgent need to pour out all she felt to someone who would take it all away and fix it, she knew she was about to betray a secret so secret that Jo, herself, hadn't yet told her about it but she desperately needed to talk to someone *not* connected to Jo, to someone younger than Viv but older and wiser than herself. And Maddy, heart thudding in her chest, repeated what Jarrah had told her about her sister's relationship with Isabel, their mother. She even tried to explain what she didn't quite understand herself, how Jo had internalised her mother's cancer and then her suicide as a damning attestation of her own worthlessness. Jo was not worth staying alive for.

"So, how did she cope? Losing a mother's always very painful but even more so– "

"She did drugs."

Christen's eyebrows arched in surprise. "But I thought you said she was clea– "

"She was … she is. That was before. Like when she was seventeen or something."

"Before or after her mother suicided?

"Both."

"But if she was already using *before*, she would've used even more – "

"She did," Maddy answered brusquely.

"As in how much? Weed or harder – "

"Let's just say *a lot*, OK, and leave it at that," Maddy replied tensely. "Marijuana." Hard fingers made tousled peaks out of her still-wet hair.

"OK." Christen looked at her hands. She glanced up at Maddy. The lip loop glinted, snug against her bottom lip. Still finding it strangely fascinating, she looked away. "How long's it been since she's given it up, then?"

"About a year."

"Good on her." Christen smiled and then, as another thought popped up in her mind, very carefully she asked, "Maddy? Did you ask her if … uh, if she had started up again?"

"No."

"No … what?"

Maddy answered irritably, "No, I *didn't* ask her."

"Why not? Don't you want to know?"

Eyes averted, Maddy gnawed at her bottom lip. She hesitated. "Oh, fuck it. I'll tell you why I didn't ask!" Her eyes were glinting. "I was afraid to. *There!* I've said it! I was afraid to hurt her feelings in case she hadn't and I was afraid to hear her say that she had because if she has, then … "

"Then what, Maddy? What do you think might happen if she's back to blowing sticks?"

Maddy snapped, "How would I know, huh? I don't have a crystal ball, do I?"

"True, you don't know, but the idea's worrying you all the same."

"It's just that … I just don't think that being on the streets *and* high's a good combo, OK?"

"Fair enough," Christen sighed. "You're right, it's not a good combo."

Maddy lifted the bottle of beer to her lips.

"You look a bit stiff, Maddy. Been working out?"

"Been swimming."

"Must've been one hell of a swim, then."

Relieved at the turn in the conversation, Maddy told Christen how she had burnt herself dry on an overdose of laps the night before at the U of Q pool which is why, she went on to explain, she had been so ready to cut the day short straight after work.

"Oh, look. One thing I'm really good at, I mean even better than target shooting, is massage."

Maddy answered distractedly, "Right. Well, good on you."

"No, look, seriously. I have three brothers and they always pull this or that muscle, if it's not a hamstring it's something else. And, well, you know, boyfriends being boys, they'd always have sport injuries too, right?" Christen shrugged. "So, what say you let me ease a bit of that tearing and swelling? All I need is whatever oils you have and– "

"I don't have any *oils*."

"Oh, hell, you've got a kitchen. Means you cook. Means you gotta have oil. Canola's fine. Olive oil stinks a bit. What's your cooking oil then? Sunflower? C'mon, it's Show and Tell time. Take me to your pantry," Christen enunciated solemnly as if she had said, 'Take me to your Master.' Maddy chuckled.

Lying on her stomach, hands flat on either side of her shoulders, Maddy would occasionally emit a little groan of pleasure. Christen, once armed with an almost full bottle of sunflower oil had decreed that first a dry massage, a little something to stimulate the spine, would put Maddy's *back* right in the groove.

"Now, I've only heard about that move like, not long ago and well, I'm on my own at the moment, right, no boyfriend on whom to practice, so … " she had said to a dubious Maddy. "But anything that stimulates the central canal's got to be good for something."

Using the heel of her hand, Christen had begun rubbing vigorously up and down a small section of Maddy's spine. Up from a spot right above her buttocks. Down from a spot between her shoulder blades and back, until both her hand and Maddy's back, along the spine, began to produce heat.

It was the heat build up that had Maddy moaning. The sensation was delicious. Her spine felt all tingly and whatever reservation she had had about letting herself be massaged by *anyone* had not lasted longer than a ball of snow in sunshine.

It's only once she felt Maddy disconnect that Christen oiled her hands and began kneading the strained muscles along her back and arms. Firmly, she traced the trapezius that swept down from Maddy's neck to the middle of her back and up over her deltoids and triceps and across her latissimus dorsi that fanned in the two identical slabs which then tucked smoothly against the ridges of intercostal muscles.

The firm pressure exerted by Christen's fingers, palms and heels of hands were breaking through the mesh of pain that had gripped most of Maddy's muscles. Eyes closed, she gave up the fight, even the fight she hadn't yet named. Eyes closed, muscles and spine atingle, Maddy let herself melt against the sheet. She let Christen generate more of that heat over the triangle of her back while she burrowed, more deeply against the mattress. A while later, slightly disoriented, she said, "Chris ... ten."

"Yeah?"

"Your arms must be getting tired, huh? Feels *sooo* good. I'm like, all melting. Kind of drifted off."

Still straddling Maddy's buttocks, Christen leaned a little forward, closer to the side of her face. "Had many massages before?"

Maddy took her time in answering. "No. None that I can remember."

"Oh, real shame."

"Sure is," Maddy replied languidly.

"*It is* ... but ... " Christen hesitated, "I was meaning that more from the point of view of the masseuse." Eyes scrunched up, as in anticipation of a blow, she lifted her hands off Maddys' ribs and held her breath.

"Meanin' what?" Maddy asked drowsily, face still against the mattress.

Here goes, thought Christen. She groaned inwardly, top lip drawn in, fighting to postpone saying what she knew she just had to say.

"Well … Like, I've massaged a lot of friends, right? A lot of men, like I said – "

"Yeah. Cops and boyfriends. Oh, and brothers. I remember."

"Yeah well … Look, Maddy, I don't know how to … Like it's really so strange and … Well, I just never thought that – " She stopped. "I never thought that a woman's body … could feel so … Well, a body like yours, I mean … all muscly and yet so *yielding.* So … manageable," she added, painfully aware of the inadequacy of her words.

Maddy twisted between Christen's hips to face her. "Whassup?"

"What's up?" Christen repeated unnecessarily. "Fancy *you* should ask." Her grin didn't linger. She squinted at Maddy, teeth hard on her lip. "Look, it's easy for you when it happens, I mean you're gay and … " Maddy made herself focus on the woman's words. The breaks and silences clued her that she was trying to communicate something important. "The thing is," Christen continued awkwardly, "if I was a bloke, well, *it'd be up* all right." She sat back on Maddy's shins and placed both hands on Maddy's kneecaps. "Maddy, I'm really turned on," she said too quickly, scrunching up her eyes.

Oh shit, was the only thought Maddy was able to muster. From inside the massage- induced languor, she simply grinned inwardly at the warmth that was radiating from her spine to her vagina. She berated herself drowsily for it but the delicious ache of arousal was hot inside *her* groin, there was no denying it.

When Christen finally opened her eyes Maddy's, round and blue, were ready to meet hers. Round and blue, Maddy's eyes were serious. "Me too, Christen. I'm … yeah, hot." She paused briefly. "Don't know what that massage did to me," she grinned quickly, "but … yeah … Thing is … " she hesitated, "nothing's goin' to happen."

She saw Christen swallow hard and look away. "No, of course not."

"It's not going to happen because my head's like, taken up, you know … by Jo." Maddy shielded her eyes with the crook of her arm, bringing her other hand over her stomach, close to her sex. Christen slid off the bed.

She looked down at Maddy's body, naked except for the little pair of pale blue knickers. She closed her eyes again as one draws curtains over something that should remain unseen. She closed her eyes, too, against the new spiral of desire that was already heating, deep inside her sex. Christen had to close her eyes, too, because she had never *desired* another woman, whether in uniform, in a bathrobe, or naked. Not at the beach. Not at the gym. Not in the locker rooms. Not anywhere. *And god knows I'm always surrounded by dykes a-plenty.* The Queensland police force was no different from any other police force and a noticeable portion of the women, from constable to officers, were lesbians.

Christen had never thought much about the *fine* line between curiosity and action. She had always assumed herself so unquestionably and exclusively heterosexual that she would dismiss with a grin and a shrug the occasional curiosity aroused by whatever woman she may have sat next to, naked in a sauna, on a locker room bench. Though she had never *touched* any woman while in that state of semi-abandonment, she had occasionally wondered what it must feel like to be a man making love to a woman, but when teased or asked about *her* sexuality, be it by male or female colleagues, jokingly, she would often reply that she considered herself one of the force's endangered species.

Yet, the feel of Maddy's smooth body, hard but yielding and softened by her touch, had ignited her curiosity beyond reason. *The feel of her buttocks so firm under me, that's what must've contributed.* While Christen struggled to find the source of what had to be an accidental arousal, Maddy looked at her, unsure as to what she should say to make light of the moment.

At twenty-five, Maddy was exclusively ghetto-gay when it came to her socialising pool. Straight women didn't come on to her. She hardly ever came across any. When it came to wheels, tyres and retreads, Maddy was convinced that whatever considerations were necessary, they were beyond most straight women's understanding as hardly any came unescorted by a male. So she waited, looking at Christen looking at her.

The blend of strength and vulnerability that exuded from beneath the paleness of Maddy's skin where it wasn't dusted with freckles, the firm vulnerability of her young breasts, the freckly knuckles over the smooth definition of her abdominal muscles moved Christen like no male body had moved her.

No, never. Christen shook her head as she finally dragged her eyes away but not yet ready to raise them to where she knew Maddy's were waiting. She tightened her sex against the spreading heat but the heat didn't go away, instead it became more focused, less bearable. Her hand reached to brush the skin on Maddy's thighs as she had begun pushing herself up to a sitting position. Mattress-flattened hair swept towards the left side of her head as by a wind storm, Maddy also pushed herself up and leaned her back against the wall, bringing her knees to her chest. "Christen," she called out softly. "We're not ... It's not gonna happen, you know, the making love bit but," she patted the mattress near her hip, "we *can* talk about it."

They had talked about *it* briefly and somewhat abstractly, but Christen was secure enough in her sexuality not to be freaked out by her body's strong reaction to the young dyke. She knew that homosexuality was not caught like a rash you got from having brushed against nettles. Because she had only been fleetingly curious about how it might feel to touch intimately a body that had neither body hair nor penis, she had not stopped to explore such thoughts long enough to consider that, per-haps, a first foray into woman-to-woman sex might work on her like chocolate mousse for the Eskimo who only ever has snow icecream for dessert. And they had sat cross-legged across the bed, Maddy with her T-shirt back on, covering her thighs way below the pale blue knickers. They had been able to look at each other and when Christen had reached for Maddy's hand, Maddy had let her hold it. Over another beer, they talked some more about Jo, and Christen said something that had all but squeezed Maddy's heart like a gigantic fist.

Back on the tack that some people take to the streets by choice, that the homeless are not *always* people who don't have a home to go to, Christen admitted to having done a little research after she had heard from the New Farm cop shop that Joanna Brenner had been informally ID'd in the park. She had made a few phone calls and even managed to get a hold of the woman who ran the MICAH, umbrel-la name for a variety of organisations that looked after the homeless in Brisbane.

"You see, Maddy, you, me, just about everyone we know, I'm sure we'd begin freaking out after the third or the fourth night out there. Imagine sleeping on the ground, not on the sand, not on a camping bed, right? Think of all the ... Think of how uncomfortable that has got to be." Her eyes held Maddy's. "Now, think of the daily hygiene thing. It's one thing not to shower like every day when camping on the beach or by a river ... because, well because we get to, at least, rinse off, right?" Maddy nodded almost imperceptibly. "Even if it's not a thorough wash, it's still … cool and pleasant and *fun*, right? Now what would *I* do out there on the streets, when I feel like a beer, or a coffee, or like when I want to read in bed and munch on something? Like, if I can't choose what to eat? And I have to eat it with my fingers, squatting on a piece of brown grass like Jo must be doing if she's not checking in at the Salvos. Well, look, honestly, I could do it for a week, right, because I'm not a total wimp. I could pretend I'm having a nightmare camping trip, or more likely that I'm doing covert surveillance. So, I'd be there, I'd do it, but I'd be resenting the hell out of it and counting the seconds.

"Now, it seems that some, *a few,* are out there because of a weird sort of choice and I don't mean the Aborigines. For them it's different again. Many are there, on the one hand, because they feel a connection to the land through any parcel of natural ground. On the other, because they feel disempowered. Others choose to remain homeless because they're doing their best not to abide by laws made by a white Australian government and so on." She paused to consider her next line of argument. "So what I'm thinking about is a different type of transient person, one who adapts … *down.* Someone not bugged by the limitations, the risks, what they are missing out on. None of that *really* gets to them. For them, it's not more than pesky annoyances, a part of their day-to-day routine, like for us catching a cold, or maybe like the gas heater that carks it in the middle of a shower. Or the TV goes on the blink. They might grumble about it all and moan that the world is a callous place but they're not bothered enough to say, Screw that, I'm going home. *They just adapt down.*" Christen repeated emphatically but when Maddy nodded, she resumed her thought. "They're not bothered enough by *long-term* filth, hunger pangs and spreading rashes, not to mention lack of intimacy and chronic illness. It doesn't get to them *enough* to want to reintegrate and seek proper psychological help from whoever's out there for them, or tap into whatever personal resources they've had all along."

"Why are you telling me all this?" Maddy asked, eyes averted.

"Because it seems to me your lover might be one of them."

Maddy's voice was too low. "What makes you think … that?" she asked.

Christen counted on her fingers. "For one thing, she refused your mobile. To me, it suggests that she's decided to face anything that'll come her way, all on her own. If she's not stupid, she's got to know that the streets are not safe for a woman alone at night. So maybe she thinks she can run and kick faster than most chicks out there but that's when she's awake." She paused and Maddy forced herself to breathe. "Even Jo needs to sleep, right? Asleep and on her own, she's totally vulnerable. She's already been out there three weeks.

"Then, you said her clothes were starting to grot up as they would after so many days, even if she's careful and tries to rinse off fresh stains. It's thirty-three degrees out there so whatever she gets wet would dry up quickly but ... really, how well can she wash *anything* while she's wearing it, huh? And yet, you said she didn't immediately grab the fresh clothes you had for her. You see, she could've changed in the loos, right, and given you the dirty ones to take home and maybe even ask you to swap dirty for clean every time you'd visit. But she didn't. She could've asked you to 'drop in' again for a chin-wag, an opportunity to sit down somewhere more comfortable with you, to enjoy company, a glass of wine, a free feed, something different from what she's able to do or scrounge on her own. She could've asked you to bring her some money, yours or hers. She could've accepted a couple of bills from you, too, right? Even more simply, she could've just given up the fight, now that she'd been found and has made ... a point ... about something or other, if only to herself. She could've gone home with you, if only to shower. If only for one night. For a decent sleep. If only for a well-deserved break from hell." Christen skidded to a halt but Maddy knew she had more to say. After a brief moment, Christen added, "Look, you just don't know how long the nights out there can be when you can't go anywhere, not for a coffee, not to the movies, not to the bars. No TV, no books, no hobby, no intimacy ... I mean ... occasionally I have a taste of that when I'm on a stake-out ... " Christen had almost reached the end of her argument. "I don't know, Maddy," she added, "but something tells me that Jo might be tackling this in a hardcore, almost fanatic sort of way." There was still one other factor that Maddy had to consider. "Do you really believe that she's doing all that ... straight? I mean as in *clean?*"

Maddy drew in her bottom lip. With a slow shake of the head, she said, "I don't understand."

"Maddy, I'm ready to bet that Jo's doing drugs and ... " she hesitated, "if she's done drugs before, I'm ready to bet she's back to using in a big way."

Some time later, Christen asked Maddy to show her around the rest of the house and garden.

"Wanna check out my Ikea specials?" Maddy asked derisively, in reference to her simple furnishings, and they found themselves under the house in the makeshift garage area.

At their feet was the big blue plastic tarp on which Maddy had spread all sorts of bits and pieces. Christen, taking her cue from Maddy, stood in silent, almost reverent contemplation of the assemblage of nuts, and spanners, and hubs, and sandpaper, and spokes, and spare parts, and old parts, and brake pads, and pedal plates, and disks, and fixing bolts, and reflectors, and chrome paint, and brake fluid in a tin, and matt-black paint in spray cans.

"So what d'you think about that, huh?" Maddy grinned expectantly. "It's like what you were saying just before about time dragging on, like when you can't get into anything to make it go by faster. Well, at the moment that's how *I* kill time."

"It's ... a bike, isn't it?" Christen asked, guided in her educated guess by the somewhat recognisable shapes of pedal plates and break handles. "What exactly are you doing with all that? A ... heavy-duty mobile? A sculpture for a city council bike path?"

Maddy rolled her eyes comically. "Should've seen it when it was still standing and you wouldn't be asking." She beamed a smile. "Yeah, it's a bike all right. It's Jo's. Old and rusty like a nail buried in mud. It's all there, though. Every single bit of it and I'm de-rusting and repainting and fixing it all up for her. For later."

A short while later, as the two women made their way back upstairs, Christen called out softly from behind Maddy, "Maddy?"

"Mmm?"

"I'm still ... I'm still feeling it."

Maddy had reached the landing. She stopped abruptly and Christen, who was only one step behind her, bumped against her back.

"Feeling what?" Maddy asked, as she stepped back to face the woman still one step below.

Round blue eyes, still in too pale a shade, scrutinised Christen's face, enjoying the rare occasion she could look into one of these tall women's eyes without having to lift her chin.

Christen spoke quietly. "Maddy, I want you."

"You want *me?*" Maddy peered into Christen's face, into her eyes, blue, too, but very different from her own. "Aren't you a Miss Cheerleader-joins-the-police-force chick?" she asked seriously.

"I am. Not cheerleader but, yeah, Miss Surf-lifesaver. Then, there was the serious … appeal of a gun, heavy and securing. But … Maddy, that's got nothing to do with anything, not the way I see it." Christen met Maddy's scrutiny without flinching. "I feel … Uh, I want to touch … Oh, fuck it, I want to make love," she concluded in a 'There-I've-Said-It' tone.

"You want to make *love?*" Maddy repeated incredulously, bringing her face closer to the woman's. The shoulder-length, sun-blond hair, though feathered around the face, reminded Maddy of the wild mane she had once seen on a palomino out in a bright, sunlit field. Christen's high cheekbones and tawny complexion could have been, in other circumstances, terribly beguiling, and Maddy rested her hands on the woman's shoulders, close to her neck. The feeling that resulted from that touch, from the firm thickness of Christen's shoulders, was foreign to Maddy. She didn't recognise it as familiar so she closed her eyes to better feel Jo's narrow shoulders and slender frame against her. She breathed in slowly. Christen shuffled on her step to snuggle closer as if Maddy had opened her arms to her.

Gently, she pushed Christen back. The woman balanced herself easily by stepping down one step, and though she hadn't seen Maddy's hand move, she felt it slide under the loose drawstring of her shorts. She felt it cool against her stomach. She shut her eyes tight.

From the vantage position of the higher step, Maddy let her hand glide against Christen's skin, down to the curls. Once at the silky warmth of her sex, she hesitated but Christen gasped softly and quickly looked up, right into Maddy's eyes. Her lips moved to speak but she didn't. She needed to feel the young redhead's mouth against hers. She needed to feel her tongue. Her yearning was that of a very small child intent on immediate oral gratification. Her yearning was that of a woman aching to feel her lover inside her, anywhere inside her. Her need was to let that touch reverberate throughout her.

"Maddy, kiss me," she said hoarsely.

One step up brought her back level with Maddy but though she did not move her head to kiss Christen, Maddy's fingers were already stroking her sex, rubbing the ache out of where it had entrenched itself, coaxing it to spread and diffuse its electricity higher and lower and deeper. Christen, face buried against Maddy's neck, tightened her embrace around Maddy. Together, body against body, for a brief moment, they swayed at the top of the stairs.

Christen's breath became ragged and abruptly, she arched backwards. Maddy's arm was there to support her but the movement took them both off to the side, and Christen's back slammed against the stairwell cladding, taking Maddy with her.

"Oooh, kinky," Christen said on a quick grin, eyes tight.

Maddy explored Christen more deeply now that she was no longer balanced precariously on the flight of stairs. Under her fingers were the hardened nodes that contained the woman's arousal. So Maddy buried her face against the warm blond tangle of Christen's hair and, a heartbeat later, felt her come around her fingers, hard against her hand.

Trapped inside Maddy's mind, Jo – grey eyes fuzzy and breathless from her own orgasm.

Christen briefly closed her hand over Maddy's and guided her out of her shorts. Short of breath and flushed, she ran the tip of her tongue over dry lips, raked her fingers through the tangle of her hair, pushing it back away from her eyes. A grin fleeted over her lips as she leaned heavily against the cladding, one hand over her heart to steady it.

Maddy had sat down on the step level with Christen's knee, so Christen inched downwards against the wall till she felt Maddy's shoulder under her hand. "Don't know if it's the balancing act on the stairs that did it but … " She shook her head, "Truth is … that was one hell of an– "

"One hell of a fuck, Christen." The woman glanced down at Maddy. "That's all it was. That's all there'll be."

"A fuck," Christen repeated flatly. Then she understood what Maddy meant. "Just *a* fuck? As in only *one*? As in *that's it?*" She, too, sat down on the step. "But Maddy, please, let me touch you. I mean, that was the point of what I was saying befo– "

"Wish I could, Christen. I'm sorry." Maddy wrapped one arm loosely around the woman's shoulders. "Wish I could kiss you, too." She looked at the stairwell gaping at her feet and shook her head. "Wouldn't make a difference. Might even make things worse." She turned to face Christen, eyes into eyes. "Look at you," she said, one hand against the woman's cheek. "*You* … " She hesitated, still debating loyalties. But as she looked into Christen's eyes again, what she saw was no longer a cop, no longer a woman who wanted to touch her, no longer a woman who could help her deal with Jo. What she saw was the face of a *woman*, the face of a vulnerable woman, the face of a woman who looked bruised. And because of the bruised look in Christen's eyes, Maddy added, not just to make Christen feel better but because she totally meant it, "Christen, you could've been *my* drop-dead, gorgeous *older* woman … romance." Had a tinge of regret crept into her voice? She wasn't sure but she looked away all the same and, dry-mouthed, she began wiping the constellations of freckles over her fingers with the hem of her T-shirt. "But, the thing is, while Jo's fucking with my head, please, Christen, let's not go *there* again."

*****

SIX

Jo – a solitary figure by the great rose garden. Earphones dangling around her neck, arms at her side, she was undecided. Last night had been rough. Last night, she had had a panic attack and, as she stood motionless in the morning light, her indecision stemmed mostly from *not* wanting to focus on why she had been thinking so hard about Maddy. So hard, ever since she had come out of last night's bad trip. A succession of cones had left her zonked in a weird way. And so in the morning light she stood by the rose garden, itself looking like the bad side of a bad trip, mangy-brown and headless, except for a couple of thin stalks dubiously crowned by wrinkled roses. She looked at them dully, wondering whether their sad state was because these were way too early for the season and had died before their time or because the season had already come, gone and left them behind.

"When?" she asked perplexed. "When do roses bloom?" She tried to remember the roses her mother used to tend with loving dedication but her mind had lost the scent of her mother's roses. So Jo flicked a dried-up rose with her fingers. *Dead rose standing*, she thought grittily. **Dead rose loses head in New Farm Park**. That little headline made her chuckle as she watched the few remaining petals flutter to the ground.

That small diversion over, Maddy popped back inside Jo's head. The thought that Maddy was holding on made her frown. She decided Maddy was just like those roses. She was like the roses in the sense that their season had come and gone and, yet, neither Maddy nor the roses seemed to have cottoned on. Teeth clenched, one by one, Jo's long fingers pulled at another rose's petals. Deliberately, slowly she did it, one parched petal at a time, with the same nasty intent as the little boy who pulls the wings and the legs, one by one, off a grasshopper.

Once the rose's petals lay on the dirt totally separated from its heart, Jo resisted the urge to bruise them under her rubber soles. She resisted the urge to trample them, pricked by the realisation that, if Maddy was on *her* mind, it could hardly be Maddy's fault. *If* the white-flash of insight gained from last night's bong-blaze had dissipated as rapidly as the morning dew that had gathered around her during her fitful few hours of sleep, *if* thoughts of Maddy were back in her head, it was simply because *she* hadn't yet successfully exorcised the dependency Maddy represented. *More's needed. More time's needed. Was never meant to be easy,* Jo reminded herself.

Jo settled on a thought from the past – no long-term illness ever gets cured overnight. Miracles didn't exist. Touch-healings weren't miracles, she insisted, only hoaxes, vertical scams for suckers desperate for an illusion, desperate for something to hold on to. She reminded herself that her self-diagnosed illness was no different from the one that had sparked such debilitating pain inside her mother's joints. In her legs mostly, but in her arms, too.

Jo went on arguing with herself. *Not any different from the douche-bags who buy pretend fireplaces just to watch fake flames dance, right, more like flicker, over fucking fake log.* Some, she understood, needed to do that to feed an illusion, just as being with Maddy had fed *her* illusion that a woman's love was a safe place for her. Safe, in a way her mother's love had not been.

To hammer in that thought further, she connected with the rule of thumb she was familiar with back in her St Joan days, in the days of her mother's illness. If a disease has been allowed to settle and progress for a few years, it will take at least one year of intensive treatment, not just to control it but to wipe it out. If her illness had been left undiagnosed, she reasoned, and untreated for so many years, then surely it would take more than a month, more than a year, more than two or three even to zap that crap out of her guts. Her sick thoughts needed to shrivel up like a cancer inside radiated cells, that much she knew. In fact, she agreed, they needed to shrivel up and die like those bloody mummified roses she was still looking at.

The malignant degeneration of her mother's bone cells had slowed down. It had become controllable but it had left her emotionally damaged. Always scared, all through remission, that it would return. That it would cause her to lose a limb or two. An arm and a leg, literally. Jo snorted at her own *humour noir*. Permanently scarred by that fear and by the fear of her husband tossing her on a refuse heap.

Isabel had died but her suicide had been motivated by one or both of her two fears. The irony was that it was one of those fears that had fed the other, the one that drove *her* away from her husband. That same fear had driven her away from her young daughter, too.

If she *discarded* herself, if she rendered herself unusable, Isabel must have reasoned, the fact that it would be a result of *her own doing* would take some of the consequential pain away. And Jo remembered, as she stood still by the rose garden, the gradual receding, the ebbing of her mother's pain giving way to a drug-induced lethargy, only broken up by repeated patterns of melancholy, only broken up by erratic mood swings exacerbated by alcohol.

Jo returned to her initial thought which centred around Maddy still pushing her buttons. The idea that she, Jo, was actually doing active pain management, pain management for a deep-seated heartwasting disease suited her for the moment. "Protect the heart. Protect the heart," she repeated to herself. And then, "Maddy, please, leave me alone," she enunciated clearly, carefully as she would an affirmation. "Please," she added so softly the word failed to reach her ears. She looked away from the rose garden, jaws clenched on the determination never to allow herself to be made vulnerable. Not by Maddy. Not by anyone else. Not ever.

Jo shoved aside the image of Maddy with her hand. Disbelieving, she stared at the back of her hand where a rose thorn had just scratched her and shook her head. Even *dead*, they still fucking bit. Tiny beads of blood stood diagonally across the back of her hand, pale under the delicate fork of raised veins that was always vulnerable to knocks and grazes. She frowned at the angry red mark, not because it hurt but because she had already decided that the hardest thing to keep clean were her hands. She knew it was from sitting on the ground so much, from spending so much time around grass, dust and dirt. She looked at her fingernails. The thin crescents of grime were wider under the nails of the index and middle fingers of her right hand than under any other.

A few days ago, Jo had slipped on the Indian cotton skirt that Maddy had brought her that first time they connected in the park. Jo had been on her way to the Centrelink office to register for the Newstart Allowance, the unemployment benefit she thought she might qualify for, being over twenty-one and unemployed. She had a cake of soap in her bag that she kept wrapped inside a plastic bag, the same supermarket bag that had contained the mangoes she and Maddy had shared as dessert, seated at the little picnic table that faced the apartment block on their last night at Burleigh. Jo had washed her hands thoroughly, scrubbing with her new nailbrush under and around the cuticles. Distracted and tense, she had forgotten the little brush on the washbasin of one of the public park toilets.

She was distracted and rattled by the prospect of having to hem and haw about her present circumstances. She was rattled because she knew that, away from the park, away from the Brunswick, Sydney and Merthyr Streets area that had become her turf, she wouldn't be safe. Not safe from the eyes of others. Not safe from their *knowing* eyes. She knew she no longer looked right. She knew that, though her skirt and T-shirt were clean, there would be something about her, even if her fingernails were clean, that would make her beep – unhinged. Feral. And she was edgy too, because she knew they'd give her a form to fill in with boxes she wouldn't be able to complete. Like, for starters, the home address and phone number boxes. Like the emergency contact box. Like the box in which she'd have to write her tax file number though she did have a tax file number. It's just that her tax file number, along with her driving licence, the few personal papers she had brought back to Brisbane some thirteen months earlier, and her most recent pay slips, had been jettisoned at *Fairfield House*. Seconds later, though it didn't solve her predicament, she remembered that they were, in fact, safe at Maddy's.

Later, Jo had gone back to the toilet block hoping that the little pink nailbrush that had become so important to her would still be where she had left it, on the edge of the washbasin but, no, the little pink brush was no longer there. Jo hadn't bought another one because when night came, she knew that the ganja she'd be scoring behind the Village Twin Cinemas would, after all, do a lot more for her than a little pink nailbrush could ever do, at least in the short term. And though a nailbrush only cost a few dollars, every cent she had, she needed to save and shell out for another stick.

So Jo looked again at her fingernails, graphically gross in the strong morning light. Stuck, like under laminating plastic. She had always worn her nails short but since she had lost her nailbrush, she cut them almost to the quick.

Standing still by the rose garden, she frowned wearily at the tiny beads of fresh blood that dotted the back of her hand, wondering how she could keep the scratch from getting infected without the help of an antiseptic and Band-Aid combo. The idea that she'd have to shell out at least a $10 bill for the two didn't sit any better with her than forking out whatever it would cost to replace her lost nailbrush.

When Maddy had again found Jo in the park, she had led her to the other side of the park, to the other side of the Powerhouse Entertainment Centre. Alone on the grass, away from prying eyes, Jo had let Maddy take her hand in hers. And Maddy had gently rubbed the soft veins on the back of Jo's hand. She had held Jo's hand in hers as if it had been a dead bird, still warm to the touch but dead all the same. Like a dead bird that might be revived if she kept it still, if she were able to instil some of her warmth into its feather-light body.

Maddy had looked at Jo's hand. She had let her fingers trace the inverted trident of blue-grey veins that spanned the back of her hands. The main vein snaked backwards from her middle finger to cruise over her wrist and the inside of her forearm.

"You know, Jo, it's weird, that," Maddy had said, caressing that one vein that stood out the most with the ball of her thumb, "but *that* vein is one of the first things I fell in love with. From the start." She was not looking at Jo. "I thought those veins made your hands like, *so* ... sensual." What Maddy really wanted to say was that the veins that coursed the back of her lover's hands made them, made *her,* seem vulnerable. Long, thin and vulnerable. Exposed. So vulnerable that her heart ached to protect her and them. Way back then and, even more so, at that moment.

That afternoon, Jo had looked at the back of her hand. She didn't see the attraction but it was true that for as long as she remembered, her veins had always stood out on the back of her hands. Even Amber, her best buddy back at St Joan's, used to tease her about them.

"Most of us have our palms read," she said one day. "But any fortune-teller will *pour* your life out just by looking at these veins of yours." And Amber had looked at Jo. "You get it, don't you, the joke? *Pour*, like from veins. And *pour out*, you know, like gush out too much information? No? OK. Bad Joke. Rewind. E-rase."

Then, another day, Amber came up with a different thought about the veins on the back of her friend's hand. "OK, so most everyone would know to slash their *wrists,* right? I mean, if they kinda wanted to off themselves, right?" Jo had nodded cautiously, unsure as to where the conversation was leading. "'But you, girl, you'd only have to slash the *back* of your hands and that would do it, wouldn't it?"

"Guess it would," Jo had replied non-committally. "But vein slashing isn't the way I'd go about it, uh ... if I wanted to waste myself."

"Oh, right. So how would you?" Amber had asked, her tone daring Jo to talk seriously about the *untalkable.*

"Well, that's the thing. I haven't figured it out yet."

Amber's eyes opened wider on the *yet.* Had her best mate been entertaining some thoughts about the taboo topic?

Jo, for whom the topic was neither remote nor taboo since she was living in dread of her mother's suicide, had indeed spent many a moment thinking about how she would like to handle *her* last seconds of consciousness. And in all simplicity, she had unravelled a little more of what she had worked out for herself. "I know I wouldn't use a razor, that's for sure. Too gross. And I know I wouldn't use a gun. Too sloppy. And, yeah, messy … like for the cleaning lady," she added, attempting a little humour to make Amber smile. "Wouldn't use rat poison and wouldn't use a noose. Same reason. Nasty to find, right? And I think the rat poison thing would be *so* painful you'd want to rewind for sure, just because of the pain, but it'd be too late and– "

The way Amber had cut her short with a "Oh right. You're *so* funny, Brenner!" had kept Jo from confiding that her mother actually had her own suicide kit well prepared. Even after her mother's death, Jo never told Amber about the vials of morphine Isabel had been collecting in the cigar box in the corner of her wardrobe. She had not referred to Isabel's death as *suicide*.

Jo looked up, sensing someone walking towards the rose garden. Clearly a woman. Dark hair cut straight below the jawline. Jeans, white tee. Backpack over her shoulder. Jo watched the woman, almost absent-mindedly, before realising that she was, in fact, walking straight towards her. The woman advanced quickly but only because she took long strides, not because she was in a hurry. In fact, the woman didn't seem in a hurry at all. As she came closer, Jo noticed chunky leather boots below the hemline of faded, wear-fringed jeans. And she thought of her favourite combat boots left behind with the rest of her gear. Already hot, herself, in her black Converse trainers, she figured that jeans would be mega hot too. Jo had only worn the jeans Maddy had brought her three or four times, not so much because, until recently, daytime temperatures had been hovering around thirty-four degrees Celsius but because denim, being so thick, took too long to dry at night in the humid air.

In the privacy of the parcel of garden that she now considered her safe turf, nighttime was when Jo had taken to cleaning her clothes. Partially hidden from the street by the concrete wall, overhanging branches and shrubbery, she would strip and, with cold water from the garden hose and her thinning cake of soap, she would try to remove the most obvious stains while still fresh. And though the jeans had had most of the night to dry, because she hadn't dared throw them *over* a branch for fear they'd be as visible as a flag up a mast-pole, she had only laid them to dry on a patch of grass. By morning, early morning, when she jumped over the garden wall and back into the street to avoid being sprung inside a garden where she had no right to be, the jeans, rolled inside her rainbow bag, were still quite damp. She hadn't intended wearing them that day, preferring to save them for cooler days and cooler nights, but she didn't like the idea of them damp inside her backpack, like mildewing, either.

The woman stopped in front of Jo. "Hey," she said, lips curled into an easy smile.

One cheerful chick, Jo thought. "Hey," she replied non-commitally.

The woman's hand flew to the top of her head to back-comb the dark hair that was falling over her eyes. "Looks like we're in for another hot day. No cooling respite from last night's rain after all," she seemed to sigh, green eyes bright in the morning light.

Jo figured the newcomer to be about her height but broader, much broader in the shoulders. But again, so was just about everybody. The notion of shoulder breadth brought in a heart-twinge that caught Jo by surprise because Maddy had appeared like a hologram over the rose garden. Jo winced into the sun until it made her eyes water.

When Maddy had asked if Jo would like her to come back the following day, Jo faltered. Her impulse was to say Yes, of course. Why not? We could – I will – But she heard herself say flatly, "I don't think so. Listen, Mad," she added more gently, "I appreciate the effort and all but … You've worked it out, right? I got a lot of shit … issues to process. Stuff I didn't deal with before, like before we got together, you and me." But then the spike of anxiety that was rising steadily at the thought of letting Maddy go had made her add somewhat apologetically, "I dumped it on you like it got dumped on me, right? But … I … Listen," she finally snapped, "you just go and let me spin my things through. In peace."

"Fuck it, Jo. Look at you! You look like shit!" Maddy had yelled back because, rainbow pack dull with dust dangling from her wrist, Jo was already walking away from her. "And what do *I friggin'* do while you crash and burn, huh? Besides watch?"

"'Fuck knows," is all Jo had answered over her shoulder.

"Close to 28° by noon is my bet," Jo said pleasantly to the woman she estimated to be in her late twenties. "I was just thinking that it'd be hot gear what you got on … "

The woman looked at her denim-clad legs. "T'is a bit … but again it doesn't make sense. It's like these things are *desert* boots, right?" she said, scuffing the thick leather toe of a boot into the dirt. "So … it's like, I don't get it. I mean, if they're to be worn in *deserts*, right, where it gets up to like, way over forty, why'd they be so bloody hot down here?" Jo liked the stranger's husky voice. It was warm and throaty and she watched the woman with a little speculative smile. She had picked up on the accent, one that is automatically attributed to English private school education. "Same with jeans," the woman carried on, encouraged by the tall girl's relaxed stance by the rose bush. "But good news is the temperature's finally due for a proper drop by the end of the week. And more of that beautiful rain."

The mention of the weather changing brought a dryness to Jo's mouth. She tightened her body against the memory of the chill that had kept her awake most of the night.

It had rained in the evening but the rain hadn't been cold. Some time later though, some time after midnight, the south-easterlies cooled the night air. Jo had had to leave the safety she had gotten used to, the safety of the dark corner of the garden, the dark protection of overhanging branches, and risk being detected as she ran, light as a shadow, up the steps to the rickety back porch. No one stirred inside the house and Jo huddled under the overhang. The T-shirt that Maddy had brought her, slipped over the one she had been wearing, was not enough to keep the chill air from seeping deep into her bones. She had wrapped the sarong, then the Indian cotton skirt, as shawls around her narrow shoulders. Arms crossed over her breasts she had waited for dawn to come.

The newcomer noted the tall girl's attempt to control whatever emotion had just overtaken her.

"So … anyway," she continued, "the jeans instead of, you know, a pair of shorts, well … that's because … " She hesitated, glancing surreptitiously at Jo. Wrecked, she decided on evidence of the soft pink smudges under the girl's eyes. It was obvious to her that the girl needed to eat *and* to sleep. "Well," she began again, cat-eyes smiling, "truth is they were the only things not already in the dirty laundry basket." She shrugged her swimmer's shoulders and grinned. "Listen, uh … I'm Tamara." Tamahrah, it had sounded like, with the emphasis on the second syllable. "Tahm."

Grey eyes on green, Jo smiled back. "I'm Jo. You're English?"

"From London, yes. Been living here forever though. Right, well," Tamara said shifting her boots in the dry dirt, "it's a good thing I decided to cut across this way from the ferry landing, then. No need to work up a sweat snooping behind bushes. Anyway ... Jo? Right! Well ... as it turns out, you're the exact person I was hoping to connect with."

Tamara had made it a point to speak face to face with the woman who had placed the call, before going to look for the transient herself. She found Maureen Leal in the riverfront restaurant she managed, busy organising the logistics involved with a large lunchtime booking. The woman seemed genuinely relieved to have someone from Queensland Health looking into the matter of *young Jo*. Maureen Leal tucked a strand of greying brown hair behind an ear and her expression was clearly one of concern as she had greeted Tamara.

"You've just missed her," she said, "but she's probably still in the park. I think that's where she spends most of the daytime hours. Don't think she actually sleeps there, though. She hasn't said, but I sure hope she doesn't." Maureen shook her head in a way that suggested total incomprehension. "Oh, you'll be quick to spot her. So young and so ... " The woman frowned as she ticked off a series of descriptors before selecting the one she thought most appropriate. "I guess, yes, you could say she is *interesting*. I mean, *visually* interesting. Not much of a talker at all but I'd say she's had a good education. Maybe that shouldn't be important but I can always tell as soon as someone opens their mouth, especially young people who come here looking for table staff positions. Sometimes it even just shows on their face that ... Well, either they're not very bright or they have no polish whatsoever. And what with the clientele we attract, the staff here need to project absolute – Oh, look, I'm going on and on and ... " The manager guided Tamara towards a corner table. "Well, yes, back to the girl, Jo. A rather tall girl, she is. Like yourself or taller even, but much thinner." The woman held up the pencil she had been using. "Thin as in thin-thin. Dark hair, short like a rat's gone through it. Unusual grey eyes." Maureen Leal paused. "Of course, she's looking grubbier now than when I first came across her. I mean her clothes, pretty much always the same khaki greens ... dirty. Well, yes, they'd have to be, wouldn't they?" She nodded. "I can't possibly imagine how she manages. Must all be so terribly uncomfortable for her this ... " She held her meandering thoughts in check and directed them back to the essential. "I'd have to say the clothes are *dirty* but not, how should I say? Not *filthy*. Not ... *smelly*," she whispered conspiratorily. "And there's something about her that, somehow, makes you want to do something to help but she doesn't *want* anything. The thing is, just looking at her, even in that state, you know she'd scrub up so nicely." The manager explained that she had tried to find out why the girl was hanging around the park, why she didn't seem to have a home to go to but she concluded, "I suspect she's like one of these wild possums, you know. You can only get *that* close." She showed a small gap between thumb and forefinger. "And not an inch closer. But it's not like she's scared, or dangerous, or anything like that. I just mean she closes up."

Jo flicked a glance at Tamara. "Why you want to connect with me?" Her easy smile had vanished.

"Why was I looking for you?" Tamara slipped her backpack off her shoulder. It made a heavy klunking thud as it hit the ground. "Ah well … A bit of a long story but … " She shifted her weight onto the other foot. "OK, it goes like this," she began, catching Jo's eyes and holding them. "Yesterday, one of my colleagues, she gets a phone call from some woman, a Maureen Leal, who runs a restaurant down here by the river, right?" Tam pointed backwards with her thumb. "And it appears that there's this chick in the park that's looking a bit feral, right?" The easy grin on Tamara's lips cancelled any pejorative meaning her words might have carried. "And her name's Jo. That's it, just Jo. So, it's like the woman back there's given this Jo person a little job or two and a feed or two but now, the woman's worried about the young transient." Serious green eyes watched Jo.

"That so?" she asked cynically.

"Absolutely. But what I find interesting is that the woman, back there in the restaurant, she's worried because she wants to help the girl and it looks like the girl's not wanting help, not hers, and apparently not anyone's. And she's not like, looking to go home either. As in not any time soon. You with me?"

Jo's eyes narrowed again. "You're with the cops?" she asked suspiciously, bypassing the question altogether. "Why'd she ring *you?*"

"Ah … that's easy. As I said, she likes you. Wants to help. So the thing is she's heard somewhere that many of the women who like, sleep rough, are usually doing it because of two things. One of them is that they're on the run from home. Well, not so much from the house itself as from the violence they face *inside* it. You get what I'm on about, Jo?"

The tall girl nodded.

"Right, well, I'm working with such women. Women who need help because of that domestic violence thing. So, that's why Maureen Leal called the division. Queensland Health Services, Domestic Violence Division." Tamara gave Jo a keen glance. "So let's cut to the chase, Jo. Is that why you're here? On the run from your partner?"

Jo's smile was twisted. "Could say that, yes." She hesitated. "Yes, I guess you could say I'm on the run from my ... my lover." Jo saw the expression shift on the social worker's face, like one moment the woman was relaxed and cool, the next she was totally focussed like a cat listening for sound. Jo felt she had to redirect. "Could say I *am* on the run, but not *that* way. No violence." She shook her head before adding with a curl of the lips intended as a smirk, "So ... shit, girl. You've wasted your time travelling all the way here. I don't have a boyfriend, you see. Don't have a dude to be running from." She shrugged. "Wrong story for the wrong girl."

"Sweet!" Tamara exclaimed, undeterred. "Good to hear. So what are you running from then?"

A little line of tension appeared, upright, on Jo's brow. "Who says I'm even running, huh?"

"Well, the way I see it ... you'd bloody have to be running from something big time to accept the trashy little job that restaurant woman's been throwing your way." Tamara shifted her eyes back to the young woman with the funky hacked off haircut. *Feral but, yeah, the manager's right. Real spunk appeal.* "Said she offered you a waitressing position some three weeks ago," she added. "Said she liked your style. Said you weren't interested. So, what, instead, you clean gunk off that same restaurant's floor? Like at 7 a.m. every morning?" Tamara's green eyes softened. "How you stomach *that?* Before or after your Milo? Or is it coffee? tea?" She waited but no answer came. "Where do you have breakfast, Jo?" As an afterthought, she added jokingly, "Can't believe the waitresses' uniform sucked that much. Did it?"

Jo shook her head. She wasn't frowning anymore but she was still wary of the stranger. *A social worker,* she thought, trying to avoid looking at the woman, almost hoping she would disappear. *Fucking hell!*

But there was something about the woman that kept Jo there and still listening. Maybe it was because Tamara, despite her role in social welfare, seemed close enough to her own age, closer than even her sister. Maybe it was because the woman's demeanour seemed genuinely casual, non-threatening. Maybe it was because the green of that woman's eyes was so very green that her eyes reminded Jo of a cat's.

For whatever reasons, Jo didn't shut her right down and that may have been, too, because in spite of herself, she was actually *enjoying* the woman's presence. So what if she was on to Jo? It seemed unlikely, to her, that the woman would lecture her stupid before goading her to some office or other to be processed. Besides, though Jo was, at the best of times, introverted and quiet, there had always been at least one significant other person with whom she could talk in a meaningful way, one in whom she could place her trust. To varying degrees.

For most of the past year, that person had been Maddy, her lover. Until recently. For the previous six years or so, that person had been Jarrah. And to a much lesser degree, occasional lovers who had come and gone after Amber and before Maddy. Even back in the St Joan days there had been Amber *and* Gabby, the goalie, along with a few other girls, more on the Hockey team than the Netball team but, mostly, it had been Amber.

Since she had taken to the streets, Jo figured, she might just as well have forgotten how to talk. Even when Maddy came around, Jo didn't say much at all. She couldn't. She didn't know what to say anymore, let alone how to say it. Maddy was confusing her. So days turning to weeks, Jo only spoke briefly with Maureen who ran the restaurant and said even fewer words to the dealer she visited most evenings. Sometimes she would find him behind the Village Twin Cinema. At other times, she would walk the extra kilometre up to the Brunswick Street train station to find him lurking near the toilets. On such occasions she would make the most of her walk there and insert a couple of coins in the slot that afforded her a timed shower.

Under the hot spray, toes curled up away from the dull sheen of the tiles, the marooned hairs and floating pubes left by whoever had preceded her into the cubicle, she felt like a cat stretching, puffing itself out, curling and uncurling, exposing its tummy fur, eyes closed, to the warm caress of a gentle sun. However, because she didn't have a towel, Jo had to put the clothes back on her wet body and *that* just about spoiled the benefit of the shower. Clothes, be they dirty or clean, on her wet body, was an experience far worse for Jo than that of sleeping on the ground, tucked out of sight, in the darkest corner of a garden she had no right to be in but that, so far, was keeping her safe while she slept.

When she talked to the restaurant manager, Jo didn't say much at all. At first, it had been just enough to let Maureen Leal feel that she was neither dangerous nor sick. Just enough to let her know that she did appreciate the free food and the menial tasks given to her because they afforded her *only* the lifestyle she desired – a few dollars daily that allowed her to score regularly and a take-away meal. Jo no longer aspired to anything beyond that. Anything beyond that would suck her back into the mainstream. With a mainstream MO.

Taking the lid off the plastic container was always a special moment for Jo. Immediate gratification. Food very quickly becomes the absolute focus in the daily routine of any transient. Jo figured that food could also become a small source of power for the one who had some to enjoy, to sell or to give away. An object of desire, too, for the one who didn't. Food and safety while asleep were two of three focal preoccupations. So Jo would close her eyes before she opened the container and, eyes still closed, she would bring the food to her nose and inhale deeply to guess what her *plat du jour* might be.

Some mornings the container was filled with something French like *saucisses gratinées,* a tasty but non fussy dish, and though Jo knew rice was all that *usually* came with most other meat dishes, Maureen always added a few vegetables on the side. Other times, it might be a Risotto or pasta and, always, extra vegetables or a bit of salad. And a cup of wonderfully aromatic coffee in a Styrofoam cup.

Jo would sit at a park table and make the contents of the plastic container last from early morning till well into the night. She would eat the vegetables and salad first because she had read somewhere that if vegetables weren't refrigerated within two hours after they were cooked, they could grow harmful bacteria. She had to take her chances with the rest and so she always left her bag in the shade. She would suck on the last morsels of that dish in lieu of the sweet munchies she was, after the last bong of the night, craving almost irrationally. She had to make some of the dish last till *after* she'd emptied the juice of her dead bong at the base of the furthest tree in the darkest corner of the garden.

"What say we sit down like somewhere in the shade, uh?" Tamara was already lifting her bag off the ground. "And hey … " she began meeting Jo's eyes, " … you could show me where you hang, I mean, around here."

Jo squinted into the sun before glancing back at Tamara who was nonchalantly hoisting the bulky bag over her shoulder. "Don't you have anywhere *you* should be going?" she asked, lips twitching. "This doesn't feel like a Saturday morning when people like you drop in for a look at the river and a picnic." She scanned the park. "Not enough joggers around for it to be a weekend morning. Sunday's even worse but I don't mind. And if this was Sunday, there'd already be some action around here." Jo wheeled around slowly, looking for evidence that it couldn't possibly be a weekend morning at New Farm Park. "Dads and sons, they'd be tossing around the footie, like over there." She pointed to the flat grassy ground on the other side of the rose garden. "Then more dads and more sons and some uncles, they'd be into a bit of pretend cricket with plastic bats." She rolled her eyes. "That's when the little girls run on the edge of the ... the action and what they do is run after lost balls with Pooch-the-dog running after them. Or ... " Jo cocked her head towards the circular drive, "we'd have boys messing around with skateboards on all the concrete bits they can find while little sisters ride little bikes. Pink usually. *Still pink* after all these years," she added, in the tone she would use to someone who made it a habit of eating tinned fish months beyond expiry date. Uninterrupted by Tamara, Jo continued pulling together impressions out of past observations. "Now I've got a real decent bik– Uh, well, *used* to have one." Tamara heard the snag in the voice but, mind ticking, she kept on walking silently half a step off to Jo's right. "I think it used to be purple or something but I'd say its basic colour was definitely rust." With a faint twist of the lips, Jo continued. "I mean, as in real rust. In fact it's the rust that held the damn thing together. But ... if I ever had another bike, I'd only get something like, yeah, black. All black, no decals. No name, nothing. You got a bike?"

While Jo talked, from her references and inferences, Tamara had been attempting to put together a composite picture of the girl's emotional make-up. Caught off guard by the question, Tamara glanced at the girl. "A bike? Me? Uh ... no. I drive. Or I Rollerblade."

Jo stopped walking. "That's what you got in there? Skates?" She tapped the backpack that had made an unusual klunking sound when Tamara had first dropped it on the ground. Tamara nodded and Jo rubbed her scalp with such vigour that her nose crinkled in the effort. Tamara blinked, unsure as to what that gesture might mean and, to get things moving again, she explained how she used her blades whenever practical and it was very practical to use them whenever she came by ferry, from her office in the city, to this particular neck of the woods. She laced up during the crossing and skated from the landing.

"Cool," Jo interrupted too quickly. "Well, *here* on weekends, what happens is that the mothers get to fuss with whatever they've packed in the esky. On face value ... " she added flatly, to signal a pre-drawn conclusion, "all's peachy pink for the nuke family."

Tamara glanced again at the young woman and, though she was not walking level with her, she detected something akin to tension, a different type of tightness in Jo's movements, in the swing of her arms. She wasn't sure whether it had been the mention of the old bicycle that had subtly altered Jo's mood. Or if Jo had been caught unprepared by *her* freedom to get places on rollerblades, to catch a ferry, to work in the city, to visit friends. Tamara thought that, perhaps, *her* freedom of movement had made the tall girl more keenly aware of the airtight pocket in which she had locked herself. *Maybe,* Tamara speculated, *maybe she envies what she perceives as my ease to live the life that she's finding so difficult to grab herself.*

"Yeah ... peachy pink but that's only until someone chucks a tantrum. And *then*," Jo added neutrally but, Tamara suspected, more out of a need to fill the silence than impart crucial knowledge, "there's the lovers. Now I'd say they rock on here for a bit of privacy, right? But they want it scenic, sexy and, like surrounded by a zillion people? I don't get it. Where's the fun value, huh?" she asked, clearly directing her question to Tamara who opened her mouth to answer but Jo needed to add more. "Not riveting watching, any of it, but definitely dis-trac-ting. Dis-con-nec-ting," she enunciated slowly, nodding her head to the beat of each syllable.

"You're right, it's not Saturday," Tamara jumped in, wishing she had more on the girl. "Not Sunday either. Only Thursday. And there's someone, an ex-client actually, that I need to visit not far from here. Which, by the way, is why I told my colleague, you know, the one who got the call about you, that I'd scoot around here myself on the way to Moray Street. Which way for now?" she asked, before adding, "I don't have to be there for another hour or so."

"Let's go sight-seeing, then," Jo replied lightly, angling her steps towards the river. "I guess I can afford to take a little time off *my* busy schedule, too, huh?" she grinned again. "Mental health stuff, right?"

Like a passing cloud, the unpleasant connection that had fleeted through Jo's thoughts seemed to have vaporised high above her tousled head. *Gone for good or to return later?* Tamara wondered.

"Absolutely. Mental health rocks." She smiled back. "What were you listening to?" She pointed her chin towards the headphones dangling against Jo's neck like a thin liquorice stethoscope.

"Seattle sound. Nothing you'd know."

"Oh c'mon, kid. This grandma's not quite out of the race yet," Tamara answered playfully. "Seattle sound circa what, mid-late-eighties? Early *Nirvana* stuff? Garage-grunge ... Am I on the right track?" she asked, taking what cue she could from the print transfer on Jo's black T-shirt.

It's gonna be too dark to sleep again   Cornell, Seattle,'91

Jo grinned. "Close. *Soundgarden.*"

"Ha! See?" Tamara hammed on. "Got one of their CDs. *One.* But they're like defunct, right?"

Poets of alienation. Tamara remembered the tag that had attached itself to groups like *Soundgarden, Alice in Chains*, and *Nirvana,* whose sound and lyrics, like pied pipers, had compelled hordes of Gen X, disenfranchised teenagers, to ditch their Nintendo consoles and get back to a basic, almost tactile, focus on their disillusionment.

The in-your-face disadvantaged look, worn proudly, had been a must-have, particularly for the ones who had been *unfortunate* enough to be born privileged. A certain type of equality had been sought through second-hand gear, the flannelette-look, long over-sized, moth-eaten cardigans and clunky mountain boots.

Genuine grunge, as a sound, had lasted only a few years as bands like *Nirvana* and *Pearl Jam* found the mainstream popularity too enticing to remain permanently entrenched in their roots. The rest is history. But for the genuine souls, the teenagers who had not just followed a trend but had felt their alienation as a state of emotional deprivation, the ethos had remained intact. And Tamara suspected that in view of her youth, Jo had probably discovered the Grunge ideology *after* it had begun ebbing. Still, she reckoned, Jo could have embraced it all the same. Tamara thought that Jo's taste in music might be an important clue as to what made her tick and that perhaps she was emotionally arrested. As in still trapped in the warp? Feeling a deep-seated hopelessness in response to a sense of betrayal? Would that render her unwilling to have anyone pull the rug out from under her? Unwilling or unabl –

"Correct." Jo nodded duly impressed. "Disbanded in '94." After all *Soundgarden,* though one of Seattle's first grunge bands, had never achieved *Pearl Jam's* or *Nirvana's* status. "But," Jo was happy to explain, "they were right there at the creation of the original grunge sound, you know, garage, dirty and smudged, along with *Green River.* Which album d'you have?"

"Uh … " Green cat-eyes narrowed in concentration. "It's like I haven't listened to it for a while, mind you, but– "

"What song d'you remember?"

"Ah, that I can answer. Used to really like the line that said something like, *'Now I wouldn't mind if you swallowed my pride.'* The first time I heard it," she turned to face Jo, "I thought, Shit, that's so cool because it's *our* own pride, right, that we're normally told to swallow but *You* can swallow *mine* … Yeah … there's something satisfying about that like, about it being done. And there's a track I think's called Hunted Down or something." Tamara wondered how deep Jo was into this thing. Her gut feeling was that Jo, perhaps unfortunately, was not just a poseur.

"That's on the Screaming Life album. That one was released as a 12 inch. Six hundred copies on, ready for that?" Jo grinned like a schoolgirl. "Orange vinyl. In '87, I think."

"And which you've got with you, then?"

"*Badmotorfinger*, their number four. Pure hard rock. The thing with them is that they didn't go commercial and they didn't even stay with the real dirty, gritty garage grunge sound. They polished up what they had but they still moved their own way and, for me, the appeal's mostly about what their music does inside my head. Like Rusty Cage. I mean, it's a real old cover but the way they do it, it's like *so* … out there," Jo went on explaining for the sheer joy of talking about something she liked to someone she was beginning to like. That combo, or anything remotely close, hadn't happened since she had left the picnic table at Burleigh Heads. And of course, then, she had been talking to someone she loved about making love. "Should give the *Badmotor* thing a whirl, you know. I'm pretty sure you'd like it. *Big sound.* Chris Cornell, the lead guy, he sounds a bit like Robert Plant … but the sound's more like *Zeppelin's.* Might have to go second-hand to find it, though."

"Or I could order it if it's not on the shelves."

"True. Uh … I mean … " Jo felt awkward. "If we were neighbours or something, I'd lend you my copy but – "

"Hey, that's cool. I wouldn't have you separate yourself from that disk. No way, even if we were neighbours," Tamara replied earnestly. "What I'll do is give the Music Shop a ring and see what they can do to … uh … to further … my education before I'm like, totally past it."

Jo smiled, though she was back to looking straight ahead. They kept on walking, almost side by side, Jo only half a step ahead. "Actually," she said, returning the conversation to Tamara's first query about sightseeing. "I'm not going to take you where I hang." She paused to consider Tamara's reaction. As there wasn't any, she continued. "But there's a place I like that's probably not all *that* cool, I mean, to go there on my own." She rubbed the side of her nose and Tamara noticed the ingrained dirt under Jo's fingernails, and if Jo hadn't been looking straight ahead, she would have seen the social worker wince in spite of herself. "Oh, it's not like it's cut-throat or anything. It'd be OK if I stayed … aware and all but … " She paused to consider what to say next. "That kind of defeats the purpose though, doesn't it, prime real estate position, scenic surroundings by the river and … on the lookout for dicknose males looking for a– " She broke off abruptly. "Well, let's just go there and see." Jo looked at the back of her hand and touched the bite left by the rose's thorn.

Tamara saw her wince at the graze. "What have you got there," she asked. "A cat scratch?"

Jo looked at her blankly. "A cat? Here with me? No cat," but she felt compelled to add, "A rose."

"Right. Still," Tamara saw the edges of the scratch were red and slightly swollen, almost curling over beads of dry blood. "Looks a bit, like, angry if you ask me."

"Nah, just a scratch."

They crossed the park diagonally, keeping the bandstand kiosk on their left. Jo aimed her steps towards the Brunswick Street cul-de-sac.

"We going to the old ferry landing *toilet block?*" Tamara asked jokingly, once it became obvious they were about to run out of park. "Thought you said *prime* real estate."

"Close enough," Jo replied. "We're going to the old ferry *landing.*"

And she lead Tamara past the old landing's white concrete shelter and wooden benches, down a few steps to a concrete ledge *behind* the toilet block but built right on the bank of the Brisbane River. From that ledge, the body of rippling water seemed unusually dark.

Transparent clumps of thin mangrove trees tried valiantly to obstruct the view here and there but there was no doubt about it, they were indeed on a prime piece of land. Very narrow, and only a few metres in length, but prime.

"Just as you said." Tamara lowered herself to the ground and, at once, offloaded the weight of her bag just as Jo had, except that Jo had already gathered her thin body into a squatting position, linking her long arms around her shins.

Jo pointed to the opposite bank. "Check out the house."

Ankles crossed, the ridged soles of her desert boots pointing in opposite directions, Tamara squinted across the river at a massive white 1920s vintage high on the hill. "Damn. A hell of a lot of Aussie dollars even just for the smallest ones. Like those under the ramshackle arrangement, just there."

At mid-height on the grassy cliff was what could only be described as an eyesore – a long building of old bricks and a ramshackle collection of scruffy chamferboard cottages that, elsewhere in the world, would have been torn down a long time ago to accommodate premium real estate. Closer to the river's edge, larger houses, evidently renovated quite recently, had proudly staggered themselves in an uppity sort of way. "OK, look at it this way," Tamara chuckled, "they have the river at their feet but they also have a splendid view of this *toilet block*. So, all things considered," she added, "your view's much better than theirs and it's free." Tamara threw a quick smile in Jo's direction before leaning her back against the toilet block wall. "Well done." She closed her eyes. Jo smiled a smile that brought on two little creases near the corners of her lips.

Although the *new* ferry landing, also white, was only some sixty metres to the left, on a weekday Jo's pozzie would remain fairly deserted until about lunchtime. In fact, once seated on the ledge, nothing was visible except for the scraggly clumps of trees, the Hawthorne-side of the river, a few sailboats on narrow tacks and the bright, hot, morning sun in a clear blue sky. Hard to imagine the park was inner city.

Though the view behind the old toilet block would be entirely wasted on a druggie, at that time of the day the ledge was an ideal place to shoot up because of the visual privacy it afforded. A very private place, too, at night for individuals out for quick sex and, too, for any predatory male out for anything else. Jo was right. No matter how disconnecting, this place had a wildness about it that could be dangerous for her once lost inside the maze of her *raison d' être,* while big bass and big drum sounds boomed inside her head. Questions peeled off each other like so many onion layers while Tamara gazed at the view without seeing it. She wanted to know how truly resilient Jo was. She wanted to know if she was the 'At Risk' type who downgraded easily and could settle for very little for very long. She also wanted to know why Jo was there in the first place. Was it her way of searching for something authentic to hold on to? Tamara was grasping for clues as to how the girl could be helped.

Still in her birdlike crouch, Jo broke the silence. "See, it's not like New York out here, I mean for the homeless. We don't have to fight each other for a shelter or for the privilege of sleeping on a hot air grate. We don't even need a box to crawl into, right?"

Tamara half-opened her eyes without moving from against the wall. "But the nights are getting cooler, aren't they?" she said. "Down to what, twenty degrees? Maybe a bit less already. In a few weeks' time, it'll be down to fifteen degrees. And fifteen degrees at night while you're trying to sleep *feels* a lot colder, I bet, than the same fifteen degrees in the sun, tucked away from the wind." She glanced at Jo but if her warning about the changing weather conditions meant anything to her, the loose way in which she balanced herself on her heels did not reflect it.

Some time later, Jo did unfold her legs from under her to sit on the ledge near enough to Tamara who only glanced at her before returning her gaze to the sparkling water.

"But you're right about the New York thing. You don't have to go begging for food either. I suppose people around here are, on the whole, helpful enough."

"To me, yes. But you see," Jo added reflectively, "I'm not black."

"True again," Tamara agreed, "You're not black and because you're so tall and thin– "

"I bring the best out of the bleeding hearts. Like Maureen," Jo remarked deprecatingly.

"*For now.* Because the Brisbane number of homeless is still very low. Like what, between three and five hundred, max. Hard to be exact but it's within that range and scattered in so many wide open spaces. Like even in this park, I bet there's hardly anyone here at night." Green eyes narrowed on Jo's profile. "Jo? Who *is* here at night? Are you?"

"Not at night, no. I don't like it here at night. But I know there's often a few Aborigines under the big trees, opposite the bowls club. And the usual white trash that fall into drunken stupor by 4.00 p.m. The police move everyone out but– "

"Got a house to go to?"

Jo shifted uncomfortably. "Me?" Tamara nodded. "Well … yes and no."

"Jo, *how* do you shelter *proactively* for the night?" Tamara asked pointedly.

Jo gave the social worker another of her speculative glances. Eyes narrowed and lips puckered, she crunched through what she could afford to tell her. "Look, there's this house … " Jo began and stopped. She wavered but decided to continue, figuring she *could* afford to tell Tamara how *proactive* she was at night. After all, Maddy already knew about the garden though Jo had yet to tell her where it was. "I've come across it from the start, right? Beginner's luck and all." Jo shrugged. "Never anyone around but no heap of junk mail falling out of the mailbox, either. So, I'm not sure what goes on during the day-time. It's all neat except for the backyard. But there's never any light on but, again, I never go there until well after midnight. So, anyway," she added, squinting into the steady-blue sky directly above her head, "what I do is squat a corner of the backyard that's got one of those thick Besser-block concrete walls pretty much all around. That's as safe as I … Well, it's safe … I mean, while I'm doing … this." Shards of refract-ed sunlight glistened on the river's back.

"How long you gonna be able to hold on to that crib, you think? I mean, what?" Tamara spread her hands. "Whoever lives there's away on holiday? Or they're pensioners who go to sleep after the news. Or … *what?*"

"Don't know," Jo answered testily. "Who cares, right? I enjoy the lull." More gently, she added, "While I have that option open." An Ibis flew heavily across her line of vision, white feathers dingy white, curved black beak curving back towards its belly. She frowned at it. She didn't like Ibises. There were a lot of them in the park like in every other park and they made her uneasy. The Ibises were always grubby. They scavenged in the bins, under benches, even in between blades of grass. They were the only dirty birds she had ever seen. Jo thought of birds as she did of cats: never dirty, always shiny and beautiful. Even pigeons were clean, not that there were any in New Farm Park.

As far as Jo was concerned, Ibises were as brazen as they were ugly with their tiny shrivelled up black-skin heads and overstuffed bodies plonked on shortened heron legs. She thought they were a sad bird specimen and that whoever had put the prototype together must've run out of good parts.

A little sailboat turned on a starboard tack. A tiny toy-soldier figure moved at the base of one of the houses across the river. "When my good luck runs out … " Jo resumed, "I'll *pro-activate* somewhere else. Not at the Salvos, though, that's for sure. Too many weirdos there." Eyes lost on an inward thought, she added, "Like me. They look like me … a few years from now. But not me now." She rounded her shoulders against a shiver. "Not me just yet."

Tamara let silence settle over them once again but it was more a non-silence. There was the lapping sound of the river losing ground under the pull of the outgoing tide. There were the loose rigging sounds of sailboats at anchor. There were the muted sounds of the park and Brunswick Street's cul-de-sac only a few metres away on the other side of the toilet block.

"Anyway," Jo started again, "You're right. Generally people around here are nice and helpful and– "

"And you must be one of the very fe– " Tamara swivelled on her hips to face Jo more squarely. "No, let me say that again. I'm ready to bet you're the only woman out here on her own, right?" Before Jo had a chance to answer, Tamara added, "The only *white* woman, right?" Jo shrugged her thin shoulders again. "You see, Jo, from what I've been reading … " Tamara added, intent on finishing her thought, "white women tend to take to their cars– "

"That's where they all are?" Jo asked, as if that answered a long felt question. "Bunkered *inside* their cars?"

"Or they shack up for the night and a place to showe–"

"Oh. Right. Probably safer being fucked by a relative stranger than raped by a total pervert lurking in the park," Jo said.

"No doubt," Tamara added caustically before letting the conversation drop out again. She needed to buy herself time while she thought of another tack that might give her a better handle on the young woman.

For a brief moment they both fell silent until Jo ventured a new thought. "You said there were a couple of reasons why women ended up on skid row. I mean, earlier you said that." A little crease of tension sat upright and thin between her eyebrows. "So, besides running away from like, domestic shit … What's another reason?"

"Mental illness." Tamara kept her voice to a mellow conversational tone as she glanced at the young woman to gauge whether her answer might have stirred something in her.

Jaw muscles bunched, aquiline nose sharply sensual against the blue sky, tufts of ratty jet-black hair at odd angles, Jo swallowed hard. Tamara did not attempt to fill the new silence with words. The slack-mouthed sounds of the water, as it licked the black rocks at the women's feet, as it curled and uncurled around the thin tree trunks, the gentle sussurus of tree-leaves busy straining the breeze through their thin surface, *that* and the occasional cackle of a bird overhead were all Jo needed to fill her ears. That was all she needed but she needed that much to wrap around the thoughts that had begun a bumper-car ride inside her head. She rested her forehead on her knees to better hear all the sounds inside her head.

Mental illness! What kind of a fuck answer is that? That question screamed inside her head because she had already worked out about the panic attack that had ripped through her back at Burleigh as the light had gone off, somewhere on the sixth floor of an apartment block. She had also worked something out of the subsequent or had it been the *simultaneous* explosion of adrenaline that had electrified her into bolting erratically into the night. What she had worked out for herself, one long nighttime hour at a time, one excruciatingly long hour overlapping another and another into dawn, into weeks and beyond, was that both reactions had to have been spurred on by a freaked-out brain.

The same freaked-out brain that was keeping her entrenched in the park, wet, cold and alone, instead of being comfortably curled up, forehead tucked against the rust-red hair on the nape of Maddy's neck. Hips and sex curled around the warm firmness of her buttocks. One arm wrapped over her lover's body. Besides, Jo had worked out that entrenching herself in this fucked up way of life on the edge of the park, *by choice,* was the proof that something very warped lived inside her head. Mental illness. Jo was not, however, that far gone not to know that the social worker was right. And so, she kept on peering over her kneecaps. Tamara saw her straighten her shoulders and breathe in deeply but quietly.

Imperturbable, the fluid body of water moved on. It shifted. It changed. It reshaped itself. Maddy had used different words with Jo but her words had yielded a meaning similar to Tamara's, except that Jo had let *Maddy's* words fly past her like mere debris lifted by the wind.

She had done so because she had been afraid to close her hand over any one of Maddy's words, around one of the thoughts it triggered. She had been afraid to grab it, to pluck it out of the storm. A child too afraid to uncurl her fingers to see what the bug, snatched out of the summer light, actually looked like now that she, perhaps unwittingly, had interrupted its flight. Afraid of her own inability to deal with whatever awareness would stir inside her. Afraid to deal with it even for Maddy's sake. But Tamara had spoken the two words out loud and *they* clung to her.

The scarab clung. It dug its tiny spiky heels into the palm of her hand, not wanting to let *her* go. And Jo chickened out. She didn't trust herself to toss Tamara into the slippery vortex that had sucked her away from the picnic table back at Burleigh. She didn't trust Tamara enough to entrust *her* with what she *knew* had unhinged her. So she asked, "And the third most common reason?"

"Drug addiction." One boot on the ledge, the other resting lightly on a black rock still shiny from the receding tide, Tamara sat sideways to better see the girl. She noticed Jo sag a little more.

The bright sun flat on Jo's thighs was unforgiving and, for the first time, Tamara noticed the many stains that dotted the thin cloth of her army-styled trousers. Actually, what Tamara saw were the *ghosts* of past stains. She was seeing the residual imprints that remain when simple soap is not enough to lift dirt, when only the alkalis and enzymes of a laundry detergent will shift ingrained stains.

"Abuse, too. Not necessarily physical," Tamara added carefully, tuned-in to Jo's non-verbals. "Emotional abuse can have devastating, delayed repercussions on one's psyche." She pulled her other foot up on the ledge and hugged both knees. "And that *can* get tied up to the mental illness thing. *And* to the drug abuse thing." She snuck a glance at her watch. She'd have to be leaving soon.

Jo nodded imperceptibly and settled in another silence before she smiled unwillingly. "OK, let's just say I'm pro-choice."

Tamara blinked. "What? You're out in the friggin' streets because you're pregnant?" She unlinked her arms from around her knees to lay both hands flat on the gravelly ledge.

Jo looked at her. Grey eyes on green. They stared at each other, each one confused by the other's silence until Jo said, "*Pregnant?* Me?" She couldn't resist adding, "I'm gay." And like a schoolgirl pleased with herself, she ginned smugly. Like a schoolgirl or like the cat that got to lick all the cream. "C'mon," she said, misreading Tamara's expression. "Gimme a break. That's *got* to be the best protection against the violence thing you're so worried abou– What's so fuckin' funny, huh?"

"Hey … I'm not laughing, I'm smiling. Not the same thing at all," Tamara said, back-combing her hair away from her forehead.

"So why the big smile, then? What's so– "

Tamara's hand flashed instinctively towards Jo's arm but stopped short of touching it. "Listen," she said seriously, "I'm smiling because of *all* the fucked-up decisions you seem to have been making lately, the fact that you're gay is like, *so* bloody *sane!*" Green eyes grinned. "Finally something *sensible* from you. Probably because the gay thing goes back further than like, the recent crap you've chosen to put yourself through."

"What, gay's sensible?"

"Absolutely. Why? Don't you think it is?"

"Oh, it's fine," Jo replied, one eyebrow arched, "but it's not like I've busted a gut getting there or anything. And it's not something I've had to decide about. It just is. Anyway," she shrugged, "why would a straight chick think it's so cool, huh?" she asked suspiciously.

"Wouldn't have the foggiest why a straight chick might think dykes are cool. But I'm not straight, so *I* think it's real cool."

"*You* gay?" Jo's gaze weighed up Tamara. Her eyes were as close to saying, You havin' me on or what? as her mouth was, but the woman was already moving on.

"Been a dyke for the past what, thirteen years or so." And she added something she thought would make Jo smile. "Can't remember for sure 'cause you know what they say about time like, *screaming* past when you're having such a blast of a time, right?" Green cat eyes gleam.

"Yeah." Jo nodded. "I know all about *lol*," she said using the chatroom abbreviation that 'connected' lesbians feel compelled to type as an adjunct to just about everything that may otherwise be taken seriously. Each time Jo came across yet another lol posting, she'd think caustically that surely life for all the dykes out there in good old Briz/vegas couldn't provide them with so much comic relief that they just had to laugh out loud after each of the most mundane utterances.

"*Laughing Out Loud?*" Tamara ventured.

"Yeah, lol. Like me and myself, right, we do a lot of that lately," Jo snorted. "A lot of laughing out loud. Should though." Nodding to herself, she added, "Good for the brain cells. Laughing's good to remain … focused, right? So, Ms Social Worker, how old are you?"

"Oh ... so who's getting personal now, huh?" Tamara teased. "Just turned thirty." She tapped the steel casing of the watch that sat loosely over her wrist. "Birthday present. From my lover. Emilie," she added lightly as a trust thing, hoping that Jo would be attuned to it. "She thought like, me turning thirty was about the right time to turn up to places on time." Cat-eyes smiled. "Used to have a bit of a history about keeping her waiting and she'd worry and ... yeah," Tamara slid a finger under the tan sharkskin leather band to centre the watch-face on her wrist.

"Cool watch." Jo meant it.

"Right," Tamara continued, "so that little three-oh celebration pops me right on the *other* side of the hill. What do you reckon?"

"I don't reckon anything." Jo's voice was thin. She returned her attention to the river before adding, "I bet *you* already had your head together the day you were born. Mature, stable and wise." She opened her mouth to add something else but didn't.

"Oh right. Thanks a lot," Tamara exclaimed. "That makes me sound like I've been a wizened old gnome all my life. Seriously not true. But OK," she redirected seriously, "back to you – what's the pro-choice thing about then?"

Jo fiddled with one of her grey shoelaces before facing Tamara again. "It's about that I've chosen to abnegate all *comfort* but that doesn't make me a charity case. And that doesn't make me suffering from some disease I need to be rescued from either." Her voice rose. "Same as I'm really getting right fed up with people giving me their two cents worth of advice on how I should run *my* life." A familiar coldness seeped through her. "I've chosen to live the freedom, that's all. Fucking harmless, really."

Tamara inquired calmly, "You do pot?"

"Why? You think I'm *using?*"

"Just what you said before about 'living the freedom'. That's a druggie thing to sa– "

"Oh, right. Well, never mind that, then," Jo snapped.

"Listen, Jo, thing is that I don't believe you can keep on doing what you're doing. Yeah, like you said, the abnegation of all comfort, day after day, without spicing up your days with something. Well, it's like I don't believe that's possible for anyone, not just you. Aw'right? Now," Tamara continued steadily, "the cheapest alternative would be to stick your head in a paper bag and chrome, right, as in inhale, take that shit inside your brain, but like, you don't come across as a huffer. And you're not the Methylated Spirits type. So ... up the quality ladder, there's cheap plonk by the four-litre cask. Much cooler, while you still can afford it, I'd say grass would be the thing for you." She opened her mouth and shut it before starting again. "I'm ready to bet you're not laying tracks. Not yet. How accurate am I then, huh? Do I get at least one jelly bean or something?"

Jo's eyes met Tamara's. She flashed two fingers. *"Two* jelly beans. You're right. Nights are so fucking long after each already bloody long day and yeah," she snorted, "let's just say that I self-medicate, OK?" Realising she had used one of the terms her mother had used to justify her alcohol dependence, Jo looked away. "Herbal pain-management therapy."

"Why *pain* management?"

Jaw muscles once again tight, Jo squinted at her hands and slid them flat over her thighs, over the ghosts of past stains.

"Jo." Tamara pulled her eyes away from the scratch that straddled the inverted trident of veins on the back of Jo's hand. Though the beads of blood had dried up, the seam looked a little too red and angry. "Why don't you tell me a little bit about the pain management thing?"

Jo curled her fingertips against the palm of her hand. Slowly she uncurled them, one millimetre at a time, and again, temporarily involving herself in a child's game of Now You See The Dirt - Now You Don't - Now You Do. Four crescents of dark grime in the bright sunlight. She looked at the social worker. "What can *you* do to me?" she asked in no more than a whisper.

The naivety of the question caught Tamara by surprise. "What can I do *to you?"* Green eyes seeking grey. "Nothing at all, Jo," Tamara protested. "I, we ... Queensland Health, we can't really do anything *to* you. Or for you." She smiled a quick smile that failed to reach her eyes. "You're not a child anymore, Jo. Not a minor. It's as you said – a choice thing ... as long as you don't slide into the serious self-harm thing." Tamara locked eyes with Jo. "The only thing anybody can do is *try* to knock some sense into you. Reinsertion into the mainstream, Jo, the sooner the better. That should be your first and foremost prior– "

"Oh. Right," Jo snarled, straightening out her long legs. "So you're going to fuck with me after all."

Tamara weighed up her options. "Uh, no, Jo." She shook her head. "I ... it's ... I'm actually not in the line of work that deals with young adults who are homeless *by choice."* She hesitated briefly. "Look ... Jo, reality is a lot simpler. All I *can* do is like, listen and suggest."

Jo glared at her and shook her head slowly, listening to something inside her head. "What say you hold back on the suggesting, then," she said gruffly, "and stick to listening." Her lips twitched into a conciliatory smile. "Deal?"

"Deal."

Navy-blue school uniform skirt tucked in between her thighs so that it didn't get messed up in the grass, Jo is all folded up on her haunches. The sun has just gone down behind the tree-line that visually delineates the garden, separating it from the horizon. The big house behind her made her feel sad so she retreated to that place where she knew she would remain disturbed only by her thoughts. *Too fucking big for just the two of us,* she thinks, momentarily forgetting that her father also lives under that roof and that Jarrah still has a room full of her own high school stuff. She hardly ever sees her father anymore. *The fucking bastard's got to be having a mistress tucked away somewhere.* She sighs. She resents her father. She resents his lack of involvement, his distance. Not from her as much as from her mother. The effort required to resent her father *that much* makes the blood rush at her temples. The thought of Isabel makes Jo unfold herself out of her squatting position and simply plop on the grass. Isabel doesn't like to see Jo squatting. If in a good mood, she might tell her daughter, "Little Jo, darling, you really need to sit down properly and make use of that built-in padded seat that the good god's given us." And Isabel would pat her own slim backside. And Jo would playfully answer something along the lines that if the good god above had wanted *her* to sit on *her* butt, he would've given *her* a lot more padding just there. And Isabel would chuckle. She would tousle her daughter's jet-black bob and, sometimes, she would sit beside her, often in silence.

At other times, either mother or daughter would engage the other in a conversation suitably light-hearted. Suitably light-hearted meant nothing said about Jo's father. Nothing said about Jarrah who never visited often enough. Nothing said about Isabel's fears that her cancer could return to chew at her joints, that the reality of life as an amputee would kill her. Nothing about Isabel's growing dependence on the nightly vodka and tonics and, *suitably light-hearted* also precluded talking about the choleric bouts that plagued more and more of the evenings Jo desperately wanted to spend at peace inside her world, at peace inside her mother's world. So mother and daughter would talk about the mother's bridge games, the few of her friends she still saw regularly and occasionally entertained. And they would talk about the daughter's netball and hockey games, and they would talk about her young friend, Amber, who, Isabel didn't know, had just become Little Jo's lover. Mother and daughter would also talk and dream about Jo's future as an architect. 'As a brilliant architect,' Isabel would reiterate.

One evening, Jo was sitting on her haunches while reorganising the collection of CDs she had spread at her feet. From that slightly elevated angle she could read the titles more easily. She was trying to figure out which was better– ordering them by album title or by the performer's name – when kaboosh! She felt a sharp dazing shock against her right temple. The bright blue and yellow colours on a paperback cover crash-landed on some of the CDs close to her foot. Stunned, Jo watched on with some sort of slow motion awareness as a few CDs slid and scuttled on the parquet floor to collide against others. She didn't stand up. She didn't turn around. She didn't say, What the f ... in total surprise because she *did* know what had happened. She simply bit her bottom lip and slid to sit on the floor. And then came Isabel's vicious, booze-altered vituperations.

"How many times! Jo?" Jo didn't turn around because she had seen it too many times already. She closed her eyes and still she saw it, her mother's face tight with anger. She saw them, the veins that had popped on her forehead, that corded along her neck and throat under the effort it required to shout with such dark intensity, with so much venom. Jo could have stuck her fingers in both ears to block out the cracking notes of her mother's ranting but she didn't. She didn't bother with that anymore because, just as her mother's face had learnt how to creep under and behind her closed eyes, her mother's voice had learnt to creep inside her ears, no matter how deeply Jo inserted her fingertips. "How *many* times, Jo? Why the fuck do you carry on like a bloody native? My daughter, a fucking island native from some tribe so ... so ... forsaken they haven't yet been *granted* the intelligence to figure out that *a rock*, for goodness sake, a fucking rock, is what they need to be sitting on. They haven't figured out yet that this *other* position is the one they bloody shit from! Where d'you learn *your* manners, Jo?" Isabel yelled. "Who in that fucking school of yours sits like that, huh?"

Jo knew it wouldn't do any good, possibly quite the contrary, to agree that no one at her *fucking* school sat that way. The Senior girls at St Joan's had taken to calling that manner of sitting the Joanna Brenner Squat, the JB Squat for short. But *they* did it in good humour, more fascinated by the tall girl's ability *not* to topple over than anything else.

The thing was that the older girls didn't *really* mind sitting wherever during their lunch breaks, be it on the concrete slab of a tennis court, or on the sparse grass under a shady tree, or in the middle of the oval, even if they shrieked and carried on each time one of them had to pick a prematurely discarded lolly or a sticky bit of wrapper from the pleats of her navy-blue skirt.

Nose crinkled up in amazing pantomimes of distaste of truly gagging proportions, the girls would pick at the sticky matter that had once been a much-chewed piece of gum. Under their fingers, it would stretch and yield compliantly but would not detach itself, not completely, from the cloth. Jo didn't get the shrieking thing and Jo minded sticky matters attaching themselves to the back of her skirts. The JB squat worked for her.

"Anyway, the thing is," Jo tried to explain to Tamara, "it's that seesaw of … of emotions like, not knowing when she'd cuddle me and call me Little Jo, I mean as she had for the best part of what, seventeen years really. Or *screech* … It's the screeching and the words … That's what hurt the most. Each time. From the day it all began when I was nine or ten to the day I found her … dead." Jo slammed her eyes into Tamara's to counteract the flutter of uncertainty she saw in the cat-green eyes. "Yes, dead. Dead on her bed. The cigar box on the bed beside her, empty. And empty, too, the bloody vials. All of them. All six. Morphine," Jo explained realising that the woman seated by her side would be as familiar with the intricacies of Isabel's story as an Eskimo with jungle lore. "And the syringe … empty too. I *still see* the moist stain on the sheet near my mother's hand, you know, where the sheet had come up to touch the point of the needle where it had … where it had fallen after … afterwards." Jo straightened out her back and blinked into the sunlight. Tamara watched her swallow hard. She watched her draw in her top lip. She watched her as one watches, breath suspended, a funambulist on her tightrope. "And I'm sure she did it … not long before I got home from school."

Jo's aquiline profile was all Tamara had to look at but the tension in the jawline and the tension around the eyes and the tension in the balled up fists that Jo held locked in tight between her knees, all of that told Tamara all she needed to know. She didn't need to see the naked, unadulterated, raw pain in the girl's eyes. She didn't need to *see it* to feel the depth of the fracture as accurately as if, like a doctor, she could run her fingers along the jagged edges of her wound and feel the anger swell from underneath. "Like, well ... yeah ... there was the moist ... the morphine stain on the sheet and ... She would've known it'd be *me* finding her. And she didn't even bother to wait till I got home and ... " Jo continued, perhaps seeking a release, *there,* as they both sat side by side facing the river. On opposite sides of a river that was overflowing its banks inside Jo's mind. "She was still warm ... a bit." Jo's brow tightened again and she didn't turn back to Tamara. "And ... You see, I could never tell what would trigger her anger. Not each first time. I was never ready for it. And she scared me so much when she was ... like that ... angry and ... *so freaking me* out. And then she went and killed herself."

The water licked the base of the dark rocks it could no longer submerge. Riding aimlessly on the back of a current, a bright red wrapper floated towards the thin tree trunks. Silently, Tamara watched Jo watch the bright red wrapper. "And the night before she suicided ... " Jo's voice was low. "She had been so mellow. She didn't even have *one* drink." Jo jerked her head and her eyes latched on to Tamara's who, though she had been waiting for it, blinked under the intensity of the contact. "I had offered to make her one, you know, to mix her the usual before I went upstairs but she said, 'Not tonight, darling. Not tonight." Jo returned her gaze to the river, to the red wrapper that had wedged itself between two thin tree trunks less than a metre away from Jo's rubber soles. "I remember that I looked at her. I still see her, book in one hand, stretched out on the sofa in her pale ... pale silk kimono, the one with the embossed flowers, her favourite one. Jarrah and I had bought it for her ... years before. She asked something about my homework and I told her I hadn't gotten around to it yet. 'So, off you go,' she said. And I just went up to my room, as I usually did, to get on with my homework. And that was that. I didn't think about it anymore. Can you believe that?" Jo asked, stricken. "Can you believe that I didn't hang around. That I didn't say anything about her *not* drinking? Not one fucking single *positive* thing? I didn't even think anything about it. I guess I just ... I ... I just assumed she'd get one for herself a bit later and ... But that wasn't it, *was it?"* Jo's pain slammed into Tamara who looked back, too aware that she could *only* be there and she could *only* listen. She could only be *there* like a gnome in a garden, as useful as a rock stuck in the middle of the river that was flooding its banks inside Jo's heart. "She was preparing herself to die ... To die sober. *To die!"*

Grey eyes awash with panic, the panic of the helpless, the panic of the one about to be swallowed by quicksand or suffocated by the clinging mass of a mud swamp. "And I didn't even realise." Once the bright red wrapper was no longer free to float light as a feather on the current's back, it had become waterlogged. Lapping water weighed more and more heavily on its surface. "What I did was close the door to my room as I always did. Open the window." Jo mimed the gesture, long arms opening an invisible window that looked onto the river and the blue sky. "Slipped on the headphones," she said, covering her ears with both hands. "And lit up." Thumb and forefinger pressed together, Jo sucked on an invisible joint and inhaled. She held her breath, eyes closed. A few seconds later, ten perhaps, she exhaled and returned her attention to Tamara, eyes too shiny. "And I got down to doing my fucking *homework* because I was going to be an architect." Jo's shoulders slumped. She raked her chewed-up hair backwards. "A brilliant one, my mother always said."

Silence had to settle between the two women before Tamara found words that might be of some usefulness to Jo, but what could she have said that Jo could have used *right* at that moment? Her impulse was to scoot right up to the tall girl and hold her tight to confer to her some of the strength that *she* had in excess. Some of her strength with which to cancel out some of Jo's bone-deep pain, but Tamara didn't move towards Jo because professional counselling is not done by hugging distressed cases. Instead, she talked to the girl.

Jo listened quietly but what could she have heard that could have lessened any of the hurt that rode inside her?

After the bright red wrapper had finally sunk below the surface, Tamara asked about a lover. Did Jo have a lover? Jo had a lover but she had run away from that lover. Why had Jo run away from her lover? She ran away from her lover, Maddy, because, unbeknown to her, Jo had begun to become emotionally dependent on Maddy. That had *finally* happened because Maddy had made Jo feel safe. Maddy had made Jo feel loved. That had happened only because Maddy was strong and Jo loved Maddy's strength. It was a quiet, sensual strength.

"A gentle strength," Jo said. "A beautiful strength."

That was what Jo thought as she did her best to explain her lover to Tamara, and her guts churned and she knew why her guts churned. They churned because she loved the way Maddy made her feel safe *and* loved *and* appreciated. And she loved the way Maddy made her *body* feel when she made love to her. Jo knew that sometimes, too, Maddy was able to reach her core when they made love. And *that* was beautiful. And *that* was wonderful. And *that* was scary. It was so scary because it was all *so* conditional. And Tamara asked why Jo thought that Maddy's love was "like, *so* conditional."

"Isn't *all* love conditional?" Jo replied. The breeze from the river touched her hair. She looked up and for a moment, watching the little white clouds that had appeared at the east. Jo knew that Maddy *would* withdraw all that felt good to her. Jo knew, too, that Maddy *would* do that the minute she realised that her lover had only *so little* to give. She *would* do that the minute she realised that Jo had so many hang-ups. She *would* do that when she realised that loving Jo was not as easy as loving chocolate, or beer, or the light puffy clouds that had drifted in the otherwise blue sky above the river. Jo explained that Maddy hadn't yet realised that there was nothing much worth loving in her. "It's just a matter of time before she does and she'll cut me out of the loop."

"What is it about you that makes you think that Maddy doesn't really love *you*?" Jo didn't answer. "Jo, how do you know she hasn't already figured you out and … still, she loves you just the way you are?"

"You can *love* these little puffy white clouds because they're pretty. They're lovely. I'm not pretty. I'm not lovely. I'm too tall and too fucking thin. And I'm all screwed-up." She faced Tamara squarely as she added, "I'm anorexic. I know I am but I don't think Maddy's realised it yet. Isabel never did but then again, Isabel never knew that Amber and I had become lovers either. And Isabel didn't know that I knew about the cigar box." Jo returned her attention to the little clouds. Maddy might like little puffy clouds because little white clouds aren't threatening. They evaporate. They vaporise. They dissipate. *I wish I was a little puffy white cloud,* Jo thought. *Phhtt … gone. Not even important enough to rain down as they go.* "All I can do is take my … my … all my crap far, far away from Maddy. Far from her *before she finds me out.* Before she stops loving me." Jo stopped and swallowed. She looked at Tamara with the stricken expression of one who knows she is doomed, tightening and pulling the edges of her young face. And then, Tamara said something that sounded disjointed. "Jo, look. I hear you," she said. "I see you, I'm not an emotional retard but there's still like, this thing I need to ask you." Jo let her eyes travel back to the voice. "Uh, Jo … how does taking to the *streets* fit in with your pain?" Jo squinted. "I mean, how does it link *back* to Isabel? I don't get it. Why not just break up with Maddy?"

The eager schoolgirl expression had returned and Jo replied too readily, "Easy, Tamara. It goes like this." She said it confidently, using the social worker's name for the first time. She filled her lungs and, as if voicing a negatively worded healing affirmation, she said, "I don't *ever* want to be dependent on anyone. Not for love". Dark eyebrows tight, she glowered. "Don't ever want to be dependent like a bloody lap dog. Not on anyone for affection. Not for attention. Not ever again. Not for … not for … Not for any fucking thing, right?" She held Tamara's gaze before returning her attention to the spot of water that had swallowed the bright red wrapper.

Tamara's forehead furrowed in concentration as she struggled with mixed thoughts. Jo was not one of her clients. Their exchange was not prompted out of the usual rather stilted protocol that, too often, shrouded the personal history part of the depositions that victims of domestic violence had to share with her before she could, through Queensland Health Services, help them secure a Protection Order against an abusive party, or relocate. This was different. This was spontaneous. This was outside any intervention framework. This was not an intervention. There was nothing for her to intervene about. "OK. I'm not arguing your need to establish an emotional distance." She hesitated. "Listen, Jo," she started again. "I don't *know* your pain but I think I can understand it." She paused. "Do you believe that's a possible thing, that? To *not* know and yet be able to understand?" Tamara was struggling to find words that would resonate in Jo who was rubbing the soles of her Converse trainers on the black rocks newly uncovered by the receding tide, backwards and forwards, like a downhill skier at the starting gate. She watched Jo consider the question. She watched the young woman's profile, her aquiline nose, her pale cheekbone, and the dark ragged tufts of hair that fluttered ever so slightly in the breeze. She watched the long thin hands resting on her thighs at the end of long thin arms. And the dark red welt.

Though Jo had indulged in years of self-criticism and had under-fed her body for years, she had not yet become emaciated. She had not yet crossed the point of no return. She was *still* a borderline anorexic. Tamara let her eyes slide back to the red and angry arc that the rose thorn had scratched across the back of Jo's hand. Her immune system would be very low. And as thin as she was, the night breeze, the wind, the drop of temperature would go right through her.

Tamara dropped her eyes to the naked ankles that showed between the black cloth of the runners and the green cloth of Jo's army greens. She considered again the thin and clingy T-shirt that ended above the low waist of Jo's trousers baring the lower part of her back as she sat on the ledge. Jo ran her hands over the stains ghosted on her trousers and lifted her face to the sun. Tamara watched Jo hug herself under the hot midmorning sun. Making herself sit more upright, she squinted into the sunlight before she turned sideways to face Tamara, eyes clear.

"Yes, I guess it's probably possible for you *not* to know, not intimately, something but still understand it. Which could happen at an intellectual level. Yes, *you* … maybe you understand."

Tamara nodded. "Right. So my question's the same. Why the street thing? Why don't you take time to figure out what you need to do from a safe place, like a room som– "

"No. Stop. I know what I have to do, Tamara." Fiercely adamant, little crease firmly in place in the middle of her brow, Jo replied, *"I'm doing it,* don't *you* see? I'm turning inward and I'm not depending on others. Not on anyone. Not for anything."

"Sure," Tamara agreed, caught wrong-footed. "I understand what you're doing but I see it as, like, extreme. Overkill." She considered the young woman and abruptly pushed herself up on her knees, narrow waist almost level with Jo's eyes. "For fuck's sake, Jo," she exclaimed, pushing back her hair in a gesture of total frustration, dropping the modalised language of case-worker and client. "C'mon, look at me." She touched Jo's shoulder. "You don't need to squat a friggin' garden or a park bench forever just because your beef is about avoiding emotional entanglement, emotional debts, emotional deficits and emotional blackmail." Now that she was launched and moved by some personal impulse, Tamara skidded further into what she had refrained from saying all along. "C'mon, Jo, don't look away!" she said. "Listen, if your thing was to make a stand against the inflated price of rentals or real estate, yeah, OK. Squat a friggin' bench. Make yourself a sign like, about abusive landlords and see what gives. *But that's not your cause,"* she concluded, dropping back on her heels, shoulders forward, hands flat on her thighs. Head cocked, eyebrows pulled close together for the nth time, she sought out the young woman's wavering gaze. "OK," she started again, more gently this time. "Here's how I see it, right?" Dubiously, Jo nodded. "You can *zombie* in to work. You can zombie back to your own *safe* turf, a friggin' room somewhere. OK, so you don't deal with love because you don't want pain. You want to avoid the grotty part of human contact and you *can do* just that. Jo?" Tamara tapped gently on Jo's knee. "You want to bypass the emotional bit. Cool. You know that old song from the '70s that says something like, 'I am a rock. A rock feels no pain. An island never cries'?" Jo shook her head. "Right, never mind." Tamara reined in a thought and closed her mouth. She looked at the rocks, black and shiny where the tide was still licking them further away from the ledge, further away from Jo's feet. "OK, it *can* be done," she said in a conspiratorial tone, palms outstretched in front of her, moving the width of her shoulders back but keeping herself totally open to Jo. Eyes squarely on the young woman, she repeated, "It *can* be done. I *can* understand that you might want to do life that way. It's the street thing that I don't see. Why the friggin' extreme lack of comfort?" Tamara shook her head and her hair fanned around her face, she raked it back. "The only thing I *really* don't get is the transient park thing. I don't see it as, like, relevant to … not to anything."

Jo let those words die. Disturbed in her entrenchment by the woman's intensity, she stared at her before turning away. She let the river butt up against the thin tree trunks. She let it split itself around each one only to meet itself again. Whole. "I've done the *room* thing," she said very quietly. "I had a room in a boarding house … by choice … for months." She hesitated. Her tone lowered. "But I was about to move in with Maddy." She looked away. "What you *don't see* is that, unless I do without *everything*, until I reduce myself one hundred percent to … to this…" She pointed at her rainbow cloth bag, "I'll never be truly out of the loop." She ran a hand across her face as if to wipe it clean of silk-thin spider-web threads. "That's why I don't even want the dole," she added reflectively. Catching sight of her hands, of the red angry welt that sat like a red caterpillar on the back of her hand, she caught sight of her grimy fingernails. She swallowed and sighed, shoulders slumped. "As if they'd give it to me," she spat defensively, though already that other day, when she had made herself go to a Centrelink office because it was a mainstream thing to do, she had known she wouldn't want any government assistance. "I'm only a wuk to them," she snorted. "One among– "

"What the hell's a wook?"

"A wuk? W.U.K. Whereabouts Unknown. So to help the wuk, at Centrelink, they say they can write me care of the post office, right? Like I'm going to check the local post office every day to see if *they've* written me to ask me to bring in the paperwork I don't have to give them." Jo brought one knee back up and rested her chin on it, eyes on the river past Tamara's side. "I don't want … I don't want to ask Maddy to bring me those papers. Bottom line, I don't want the dole." She brought up her other knee and hugged them with both hands. "Just like I'm not interested in fixing up the six years I've already wasted since my mother died. Like I don't want to be an architect by the time I turn thirty. Like I don't want any of that shit because if I get back into it, it'll take me back to where I was *before* my mother bailed out on me, before she killed herself, to being a kid not good enough or not lovable enough to make her want to hang around. Dependent." She hesitated. "I didn't do all that *to Maddy,* all these weeks, for nothing." Her voice cracked. "I gotta fucking make it count. It's a twenty-four/seven commitment to the streets."

"Awh, for fuck's sake, Jo!" Tamara unfolded her legs to sit with her back to the river to better face Jo. "The temperature's dropping. It'll soon get down to fifteen degrees at night." Forcefully, hand brushing her hair back, she added, "Jo, it'll go down to three degrees on any winter night from June till August. You know that. You're not a tourist. What will you do to stay warm, huh?" she asked. "There won't even be a bed for you at the Salvos, even if you wanted one. Not at the drop of a hat. As you said," Tamara spoke more gently, "this isn't New York. *No* brazier at street corners. *No* grates blowing hot air."

"But, hey, there's quite a few shops around. With lots of cardboard boxes," Jo said flatly. "I'll always be able to score a box and curl up into it."

"If you say so." Tamara shrugged her shoulders in resignation. Her watch said it was time for her to go. It was after all a Thursday morning, not a weekend morning. And Tamara had to get back to the city, back to her office. She had to move on and both women stood up. With thumb and forefinger she pulled down on her jeans to ease them away from her crotch, smoothing the cloth over her thighs. Jo tugged on her little T-shirt but it still only barely covered her navel.

Arms open for a hug, Tamara took one step towards Jo who let herself be enfolded by the older woman's firm embrace. Jo's ear brushed against the woman's cheekbone. She closed her arms around Tamara's waist and her heart flip-flopped because, though Tamara was much taller than Maddy, there was something about the woman's body, its tautness, the wide shoulders, the narrow hips that made her long for her lover. And when Tamara's full breasts pressed against hers, Jo became conscious that she hadn't had a hug, not a proper one, since she had left the picnic table at Burleigh. A prickling sensation gathered behind her eyes. She swallowed hard and blinked. She yearned to let herself go limp against Tamara's neck and burrow inside her arms and that yearning caught Jo by surprise. When, eyes closed, she caught herself inhaling Tamara's scent, wanting to find Maddy's, she pulled away from the hug, pale cheeks pink with blush. Tamara's fingers barely touched her cheek.

Jo knew what she wanted. She wanted to get strength from the woman's strength. But what she needed was different. She needed to turn away, heart beating too fast, heart ready for flight because that feeling, that want, that dependence, were the exact emotions she had to excise from her being.

Once Tamara had gone, Jo stepped off the ledge and on to the rocks left behind by the tide. Carefully, balancing herself, long arms raised at shoulder level, picking out one rock at a time, she stepped onto it, feeling each under the rubber of her soles. At first, deliberately but carefully, she picked her way over the smoother ones, over the flat and dry ones, over the pointy ones, then closer to the edge of the receding tide, she set her soles over the odd angled ones and the glistening ones.

When the water lapped against the rubber strip of her soles, Jo stood still. She looked across to the big houses on the other bank. Carefully, she turned to face down river. All the little boats had gone away. The only ones that remained on the river were tethered to the house-pontoons. Balancing on the rocks, she looked up, one hand raised to her forehead, shielding her eyes from the sun. The little puffy white clouds were no longer there. They, too, had gone away. *"Phhht,"* she said, *"Gone. Everyone gone."*

Moving carefully, sliding one foot in front of the other, picking her way over rocks that were slippery dark, slippery wet, slippery submerged by spilling river, she kept on walking downstream, arms outstretched at her sides, like a crane about to alight. Eyes closed, Jo is at the edge of the river's shifting watery flank, trusting only the rubber toes of her soles to guide her downriver.

Jo is thirteen all over again. She comes home from school, drops her bag at the base of the stairway that leads upstairs to her room and goes looking for her mother. She doesn't call for her because Isabel doesn't usually like it when her daughter calls out. Eventually Jo finds Isabel at the bottom of the garden, where no one ever goes anymore, peering inside the much-neglected pond. So as not to startle her, Jo, still a little distance away, says softly but clearly, "Hey, Mama. What you up to?"

Still on all fours, Isabel turns her head to meet the voice, "Oh good, Little Jo's home. Come, come," she gestures with her hand. Isabel sits up on her haunches to make room for her daughter. She pats the space in front of her. "Here. Sit right here."

Jo crawls into the space opened up for her on her hands and knees and, with her back to her mother, peers cautiously into the algae-green water. She peers into the water and her mother peers over her shoulder and finally Jo exclaims, "But there's a fish in there, Mama. A fish! A big bugger of a fish." She turns to her mother and meets her mother's oyster-shell eyes.

Smiling eyes. "I knew it would make you happy, seeing a live, healthy fish in this pond. No idea what it is though."

"Well, it's not a goldfish, that's for sure. It's not even orange at all," Jo says, scrutinising the water for another glimpse of the fish that's no longer visible. "It's a grey thing, isn't it? A *real* fish from the deep. It lives in the dark caves beneath the water of *our* pond,' Jo adds, following her own narrative. "And *you* found it. I'll make you a plaque like they do for ... uh, for discoverers of things." Again, she turns sideways to look at her mother. "What brought you down here anyway?"

Isabel smiles and brushes the wild strands of hair away from her daughter's cheek. "Well, since you're so rude as to ask," she says, smiling gently, "I just got up from my nap wondering whether that pond was still full of water or whether it had ... dried up. Jo, would you believe that I couldn't, not even to save my life, remember if anyone had done anything to it, like you, the gardener, or even your father."

"Cool, but what made you think of the pond?"

"No idea. But I knew you would be home soon and that, eventually, you would find me here. What I didn't know is that I'd end up finding our dinner at the botto– "

"Mama, don't you dare!" Jo exclaims, but not too loudly. "He's too gorgeous to even make frying pan jokes within *gill*-shot." Jo squints at her mother. "Get it? Gill-shot, earshot?" Her hair is cut in a smooth, young ladylike bob. It is black and shiny under the late afternoon sun.

"Mmm ... " Isabel pretends to think. "Uh, ah, yes. I get it." Grey eyes sparkle. She tousles her daughter's hair. "Now, do you think that this grey creature that lives deep inside the pond might appreciate a little bread? You know, as a reward for having grown so big all on his own."

"Oh yes. Of course, it couldn't have been easy for him. It's quite lonely out here." Jo's already up on her feet. Dried bits of grass cling to the back of her navy-blue uniform. Isabel picks off a couple of the larger ones before her daughter starts back up towards the house. Abruptly, she has an afterthought. "I'm sure he'll like the bread," she says, "but Mama, … d'you think it's OK to give him people food?"

"Ah, yes." Eyebrows screwed up in thought, Isabel turns to face her daughter. "I mean *no*. I mean, you're right, if it got that big on its own, it probably doesn't need our help now. Didn't have that mean and hungry look about him anyway, did he?"

"Can't say that he did," Jo chuckles.

"Why don't you come back here then, and we just see if he'll come back up for air. Or to have a better look at us."

Mother and daughter peer back into the dark pond. Isabel's arms are around Jo's thin shoulders. Under her hand, she can feel her daughter's heart beat. She nuzzles Jo's black hair. Two peas in a pod.

Jo is fourteen. The light from the garden is trapped inside the glass. Jo watches the refracted light as it spins, as the spray of transparent liquid curves outwards and back. She's already traced its path. She won't have to duck for *this one*. In her mind, she snap-freezes it in mid-air for half the time it takes to blink. In rapid-fire impressions she thinks, *Would hurt real bad but won't connect. No excuse to invent for school.* So she watches the glass spin in slow motion. She watches it spin free of its transparent content wishing that, before it crashes at her feet, she could truly freeze its trajectory and rewind the last seventy-nine seconds.

The thing is, Jo doesn't know, not fully, why her mother has hurled the glass at her. And it is the *not knowing* that makes her a bad daughter. A bad daughter who precipitates her mother's bad moods. *Bad girl. I'm a bad girl,* she reprimands herself silently.

Jo is convinced that she *and* her carelessness are the triggers of her mother's erratic behaviour. It is she who, after all, had chosen the moment, though she knows that mornings aren't necessarily the best times for her to approach her mother, if she is awake, since the medication she still takes before bedtime often leaves her with a terrible headache and an upset stomach. Nighttimes she knows, too, were best avoided in the sense that, like the mornings, they are not the best time in which to sidle up to her mother to ask her a favour although, of course, *most* mornings and *most* evenings are fine. It's just that she's too dumb to avoid picking the *one* bad one.

The glass splinters on the brushwood floor. Jo jumps backwards. Shards skittle and scatter, some fly upwards. Isabel is beside herself with rage.

"You, idiot!' she screams. "Don't you know that I could die while *they're* here? How would your little friends like it, huh, if one of them found me *asleep?*" Isabel's smile is nasty. "Asleep right here on the sofa. *A-sleeep* forever. *Forever dead*. Sleeping the sleep of the dead, huh? You think you'd be Miss Popular after that, do you?" Once launched, Isabel is relentless. "I've brought you up to think. I've been paying good money after bad to have people, all your fucking teachers, teach you some common sense. A *little* common sense is all I ask of you. And all you're thinking about is a fucking *slumber* party?" Mouth twisted, she glares at her daughter. "Now, don't just stand there like a retard. Pick up the fucking glass. No!" she yells at Jo's retreating back. "You just get on those hands and knees and you pick it all up. To the last shard, you hear me? To the last shard!" Strained muscles, tendons and arteries entwine like cables along Isabel's neck. "Let's see you do *one* fucking useful thing with those hands of yours. One thing that goes beyond holding a pen or a fork. You show me what they can do. And wipe that stupid look off your face, you hear?"

Jo's eyes are still closed. Her face is lifted to the sky. A blind girl hugging the river's ever- shifting watery flank, trusting only the rubber toes of her soles to guide her, she walks deeper into the river. It is a sunny Thursday morning.

*****

SEVEN

Dark, rust-red hair standing on end, round blue eyes made more round by mocking incredulity, Maddy is angry. "I mean, fuck! What gave you the right to spy, huh?" she glowered. "I thought I could trust you, like, you know, TRUST! And what *you* do is go abusing your power and– "

Christen frowned. "I didn't abuse my *power,*" she retorted flatly. "I didn't *abuse* anything." Maddy's blue glare was ice cold. "What?" snapped Christen. "I didn't *do* anything to her."

"Right. Nothing at all," Maddy said frostily, bottom lip split by her gleaming lip loop.

"That's correct. Nothing except shadow her for a while."

"To spy on her," Maddy snarled.

"Well, no, Maddy, I … I wouldn't say *spy*. I'd just say followed *and* watched."

"Oh, big difference!"

"I think there is … at least *some* difference. Spying implies–"

"Spare me the dictionary session, Chris." Blue eyes glaring, Maddy walked away. She didn't want to see Christen's face anymore. Not just then.

"Oh, hell, you don't need to make me the bad guy." Christen pushed her sun-blond hair away from her face. "There was no nasty intention on my part." Maddy ignored her. "What I thought was that if I had a look at her, I might come up with an idea … Something that might help her come around and ... and reinsert. I mean, it's difficult to– "

Maddy glared back at her from the deckchair where she had flopped under the overarching poinciana tree. "Yeah, sure," she grumbled cantankerously. "And how did you even connect with her, huh?" she asked belligerently, twisting her neck to look at Christen who was still standing outside the back door.

Christen had phoned to see if it was alright for her to drop by, as she was once again in the neighbourhood, and Maddy had replied, "Yeah, I'm home. Not doing anything much. Just fiddling under the house with Jo's bike."

When Christen had walked through the squeaky back gate Maddy, squinting into the sunlight, had popped her head from under the house. "Grab a beer," she had said casually as she would to an old friend. "I'll be up in a tick. Just need to spray a second coat of chrome on the handlebars."

"OK. Don't go inhaling the fumes. They're vicious," had replied the older woman.

Christen had reached into the fridge, popped the cap off an ice-cold beer and had returned to the patio where she sat at the wooden table under the kitchen window. She stretched her legs, crossed her ankles, and sighed. She took a sip from the bottle and ran the tip of her tongue over her lip. She smiled to herself, closed her eyes to listen for the tiny sounds and flutters that filled the air inside Maddy's backyard.

A short while later, when Maddy dropped a hand on the woman's shoulder and said, "Hey," Christen opened her eyes and smiled at the young redhead.

The loose turquoise muscle-shirt Maddy had thrown over a pair of faded low-waisted jeans enhanced the width of her shoulders. Its open sides clearly revealed that Maddy was not wearing a bra and the firm slab of the back muscle that curled gently to touch her ribs made Christen smile differently.

Maddy's hair, near her temples, was flattened damp with perspiration. Like a tribal tattoo, a double smudge of dark grease crossed her forearm. Her hands were stained by silver chrome and black paint. "I've finally reached the fun stage of this thing," she said, grinning broadly. "Sanding and de-rusting and undercoating all the small bits *and* the frame, that wasn't great fun but now, it's all hanging well. I'll take you down for a look later."

Christen answered enthusiastically, "I'd love that."

Maddy went inside to scrub her hands clean, and came back to the patio with a bowl of olives in the one hand, one of cashews in the other, and a beer caught between two fingers. All traces of grease smudges had disappeared but as Maddy sat across from Christen, the angled sunlight that bounced off her cheekbone revealed a faint trace of glittery chrome. Christen made herself look away and the two women chattered on easily until the blonde one said, "I saw Jo."

Maddy started and blinked. She drew in her bottom lip and she stared at Christen. "Jo? *My* Jo?"

"Yes," Christen smiled. "Jo Brenner, your Jo. I don't know any oth–" she caught Maddy's suspicious squint. "What?"

"How the hell did that happen?" Maddy asked too sharply, but Christen went on to explain that that particular evening after her shift, she had driven up from Burleigh to visit her mother who, at the moment, was not at all well. About to turn her car towards the highway, Christen had hesitated. On impulse, she had turned the car around while she still could.

"I thought that … well … you know," she said, focusing on the long spiral of clear perspex that, hanging from a low branch, was spinning swirls of light. "Well I thought about it, you know, as I was driving back on Cornwall … and then I thought it'd be best not to, I mean not to call you. Better if I didn't try to see you. I mean on the off chance that …"

And it had only been *then* that the connection had happened. If she shouldn't see Maddy, Christen thought, maybe she could see Maddy's *lover*. Maybe she could hang around New Farm Park and see if she could spot her. Christen admitted that she had been curious as to what young Jo looked like but she also thought that seeing her in the park, or in the streets, might help her think of something constructive that could be done to help her leave the park and resume a more practical lifestyle.

"To be honest," she shrugged, "I can't say that I *connected* with her at all. It's not like I talked to her or anything. She didn't even see me."

"So how you know it's her, huh?" Maddy asked, not yet ready to let her anger drop.

Christen looked at her incredulously. "Oh, like you think she's hard to spot, do you?" Maddy lowered her eyes. "How many young chicks looking like her have we got hanging around the park area, you think? Like here in Brisbane?" Maddy shrugged. "Anyway, from your MP report, I knew I was looking for a dark-haired twenty-three year old, about five-eleven, wearing army greens and carrying a rainbow cloth bag."

"Ah yes, the report that no one but you took seriously."

The blonde woman waved her hands in front of her chest. "No comment."

"Right."

"What?" Christen asked again, in response to Maddy's hard stare.

"Nothing. So, uh … when was it, then?"

"That I followed her?" Eyes away from Christen, Maddy nodded. "Two nights ago. Last Wednesday. Why?"

Maddy shrugged again but this time she turned her attention back to the policewoman. "I haven't seen her for almost a week. Last time wasn't too good."

Silence settled between them. Directly in Maddy's line of vision, dangling from a low branch, the long spiral that Jo had given her on the night of their six month anniversary, twirled under the soft breath of the breeze, and the dappled sunlight rippled and shimmered on its curved acrylic surface. Elongated discs of transparent light materialised out of the air below to rise languorously in slow succession, only to die and disappear back into the nothingness at the other end of the long spiral. Again and again, on an upward travel, on a downward path, sparkling light cascaded and rippled the length of the spiral. Maddy pulled her eyes away from the magnetic attraction. "Chris," she said softly.

"Mm?"

Maddy patted the deckchair next to hers. "Come here."

Until recently, Maddy had only had one garden lounge but for some reason, though there were a couple of tubular plastic seats scattered in the backyard, one particular afternoon when she had been thinking of Jo, she had decided to buy another lounging chair. *For Jo.*

Silently, Maddy snorted. Leaning back, she closed her eyes and sighed. She heard Christen's footfalls move towards her over the tiles. She heard the frame creak as Christen settled on the striped mattress at her side. Neither woman spoke. Not for a long time. Anyone peeping inside the garden would have thought them asleep.

Finally Maddy shook her head, slowly, sadly. "I just don't know what to do any more," she began wearily. "When I see her, sometimes we talk but … it's not about *it*. It's not about why she's there or what she thinks she needs to do before she can come back." She let her eyes be drawn again by the spiral and Jo's voice flooded her eardrums.

'I'd like you to hang it right there,' Jo had said, pointing to the low-hanging branches of the tree. *'Just so that … when you're out here, gazing into space, the spiral, you know, the way it catches the light, twirling it around and all, well, I'd like to think that it'll bring you … your thoughts back to me.'*

Maddy pulled her eyes away and sat up on the striped mattress. "It's not even like I've ever said that she— that we need to carry on as *Oh, let's pretend nothing's happened*. I mean, what I do tell her is that she can get herself another room. That's to help … if it's the idea of the two-lives-joined-at-the-hip thing is what's making her flip. I tell her she needs to start using some of the money she has at the bank for …

for basics. I tell her she can go back to her sister's. I tell her I'm there for her, even if she doesn't want *me* … Well, yes, even if she doesn't want me as a lover anymore. And all she tells *me* is that she can't go back to her old life anymore and that means *no* to a room, *no* to Jarrah, *no* to regular work, *no* even to the dole." Maddy shook her head and nibbled on her bottom lip. "So, I'm like, *So … what, Jo?*" She frowned, intent on her flashback. "So I ask her if *all* she wants out of life, like now, is to work *one* hour a day, sit on a park bench for the rest of her life? And sleep on the ground? And all she gives me is, 'Look, Mad. You don't understand and I can't explain. So just leave me alone.'" Maddy turned her face towards Christen's. Hurt and incomprehension in round blue eyes. "She says, 'Just walk away and leave me be.'" For a moment, Maddy remained in silent contemplation of her knuckles. The middle one was skinned but it had begun healing over. Maddy ran the thumb of her other hand over the scab and frowned again. "She looks like shit. Like totally wrecked and she's gonna get sick. So she mops the floor at that restaurant. Cool! So what does she do the rest of the time, huh? Used to be so active before all that. What does she do with her money? Obviously she's not spending it, not even on a fucking nail-brush," Maddy spat bitterly, as if Christen's silent presence allowed her to *finally* think outside her head. "And she's such a hygiene freak. Having dirty nails … That'd be driving her … *crazy.* And well … I don't know where she washes or showers. Where *do* you wash? I mean, *how* do you fucking wash when you don't have a fucking bathroom, huh?" Maddy glared at the spiral. Her hand raked through her hair. "I just can't work it out anymore," Maddy finished in a big sad sigh.

Christen hesitated. She looked at the young woman, feeling her confusion, feeling for her. She opened her mouth and leaned forward to speak but she changed her mind. Instead, she let her eyes be drawn by the mesmerising swirls of sunlight that spiralled in and out of the air ahead.

Still thinking out loud, Maddy broke the silence. "OK, so even if it takes her like one hour … or two, you know, to clean and mop the floors at that restaurant, she must be getting at least the minimum hourly rate, right?" She asked, waiting for Christen's nod before continuing. "What's that then? What, about fifteen bucks?"

"Was, last time I checked."

"So she makes about twenty dollars a day, give or take. She doesn't spend it on food. She's even thinner than before. She doesn't spend it on laundry powder, I mean like, she doesn't do the Laundromat thing, that's pretty obvious by now. Anybody looking can tell her clothes are not– " Maddy heaved another great sigh. "So ... what does she do with what she gets every day, huh? I mean, by now, she probably shouldn't be carrying that much cash around, right?"

"She's not."

Maddy eyed the blonde woman. "She's not what?"

"She's not carrying that money on her person."

Maddy opened her round-blue eyes wider. "Oh, right. She's depositing it at the bank, then?" she asked superciliously.

"She deposits it but not at– "

"Oh, fuck it, Chris." Maddy swung her legs on to the ground to better face the woman. "What does she do with her money?"

"*Spying* sucks big time," Christen replied with a smile that crinkled up her nose, "and now you want me to– "

Maddy ran her freckly fingers through the short length of her hair. "Oh, fuck it," she said in frustration. "Look, I'm sorry about ... about before. I was out of line ... in a big way," Maddy replied with a quick apologetic grin. "I ... look, Chris, what do *you* know?" She sucked in the silver lip loop and waited, an apprehensive squint tightening her eyes.

Christen pushed herself up on the mattress and gave the redhead a measured look. "Look, Maddy ... " She hesitated one last time. "It's not good. You don't wanna go there– "

"Spit it out, Chris. Tell me! Please."

Eyes turned away from Maddy, Christen replied flatly, "She spends it on drugs."

Silence. "On *drugs?*"

Christen nodded. "On shit. Grass. Weed."

"And?" Her hand raked through her short hair.

"And ... nothing. That's it." Christen shrugged. "You wanted to know what she does with her money, so now you know. She blows twenty-three dollars a day."

"Twenty-three?" Maddy bit on the lip loop and considered Christen. "How do you know it's twenty and not ... fifteen or ... five?"

Christen chuckled. "Maddy, you can't buy dope for five bucks, this is not Bolivia. Besides, I've been spying, remember?"

"Yeah. I've apologised for that." Maddy snorted and looked away. She nibbled the inside of her lip.

"OK, I've tailed her, yes and– Well, I've found that garden hideout where she hangs at night, and I spotted her connecting with a small-fry dealer, one James Mirren, who operates from Oxley Lane behind the Village Twin Cinemas." Christen looked at Maddy. "The boys at the New Farm station know all about him, that's how come I know who he is, but they don't want to make an arrest. No long-term benefit in it," she explained. "Another one would be standing at the exact same spot in a matter of days. Same old stor– "

"Jo *buys* from this dude?"

"She does. A foil. Twenty-three dollars."

"Twenty-*three*? Like what? They don't do even numbers? Would be simpler."

"They do. Twenty-five dollars is the going price for a two-gram deal but for his … " She considered Maddy. "He gives his regular customers a bit of a discount."

"So … she's a regular."

"She is. Has been for about six weeks."

Jo. Back on drugs. Abruptly Maddy stood up and paced. What was it that Jarrah had said about it, about her sister's habit at the time of their mother's suicide. Jaw muscles bunched, Maddy squinted from the effort of bringing back the words Jarrah had used. And when those words came back, she winced. She felt winded. She shut her eyes against the unsettling image.

'She attached herself to the bong *like a mare to a feeding bag,*' is what Jarrah had said.

Harsh words, Maddy had thought at the time, but at the time she knew Jo had turned her habit around. Jo was clean. And Maddy hadn't had to see what Jarrah had seen. She hadn't had to put up with what *she* had had to put up with during the year that followed their mother's death, the year Jo spent with her older sister. But as Jarrah's words overlapped with Christen's, Maddy felt sick. Sick with apprehension.

"So … uh, what does she … What does she get for twenty-*three* bucks?" she asked slowly, voice faltering.

"Enough for three or four joints. Depends how tight she packs her bong."

"A day?"

"A night. Jo's clean during the day. She only lights up at night. After midnight."

"You know this, do you?" Maddy asked acidly.

"I know that."

"You'd better tell me all of it, Chris."

Christen had ID'd Jo last Wednesday night as she skirted the Sydney Street side of the park. It was well past midnight and Christen had been cruising for quite a while already. She opted to keep watch from inside her car until thoughts of Maddy, the same that had been playing on a loop inside her head for the last two weeks, almost tempted her into something silly. Lulled by the false security of her tinted windows, she had let her hand wander away from the inside of her thigh and over the crotch of her jeans until she laughed to herself at the imaginary head-line:

Predator Police Sergeant Caught Clit-in-Hand.

"Damn," she had said softly, as she did each time the memory of the orgasm brought on by Maddy's fingers overlaid itself on much more relevant but much less exciting thoughts. So that night, she stepped out of her car to walk briskly along the circular drive that hugged the river. She jogged to a clump of fat-bellied bottle-trees and patted their craggy grey skin. When she reached an old whitewashed block of concrete, she applied the palms of her hands against the rough texture of the wall and did a series of quick press-ups. *You're such a jock, Jensen,* she thought mockingly.

Forwards and backwards, like a footballer in training, she skipped over the ten steps that led from there to the river. Unfamiliar with the area, she *guessed* that this had to be a disused ferry landing. As she hopped lightly from one step to the next, she noticed the narrow ledge that butted against the toilet block and suspected that, secluded as it was, the spot might be a local magnet for all sorts of illicit night-time activities. Curious as to what lay beyond, she stepped on to the ledge and almost tripped over a shape half sprawled on the ground.

A man, dishevelled and grubby, half lay, not unlike a broken puppet, propped against the toilet block wall, half of his legs dangling off the narrow ledge. On the ground by his hand lay half a bottle of rum, four empty beer bottles and numerous cigarette butts. Near the very dirty loose cloth of his pant leg, level with his knee, was a crushed red and white pack of Marlboros. Christen waited a few seconds until she heard breath gurgle hesitantly inside the man's throat. Relieved that the man was only away with the fairies, she grinned inwardly. She stepped over his knees and walked to the end of the ledge. A yellow and black sign warning about submerged electrical lines was fastened high above the bank to two tubular posts but no one else was in sight. A little chill ran through her, not just because the night was getting cooler but because totally unhealthy vibes emanated from the area.

Confident that she would be quick to despatch any would-be aggressor, even a sober one, into the river, be it at low or high tide, Christen was not worried about being mugged. And so, the chill that made the fine hairs on her arms stand on end was due to her awareness that it was in such isolated places that too many women came to grief. Women who, unlike her, could be rendered helpless by the simplest of methods, the oldest one in the world – being trusting of their partner. The other – being victims, first, of the element of surprise.

Of course, she reminded herself, men in a comatose state like the one at her feet were also at risk – being bashed just for the fun of it by prowling gangs of youths. From a half-crouched position above him, Christen pulled at the shoulder of his stained shirt until the man's upper body leaned more squarely against the wall. In this adjusted position, the derelict appeared less comatose, though a little slobber ran unimpeded from the corner of his slack-jawed mouth.

Rubbing her hand against the seat of her jeans, Christen turned her back to the old ferry landing. She lifted her face to the night sky. The breeze played softly with her hair. The nights were getting cooler. She grinned, remembering the walks she used to enjoy in the Melbourne hinterland, in autumn, in winter. That was before her mother had retired to Brisbane, closer but not *too* close. And the one thing she missed the most was the colour change nature underwent at the end of every summer. She missed the crunch of yellow and red leaves underfoot, the crispy clean feel of the air against her cheeks.

In Brisbane, in *Queensland*, most trees didn't lose their foliage except for the odd liquid amber and other European imports. Gum trees, be they spotted or ghost, palms, ferns, bottle brushes, bunya bunya pines, may shed their bark, drop branches, fronds, cones or pods, some of enormous proportions, but with the exception of the wattles, jacarandas and poinciana that sport tiny round leaves, none wider than a few millimetres, Australian natives are not great leaf-shedders. They seem to be perennially green. Often dusty, almost khaki green in the sunlight.

So, in New Farm Park under the competing lights of lampposts and half a moon way up in the sky, Christen jogged up and down the grassy banks that hugged the river. She made a little detour by the Powerhouse Entertainment Centre to pick up a programme guide. Taking her time inside the softly lit foyer, she flicked through the pages until a title, *The Vagina Monologues II* caught her eye. And like a magnet pulls in pins, her mind pulled in more thoughts of Maddy. She wondered what she did when on her own, when she was not pulling apart old bicycles.

As she lingered near the box office, she considered other advertised events and came across the mention of the Brisbane Queer Film Festival. She pondered the contextual meaning of the word 'queer'. Queer as in odd? Or queer as in gay? She read the short accompanying blurb but was none the wiser, although the word *queer* had been repeated a few times.

Christen attempted to distract herself away from anything either vaginal or gay but only came up thinking that if this festival was about dyke films, she could maybe – just a thought that made her heart-beat pick up – ask Maddy for a date. And then came the heartbeat moment when, imagining herself safely ensconced in the darkness of the theatre, she imagined reaching for Maddy's hand. She imagined settling that hand flat on her thigh and, on a slow intake of breath, she imagined covering Maddy's hand with her own. All these unsubtle thoughts combined, made Christen blush but did absolutely nothing to ease her ache.

So she went back into the park to sit on a bench. She looked at the boats anchored to the other bank at private pontoons and decided that, except for the view of the river, the area was too close to the city to be appealing to her if she ever had the money to invest in water-front real estate, anywhere.

Christen sat inside the bandstand gazebo and breathed slowly through her nose. She attempted clearing her head from the still over-lapping thoughts of Maddy by letting in a work-related clutter, snippets related to the new drug diversion initiative that gave Marijuana users the option of undertaking treatment rather than getting caught up in the criminal justice system. Then, she thought of the article in the *Australian Police Journal* that explained why women police officers were substantially less likely than males to attract a complaint from a member of the public.

The article confirmed what she already knew, that women cops relied more on communication skills than coercion and were less likely to be provoked or feel their authority impugned than their male col-leagues. She did all that and yet thoughts of Maddy nudged all the other bits and snippets aside because, no matter what she tried to do, Christen was still seriously fixated on the insidious craving for a place-bo – that of running her hand over her own sex. And no matter how, since the balancing act above the stairwell at Maddy's, she had tried to divert her mind from *that* thought, reality was that she had not stopped being hungry for the feel of Maddy's fingers softly firm against her.

When Christen's mother had asked her to drive up to help her rearrange some living room furniture to accommodate a new sofa and a huge TV set, Christen's first thought had been that she had just been handed the prompt she needed to *also* stop by Maddy's. But she hadn't done that. She had turned the car around after saying goodbye to her mother. She came to the park instead and her body was strongly protesting that change of plans.

So the *other* craving that had taken far too much space in her consciousness was that of running her hands freely over the young woman's body, over the warm alabaster smoothness of her skin. And she smiled at the memory of Maddy's multitudinous freckles. She remembered the dense spray across her shoulders which she had first noticed the night Maddy had appeared at the station, disoriented like a child woken from sleep. She remembered, too, the dark-russet constellation, solid but moving under her hands, softening under the palm of her hands, that one afternoon, as she had kneaded the stiffness out of Maddy's muscles. Christen chuckled, considering that, *perhaps,* her freckles knew no boundary. *Except on her arms. She doesn't have many on her arms.* She closed her eyes to better let her eyes roam once more over the memory of Maddy's prone body. Again Christen lifted her face to the river breeze to feel its cool brush against her face because, then, she needed to know *where* on Maddy's front lay more freckles.

She stood up. She made herself enjoy the calm of the park and the halo of serenity that emanated from the moon. Half of it was full and white like one half of a communion wafer, while its other half was ghosted. Ninety percent transparency. The trees, far too tall to make a sound, brushed silently against the sky and Christen remembered why she was sitting there, in New Farm park, well past midnight. She wasn't there for Jo. She didn't know Jo. She was there for Maddy. She was there to help Maddy figure out a way to reel in Jo.

A boy, lips rimmed in blue paint, similar blue stains smeared on his hands and clothes, had ambled unsteadily over to her but it was the paint fumes emanating from him that had alerted her to his presence. One hand holding up his baggy trousers, the other clutching a blue-streaked freezer bag, the young huffer had sniffed. He had sniffed some more and wiped the frayed cuff of an oversized sweatshirt across his runny eyes. *Shit, she thought,* working up a smile for the boy. *Chronic chromer symptoms.*

"Hey, lady. Got ... got ... three bucks?" he asked shakily.

Christen had shaken her head trying to figure, right there and then, what it was she could do for the boy besides *not* give him the couple of bucks he needed to buy himself another spray can, come opening hours tomorrow. Looking at the boy's hands, she estimated him to be no more than fifteen.

Dwarfed by his too-large clothes, he almost looked like a sleepy child. But he was not a sleepy child though his hair was tousled. *Could be dead tomorrow. Cardiac arrhythmia. Anoxia.* She wanted to reach out to him. *But he's not a puppy,* she admonished herself. *Not a stray looking to be picked up. He belongs to someone. He's got rights. He's got the right to be here. Got the right to sniff his little brains out.*

In the police, everyone was acutely aware of the societal problem these youngsters presented. Boys, mostly, because girls don't like getting their clothes sticky with paint. But the police had no right to pluck them off the streets, no right to drag them through a detox programme.

At best, youth workers doing night prowls might manage to pick up some of these children and bring them back to a centre to sleep off their paint-induced stupor, but basically, what these kids were doing to themselves was not illegal. It stemmed from a lucid and deadly need to escape but it was not illegal. There was no regulated response to such self-destruction.

Christen talked to the boy, prepared for the eventuality that he might become violent. She knew that the safety of staff and carers dealing with chronic chromers was a recurring issue, as a chromer's explosive strength doubled under the influence. One golden rule was to never interfere with a chromer in the act of chroming. His reaction could be as unpredictable as violently erratic. But the boy who had zombie-walked from behind some bush had already had his fix and so Christen had talked to him, though she knew that not much of what she said would be heard, let alone remembered. Chromers, she knew, couldn't see the big picture. Not in the middle of a high and even less from deep inside the trough on the other side of that high, not when all thoughts that could still connect were harnessed by the irrational impulse to plunge back, head first, into a plastic bag.

"Hey ... lady," the boy had sniffed. "You don't ... you don't know yo' own shi...it." His speech was slurred by the volatile substance and adrenaline combo that had already been sponged up by his lungs. "I'm … I swear … lady. I'm fuck … fuckin' bull … bulletproof."

Again the boy wiped his runny nose on the back of his paint-smeared hand and, with a faltering step, he had turned himself around. Brain properly fumigated by solvents, he had returned to the night.

By the time Christen completed another circular lap of the park, a small group of Aborigines had occupied a section of the ground near a hedge on the Brunswick Street side. The three of them, one female, two males, were already seated on what seemed to be a foam mattress thrown on the ground, backs to the bowls club, under a clump of massive, heavily branched Moreton Bay figs. A bottle of clear liquid was being passed from lips to lips. The old 'goom,' Christen guessed, metho, at $ 2.95 a litre much more affordable than vodka or gin. She sighed thinking of the violent delirium tremens that accompany brain damage. The park at night was not a happy place.

The female cradled the square shape of a cardboard cask of wine between her knees. On the ground between them, only a few dingy plastic bags, but Christen sensed they had come here to spend the night. When alcoholic stupor would ultimately overtake them, the ancient thickset trees that reached high and spread wide would shelter them from the night mist and drizzle and to some extent, too, from the cool breeze that still blew from the river. Good shade in the middle of the day, too.

From where she stood only a few metres away from the trio who were totally oblivious of her presence, being partially camouflaged by the high and flat buttresses of a tree trunk, Christen observed their stillness.

Eyes loosely focused on the ground that separated him from the woman and the older man who, Christen thought, might be either uncle or cousin, the younger man broke the silence. In the Indigenous way, not all information needs to be shared quickly. Not everyone needs to interact at the same time.

Christen watched on, observing some of that culture she knew so little about. Moments of silent contemplation mixed together with carefully calibrated eye contact. She nodded to herself. How much more civilised than the way we socialise. Less energy scattered everywhere.

"By the river he come with his monkey blood got from his mate at the pub," the younger man said in a low tone. "All these migaloos were there watchin' and the other koliman, he come ... shame."

Aboriginal English, she surmised, remembering that, as Indigenous Australians came from a multitude of language groups, close to four hundred, some said, they had had to adopt an English-based lingua franca, as they began venturing away from their different 'countries' within Australia to migrate to the cities. Christen leaned more closely against the huge trunk, totally fascinated by the trio's almost contemplative demeanour as, like most white Australians, she seldom if ever had an opportunity to observe them unimpeded.

As a young Constable destined to at least *begin* by following orders, if she was ever going to wear stripes on her shoulder-boards, she and hundreds of her contemporaries on general duties had had to move indigenous people on many times and slap a vagrancy charge on them. They had had to swoop down on others to restrain them, to lock them up for drunken and disorderly behaviour. That was back in the days when too much 'Aboriginal behaviour' landed them in jail, particularly when it involved offensive language aimed at an Officer of the Queensland Police Services, though young white males were usually simply summoned for the same infringement. That was back in the days where the use of a summons instead of an arrest was not perceived by many in the force as necessarily applicable to young Aborigines. That was back in the days when the nature of police intervention was still highly discretionary.

She knew that more recently another trend had emerged in spite of a greater emphasis on prevention, planning and counselling in conjunction with Aboriginal communities. More and more Protection Orders now have to be written up against Aboriginal males involved in acts of domestic violence, especially those under the influence of alcohol. In North Queensland, a tendency was emerging whereby young boys, not yet teens, were so affected by relentless domestic violence that physical and emotional abuse had already become accepted as normal behaviour in and out of their peer group. Around Cape York Peninsula some men were, according to another journal article, trying to corral wives suspected of possible infidelity by knocking their eyes out with a broom or sticks to render them less attractive to passing strangers. But Christen knew there was still the problem of over-representation in custody, and the problem of not enough under-bail release provisions. And that all these discrepancies were linked to the lack of general appropriateness of the bail system for their lifestyle.

Christen tried to follow the gist of the trio's interaction. She groaned at the sad irony of considering homeless Native Australians at play, despite their suckling of bottles of gut-rotting Methylated Spirits, simply because they happened to be sitting under a beautiful canopy of foliage in almost idyllic nighttime surroundings. In Brisbane, Aborigines did not sit at sidewalk cafes. They did not go to the movies. They did not live where she did, even when they didn't live in a park. That was because the majority of them had refused, and still did, assimilation on the *whitefella's* terms. Their choice, some would say. Others, even less enlightened, would say that it was because they've never understood the *whitefella's* effort to protect them from themselves. Not back then in 1770 and still not at the turn of the twenty-first century.

So, that night, Christen was mesmerised by the strength that emanated from their strong brows glowering above a dingy kerosene lamp sat on the ground almost at their feet. She trained her ears to the unusual sounds interspersed, as it were, by so many hand movements that she thought of sign language when, out of the darkness at her right, she spotted a very tall and very thin figure moving out of the shadows. A rainbow-coloured backpack dangled from a long arm. Having immediately ID'd Maddy's Jo, Christen decided to hang back half a street block behind her.

The streets in that part of town were not crowded, the relative mid-week restaurant bustle having long died. The moviegoers had already returned to the comfort of their homes. Only a few pedestrians were still about, drifting like leaves in the breeze, and the occasional prostitute hugged what shadows she could find in the well-lit, wide street. Suspecting that Jo had returned to a marijuana habit, DS Jensen, before pulling up by the park, had made a quick stop at the New Farm police station where, after a quick flash of her ID, the boys made it their pleasure to enlighten the tall, blonde, strapping woman about the shadier aspects of their district's night life. By the time Christen returned to her car, the three police officers on duty were privately thinking that some time by the surf was long overdue. And it hadn't been long before Christen figured out that the willowy young woman was aiming for a spot behind the Village Twin Cinemas and that a certain James Mirren would, in all likelihood, be her contact.

Walking a short distance behind her, Christen had every opportunity to ascertain that the girl was still straight by the time she left the park. She watched the tall silhouette walk almost purposefully up the street and slow down her pace only as she approached the end of each sidewalk. Maybe it was the khaki-green trousers and the small dark T-shirt that made Christen think of a graceful seaweed.

After a while, still behind Jo, Christen crossed the street to break into a jog and cut back towards Jo, who didn't even look at the blonde woman who had slowed her stride as she passed her. The lanky girl with the oddly cut hair seemed lost in thought and, though her arms were covered by the tight sleeves of a T-shirt, Christen doubted she was a junkie. She was, however, quite sure that she was on the edge of full-blown anorexia. Her first impression had been that Jo still had some muscle tone on her forearms but something about her overall stringiness made Christen think of thin frog legs. Not sinewy. Too thin to be sinewy but not yet emaciated. Not yet wasted.

"So," Maddy broke in, "How did you follow her?"

"Back down to Merthyr Street from the cinemas and into a side street. Welsby."

"And then?"

"Ah well ... that's the part I'm not ... " Christen hesitated. "Listen, Maddy, maybe it's best if you don't go ther– "

"Don't even think about it, Chris. You tell me the *whole* fucking thing." Maddy glared at the policewoman. "And what *I* do is tell you when I've had enough. Deal?" Blue eyes gentle again.

"You're the boss, Boss," Christen sighed. Eyes on the spiral that cascaded downwards from an over-reaching tree branch, she began on a deep intake of breath, "OK, so as it turns out, that street's pretty long and a lot less lit than Brunswick, right? Like there's only a couple of restaurants at the other end of it, or maybe even just one near the old sugar factory. In between it's mostly all chamferboard cottage stuff. A bit like yours here. So, after a while, I see Jo stop. She looks around and, hop, she throws herself to the other side of a garden wall."

"Uh ... right."

"So I'm like, Great! What do I do next? And yeah ... Well, I thought it might be helpful ... " Christen peeled her eyes off the twirling spiral to glance at Maddy, "I mean for you, to have a bit more on what she gets up to ... after she leaves the park for the night, right?" Bottom lip drawn in, Maddy nodded, eyes intent on the woman who seemed to know so much more about *her* lover than she, herself, did. She swallowed to push that thought back down. "OK, so I waited a while and did a little recon of the immediate vicinity," Christen explained. "Very quiet street actually. Most lights off. Nothing stirring, not even a stray cat. So after a while … well … Look, Maddy, the thing is I jumped into the garden, too. At worst, I figured, she sees me. That gives her an almighty fright but all that happens is that I jump back into the street, blend with the shadows and that'd be the end of that. Right?" Maddy nodded for Christen to go on. "But as it turned out, the garden is really quite big with lots of trees along the back and sides, and lots of bushes. And most of the ground in the back corner is pretty much hidden from all viewpoints except from the back rooms of the house. But as I said, it was all buttoned up in there. All dark. So … I make out Jo's shape crouched under some tree in a corner of the garden. I stay put and after a while I see her get up. She goes for the garden hose. I see quite well once I adjust to night vision and, with a bit of the street light that filtered through, she stood out real pale against the shrubs. So she'd taken off her trousers.

"Quiet as a mouse, she drags the hose under some hanging branches then she goes back to turn it on. Not much, like not on full throttle at all. She squats and starts rubbing at something, one of her pant-legs I think it was. Then she drags out a bucket from under another bush and she fills it up. That's … uh … that's what she uses to wash herself. I mean, yeah, the armpit thing and arms and hands but she hadn't removed her top totally. Like she still had it around her neck and she pulled it back on once she was done. Then she … " The stricken look in Maddy's eyes made Christen hesitate again.

"No, look … It's OK. I can do this." Maddy's tone suggested an attempt at auto-persuasion. "I mean … I try not to think about that, you know but … if she's like, determined to do it rough … " Her voice trailed off.

"Well, give her credit. This is one woman that's really doing what she can to stay clean. I mean … yeah, can't be easy for her. So anyway," Christen began again, "she squatted above the bucket and … washed herself. Thing is … I don't think she has a towel. It looked like she was dabbing herself with something small like a T-shirt, a spare one maybe. And then, she spread her fatigues on the grass, hoping they'd dry over night, I guess, and she pulled on another pair, might have been jeans. But," Christen squinted at the curling spiral, "it would've been a bit cold out there, you know, what with her being still wet or damp and with the breeze and not even a cup of tea to warm– "

"Right," Maddy interrupted too quickly. "So that explains how she still looks … more or less together. But there's more, right?" Round blue eyes squinted. "That's not really the part you thought I'd get upset about, is it?" Maddy thrust her chin forward. A late afternoon mosquito, one of the kind that rarely travelled alone, buzzed near her ear.

Christen shook her head slowly. "There's more. OK," she continued but, eyes sliding off Maddy's, she talked in the direction of the light-catching spiral, straight in front of her. "To get to the point quickly, let's just say that she lit up a bong." She paused, wishing she could ease Maddy more gently into Jo's night-world. "She lit it up and threw a sarong over her head– "

Maddy frowned. She opened her mouth and closed it before asking a croaky, "What for?"

Christen considered her for an instant. "At first," she said slowly, as if slowing down the pace would lessen the bite unintentionally carried by her words, "I thought it was to … to contain the … the … aroma, you know, of the weed burning. But later, I worked it out differently. I'm sure it was to make like, the most of each cone. So that she'd inhale not just from the bowl but also from what got trapped under the– "

"Oh … *fuck!*" Maddy exploded between clenched teeth.

"What?"

Round blue eyes tightened around some visuals Jarrah had provided the night of their conversation, back in Toowoomba. Visuals that Maddy, herself, had never seen. Visuals that, even if only palely imagined, had made her stomach tighten with anxiety.

"Jarrah, that's Jo's sister, she said that after their mother killed herself, Jo went on a binge." She drew in a corner of her lip and nibbled it. "What did she call it when … She said Jo'd smoke inside the car, windows rolled– "

"Clam-bake?" Maddy shook her head, brow tight. "Hot-boxing?"

Maddy bit her loop and remained silent. She felt the mosquito flutter against her cheekbone. In an unfocused, instinctive manner, she swatted at the side of her face.

"Hot-boxing?" Christen asked again.

The dark spot of a mosquito in full flight hovered in front of her face, looking for somewhere to land. Maddy nodded. "Yeah, that." She slapped her hands together but when she looked at her palms, they were free of any mosquito debris.

"Well, she's back to doing it big time. She lit up three cones and smoked all of them under the– "

"But this is all about *not* feeling, isn't it? Chris?"

"Probably, considering what she's embarked on. Otherwise, I'd say there'd have to be more comfortable ways to zonk out."

Maddy slumped. "And then?"

"Look, Maddy," Christen waved her hands in front of her chest. "It's not like I had to see more. I … I really feel like, yeah, you were right earlier, I felt like I'd been *spying* on her. I mean, it's OK tailing someone to gather intel on a suspect as … uh … as a surveillance thing but Jo … she's *not* a suspect in anything. Only a citizen going about her private business." Christen brushed blonde wisps away from her face. Maddy read tension around her mouth, tension in the tightness around her eyes. "I was free-lancing, right? And when I started off behind her, I never thought I'd end up *seeing* so much like, just there, in the open. She's out there with only a few trees and a fence to protect her from the street and well, I felt … it made me feel a bit sick. Like I'd been perving on her or something." Christen shook her head but looked straight at Maddy. "Jo has a right to her privacy and I blew that for her, so … yeah … Well, that's it really. That's all there is to tell." Christen slapped her forearm with her left hand. She flicked off the dark flattened insect. Silence settled over the garden. Eyes blurry, Maddy teased her lip loop and Christen closed her eyes until Maddy stirred.

"Uh … Look, Christen, let's go inside. The mozzies are out in force already and I'm like right out of citronella oil." She scratched her ankle.

"It's the season. They come out earlier as the days begin to shorten. They get ready for whatever they do at dusk and–"

"Yes, well … they've already got me a couple of times." She got up from the deck-chair. "Come on," she said, holding her hand out to Christen. "Let's just go inside."

*****

The next morning, at 7.00 a.m., the first thing Maureen did, as soon as she saw Jo's tall silhouette striding through the doors of the restaurant, was to hand her a very little package: brown paper tied with simple twine and only bearing two letters printed in even black block letters:

JO. Jo did not immediately open the package. Instead she started on what had become her 7.00 a.m. routine.

From the wide kitchen floor, she moved everything that could be lifted, dragged or slid out of the way. Into a red bucket, she poured very hot water on top of two measures of an industrial strength floor-cleaning product. Because Maureen was hovering nearby, Jo slipped on a pair of pink kitchen gloves that were both too short and too wide for her hands. If Maureen hadn't been hovering around, she wouldn't have used the gloves because she would've dipped her hands into the hot detergent to ease away some of the grime under her fingernails. She had found that, though the grease cutting detergent dried her hands terribly, if she wrung the mop by hand, digging her fingernails into the strands instead of using the pedal wringer, her fingernails came out considerably cleaner. But because Maureen was hovering nearby, Jo wore the pink gloves and used the pedal wringer to wring dirty greasy water out of the mop. And when the floor was shiny-wet and properly rinsed, she tackled the tiled dining area. Someone's job defi-nition must include stacking all the chairs by the end of the night shift, because Jo always found all the chairs stacked in tidy columns in the back of the room. When that was shiny-wet too, and rinsed, she went to the toilets. With a different cleaning product, she wiped the seat and under the seat and under the lid before mopping the floor around the toilet and the sink. Then, armed with the toilet brush, she squirted an arc of lemon-fresh deodoriser, spread it with the brush and scoured the bowl. Once the first cubicle was shiny-wet and rinsed, she moved to the second one and then she moved next door to the men's toilets.

An hour and a half later, she was once again out in the clear morning light, seated at one of the wooden picnic tables. With eyes closed, she embarked on the second phase of her morning ritual. She inhaled deeply a few times before deciding that today's dish was some sort of fish. Once she had eaten what amounted to her morning intake, eyes half-closed against the sunlight, she sipped her freshly brewed cup of strong coffee from the white Styrofoam cup. The first and last hot drink of the day. Then, and only then, did she begin undoing the twine around the brown paper that covered the package that bore her name in large, black blocked letters.

Jo hadn't asked Maureen who had brought in that package. And Maureen hadn't volunteered that information. Out of the folds of brown paper emerged, first, a little blue plastic fingernail brush. Under it were two little bright blue square boxes of Libra Regular tampons.

Underneath that was a little box of Band-Aids. Underneath that, a small box that clearly contained a medicinal product of one sort or another. She lifted the glossy white and pink cardboard box to eye level: *Antiseptic First Aid Powder*. And underneath, the hand that had stacked all these small and light objects so neatly had also lain a tiny little pouch of raw silk that Jo recognised as the type used by Philippino jewellers. It was *their* custom to slip every purchase into such soft silk pouches, not in boxes. Philippino jewellers have lined-silk pouches of all sizes and colours. Pouches small enough to make one ring feel snug. Pouches wide enough to accommodate bangles and watches. The little pouch in Jo's parcel was lime green. It was edged with a ribbing of a darker green. Very curious as to what could possibly be inside the pouch, she lifted its little flap with careful fingers and tilted it so that the contents could slide into her palm. Incredulous, she stared at a common-variety twelve-sided Australian fifty-cent coin. It shone like hardened mercury in the middle of her palm. On one side, the portrait of Queen Elizabeth II. On the other, the Australian coat of arms made up of an emu and a kangaroo upright on either side of the nation's crest. Jo blinked at the coin before lifting the white and burgundy business card still lying against the crinkled folds of brown paper, the first item to have been laid on it.

Queensland Health Services, Jo read silently.
Domestic Violence Division Coordinator
Tamara Townsend

She read the hand-written message out loud. "*Jo, it's OK to use the phone,*" it said. "*Please, use the fifty cents when you've had enough. Tam.*" Jo raised her face to the blue sky. Then she turned to look in the direction of the old ferry landing where she had taken Tamara, the social worker. Jo snorted softly. She looked at the Band-Aid already glued to the back of her hand, compliments of Maureen Leal. Again, she shook her head slowly but finally, slowly, a little smile softened the curve of her mouth. The smile settled and creased the corners of her lips. Two coins. *Two local calls,* she thought, as she flipped one of the heavy fifty-cent coins way up into the air. It landed squarely in the middle of her palm. She slipped the silver coins back inside the lime green pouch. She had intended dropping it inside her backpack but, instead, she let it slip off her fingers and inside the deep pocket sewn on the outside of her Khaki greens. She buttoned the pocket flap that she had never bothered buttoning before.

*****

SEVEN

A red Jeep rolled inside the workshop. Viv flashed a look at the wall clock. Four-thirty. She glanced at the day's booking and nodded as she read, **Anderson/RB/Jeep Ren.** *Good man,* she thought. *Right on time.* Viv liked for clients to be on time. She tended to greet *those* with a better smile than the ones who brought in their vehicle later than the time logged into the day's duty ledger. *Where's Drew?* She scanned the floor just as the mechanic came out of the locker room. Aware that Drew was again running behind schedule, Viv puckered her brow. She decided on the spot not to get involved and let him figure out how he was going to pass on the new arrival to Maddy which would, in turn, set her back with her own workload. The Jeep pulled up near the balancing machine.

From the window opening, the driver, a woman, inquired, "Uh, excuse me ... " Drew moved closer to the vehicle. "Is it OK to leave it here for a wheel rotation and balance?"

"Yeah," Drew answered. "Here's fine." He turned to face the office window and saw Viv looking at him with an expectant *And now what?* expression on her face. He pointed to his chest mouthing *Mine?* Viv nodded and deliberately shrugged to signify that, this time, she wasn't going to bail him out by asking Maddy to rescue him as a favour to *her.*

Pointing his weight hammer to the Jeep, Drew asked, "Uh ... it's in the books, is it?"

The woman nodded the affirmative. "Sure hope so. I made the booking early last week and ... well, I'm afraid I've let it go too long already."

"And what name's it under?" Drew asked, to buy himself some thinking time while his eyes darted towards the Toyota sedan where only a pair of overall clad legs and work boots protruded from under the chassis.

"Anderson."

"Anderson. Right. Mrs or Miss?"

The woman frowned, visibly not making the connection between what she needed done and the man's question.

"*Ms* Emilie Anderson."

Drew tapped the little hammer against the rectangular weight he had been about to reposition against an inside rim. "And that's for a rotation and a balance, you said."

"I did say that, yes," the woman replied, somewhat tightly.

Drew could tell by the woman's changing non-verbals that, unless he moved quickly, this customer wouldn't be too accommodating. She didn't look the type to be amenable to spending an *extra* forty minutes in the waiting room while he finished his current job and debriefed the owner who was due to return any minute.

"Is anybody picking you up?" he asked, hopeful.

"No. I'll just wait around. Shouldn't take that long, right?" The woman jumped out of the cabin, leaving the car door half-open.

"Right." Drew flashed one of his nice smiles. The woman smiled back but a guarded sort of smile. "Hey," Drew called out towards the sedan. "Tom!"

A muffled "Whassup?" came from under the car. A brief moment later, the chunky brown boots slid the backboard trolley forward to reveal more of the stained overalls, the mechanic's torso and finally the mechanic's head appeared from under the car. The customer blinked at the red, very red hair but her lips curled into a little smile that suggested that for her, at least, red was a nice colour of hair to have. But still unsure as to which of the two mechanics was, in fact, supposed to work on her vehicle, she looked from the barrel-chested young man, who looked uneasy, to the other mechanic still supine on the trolley. She frowned unhappily at the thought that such a youth would be laying his hands on her wheels. Leaning back against the passenger-side door, heel of one boot resting on the chrome side-step behind her, the Jeep driver's frown was still ominous though she privately agreed that a mechanic's height probably had very little to do with his ability to get the job done as everything these days was assisted either with pulleys or with technology.

"Hey ... uh, Tom. Can you spare us a hand? This baby ... " he explained tapping the jeep's hood, "What she needs is an RB but what with ..."

Maddy glanced at the red Jeep Renegade made even bigger by the chrome bullbar and the lift kit that would give it, Maddy quickly estimated, a good five inches of extra chassis clearance on deeply rutted terrain. *High enough to crawl over a fallen tree trunk.* She looked quickly at the woman who was leaning against it in a proprietary manner. She locked in on the washed-out jeans and on the loose jungle-green shirt. She locked in on the leather hiking boot casually resting on the side-step. She locked in on the woman's face. *Sporty-forties,* was her conclusion. "Getting a bit too old to keep up with the cracking pace, then?" Maddy joked, returning her attention to Drew. "Mate, that's gonna cost you *big time*."

Drew grinned and flashed a thumbs up in reply. "Lady," he said to the Jeep driver, "you'll be in and out 'fore you know it and the lil' beauty, here, she'll be all balanced up. Good as new."

The woman flashed him an undecided quick smile before returning her attention to the young mechanic who, still seated on the trolley, was wiping grease-smeared hands on a grimy rag.

"I'll only be a tick," the redhead called in her direction, as she tossed the rag into a bin.

Fiddling with her car keys, Ms Anderson looked around. Behind the glass window of what was obviously the workshop's office, a wide-faced, grey-haired woman looked up from her computer screen. Their eyes met. The older woman looked at her inquisitively. Unsure as to the meaning of the woman's look, the Jeep's driver nodded and smiled a little smile of acknowledgement. Apparently satisfied, or was it reassured, by the smile, Viv promptly lowered her eyes back to the computer screen in front of her.

"I'll be needing the key … Ma'am?"

Ms Anderson started. Momentarily lost in thought, she had lost track of the young mechanic's movements. Maddy saw the quick blush colour the woman's face. "Your vehicle's to go on the ramp. Safety regulations. I have to drive it up my– "

"Oh … right. Of course," the woman stammered as she proffered the key. "I … lost in space, I was. Uh, sorry, I hadn't realised you were– "

"I beg your pardon?" Maddy cut in with the stiff politeness of an English butler. She was quite used to customers being surprised. Men, most of them, were surprised by the fact that she was a woman doing a man's job. Women, most of them, tended to be surprised that as a woman, she would choose to do a *dirty* man's job. On the whole, though, once the surprise element was over, most customers let her get on with her work and spoke civilly to her. She could remember only a handful of customers who, over the years, had preferred to drive away rather than have her, a woman, work on their vehicle.

Most outfits open-minded enough to actually employ women mechanics, were not usually willing to accommodate such unreasonable client tantrums. As such, they were not open to orchestrating an unplanned mechanic swap and so each of these men had driven off with at least *one* "Stupid bastard" tag trailing behind him. Male colleagues, Maddy had long ago concluded, be they behind the counter or on the floor, were more often than not genuinely moved to kick into the 'protective mode thing' and rally around their "Sheila", *their* female, *their* mate, in a supportive manner.

"It's just when he, I mean, the mechanic … over there … When he called you Tom, I assumed you were a *young* man." And the woman blushed again. "A boy, really. And I wasn't sure, to be honest, that … a young man, *so* young, should be entrusted with … "

"And now that I'm not a boy?"

"Ah … well, that's different, isn't it?"

"I wouldn't know, Ma'am," Maddy answered caustically, though perplexed as to why *she* was taking the mickey out of this woman who, after all, had not been unpleasant to anyone.

"Well, it's the youth factor, I guess." The woman went on explaining unnecessarily. "My experience of it is that it usually comes with a serious lack of experience. As it should, *really,* because … experience does come with age, doesn't it?"

Maddy took in the woman's rough-cut hair. *Used to giving orders,* she surmised. "I wouldn't know that for sure, Ma'am," she answered tossing the woman's keys flippantly in the air. She deliberately over-did the swagger around the car and, one booted foot on the side-step, she hopped on to the driver's seat, careful to close the door softly but firmly.

Viv smiled behind the glass enclosure of her office. Maddy's easy banter with Drew, and the-in-your-face-dyke non-verbals she was putting on for the benefit of the woman who had driven the Jeep in, confirmed that her *protegée* might just about be over the hump. The old notion that time healed all wounds still held currency and Viv sighed over a smile of relief. She had been keeping a constant watch on young Maddy and the two of them had had more mother-daughter type conversations about Jo, whom Viv had never met, and the fears Maddy had in regards to her lover's crash 'n' burn approach to resolving whatever needed to be resolved. But, lately, during the past week or two, though Viv knew that Jo had not yet returned, something had shifted inside Maddy. She had briefly wondered whether the nice policewoman, the one who had found Jo, the same one who had phoned for Maddy once or twice, had anything to do with her return to the land of the living but, with a shrug of the shoulders, Viv had soon banished all forms of speculation.

Behind her glass enclosure, she slipped a fresh job-sheet on a clipboard. She'd have to go out on the floor and obtain all the relevant details regarding the 4.30 p.m. WRB job but, first, she had to enter a bit more data on *Terry's Tyres* stock update.

Once seated in the cabin, Maddy adjusted the seat to bring it closer to the pedals. She eased the vehicle into reverse, backed it up to turn it around and seconds later rolled it softly parallel to the woman. Strong forearm casually resting on the window-frame, Maddy beamed a smile at her as she eased the big vehicle on to the ramp. "Cute," she called out from inside the cabin.

Unsure as to what the young mechanic was referring to, the woman looked around. "Sorry?" she asked with an upward inflexion.

"This rig ... Flashy. Real cool." Maddy stepped out of the vehicle but instead of stepping down from the ramp, she reached down to the control post, hit the command that made the hydraulic hoist rise off the floor, and let it carry her some four feet off the ground. "*Cute.* Like a big toy." From her position between the axles she engaged the split-level bars needed to lift the Jeep *off* the platform. If Maddy was going to remove the wheels from *under* the Renegade, it was essential they be off everything, including the hoist's tracks. "Nice and chunky like those remote-control model cars. Your husband ... " While waiting for the vehicle to settle, suspended on its dual bars, she shot another glance at the woman. She speculated quickly that, at her age, she'd be more likely to have a husband than a boyfriend. "Your husband," she said, "he's got to be serious about cars, huh? Wranglers everywhere but Renegades, they're like hens' teeth around here."

Maddy's experience of years spent in mechanic workshops, was that women seldom owned grunt 4X4 vehicles and though many drove them in city streets, very few actually drove them off-road. Unless the women were Rangers or buffalo hunters, the bigger the four-wheel drive, the less likely it was to have been *bought* by a female. It might be the family's holiday-adventure-people mover. It might be the vehicle the woman had to drive when sharing jobs with her husband or boyfriend but it was seldom hers by choice.

"Couldn't *possibly* be my husband's," the woman corrected quickly, a faintly amused smile playing on her lips. Something about the woman's answer made Maddy look at her over her shoulder as she adjusted the impact socket on to the air gun. "But you're right, there *is* something about classics," the older woman continued, unaware of Maddy's sudden awareness of her as a person. "This model's over thirty years old. '71 Limited Series," she concluded. She looked up at the young redhead catching her side-on, lovely and strong in her cheerful turquoise but oil-stained overalls, totally looking the part of the cute dyke in charge.

"Yours then?" the mechanic asked over her shoulder.

"All mine. Have had her for years. Uh … not since '71 though. I'm not *that* old." Maddy grinned and the woman added, "She's as close to mint condition as a grandma can ever get."

"Very sexy for a grandma," Maddy retorted, eyes on a wheel-nut, finger on the trigger. The staccato cough and whirr of the air gun filled the air.

"So, what's Tom short for?" The woman asked, apparently willing to while the time away in light conversation. "Can't think of any girl's name– "

Maddy fitted the socket on the next wheel nut and pulled back the trigger. "It's meant to be Tom for Tom," she answered, setting the gun by her knee. She pulled the nut out and lay it next to the first one. "My real name's Maddy," she added, just as the gun coughed again. "And that's not short for anything," she added, pre-empting the usual question. "I wouldn't go too close to that drum if I were you." Maddy pointed the gun at the industrial barrel in which old oil was poured.

The woman automatically looked down at her trousers. The pale denim already sported a grimy smear on the left leg. "Oh. Right." And then, almost in spite of herself, the woman asked hesitatingly, "Uh, Maddy … you do look very young. I mean totally capable and all but very *young.* I was wondering if it'd be rude to ask how– "

The gun coughed. "It's the freckles, Ma'am. They fool everybody." She glanced up from the machine and added easily, "You can relax, I'm not new to this. Ask Viv." Maddy pointed the gun to a spot behind the woman. "She'll tell you."

The woman looked over her shoulder. The kindly, wide-faced woman she had noticed inside the office was walking towards them, clipboard in hand.

*****

Maddy turned into Princess Street and parked right at the top of the incline. She angled the front wheels towards the curb and pulled hard on the handbrake. She grabbed her bag from the back seat, along with the tote bag in which she kept her swimming gear.

She had planned to catch the Dutton Park ferry across the river to the university pool when she realised it had been a long time since she had last walked through the old, almost derelict, cemetery off Fairfield Road. She occasionally enjoyed walking there, particularly in winter, because cold greyness suited better the dingy unkempt grave-yard than the happy glare of bright sunshine. On a bleak winter after-noon, grey clouds over a grey sky, and the pewter-grey river below, were a more fitting backdrop to the uneven rows of mildewed-grey con-crete sepulchres.

Although the sun was still bright on that particular late after-noon, rather than park her car by the landing and cross over directly, Maddy had driven in a loop, back up past the Brisbane Corso to park on top of the hill. The thought of a walk back from the ferry and up to her car after a good hour spent in the pool did not worry her. She would need that good hour in the pool to unknot all that had become tight in her shoulders and lower back, and she would need the walk back to her car to stretch differently the muscles that she will have pushed, proba-bly again, to tearing point.

Maddy didn't have to squint against the sun's brightness. It wasn't winter yet but the days had begun to shorten and what remained of the late afternoon sun and blue sky had lost its bite.

Carefully, almost reverently, Maddy began walking in between the uneven rows of dirty grey concrete rectangles. She was happy to see that the little marble angel atop a column she always passed was still standing and still holding its tiny bunches of marble-grey roses fes-tooned against its robe. She smiled at it, sorry it was too high on its perch for her to reach up and touch it. Trying to touch its wings would have meant standing on tiptoes on the edge of the grave and that was just something Maddy could never bring herself to do, standing on a part of anyone's grave. And yet all around her, just about all the graves were fractured, collapsed, sinking. Listing and sinking deeper into the soil. Whether they had buckled up or caved in was not clear. Most ste-les had long ago given up their vigil and, like drunks into their plate, they had fallen face forward and lay flat, inert, against what remained of the grave sealing-slabs. Some lay there splintered. Most lay there cracked or shattered. Headless pillars stood blind while long-empty vases stood a perennial watch for the hand that would leave behind the bright colours of a bouquet. Cracked crosses stood steadfast, arms spread against abandon.

Louis Hardy, Maddy read, as her hand brushed against the rough edge of a slab. *1870.*

Long and hard shreds of dry eucalyptus bark strewn on the uneven concrete path lay curled up on their side and crunched under her boots.

George. Gone but not forgotten. 1893-1953, she read further ahead. She hesitated in the middle of the row before angling downhill towards the river. The delineation between tomb and pathway was unclear and, afraid to inadvertently walk over an unmarked grave, she continued further ahead until her steps connected with what was unmistakably a trail.

As she turned another corner and began walking through another row, she came across an unusual grave site. It was filled with rubble-speckled, yellow parched soil and though it kind of looked like a freshly-filled grave, in the sense that it was not sealed, Maddy assumed she was looking at an old burial place that must have become separated from its covering slab. The obvious vulnerability of the site disturbed her. *OK,* she thought, *so there aren't any grave robbers and no one's lurking around for a grave to mess around with. Still ... it doesn't seem right leaving it exposed like that.* She let her eyes travel over the curved mound. *Wouldn't want any of my loved ones lying like that, unprotected, if I had anyone dead. Like how long's this cover been missing off this thing?* She wanted to ask that question of the groundsperson but there was no groundsperson to ask and no groundsperson's office to find. A throbbing sort of irritation rushed to her ears even as she moved away. *A fucking dog could drift in here and piss on the grave!* And because she hadn't yet had to bury anyone she loved, for the first time she thought of Isabel Brenner's sepulchre. *Wonder where it is.* She would have asked the groundsman if there had been one to ask, then realised that, in all likelihood, Isabel Brenner had not been buried in a Brisbane cemetery. *Besides,* she admitted, *it doesn't look like they've had any newcomers here for quite some time. Most likely in Toowoomba.* After all, Jo originally came from there and that's where she had lived until her mother's death. *What does Isabel's grave look like?* Maddy wanted to know. *Does she lie under a drab concrete slab like the ones here? Or under a ritzy marble one? Inside a mausoleum or what?* She cast her eyes around. *Did she have an angel watching over her? Is her tombstone still upright? Did anyone ... did Jarrah ...*

Does Jo ever visit her there? The flurry of questions assailed her as she walked past long forgotten burial sites. *Is there a bouquet of her favourite flowers in a marble vase? Are they fresh or fake? Plastic or silk?* she wanted to know because the next grave in front of which she stopped had, as sole offering, an empty, dirty glass jar so obviously there in wait of flowers, that looking at it made her feel queasy. *Is she secure there, wherever she is, Jo's mum?* Maddy stole another glance towards the unsealed tomb in the other row. *Is it a loved grave, hers? What's written on it?*

"To our loving departed mother?" She had spoken out loud. A hot tingle itched in the back of her eyes and the tip of her nose began to swell. Her throat closed up and she hesitated before moving further down the slope. Arms akimbo, she turned on her heels and turned again like a weathercock under an undecided wind.

She dropped at the edge of a shallow grave. Like a struggling rubber dinghy weighed down by water, the little grave sagged, about to be swallowed up, border and all, by the grassy soil around it. One hand on its cracked edging, either to steady it or to steady herself, she let heavy tears roll unimpeded down her cheeks. They brimmed, round and wide. And she let them roll because they were so big that she didn't think her eyelids would be strong enough to keep them from spilling, even if she closed them. Anyway, she didn't want to shut her eyes against anything because everyone else around her had had their eyes shut. *Shut once but by now,* she reasoned, *they'd simply be empty and hollow with no eyelids to shut over them. Mind you, no tears left to spill over anymore, anyway.* And that thought opened the dike further and more tears coursed down her cheeks.

Some of these tears were about Jo, for Jo. Some of them were about Jo but for herself because, at that particular moment, Maddy felt very small and very helpless. More than that, she felt an overwhelming sadness.

"God," she moaned. "Look at me ... fucking feeling sorry for myself." She sniffed and rubbed her eyes like a little girl, fingers curled into a loose fist. She sat up straight but more tears splattered and died, absorbed by the thick cloth of her jeans. And new tears were for Isabel Brenner. *Such a fucked up life.* She sniffed again, more loudly this time, as she pushed the heels of both hands against her eye-sockets. *Beautiful and totally fucked up.* And thoughts on a loop brought her back to Jo. *And she's fucked up because ... Because of what? Because her mother had other things on her mind besides the living.*

She wiped the back of an already wet hand against her nose, drawing in the silver lip loop and, little child suckling her dummy, she kept it against her tongue, against her teeth. A pacifier by any other name. *Is it that simple to fuck up someone's life?* She asked herself, round blue eyes round. And then thoughts of Christen broke into her other thoughts but thoughts of Christen did not bring on new tears. There was nothing sad about Christen. *She's strong. She's solid. She's beautiful.*

That was how Maddy thought of Christen and she remembered that, if it hadn't been for the thoughts of Jo alone in a dark backyard, thoughts of Jo washing herself from a plastic bucket, thoughts of Jo, head blown by too much THC, if it hadn't been for all those thoughts, last night she would've made love to Christen. *Yes, I would've. Gently, tenderly.*

"Why?" Maddy asked, again out loud. She asked *why* because she thought she needed to work out what, in regards to the police-woman, she had finally become attracted to. Was it to the blonde hair that, by the end of the day, escaped from a sensually demure eight-strand plait to play against Christen's cheekbones and lips?

When once she had come to Maddy's straight from work and still in uniform, Christen had slipped off an innocuous tie from the tip of her blonde braid and had shaken her hair loose. For the second time since they had met, Christen's wind-blown, salt-bleached hair had reminded her of a wild palomino's mane. But maybe it was the fjord-blue eyes that Christen had inherited from her Swedish great-grandfather that Maddy had begun to trust.

At the edge of the sinking grave, Maddy sighed because basically she knew that she had already figured out the origin of her attraction to the older woman and what attracted her was, in fact, the woman's physical strength. Because Jo was so thin, Maddy wanted to believe that anyone physically strong and sturdy was *mentally* strong and sturdy, too. And Christen's solidity had begun working on Maddy like a slow-release aphrodisiac.

The previous evening, as they left the garden to the mosquitoes, Maddy had taken Christen's hand and had led her inside the house. She hadn't stopped to think whether she should have held her hand out to the woman, she just had, and she had led her up the back steps and inside the kitchen. From behind, Christen had tugged at Maddy's hand and Maddy had turned around.

It had just been a tug, such a little tug really, but Maddy turned around and her eyes connected with Christen's. Her eyes *had* connected but it was Maddy, all on her own, who had snuggled against the woman's shoulder and Christen had closed her arms protectively around her and she had run calming fingers through Maddy's tousled rust-red hair. Maddy closed her eyes and they stood still, Maddy tucked in against Christen's neck, against Christen's gym-firm body until Maddy stirred and looked up. She looked up and Christen dipped her knees a little.

The moment hovered, hesitated and became very still. As still as Maddy's breath on her lips. Then she closed her eyes again, leaning more heavily into the woman's embrace. Only aware of Christen's mouth against hers, Maddy lost track of the moment. She was not even aware that she had folded inside that embrace like a deflated rubber doll. She was only aware of the silkiness of Christen's lips against hers and the slow ache that glowered low inside her belly, uninvited but wonderfully warm all the same.

Slowly, very slowly they kissed. They kissed so slowly, so thoroughly that Maddy grew lightheaded. She needed to pull away, just a little. And as she pulled away, perhaps to look again at Christen, perhaps to look *differently* at Christen, Jo snuck inside the space.

Jo and her serious grey eyes. Jo and her rat-chewed hair. Frail and thin, Jo curled her long body around Maddy's and Maddy had had to pull away, further away, totally away from Christen because Jo was alone in the dark. Jo was cold in the dark.

At the edge of the sagging grey tomb, Maddy lifted her head to the sky. She lifted her eyes to the breeze because she thought it would be nice to have her tears dried by the evening breeze. Above her head were the leafy branches of an age-old ficus. In between those branches the sky was soft and dusky. And in between the branches there was, too, a flock of birds, high up there, in a Vee formation. The birds flew above Maddy, above the tree, above the cemetery. And she thought the birds lucky. Not just lucky to fly and be way up there but lucky because, from way up there, the birds couldn't see the grey and they couldn't see the grot and they couldn't see all the ugly things that went on down below. Maddy flopped backwards on the grassy soil. She flopped next to the old grave that had neither name nor headstone nor flowers, not even an empty glass jar in which one might drop a flower plucked from a neighbouring hedge. And Maddy closed her eyes.

*****

Jo's hand on the back gate. The little bell tinkles and the rusty hinges give the usual creak.

The driveway is empty. Jo has already ascertained that Maddy is not home early from work. Loose-kneed, Jo lopes to the side of the house where she knows the lock on one of the living room casement windows doesn't catch.

Jo feels for the little sill that juts out below the window only a few centimetres above her head. Her fingers find the vertical line where the two window frames meet. With the heel of her hand, Jo pushes, gently at first, then more firmly against the upright joint, willing it to swing open inward. The double windows stay welded to each other. She stretches on tiptoes to put more power behind the heel of her hand. And Jo realises that Maddy must have fixed the lock.

After Jo had finished her morning's work at the restaurant, Maureen Leal sat her down in front of a cup of coffee she had served in a proper porcelain cup and a stack of pancakes dripping with maple syrup. On the side of the plate lay three slices of bacon.

Jo had looked at Maureen but the woman who managed the restaurant shied away from Jo's questioning grey eyes.

"Whassup?" Jo had had to ask.

Maureen's non-verbals betrayed her agitation. She tucked a stray strand of hair behind her ear. "Look, Jo ... if I had it my way ... it'd be different." She hesitated. "I want you to know that because ... well, because it's important to me."

"And?" Jo asked, though she had already guessed what the manager was trying to tell her.

"And ... uh ... Well, James, the owner, he's found out about you ... Well, I've had to tell him I was paying you out of petty cash." Jo's eyes dropped from Maureen's face and settled on the pancake stack. The pancakes smelled sweet and smokey. She was not surprised by Maureen's news. She wanted to tell her it was OK because she'd always known that *that* moment would come, sooner or later. She knew the day would come when she'd be asked not to come back to the restaurant, that her mopping of the floors and what wages were associated with it really ought to belong to someone already on a payroll like one of the kitchen hands. Just like she knew the day would come when she'd be banned from her corner of some stranger's backyard. Beginner's luck, she'd been reminding herself on and off. Only the type of providence that watches over newbies would have provided her with these two lucky breaks almost as soon as she hit the streets. *One down. One to go,* Jo thought as she buried her fork into the stack.

"Jo, it's because he says that the petty cash is for miscellaneous, unplanned expenditures. You, coming every morning, for such a long time, he doesn't think that qualifies as either unplanned or small expenditure."

Jo turned a morsel of pancake around in the thick syrup. She inhaled its rich aroma. "Well, it *is* small," Maureen corrected, "but he's right, it's not unplanned, not as such. Not after so long. Now, Jo, you see, even *I* thought I could bail you out because … well, because I wanted to but also because even I thought, at the time, you'd only need to be tied-over, only for a couple of days. A week or two at the most. I was sure that by now … *for sure,* you'd have … well, you'd have moved on. Gone back home."

"I guess I could've told you." Jo cut another triangular bit off the golden, syrup-laden pancake. "But it's not like I have a plan or anything. It's a day by day thing." Jo smiled at the slice of bacon before slicing into it. She chewed very slowly.

"Jo … "

Jo was still chewing the flavoursome morsel. "Mm?"

"What are you going to do with yourself … now, for … uh, for money? If you don't go home?"

Jo stopped chewing. She swallowed quickly, blinking at what remained on her plate. She stayed still.

"Jo?"

Jo lay the fork carefully on the side of the white plate. "I'll go to the bank."

Jo had answered so casually that Maureen deliberately ignored the answer. After all, why would anyone become a park person if there was money in the bank?

"Will you be all right?" Maureen checked again, trying to meet Jo's eyes. "Shouldn't you go home? Now? Jo?"

Jo was not ready to look up and Maureen was not ready to spoil the moment. She wasn't, for the sake of an answer, about to risk spooking Jo by insisting. Instead, her eyes found Jo's long, dark-rimmed fingers and her slender hands. Her eyes absent-mindedly followed the inverted trident of thick veins that snaked from the middle finger, over the girl's forearm to disappear somewhere below the sleeve of her T-shirt. Maureen noticed how the skin on Jo's hands, and up to where the tight sleeve of her rib-hugging T-shirt rubbed, had been tanned by the many hours Jo undoubtedly spent outdoors. The skin where her sleeve rode up on the middle of her forearm was still pale. Maureen looked up at the girl's face. In fact, Jo's face was made even paler, her eyes made more transparent, by the darkening shadows that smudged them. She smiled a concerned smile at the rat-chewed haircut just as Jo exhaled a deep sigh through her nostrils. "Maureen, listen. Don't you go on worrying, OK? I'll be right."

"Just tell me, Jo, do you *have* a place to go home to?"

"I do," Jo answered, not just to pacify the woman but because she felt she *did* have a place to go to, if ever she wanted one. She silently updated her thought. If it wasn't too late. If it's not *too* late in regards to Maddy, she could have clarified for Maureen's benefit, but she didn't because the woman didn't know anything about Maddy. And Jo could have tacked on, *if it's not too late for me,* but she didn't because Maureen wouldn't have understood why going back home might have become a 'too late thing' for Jo. "There is somewhere I could go," repeated Jo reassuringly, though she kept her eyes lowered on to her breakfast plate.

Jo did, after all, decide to take the train from the Brunswick Street station to Fairfield and she walked the rest of the way. She didn't turn into the street where *Fairfield House* was located but she did think of her old, rusty bicycle that used to be chained by the toilet block. Although she didn't have to walk far from the station, Jo missed the feel of the breeze in her hair and the pressure of her feet against the bike's pedals now that she was back in open, former-life territory. As she pushed the rubbery soles of her Converse trainers against the bitumen, Jo wondered what had become of the old bike. She assumed Maddy had taken it to the dump along with her garden debris. She almost smiled at the thought. After all, someone else would buy the thing for what, forty bucks? Better deal than she got it for, what with the tyre that was almost still new and all.

Heel of her hand pushing against the vertical point where the two windowpanes meet, Jo grunts. Applying so much pressure from an arm-over-head position is uncomfortable and tiring, besides she's become impatient with the wretched thing that won't budge. She gives it a miss and ambles around the front of the little cottage. What shrubs Maddy had planted, whenever that was, look good and established. Little tender-green leaves scaffold their way along most of the stems. Some junk mail has slipped out of the mailbox and Jo picks up the colourful papers. *Southern News,* the local free rag. K-Mart's sale promotion. Domino's pizzas. $13.95 for two family-sized pizzas. She looks at the golden toppings and reads each corresponding description. Her mouth waters but she's not hungry. Maureen's morning pancakes still fill her stomach nicely and the take-away container that she insisted Jo take weighs nicely inside her bag.

Maureen had tried to make her promise that if she wasn't going to go straight home, wherever *that* was, then please to drop by for food. Please to not even think twice about doing it.

"*That* I can do, Jo. I don't need anyone's permission to fill an extra take-away. So ... please, take me up on the offer, will you? I mean, if you're not *really* going home," Maureen had added, Jo's hands tightly inside her own. And Jo had skilfully thanked the woman, avoiding looking into her eyes because Maureen's motherly attention had brought on a lump in Jo's throat that threatened to upset her composure. Too, she had side-stepped the promise to drop by *just* to collect a tub of food. *That* thought, the thought that one day she may have to do that, beg for food, with nothing to give in exchange had made her queasy about what the next days might hold if she didn't alter at least one fraction of her resolve.

Jo shoves the junk mail back on top of envelopes, closes the back flap to Maddy's mailbox and comes out on the other side of the garden. "Why two?" she asks out loud. There used to be only one lounge chair in Maddy's backyard. Jo remembers the many moments they had spent, entwined on the lone mattress. Her brow tightens. Jo doesn't know anymore why she came to Maddy's. The sight of the lounge-chair has unsettled her because she and Maddy have made love on it, at night, many times before. A moving light catches in her peripheral vision. She turns to face it more squarely. "Oh." Her voice is small. She moves towards the undulating spiral of light that drips from the tree's lower branch. "Oh," she says again. Her hand reaches out to touch the gift she had given Maddy on the night of their six-months anniversary. The curled strip of clear plastic is hard in her hand. There is nothing ephemeral or magic about it while she's holding it so she lets it twirl freely. Immediately, bubbles of light rise slowly upward and vaporise before materialising again on a downward spin.

Jo flops wearily on the new lounge and though her intention had been to let herself be mesmerised by the spiral of swirling light, she closes her eyes. Her body makes itself heavy against the striped mattress. She sighs and adjusts the position of her neck. She readjusts the length of her body into the firm but soft support below her. *So nice,* she moans silently. *So much better than hard ground.*

Like a marathon trekker set on her objective, she had forgotten how good a mattress, any mattress, could feel but *her body* had been yearning for that comfort. And as she lies, eyes closed, under the poinciana tree, her body just doesn't want to stand up. Doesn't want to move. Wants to lie there forever. And tears well behind Jo's closed eyelids. "Oh, fuck," she whimpers, eyes still closed, because she doesn't want to look at the spiral of light anymore. She doesn't want to think about making love on the deckchair. "Should've stayed away." The tears press heavily behind her eyelids. She has to open her eyes and let them flow. She sits up, sniffs loudly, and dabs at her eyes and nose with the hem of her T-shirt. "Fuck this!" She gets up, straining against her body's desperate longing to stay there, long and loose, safe against the mattress. "Let's find a way in and let's peel out of here right quick," she mutters.

Under the house, inside the garage and makeshift workshop, she tries the door that leads to the inside staircase. Locked too. An uncomfortable heat rises to Jo's head. She needs to get inside the house. She needs to get in but without breaking in. She could never do that to Maddy, break a window to get in, leave behind a mess for her to repair, but not leaving a word of apology. She doesn't want Maddy to know she's been around but the voice inside her head doesn't tell her why not. Seated on a packing crate, she ponders how to get inside. The answer comes to Jo in the shape of an old straw basket hanging in the far corner of the garage. She walks up to it, reaches inside, and squints at the key she's plucked out. *Yes!* That's one habit she hasn't changed, she thinks about Maddy's various hidey-holes. Having derived a degree of comfort from the thought that some things hadn't changed around the house, key thrust in front of her like a divining rod, she means to head back towards the stairwell door.

That's certainly her intention but suddenly she can't move. She can't move because her heart has just requisitioned every drop of blood from everywhere else in her body. Her heart is pumping and pumping and pumping so fast she needs to lean against the wall while she stares at the gleaming bicycle that's hanging, supported by two brackets, against the opposite wall. Jo's heart is already pumping so wildly, so erratically, because *it knew*, long before she did, that what she's look-ing at is not a new bicycle.

She understands that the gleaming black bicycle is what's become of her old rusty nail. She knows that, because on a blue tarp that she's just spotted half dragged out of the way, she sees smudges of silver and smears of black paint. And she's seen, too, little mountains of sand paper bits, spanners, worn brake pads, rusted spokes, bolts, nuts and other discarded parts and empty packaging while, off to the side, the old cracked leather saddle that used to be on her rusty bike lies as irrelevant as a discarded old shoe.

Jo stands still, totally still except for the manic pumping of her heart. Still except for thoughts that whirl inside her head. And out of the miasma, one thought spikes higher than all others. "How do you know she hasn't already figured *you* out?" The voice of the social worker. "And … still, she loves you just the way you are?"

Stepping over the scattered bits and pieces, Jo reaches to touch the bike. It's black. It's perfect. It's cold under her fingertips. Cold and smooth. And she peers closer at the frame. And she looks back at the blue tarp. Yes, it was there. It was written in dark-green smears around empty cut-out stencil. Her name. Jo. And on the bike's frame, in full stencilled-blocked letters, the same name. Hers. JO.

She screams inside her head. What if it's like the social work-er said? What if Maddy has figured her out and *still* loves her?

"What does it do to me, if she does?" she asks out loud, face scrunched up with tension. "What does it fucking mean? Does it mean she won't shut me out. Ever?" Her throat's too tight. Her Adam's apple is jammed half-way. She can't swallow properly. She's hot. Too hot. Her head hurts because it's throbbing. It doesn't hurt like a headache. It hurts like her brain is pushing, dully, dumbly, relentlessly against bone.

Over the cold bicycle frame, she lets her fingers run over her name. Gently her fingers spin the front wheel. Silver spokes gleam and blur. Hand against tyre, abruptly, almost brutally, she stops their free-wheeling splendour and, key tucked inside a clenched fist, she turns her back to the bicycle.

She slams the first two drawers shut and she slides open the next one. And the fourth. Her eyes scan Maddy's bedroom. *Where is it?* she demands to know, eyes still adjusting to the semi-obscurity. She pulls open the door to the wardrobe. Straight and light on their hangers, Maddy's going-out shirts are still as silk statues. Quiet until her hand reaches to touch one. Then they stir altogether in a mad unison. Jo slams that door shut too.

"OK, Where on earth would she have put the damn thing?" she asks the silent room. Tension is building up some more, in her, around her. She is trapped by inanimate objects. She is trapped by vivid memories that creep back slowly, that flood back, in and around the whorls of her brain. She is trapped by a scent, that of Maddy's, on the clothes inside the wardrobe, in the room. She needs to bolt away from this room. She needs to remain calm to get what she came for.

"Right," she reasons out loud, forcing her thoughts to focus. "She'd want it to be safe, so it's for sure not in the bedside tables." Jo won't look inside the drawers of Maddy's bedside tables because she knows bedside drawers are often full of discarded bits and pieces that would often be best thrown away but the hand that's put them there leaves them there because of the little secrets they contain, together and separately. Bedside tables yield secrets. Jo would simply be unable to pull open Maddy's bedside drawers. "Anyway," she mutters, "bedroom and bathroom drawers, that's the first place crooks go to." She looks around the room. "If *I* know that, she knows that. So where else would the damn thing be? *Where* would she keep it safe from a Break and Enter?" And the stillness of the room gives her the answer she is after. She makes herself calm down.

Down the corridor she strides, down the steep stair she goes and, under Maddy's workbench, she finds it. She finds it sealed inside a freezer bag. She looks at it like a transparent mollusc in the palm of her hand. She looks at the freezer bag around her wallet and she thinks of a crime scene. Lift it, bag it, tag it. "And who the fuck's died?" she shouts, fist closed around her wallet. No one answers.

Back in Maddy's room, she tears open the plastic bag and flips the wallet open. Deep inside the front pocket of her jeans, she slides the key card that will give her access to her savings account. And almost dizzy by the swirling vortex of emotions that's been sucking at her from inside she breathes in, deeply. In and out, slowly. And slowly her thoughts settle around her like leaves exhausted by a storm that's passed overhead. She has done what she came to do. She can leave now.

In the corner of the room, neatly folded on Maddy's old rocker, she spots her old, over-sized cardigan. She holds it to her face. It smells fresh. It smells clean. It smells like Maddy's winter gear. She unfolds it. "Yes," she tells the cardigan, forgetting her initial intention of leaving no trace of her visit. An object removed leaves a ghost of a trace, an invisible trace that will tell Maddy of her presence as clearly as a broken window pane. "You're coming with me. Been needing you like mad already." She cuddles it like an old friend and lays it on the bed and that gesture helps different thoughts slide in position.

Jo's been cold lately, cold at night, and though she's only come to Maddy's to retrieve her keycard, she makes the connection from comfy cardigan to strong and black combat boots. She finds them where Maddy has set them at the end of the long row made up of her own boots and trainers, still stuffed with her socks.

"Mm, nice," Jo mutters. "Missed you guys," she tells the big, black, lace-up combat boots. They are snug and tough around her feet.

About to close Maddy's closet, she hesitates. Her hand reaches to pull out one sweatshirt that is neatly folded. A standard grey variety sweatshirt and hood. Jo holds it in front of her. Its shoulder-width fills up. It fills up over Maddy's strong body, over the width of her shoulders. Maddy is standing in front of her, the grey sweatshirt reaching just below her knickers. Maddy is still in the chiaroscuro of the bedroom. Her bare legs, firm and strong, gleam dully like matt alabaster. She's right there, almost touching Jo, but not quite. She's right where Jo is holding up Maddy's sweatshirt. And Jo flops backwards on the bed, Maddy's grey sweatshirt tight against her breasts.

Squeak. Squeeaak. Squeak. Startled, Jo sits bolt upright. Her eyes have snapped open too quickly. Her brain's not following. It feels a bit seized. She's disoriented. She's forgotten that she's in Maddy's room, that she's fallen asleep holding Maddy's sweatshirt.

The back gate. She remembers now. Maddy's room. Maddy's house. She remembers where she is. She's come here to get her keycard. The backgate always squeaks. She had asked Maddy once, 'What's the little bell for, the one on the back gate.'

'It tells me someone's come in the yard.'

'Duh!' Jo had exclaimed jokingly. 'That much I had figured. The question really is, Why do you need that little bell when the hinges squeak so loud– '

"Shit! Oh, fuck! Now what?" Jo mutters between her teeth, sleepy brain wide- awake.

She's not ready to see Maddy or more to the point, she's not ready to have Maddy see her. *Not here. No, not like that,* she confirms silently. *Not now.*

Heart set, once again, on a manic rhythm, adrenaline coursing upwards and downwards, Jo stands up. *Why not? Why not* now? *Why the fuck not?"* she argues while her body seizes, waiting for her to decide which way it'll be, fight or flight? She looks in the direction of the garden. Don't fucking rush me, she'd like to tell the room. She defies the silent room to stand in her way. And thoughts slow down. They settle. There is no reason for her to feel trapped. There is no reason why she can't hang here, chill, have a beer with Maddy before returning to New Farm Park.

Jo should run to the window to see Maddy. She should knock on the windowpane and let her know she's in there. A surprise it'd be but a controlled one. A surprise with a bit of distance attached to it. One that would allow them a separate space in which to deal privately with whatever emotion Jo's unannounced visit will create for both of them.

Jo's ears have been trying to tell her something but her brain's been monopolising the circuit. Jo's ears have been trying to tell her something about sounds. Something about the sounds outside not being right.

Jo's eyes widen. Something's not right. Maddy's car. It's not coming down the driveway. Jo rushes to the window and parts the curtain carefully. She scans the garden. Back gate closed. Driveway empty. What the fuck? What time is it anyway, she asks the room, having lost track of it.

The alarm clock on the nightstand tells her it's 5.00 p.m. Already? What day? She needs to ascertain whether today is one of Maddy's days at the pool. But she doesn't know what day it is and neither does the alarm clock. Jo leans against the window.

She scans the garden again, wondering if maybe there was a Jehovah's Witness about to knock on the door. Or a Gideon leaving a bible. Or someone from the Guide Dog Association having a look around for occupancy.

Feeling someone's there, but not Maddy, makes her nervous. "What the fuck," she mumbles against the windowpane. "Shouldn't come *inside* the garden. Even if they're OK people. It's someone's fucking private property."

Jo leans to the right. She can see the edge of the lounge chair and she can see the plastic spiral of iridescent bubbles but nothing stirs. Nothing stirs until movement catches her eyes near the oleander bush.

Jo looks and she looks again. She knows what she's seeing but her brain's not processing an explanation for what she's seeing.

First a hand, then a woman. Picking flowers. Yellow flowers. Picking flowers from Maddy's oleander bush. Four, five flowers inside her hand. Jo frowns. She thinks the woman has no right coming inside Maddy's garden while she's at work. She's got no right to pick Maddy's yellow flowers. But again, if the woman needs Maddy's yellow flowers to brighten up her life, where's the harm, right? Maddy wouldn't mind. Neither does Jo.

Jo's about to slip her battered Converse trainers in the slot vacated by her combat boots when another brain message pushes through.

She strides back to the window. The woman's still there. Still picking Maddy's flowers but the back gate is closed. And what Jo's brain's been trying to tell her is that if the woman was a neighbour who had surreptitiously crept inside Maddy's garden, she would probably have left the back gate open. Jo lifts her gaze to a spot above the back fence gate. A yellow car, eggyolk yellow, is parked on the sidewalk, right against Maddy's fence. Jo blinks. That car wasn't there before or she would've noticed it.

Jo looks at the woman. Blonde. Tall. Sporty. Looking quite at home inside Maddy's garden. Jo blanches. Her blood's retreating somewhere, sucked away from her face, sucked away from her hands. She understands why the woman is in Maddy's garden. The woman is waiting for Maddy. And she thinks she understands why the woman is waiting for Maddy.

Jo's brain is finally given the message it's been waiting for. Flight! It's all systems go. Grab bag. Grab sweatshirt. Run downstairs. Run through garage. Run through front gate. Run into the street.

*****

EIGHT

As soon as she turns in her street, Maddy sees the eggyolk yellow Ford Focus. She smiles at it because she hasn't heard from Christen, not since the last conversation they had about Jo, about Jo in some dark backyard. They haven't been in touch since that day and that day also happens to have been the day Maddy had folded against Christen's body, like an end-of-race marathon runner stumbling into the arms of her coach. *It kind of felt a bit like that in a strange sort of way.* But, Maddy suspected, what she had felt, safe inside Christen's arm, safe against her body, aroused by the slow play of her tongue, had to be different from what the marathon runner would feel, collapsed against her coach. *Hey, maybe not*, she grinned, silver lip loop gleaming. *Depends what happens after training, huh?*

Though neither Maddy nor Christen had picked up the phone to touch base during the past few days, Maddy's mood had decidedly picked up. However, she had also had time to process that what she actually felt when Christen's tongue pressed against hers had been gentle arousal. *Hot, yeah, but still ... she didn't have me firing big time.* And Maddy had concluded that a great kiss had to be an amazing kiss. *That's how you can tell the difference between a fucking great pash and ... a good kiss.*

The moment with Christen had certainly been *hot,* Maddy had no problem with that. It's just that, on and off during the past few days, she had played the moment over in her mind. And her mind had tapped into specific memories stored deep inside the whorls of her brain to confirm that a great kiss had to bring on some kind of delirium. It had to trigger something like what had happened in her kitchen when *Jo* had first kissed her. *All those months ago. Big-time fireworks, then. Sudden and like, so strong. One moment I'm thinking about chips in a bowl and yeah, suddenly I'm totally open to her, I guess. I had thought about it before she rolled up on that bike of hers. Hooking up with her could be fun, is what I thought at the time. Right. That's all I was thinking.*

Maddy swings the back gate open. Christen waves. Maddy waves back. Back then, a little pash with Grunge-Chick was all that *she* had been looking forward to. What she had not anticipated was the sudden rush of desire that had her following, or was it guiding, Jo towards the sofa. *So, yeah, by comparison, the thing with Christen was ... nice. Oh, C'mon,* she argues with herself as she lets the old Commodore roll down the driveway. *Better than that. it was* good. *Uh, very good,* she finally admits, pulling on the handbrake. *But not totally out of control.*

Christen doesn't get up. Maddy's pleased to see her comfortably stretched out on the new lounge chair. Christen buries her fingertips deep inside the thickness of her hair and rubs her skull vigorously. The late afternoon light shimmers and skims over the palomino wild hair. And Maddy has to ask herself why a mad and delirious pash necessarily has to be better than a slow, smouldering one.

"Hey."

"Hey to you, too," Christen replies. Her hand glides over Maddy's forearm. Maddy squats by the lounge chair and smiles at Christen because she feels she might owe her an apology – she's just worked out that if Jo hadn't snuck in just as she had come up for breath ... they might have had a fucking great pash themselves. The silver lip loop glints.

"Been here long?"

"Half an hour max," Christen replies. Pointing at a discarded ice cream tub spilling over with yellow blooms, she adds. "But ... I picked a few flowers for you. Thought you might like them in the kitchen. You don't mind, do you?"

Maddy chuckles. "Why should I?" she asks lightly, curbing an impulse to run her hand through Christen's hair. Her resolve still is not to initiate anything. "Glad you did because what I do with them, normally is ... well nothing, really. I just look at them from here until they drop." She straightens up. "So ... beer or coffee while I have my tea, and then my beer?"

Christen smiles. "Coffee, thanks."

"Righteeo." Maddy lets her hand brush over the woman's shoulder. "You keep on chillin' here. I'll start the kettle and hop in the shower. And– "

"Let me give you a hand then."

"With what?" Maddy asks with a naughty grin. "Kettle or shower?" But she trots off before Christen can answer. "I've had to learn to manage both, you know, like quite a while back," she calls over her shoulder.

The breeze has died down and bubbles of light spiral lazily from the branch in front of Christen. She breathes in very slowly. She looks around, brings up her knees and locks her arms around them. She sits quietly while she listens for the muted chinking of cups that will soon be coming from the kitchen. She settles against the backrest and concentrates on the garden sounds until the silence that comes from the kitchen moves her to get up.

Inside the kettle's belly, the water is simmering slowly but the kitchen counter is bare of cups.

"Maddy?" she calls out. "What are you up to? Hopped into the shower alrea– " Christen listens some more and she hears it again. The soft thumping sound comes from the bedroom. "Hey … just had a thought," she says having just had a thought. "Why don't I give you another massage when you're done with– "

The sight of Maddy thumping her forehead softly but repeatedly, softly and again, slowly and again against the wardrobe door stops her dead. "What are you doing?" Already, she's at Maddy's side. "Maddy! What's up?" She encircles the young woman with both arms and tries to draw her away from the wardrobe, but Maddy makes herself heavy and she makes herself rigid and she doesn't detach her forehead from the wardrobe door. Christen winces as Maddy's forehead thuds again and again in a reverberating keen.

She doesn't want to bodily pick Maddy up to make her stop. She doesn't want to use her strength to forcibly move her away from the wardrobe so, instead, arms tightly wrapped around Maddy's waist, she leans against the length of her and waits.

With Christen's body tight up against hers, Maddy can't move her head back. She can't thwack it against the door so she leaves her forehead pressed against it. And pressed against Maddy's back, cheek against her temple, Christen waits. She waits until Maddy stirs. When Maddy turns around, a battered Converse trainer in her hand, Christen sees the silent grimace that has etched itself over her mouth, over her eyes and she moves back. She looks at the shoe and she looks at Maddy. Maddy's chin quivers. Round blue eyes brim with tears. Big round tears roll off her cheeks and Christen brings her in. She brings her in close against her. Unresponsive as a plastic doll, Maddy lets her. She lets her until she no longer can stand their combined stillness.

Christen lets her step back but cupping Maddy's elbows, she says, "Maddy, talk to me."

Maddy sniffs and swallows. "She came here."

"Who? Who did? Maddy, tell me." Maddy holds up the old busted Converse. Then Christen understands. "When?"

Maddy shrugs, drawing in her bottom lip to steady it. Hands tense in front of her chest, she pushes past Christen to pick up her grey sweatshirt off the floor along with a black wallet. She picks them up from where Jo's dropped them, near the foot of the bed. And she points to the shape Jo's head has left in the pillow. "She came *here.*"

"OK, she did, yes," Christen nods. "But that's ... good, isn't it? You do want her to come back, don't you?" And suddenly she wonders what she, herself, wants.

Black Converse still in her hand, Maddy flops backwards on the bed. She hears Christen ask, "Can I?" but the ceiling is blurry. Maddy's eyes are too full of tears, hot tears that run cold against the side of her neck. She sniffs and squeezes her eyes shut. "Can you ... what?" Tears gurgle in the back of her throat. She needs to sit up.

"Can I sit on the bed, right here?" Christen pats the edge of the bed.

Fingertips pressed against her eyes, Maddy nods. Christen sits at the edge of the bed. "Why are you *so* cut up? I don't get it."

"Chris ... " Maddy pitches the Converse trainer. It bounces up off the carpet before settling on its side. "It's *the first time* she's been here in ... since she left."

"Uh ... yes, I've gathered that but where's the problem in tha– "

Maddy runs the cuff of her sleeve under her nose. "She didn't stay."

"Well, no," she hesitated, unsure as to what Maddy would prefer her to say. "Maybe she came to pick up something and then she left."

"She didn't just *leave*, Chris. Don't you get it?"

"No, can't say that I do."

"No, I guess you wouldn't, but I do," Maddy retorts, falsely accommodating. Round blue eyes are drying up. "Jo ... she's ... neat. *Very* neat." Face tight, she glares at the wardrobe. "Probably something *else* she had to learn to keep her mother happy. *Not* make messes. *Never* leave a mess behind. So this ... " She holds up the grey sweatshirt. "And these," she points at the Converse trainers, "just like left there in the middle of the floor and her ... her wallet on the floor ... too." Maddy draws in the silver lip loop but squinting at Christen, tone hard as flint, she has to add, "You're a *cop!* Isn't that what you're trained to do ... *figure out* that something's not right?" Not allowing Christen a reply, she stammers, "She came here. She came ... for her wallet. Something's freaked her out. That's obvious. That's why the ... the bit of a mess. It's like she ran out of here, dropping her wallet, out through the garage. Didn't even shut the door downstairs."

"Right. So … what spooked her, then?"

"How the fuck would I know?" Maddy pushes off the bed and past Christen.

"Where're you going?"

"Where d'you think, huh?" Maddy's eyes tight on the woman's face dare her to answer incorrectly. "I'm going to look for her, that's where I'm going. I'm going to that fucking park and I'm going to walk around and sit there and wait for her until she shows."

Ignoring Maddy's defiant independence, Christen springs to her feet. "OK. Let's go."

"No! No, Christen." Maddy's hands are back in front of her chest, tense, forbidding contact. "You don't come with me."

"Look, Maddy, it's going to be dark soo–"

Maddy strides past the woman who doggedly follows her into the kitchen. "You don't want to be hanging there on your own in the dark," Christen says. "It's not a safe–"

"Oh, please!" Maddy scans the kitchen for her bag and keys. "You think *she's* been hanging with a bodyguard all this time, do you?"

"Maddy, it's different. She knows her way around– "

"She didn't know a fucking thing when she first got there." Christen shadows her to the garden. "Chris, no. Stay out of this." Maddy slams the car door and, forearm braced against the window opening, she backs the car up towards the gate. "Chris!" She jams on the brakes to better glare, long and hard, at the woman keeping pace close enough by the passenger door to snatch it open and jump in. "I don't need *your* help, Christen. She's *my* lover! It's me she needs, not you. Me alone." But softening her tone a little she adds, "Okay?" before throwing the gears into first and accelerating away.

*****

Welsby Street, off Sydney Street, is easy to find and Christen's previous description of the house, the only one in the street with a white concrete-block fence line somewhere near the old sugar factory end of the street, makes it easy for Maddy to identify.

Because she knew that, in all likelihood, it was still too early for Jo to be there, she had parked alongside the curb and had casually loped to where the wall was at its lowest. Deciding on having a quick look at the lie of the land, she had vaulted over it.

The garden was already quite dark, not just because the sun was starting to set earlier these days but because of the heavy foliage that hung above. Maddy spotted the corner that Christen had talked about, the corner where Jo washed and smoked and presumably slept. So she hugged the wall and sat where Jo sat. She smelled the air trapped under the foliage but whatever plumes of THC had clung to the branches was long gone. Only the wafer-thin sliver of soap almost under her foot, there, where the ground was damp, attested to a recent presence.

Maddy had then gone to the park. She had walked around looking for Jo, willing her to be sitting at one of the picnic tables or on one of the benches dotted along the river. She had sat at Rosati's, absent-mindedly nibbling on an order of Bruschetta al pesto, used as a prop, as she sipped cups of black coffee and finally a beer or two while, from her position on the terrace, she scanned the pedestrian traffic in and around the park. When around 10.00 p.m., the last of the other diners had left and the bistro staff began closing down in the kitchen, Maddy went back to the park for a final lap before returning to Welsby Street and a stake-out of the back yard. Waiting for Jo to appear.

Maddy pulls up and parks a little way up the street from Jo's squat. She turns up the volume on the old radio and observes the house that has, indirectly, anchored Jo for so many weeks. *The house itself hasn't done much for her,* Maddy reasons, *but without a house there wouldn't be a garden. She's got to be a lot safer there than in any vacant lot or park bench. All relative really but, once in that garden, tucked under the trees, she's quite safe. Not comfortable but safe.* But an unpleasant, adjunct thought sneaks in. *Safe until some douche bag follows her and … Oh, fuck,* she thinks again. *Why's she still doing that, huh?* she asks the empty sidewalk. That was one of the questions she had been returning to ever since she had spun her wheels out of her gate, leaving behind a quickly receding Christen, fist clenched in frustration, inside the rearview mirror. *Why didn't Jo tell me she'd be coming over? What if Christen's right?* What if it's me *coming home that's made her run?* Maddy hits the dashboard with a fist. "Why the fucking panic?"

The relentless rush of merry-go-round questions makes her feel dizzy. The steering wheel encroaching on her space, the unyielding seat, the hard metal of the door, all make her feel trapped, short of breath, so she flings the car door open.

She has to feel the night air. She needs to breathe its cool freshness. And she grimaces again at the thought of how cold Jo had to be, sleeping rough without even a sleeping bag. *Maybe I could buy her one. Would she let me?* she asks herself, round blue eyes made more round at the thought that, maybe, she could buy Jo one of the newfangled, light-weight, snowproof, waterproof, windproof, warm sleeping bags that roll into a tight sausage, tight enough to fit inside Jo's bag. "Maybe," she grumbles. "If I ask nicely."

Her boots hit the bitumen. She scans the street, first to the right and then to the left before returning her attention to the house. And it is only then that the dull glint catches her attention. "What the hell", she mutters. *When did it get here?* She crosses the street just to make sure, and sure enough it's there. It's green. Dark green and old but it's a car all the same. It's a car in the carport where no car had been parked earlier. *And now what?*

Maddy understands that whoever lives in that house must have finally returned from a month's long absence. *Or have they been there all along*? she wonders, startled by the thought. From what Christen had said about the house, or had it been Jo, Maddy had concluded that it had to have been empty all this time, which would explain how Jo has been able to move around the garden undetected night after night.

Maddy glances carefully up and down and across the street before vaulting over the low garden wall, for the second time that night. Crouching inside the shadows, she stops and listens before scrambling far enough into the garden to have a good view of the back façade, hoping to find it in total darkness but she discovers that's not the case. There's a light in what she suspects is a bedroom window, a light that throws an angled rectangle of light across the patch of ground near Jo's clump of trees. Maddy slumps.

Leaning back against the wall, she tries to think. She tries to figure out whether Jo would risk coming back here once she realised her squat was no longer safe. But simultaneously, it occurs to her that waiting for the household to go to sleep might be a game of patience that Jo has had to play every night before curling up in a corner of the yard. Before dragging out the hose. Before sparking her bong. *Why doesn't she squat my garden then?* Leaning against the back wall, rectangle of light almost touching the toe of her boot, Maddy moans. *What the fuck's wrong with my garden, huh? Why's she freezing me out?*

Maddy waits for Jo some more. And when Jo fails to show, Maddy drives back to the park because, that first time after she vanished at Burleigh Heads, it's where she first saw her again. By a picnic table, by the toilets near the Junior Soccer League shed. Maddy wants to know why tonight she can't find Jo anywhere. And she walks around some more. She wants to know if it's related to the car that's in the driveway of her squat or whether it's related to whatever's made her run from her place. *If it wasn't just me coming home, what else has made her run? What the hell is she doing with herself like now, this very minute?* Around the bend, sheltered under massive Moreton Bay trees, she sees a little group of Aborigines that hadn't been there earlier. And she wonders whether they're the same ones who had been spotted by the little girl riding a pink bicycle, the time Jo had appeared out of nowhere to retrieve a discarded magazine out of a rubbish bin, only to disappear before Maddy had had time to compose herself.

So, Maddy walks closer to the group. She thinks they might know Jo. She wonders if Jo might be with them. She moves closer to the edge. She can see them now. One woman, two men. All Aborigines. Seated on a thin mattress thrown on the ground with a few plastic bags kept close to their hips. *Jo's not there.*

Quite undecided as to what to do next, Maddy nibbles her bottom lip. From where she stands in the middle of the road, she watches on as the indigenous woman raises a large, silver wine-cask bladder to her lips. Tangentially, Maddy walks towards the cross-legged trio seated around a kerosene light. One of the men spots her. His mouth smiles a white smile full of gaps. Maddy knows the glint of the lip loop gives her an attitude so she smiles back.

His hand beckons her to come forward. "Fire-head lady, you got a smoke?" asks the younger of the two men. "You got a durry. Cigarette." His timbre is low but void of inflexion. "Come," he says again, brown hand scooping the air in front of him.

"Uh, no … " Maddy replies awkwardly, because she would've liked to give the man a cigarette. "I don't smoke."

Maddy shakes her head looking at the man but he's not looking back at her. She wishes he would. He's avoiding her eyes and it makes her feel uncomfortable. She'd like to ask him if he knows Jo. She'd like to ask him if he's seen her around but she doesn't because he's not looking at her. She turns her gaze to the other two seated on either side of the sooty kero lamp. It's the older man's turn to suck the silver cask liner but in between swigs he appears to be lost in thought.

Not much of a party mood going on here, Maddy thinks as, self-consciously shifting from one foot to the other, she wonders what to do next.

"Here," replies the man in the same deep and measured tone. "You sit. Heehre." He lowers a hand towards the ground.

"Uh … no, thank you," she replies, shaking her head, only to realise once more that no one's looking at her. Or are they … looking at her, without using their eyes? *Like talking to blind people*, she thinks somewhat uncomfortably. On the rare occasions when she had had to talk to a blind person, though she had felt awkward not knowing where to look, she had felt transparent and clumsy. And, belatedly, she realises it's a cultural thing, avoiding eye contact with white people. *Oh, but it's OK,* she thinks somewhat dismayed by the thought. *They can look at me. It's not like I'm going to hassle them! How do I say that to them without sounding condescending? Like totally lame?* She checks herself. She considers the woman again, trying to guess her age.

The woman's lips are shiny wet, her eyes dark, invisible almost under her heavy brow. Maddy can't decide on how old the woman might be. *Thirty, forty? Why's it so hard to tell?* She looks again at the woman sitting motionless on the hard thinness of her mattress, seeing eyes not seeing. Embarrassed by her inability to read these people as she would any other three strangers in a crowd, Maddy lets herself be drawn by their dusty, straw-dry, black hair. *It's like it's so dehydrated, like seriously dried out.* And she wonders why Australian Aborigines don't have the tight frizz all other blacks seem to have, no matter where they're from. *Best way is I don't say anything. If it's a cultural thing then, just because I think I'm a nice person … C'mon, give 'em credit,* she berates herself. But suddenly she finds herself asking, "I was wondering … I'm looking for Jo, my friend. Do you know Jo?"

The silence that settles over the group makes her wish she was someone else, because someone else might know how to talk to these people. Someone else might be OK with their drawn out silences. The hedge closest to her stirs and rustles. Maddy becomes aware of the sussurus of the tree branches above their heads. She lifts her eyes to the thick canopy of intertwined century-old branches, startled by the sound of their soft caresses. She watches as they slide against each other, sway together, and whisper to each other. And she thinks of strangely silent sailors returning to their galleon, gallons of port under their belt. And she smiles in spite of herself.

"What she like?" the man asks, in low tones.

Maddy's eyes snap back to his face but only meet his shadowy brow. "Tall. Very thin. She's got dark hair. She lives here in the park." She's growing aware of the two other people seated on opposite sides of the tired old storm lamp. She's become aware that the man's still sucking the now flaccid silver bladder and she's become aware of the woman because, though she hasn't moved, she feels her on the edge of a silent communication. Maddy senses her like an unmeddling kibitzer in a chatroom, silent but listening. A moment earlier, the woman had spoken softly but in gravelly tones to the older man, calling him Cuz, and Maddy wondered whether they were kin to each other. She had said something to him too quickly that sounded to her untrained ear like "Migaloo ... but she dugul."

"She skinny like a water reed. She come around."

"You see her tonight?" Maddy asks too eagerly. "She come *tonight?*" And she connects with her spoken words a heartbeat too late. She's heard her unintentional lapse into Pidgin and she blushes, thankful for the dim halo of light that sits smudged on the ground. She draws in the lip loop, relieved that the man's averted eyes do not show that he's noticed. If he's noticed.

"Heeh-re," he says again, stretching the word out differently but still in a low tone. And this time, Maddy understands that he's telling her to relax. *Like 'Chill'.* His eyes flicker up to her knees before returning to an invisible spot beyond his feet.

Silence settles once again and the rustle of the leaves high above her head tells her it's time to move on.

Maddy can't quite bring herself to turn her back on the one place that has the strongest connection to Jo. *Those guys over there*, she thinks about the Aboriginal trio, especially the woman's silence, *they* know *her. She comes and goes around here. Might come back later.* She begins another slow lap of the bitumen that encircles the old colonial bandstand and the rose garden. Nearer to the Powerhouse, her ears pick up clashes of oddly cacophonous sounds that emanate from it. She lifts her face to the night sky to better pick up the erratic strains and round, eyes round, she stops.

Through gaps in the tree foliage, Maddy can see the rough brick façade of the converted power plant shimmering. It's peacock blue. It's streaked with magenta and fluorescent pink while a warm virtual sunlight roams over it. Digital snuffling sounds, not unlike those made by a baby who's all cried out, bounce against the moving colours that splash the length of the huge façade and resonate far into the night. Intrigued, she quickens her pace towards the entertainment centre.

She sees hundreds of people, silhouetted against the bright sprays of emerald green and electric blue that rearrange themselves over enormous, almost transparent disturbing images. They sit or stand, shoulder to shoulder, silent boulders mesmerised by the open-air, electro-digital performance.

Maddy's heartbeat picks up. She senses Jo is near. There is no logic to her belief that Jo has got to be among the hundreds of dark shapes, there, just a few hundred metres away. But she knows it – it's as simple as that. And a wave of weariness sweeps over her. The thought of pushing herself inside the dark crowd, of feeling it press back against her, unyielding, stubbornly resisting her intrusion, is too daunting for now. At the moment, it's more than she can face. Instead, her drained brain whispers to her that Jo will come back *here,* to the park, now that she's lost her squat and that she could just wait, right where she is, till Jo emerges out of that crowd. So Maddy settles herself on the ground, back wedged against raised and ancient roots that have anchored a huge tree right where it is for more years than living memory can remember. She sits in darkness. The eclectic mix of irregular strains travels strong across the distance but reaches her ears somewhat muffled by the dense foliage above her.

As she sits waiting for Jo to appear, a century-old tree wrapped around her, she tries to force new thoughts inside her head. New thoughts that should appear in answer to her 'And now what'? question. *And now what?* The soft flapping of leathery wings makes her look up. Black against the lighter patches of the city night sky, dark wings spread taut, a bat flies above her. *So what do I say when she walks right past here? What do I need to know?*

Maddy stretches her legs in front of her and nibbles her bottom lip. *I need to know why she took off in such a hurry, right? I do need to know that,* she confirms to herself. *That's why I'm here, right, instead of being nice and comfortable in bed.* A blond palomino mane flashes shutter-quick over that thought. "Yeah," she snorts, in wry acknowledgement. *Maybe even with Christen.* Christen's fjord-blue eyes fade. *And I want Jo to explain all over again why she ran away from that fucking picnic table in the first place. Might make more sense … now.*

Maddy's thoughts drift back to the last mellow moment shared with her lover because she feels that she should open up the memories, let them surface, instead of blocking them off as she had been doing ever since Burleigh. Maybe now, because she can think back to the night she disappeared without total pain, they'd yield a clue as to what had happened *inside Jo* to make her take herself out of the frame in such an inexplicable way.

Her hand travels gently, absent-mindedly in her dream sleep, inquisitively over the dark recesses of the deep root that guards her right flank. *Rough. Gnarled.* Her fingers tentatively follow the rough edges of crevassed scars before settling over a swollen arthritic joint oddly edged by a wide patch of soft bark.

Under her hand, Maddy feels Jo's ribs. She counts them one by one. She feels each smooth ridge with the flat of her index finger while, nuzzled against her neck, Jo stays wrapped over and under her like a vine. She lets her hand glide from Jo's side over the dip of her waist and to her buttocks. Her lip loop glints as she smiles a smile of contentment.

Maddy's skin still carries the ghost-imprint of Jo's lovemaking. Her sex is still tingling. She settles her hips more comfortably between the thick, distended roots that shelter her from casual onlookers. Wing-flaps upset the rustle of branches overhead. A squadron of bats alight. Maddy doesn't see them. She doesn't hear the rhythmic soft *swoosh, swoosh* made by their stretched wings pushing against the air.

Jo's pressed against her, light against her. Her hand's resting over Maddy's sex. Though she can't see them, Jo's eyes are clear pools of backlit-grey, free of pinkish purple smudges. For the first time, Maddy allows herself to feel the memories of that morning of lovemaking, and she knows that *if* she had asked Jo to look up, she would've seen what had lain undetected for so long, dark-grey eyes tender like bruises.

Seated at the base of the wide tree trunk, Maddy stirs hazily against its rugged plane. Her shoulders are cramped between the high, unyielding roots but it doesn't matter. She can hold that position until Jo is ready to move. For now, she wants to hold her position, wrapped inside her, nestled against her neck. She wants to lie a little longer against her lover's sex, inside Jo's long legs. Later, soon, they'll go down to the beach.

Maddy wants to rent a surfkite and Jo wants to rent a boogie-board. *Sweet!* So, first they'll go looking for a kite to rent because it'll be harder to find than a boogie-board and, then, Jo will jump on her rented board and do some serious wave slicing. *Our last day here.* Though the day is still early, Maddy feels a little tug of regret. *It's been so good*, she thinks, already in the past tense. *Great weather. Cool little flat and, uh, like honeymoon stuff,* she adds silently.

Slow thoughts that follow the rhythm of her sleep slide in and out of focus, pulling Maddy closer against the protective tree roots. She drifts through her memories of that glorious morning. She frowns against the clatter of voices that rises from the esplanade below. *Why do they need to be so loud?* The electro-digital performance is over. Clusters of people spill into the park. Some, amped up by the show that they'd say was seriously awesome, talk louder than they normally would. Maddy stirs in her sleep. She pulls up her knees but doesn't wake.

She always feels a little drowsy after sex and, with Jo pressed, light as a reed against her, Maddy doesn't feel compelled to rush out on to the beach and make every minute count out there. *The sun'll still be there. The waves will still be there.* Instead she's making every minute count inside the sunlit bedroom of their rented apartment. Jo's breath flutters against her neck. *It's soft. Regular.* Maddy feels an over-whelming urge to turn inside her lover's embrace, to roll on top of her, to hold her more tightly against her, under her, but she doesn't.

Jo, drawing back her legs, shifts next to her. She caresses Maddy's stomach. *Slowly, lightly.* So slowly, in fact, that the thought that brain static is interfering with her lover's connection to the moment fleets through Maddy's mind but doesn't grip. Maddy is sleepy against Jo and Maddy doesn't open her eyes to look into Jo's. Tucked inside the protective roots of the big tree, she understands subliminally that if she had looked into Jo's eyes *then*, she would've seen what had lain undetected for so long, dark-grey eyes tender like bruises.

Jo raises herself on an elbow, only just enough to find Maddy's lips and separate them with her tongue. She runs her hand over Maddy's hipbone, over the hard plane of her stomach, on the inside of her thigh. She looks at her but Maddy's eyes are closed so she doesn't see how Jo is looking at her. Instead, she shifts under Jo's hand and stretches lazily. Jo kisses Maddy's belly button and nips at Maddy's rust-red curls. *Her lips are warm. Warm like a little puppy.* Maddy giggles quietly. *Big puppy,* she corrects herself with a smile. *Tall puppy.*

Her hand rubs Jo's back and tousles tenderly the short dark hair that stands pillow-flattened on the side of her head. She raises her hips to better meet her lover. Jo's tongue tells Maddy that Jo wants to make love again. And Maddy smiles again. She slides her hand against

Jo's sex and feels it close around her fingers. Slowly, slowly, Jo rides soft-silk lightly against Maddy's fingers. Jo's tongue is warm. It makes her shiver and Maddy wants all of Jo inside her.

"Hey? Who said you could move, huh?" Jo mutters softly. "I need more of that, more kisses. And more of what … more of what you were doing to my clit just then."

"I know you do." Maddy scoops up Jo inside her arms and holds her tightly against her before rolling her over on to the mattress. And a moment later Jo reaches *her* orgasm, one hand hard over Maddy's buttocks, one arm tight around her waist because Jo wanted to pull her down and down, closer against her clit. Her sex tightened against Maddy's fingers, around Maddy's fingers while Maddy's tongue danced against hers the way her fingers danced inside her.

When Jo opens her eyes, when she detaches herself from Maddy, she's still flushed and breathless. She takes Maddy's hand and places it over her sex in such a way that her lover's fingers curl over it. Bats squawk from inside the foliage that shelters Maddy. Their quarrel whips up the fading night air and stirs a few leaves but they do not wake her. Maddy's feeling cockily, happily connected to her lover. She grins in her sleep.

A kookaburra cackles from a distant tree. Something bumps against Maddy's shoulder. "Yurrgan. She come."

Air rattles inside her throat. Her neck is twisted from a nightlong attempt to make a pillow out of the raised root that's held her safe during the night.

"Skinny girl. She come, you hear." Dark fingers prod her shoulder roughly.

Maddy groans. Her neck hurts. She winces. She opens her eyes, round blue eyes made more round by her startle.

"What the hell– " Even before she moves her hips, she knows her back hurts too. And her hip feels anchored to the soil in between the roots.

Dark eyes. Very dark, deep-set, chocolate brown eyes peer at her from under a thick brow. Maddy blinks as she remembers the face. She tries to push herself up against the thick tree trunk but her body has seized. Beyond the Aboriginal woman, two men, shabby in their dust-grey clothes, each carrying a thin foam mattress. Grey plastic bags dangle from their hands. The night sky has faded away. Beyond the men's heads, a magenta pink and pale blue dawn. Fuzzy-headed, Maddy heaves herself upright.

"Jo? You saw Jo?"

Already the woman has returned to her companions. "She come."

"When? Right now?" Maddy asks. "Uh … last night? You *talked* to her?"

The trio walks away. Foam mattresses folded under their arms, grey plastic bags held close to their chest. The woman's sad calico skirt sways as her dark feet pad on the bitumen.

"Where're you going?" Maddy struggles to her feet and shuffles stiffly behind them. "Wait."

The woman doesn't turn around. "Bulli-men come soon. We go now."

What the hell, thinks Maddy. *What's the fucking rush.* She blinks into the clean light of dawn. *Bullymen? Bully men?* "What, the police are coming? That early?" *Shit, that's too bloody early to be having to upend yourself like that and hit the road.* "Shit," she mutters, "that can't be good for them, that." And she knows that their life is the life Jo has chosen to follow. And the body-breaking sleep she's had on the ground has been Jo's, not for one night but for night after night after night. And Maddy's eyes burn. They prickle with tears. Except for the hangover that she doesn't have, no headache has ever felt worse.

She hesitates, unsure whether she should tag along behind the city nomads. "She said anything?"

The younger man from the night before only turns his head sideways. "She says it's not safe anymore."

"Not safe?" Maddy trots stiffly to catch up with him. "What d'you mean not safe? What's happened?"

"Heeh-re, Fire-head," the man says in the low, deep tone of the previous night. "Heeh-re."

And again Maddy feels that, through the inflexion he imparts to that simple but resonant word, the man is telling her to relax, to breathe, to chill. "She say she goes away," he adds, looking straight ahead. As the little group reaches the old ferry landing, near the Brunswick Street cul-de-sac, he adds, "She go home."

"Home? Home where?"

"Home. She be safe."

*****

231

Dear Reader

If you have enjoyed **Far From Maddy**, it is my pleasure to offer you the opening pages of the third chapter lifted from ***North And Left From Here*** *(Take II)*, the remake of my first novel, soon to be released by Bookmaker's Ink.

Should **Far From Maddy** be your first encounter with my style of romance, I would also like to invite you to visit **www.ccsaint-clair.com** for the **free** serialisation of key novels, such as **Benchmarks** and **Silent Goodbyes**, a venture that I plan to keep going for your enjoyment.

Warm regards,

C.C.

DIANA

"*Ah non! Merde alors!* Not another corny plot!" I shout at the ceiling, barely resisting the urge to hurl the book at it. Anjo opens her Siamese violet eyes and blinks, tail twitching quizzically.

"Bloody asinine!" I sit up against the pillow. Anjo looks at me from her curled up position on the empty side of the bed.

I'm really sick of lesbian novels in which 'beautiful-young-dyke-meets-equally-attractive-older-woman'. All it takes is one glance across a crowded room. In the plot in point, the *magnetic* attraction takes place in a department store, two days before Christmas: how much more crowded does it get, huh? Anjo flexes her delicate front paws, curls and opens them again and again, kneading invisible dough. She's making it very obvious that she's not about to involve herself with my little upset.

"So, what have we, really, got here?" I can't resist muttering to myself. An older woman senses someone's stare; she turns around to locate its origin. Her steel-blue-grey eyes lock into those of a young sales girl. Puzzled by my muttering, Anjo fixes her violet eyes on my face, while her brown, snake-like tail whips the air. "Yeah, right on. Even *you* agree it's corny," I tell her softly. "But, wait, there's more." I quickly scan a few pages. "Ah, here they are, sitting together in a cosy little restaurant, sipping the ole Chianti and involved in a silent, deep and meaningful conversation taking place *inside* each other's eyes. Oh, please!"

Why is this pulp getting to me so? Am I so desperate for something like that to happen to me, while knowing it bloody well won't? I reach for Anjo's furry chest. A low purr vibrates through her ribcage. Sigh. Breathe, I admonish myself. I let go of that childish resentment and a chuckle bubbles upward. Who, me, chuckling?

Diana, exciting Diana, dances in front of my eyes as glorious as she had been in the flesh!

Diana Von Fahlan - perfectly at ease inside her body - the type of woman who looks gorgeous in faded denims and gorgeous in a designer gown. So gorgeous in both that I had been unable to decide which clothed the real Diana, and so I had concluded that both types of apparel enhanced equally strong facets of the same woman.

Des fois, c'est vrai, I finally come to agree from the middle of my lonely queen sized bed. There are moments, rare moments when something unexpected *can* happen. And, occasionally too, reality can rival fiction.

"Yeah," I sigh dejectedly, "but that was so long ago. In another life."

In a way it, – the older woman / younger woman thing – *had* happened in another life, in sun-drenched Mallorca, home of the magnificently convoluted century-old olive trees, a land where it never snows but where the ground covers itself in a white mantel of almond blossoms. I had been teaching at the island's Escuela Internacional de las Baleares for a couple of years already by the time Diana made her grand entrance in our staffroom.

"Folks, sorry to interrupt your lunch break," the Principal, Señor Vasquez, had announced grandly, "Let me introduce to you ... Diana Von Fahlan. All the way from the Big Apple and ... via Rio." The tone of his voice had made me wince for, in his excitement, he sounded as if he were introducing the winner of a beauty contest. "... here to take up Mrs Butterworth's place in the Chem Department. As you know, Mrs B is already on her way to Canada ... the lucky devil."

I remember having glanced at the handful of teachers scattered around the room and, to my surprise, I noticed that a couple of my male colleagues had already put down their sandwiches, while others had momentarily disconnected themselves from the bits of lettuce or pasta that still dangled from their forks.

It became obvious from where I was standing by the espresso maker that my male colleagues would, indeed, have found it difficult to find their mouths as long as the newcomer kept leaning nonchalantly against the doorjamb.

Diana had a long mane of fashionably-tousled, sun-streaked hair spilling over her shoulders and over the electric-blue silk of a blouse that was opened lower than the unwritten rule prescribed for teachers. Amazing what difference a button less can make against one's gorgeously-tanned skin.

Her legs were sheathed in a pair of white skin-tight jeans. Soft suede loafers matched the electric blue of her shirt. A scarf of iridescent material designed to flutter in the lightest of breezes was draped loosely around her neck to hang in diaphanous folds.

To be totally honest, I, too, might have had to put my sandwich down, if I hadn't already eaten it, for Diana, that day in particular, afforded us a most sensuous vision. I immediately thought of our male students who were going to approach the study of chemistry with a most ardent fervour. And then I tried to remember how long a leave period old Eileen Butterworth had bought herself

From where I stood, fiddling with the coffee machine, I watched as Diana's eyes roved from one face to the next, a pleasant but fixed smile on her lips.

"And here we have Alex Delaforêt. Alex teaches mostly English. She is French and she is our youngest staff member, by far. Alex, Diana." His introduction, though I had been readying myself for it, caught me in the middle of scooping out a second measure of coffee grounds. So, I turned towards the newcomer shaping a polite smile. Our eyes met not *quite* across a crowded room but certainly *in* a crowded and suddenly very hot room.

Anjo's looking for a cuddle. Gingerly, she walks on to my belly, little paws sinking, to settle under my chin.

"Really, little one! Isn't three-quarters of a queen size bed enough for you anymore?" I mumble into her fur already under my nose in a fait accompli. Choosing to ignore me, she tucks in her paws and closes her eyes. Her low purring vibrates from her throat to my chest. "Oh well," I sigh resignedly, "I guess that settles that." The soft vibrations intensify. I close my eyes. Nothing happening here so what the hell, let's go back to Palma de Mallorca, uh?

So there I was by the coffee machine, caught off guard by the stranger's frank open face. "Hi there," I said, a little too quickly, returning my attention to the making of my much-needed cup of strong coffee. By the time the machine finished spluttering the brew in the demitasse, Mrs. or was it Ms. Von Fahlan, I wondered, had already been whisked away, led further into the depths of our school, by the effusive Señor Vasquez.

"Hot damn! What have *we* got here?" John, the Head of Chemistry, had finally found enough voice to verbalise what most of us would've liked to say. "I volunteer. I'll be her official guide around the place, yes!"

"Down, boy!" Another male voice joined in. "Don't you go forgetting how busy you are preparing for your in-laws' visit and all. Get it, John? In-laws? Ring a bell?"

"Don't you worry about that. I can handle that *and* initiate gorgeous Diana to the nuts and bolts of the Chem. Department. And, oh, yes, she might need a little help getting the Senior class up to speed for their A level exams and– "

"Yeah, sure. Dream on, Johnny boy."

"Oh, give us a break, will you? I mean, I can still look, can't I?"

"Hey, it's not for me to say," Dan giggled, "But if I were you, I'd check with my wife first."

"What a tan!"

Tim, the only other young teacher on our staff broke in. "I wonder if that tan of hers is– "

"Don't waste time wonderin', Timothy, my boy. Tell you what. I'll be sure to find out for you."

I shook my head, totally bemused at the general surge of testosterone that had all my hitherto respected colleagues talking like juveniles.

"Must have stopped in Ibiza along the way!"

I looked across the room and Raquel, one of the Spanish teachers, caught my look. She rolled her eyes to the ceiling. "Boys will be boys," she remarked, loud enough to be heard. "Or should I say, even *wiser* old men never know that the time's come to hang it up."

"Oh, there you go. Acid Tongue strikes again. Just because you're–"

Raquel warned, "Don't you go there, John Barnes."

I tried to block out the men's boorish comments and the nervous, embarrassed giggles of my female colleagues who felt cut off by this sudden display of testosterone. Instead, I brought back the vision of this Diana person as she had appeared, wholesome and feline-like, leaning against the doorjamb.

Alex, don't be silly! I admonished myself. A totally splendid, totally sexual dame if ever there was one! But a very, very het one no doubt. How old? Early thirties was my first guess. Older woman fantasy stuff. I drew in my bottom lip to contain the soft blush that was creeping up my cheeks. The only difference, I realised, between me and my male colleagues, buoyed out of their customary casual but professional demeanour, was that I had remained silent.

I went back to my empty classroom, preferring its silence to the guys' ongoing speculations regarding Mrs Butterworth's replacement. I flopped on the chair and glanced at the semester planner already opened on my desktop. I closed it but I picked up a pen. Absent-mindedly, I watched it glide across the page, leaving behind a trail of sensuously-convoluted doodles that vaguely enclosed the space formed by a capital D.

"*Salut, Alex!*" The accent was impeccable. Clipped syllables. The 'u' pronounced through tight, rounded lips as opposed to the loose-lipped Anglo rendition. The 't' was silent as most ending consonants need to be in French and the 'A' in my name had been kept short, while American tongues usually start it off as an aborted yawn as in 'Aahlex.'

I wheeled around to face the voice. Diana was standing in the doorway, watching me through aquamarine eyes. A large but oddly compact straw basket dangled from long, woven straps of indigo leather that hung from her shoulder. Native craft from … elsewhere, I thought. But again, maybe not. There was a definite designer look to that understated straw basket.

"*Tu viens prendre un pot au yacht club*?" she asked in perfect French.

I looked at her blankly. A drink in the middle of the day?

"*C'est l'heure du déjeuner,* as in … lunchtime," Diana explained, as if I had lost track of time.

"*Ah, non …*" Just as I was about to add, But thanks all the same, the thought of a tall glass of sun-yellow Ricard, of dewy droplets running down the frosty glass, of sitting on the white and blue striped deck chairs of the local Yacht Club, of facing the sea and, mostly, of being with Diana, all beckoned me as intensely as the shimmering mirage of an oasis does the parched desert traveller.

I pushed away from behind the desk. "Hey, why not?" I heard myself replying.

"Why not, indeed. There's enough time for one slow drink at the terrace."

White sails. Cool shade under the blue sun umbrella. The gentle lapping of the sea against the boat hulls. The tinkle of riggings as they swayed above the smooth wavelets. A white wrought iron table for two. Seagulls the colour of the sky on overcast days. Yes, indeed, why not? What a wonderful idea this is, I thought, as I reached for the coolness of the glass that the white clad waiter had just set down next to a little plate of Mallorcan olives.

Anjo is twitching on my chest. I open my eyes. "Off you go, then." I scoop up her warm little body, kiss her brown snout and gently place her down at the foot of the bed.

I retrieve the novel discarded earlier, flip a couple of pages to find the spot where I had stopped reading and try to focus on the printed words. Nah. Mallorca's better. Let's stay there a bit longer. At least the Diana chapter, as I remember it … that one's not fiction! Lights off.